P9-BBQ-760

Full Throttle

ALSO BY JOE HILL

Strange Weather

The Fireman

NOS4A2

Horns

Heart-Shaped Box

20th Century Ghosts (story collection)

Graphic Novels

Locke & Key, Volumes 1–6 (with Gabriel Rodríguez)

Wraith (with Charles Paul Wilson III)

Full Throttle

Stories

Joe Hill

HARPER LUXE

An Imprint of HarperCollins*Publishers*

DEER PARK PUBLIC LIBRARY
44 LAKE AVENUE
DEER PARK, NY 11729

These stories first appeared in the following publications: "Throttle," *He Is Legend: An Anthology Celebrating Richard Matheson*, ed. Christopher Conlon (2009); "Wolverton Station," *Subterranean: Tales of Dark Fantasy 2*, ed. William Schafer (2011); "By the Silver Water of Lake Champlain," *Shadow Show: All-New Stories in Celebration of Ray Bradbury*, ed. Mort Castle and Sam Weller (2012); "Faun," *At Home in the Dark*, ed. Lawrence Block (2019); "All I Care About Is You," *The Weight of Words*, ed. Dave McKean and William Schafer (2017); "Thumbprint," *Postscripts 10*, ed. Peter Crowther and Nick Gevers (2007); "The Devil on the Staircase," *Stories*, ed. Neil Gaiman and Al Sarrantonio (2010); "Twittering from the Circus of the Dead," *The New Dead*, ed. Christopher Golden (2010); "In the Tall Grass," *Esquire*, June/July and August issues (2012); and "You Are Released," *Flight or Fright*, ed. Stephen King and Bev Vincent (2018). "Dark Carousel" was first published as a vinyl original by HarperAudio (2018). "Late Returns" and "Mums" are original to this collection.

This is a work of fiction. Names, characters, places, and incidents are products of the author's imagination or are used fictitiously and are not to be construed as real. Any resemblance to actual events, locales, organizations, or persons, living or dead, is entirely coincidental.

FULL THROTTLE. Copyright © 2019 by Joe Hill. All rights reserved. Printed in the United States of America. No part of this book may be used or reproduced in any manner whatsoever without written permission except in the case of brief quotations embodied in critical articles and reviews. For information, address HarperCollins Publishers, 195 Broadway, New York, NY 10007.

HarperCollins books may be purchased for educational, business, or sales promotional use. For information, please e-mail the Special Markets Department at SPsales@harpercollins.com.

FIRST HARPERLUXE EDITION

ISBN: 978-0-06-294420-7

HarperLuxe™ is a trademark of HarperCollins Publishers.

Library of Congress Cataloging-in-Publication Data is available upon request.

19 20 21 22 23 LSC 10 9 8 7 6 5 4 3 2 1

DEER PARK PUBLIC LIBRARY
44 LAKE AVENUE
DEER PARK, NY 11729

For Ryan King, the daydreamer. I love you.

Contents

Full Throttle

Introduction
Who's Your Daddy?

We had a new monster every night.

I had this book I loved, *Bring On the Bad Guys*. It was a big, chunky paperback collection of comic-book stories, and as you might guess from the title, it wasn't much concerned with heroes. It was instead an anthology of tales about the worst of the worst, vile psychopaths with names like The Abomination and faces to match.

My dad had to read that book to me every night. He didn't have a choice. It was one of these Scheherazade-type deals. If he didn't read to me, I wouldn't stay in bed. I'd slip out from under my *Empire Strikes Back* quilt and roam the house in my Spider-Man Underoos, soggy thumb in my mouth and my filthy comfort blanket tossed over one shoulder. I could roam all night if the mood took me. My father had to keep reading until my eyes were barely open, and even then he could only escape by saying he was going to step out for a smoke and he'd be right back.

(My mother insists I developed childhood insomnia because of trauma. I took a snow shovel to the face at the age of five and spent a night in the hospital. In that era of lava lamps, shag carpets, and smoking on airplanes, parents weren't allowed to stay overnight with their injured children at the hospital. The story goes that I woke, alone, in the middle of the night and couldn't find them and tried to escape. Nurses caught me wandering the halls bare-assed and put me in a crib and strapped a net down over the top to keep me in. I screamed until my voice gave out. The story is so wonderfully horrible and gothic, I think we all need to assume it's true. I only hope the crib was black and rusty and that one of the nurses whispered, "It's all for you, Damien!")

I loved the subhumans in *Bring On the Bad Guys:* demented creatures who shrieked unreasonable demands, raged when they didn't get their way, ate with their hands, and yearned to bite their enemies. Of course I loved them. I was six. We had a lot in common.

My dad read me these stories, his fingertip moving from panel to panel so my weary gaze could follow the action. If you asked me what Captain America sounded like, I could've told you: he sounded like my dad. So did the Dread Dormammu. So did Sue Richards, the Invisible Woman—she sounded like my dad doing a girl's voice.

They were all my dad, every one of them.

Most sons fall into one of two groups.

There's the boy who looks upon his father and thinks, *I hate that son of a bitch, and I swear to God I'm never going to be anything like him.*

Then there's the boy who aspires to be like his father: to be as free, and as kind, and as comfortable in his own skin. A kid like that isn't afraid he's going to resemble his dad in word and action. He's afraid he won't measure up.

It seems to me that the first kind of son is the one most truly lost in his father's shadow. On the surface that probably seems counterintuitive. After all, here's a dude who looked at Papa and decided to run as far and as fast as he could in the other direction. How much distance do you have to put between yourself and your old man before you're finally free?

And yet at every crossroads in his life, our guy finds his father standing right behind him: on the first date, at the wedding, on the job interview. Every choice must be weighed against Dad's example, so our guy knows to do the opposite . . . and in this way a bad relationship goes on and on, even if father and son haven't spoken in years. All that running and the guy never gets anywhere.

The second kid, he hears that John Donne quote—We're scarce our fathers' shadows cast at noon—and nods and thinks, *Ah, shit, ain't that the truth?* He's been lucky—terribly, unfairly, stupidly lucky. He's free to be his own man, because his father was. The father, in truth, doesn't throw a shadow at all. He becomes instead a source of illumination, a means to see the territory ahead a little more clearly and find one's own particular path.

I try to remember how lucky I've been.

Nowadays we take it for granted that if we love a movie, we can see it again. You'll catch it on Netflix or buy it on iTunes or splurge for the DVD box set with all the video extras.

But up until about 1980, if you saw a film in the theater, you probably never saw it a second time, unless it turned up on TV. You mostly rewatched pictures only in your memory—a treacherous, insubstantial format, although not entirely lacking in virtues. A fair number of films look best when seen in blurry memory.

When I was ten, my father brought home a Laserdisc

machine, forerunner of the modern DVD player. He had also purchased three films: *Jaws, Duel,* and *Close Encounters of the Third Kind.* The movies came on these enormous, shimmering plates—they faintly resembled the lethal Frisbees that Jeff Bridges slung around in *Tron.* Each brilliant, iridescent platter had twenty minutes of video on each side. When a twenty-minute segment ended, my dad would have to get up and flip it over.

All that summer we watched *Jaws,* and *Duel,* and *Close Encounters,* again and again. Discs got mixed up: We'd watch twenty minutes of Richard Dreyfus scrabbling up the dusty slopes of Devil's Tower to reach the alien lights in the sky, then we'd watch twenty minutes of Robert Shaw fighting the shark and getting bitten in half. Ultimately they became less like distinct narratives and more a single bewildering quilt of story, a patchwork of wild-eyed men clawing to escape relentless predators, looking to the star-filled sky for rescue.

When I went swimming that summer, and dived beneath the surface of the lake, and opened my eyes, I was sure I'd see a great white lunging out of the dark at me. More than once I heard myself screaming underwater. When I wandered into my bedroom, I half expected my toys to spring to antic, supernatural life, powered by the energy radiating from passing UFOs.

And every time I went for a drive with my father, we played *Duel*.

Directed by a barely twenty-year-old Steven Spielberg, *Duel* was about a nebbish everyman in a Plymouth (Dennis Weaver), driving frantically across the California desert, pursued by a nameless, unseen trucker in a roaring Peterbilt tanker. It was (and still is) a sun-blasted work of faux Hitchcock and a chrome-plated showcase for its director's bottomless potential.

When my dad and I went out for a drive, we liked to pretend the truck was after us. When this imaginary truck hit us from behind, my dad would stomp on the gas to pretend we'd been struck or sideswiped. I'd fling myself around in the passenger seat, screaming. No seat belt, of course. This was maybe 1982, 1983? There'd be a six-pack of beer on the seat between us . . . and when my dad finished one can, the empty went out the window, along with his cigarette.

Eventually the truck would mash us and my dad would make a screaming-shrieking sound and weave this way and that along the road, to indicate we were dead. He might drive for a full minute with his tongue hanging out and his glasses askew to indicate the truck had schmucked him good. It was always a blast, dying on the road together, the father and the son and the unholy Eighteen-Wheeler of Evil.

My dad read to me about the Green Goblin, but my mother read to me about Narnia. Her voice was (is) as calming as the first snowfall of the year. She read about betrayal and cruel slaughter with the same patient certainty that she read about resurrection and salvation. She is not a religious woman, but to hear her read is to feel a little as if you're being led into a soaring Gothic cathedral, filled with light and a roomy sense of space.

I remember Aslan dead on the stone and the mice nibbling at the ropes that bound his corpse. I think that provided me with my foundational sense of decency. To live a decent life is to be no more than a mouse nibbling at a rope. One mouse isn't much, but if enough of us keep chewing, we may set something free that can save us from the worst. Maybe it will even save us from ourselves.

I also still believe that books operate along the same principles as enchanted wardrobes. You climb into that little space and come out the other side in a vast and secret world, a place both more frightening and more wonderful than your own.

My parents didn't just read stories—they wrote them, too, and as it happened, they were both very good at it. My dad was so successful at it they put him on the cover of *Time* magazine. Twice! They said he was America's boogeyman. By then Alfred Hitchcock was dead, so somebody had to be. My dad didn't mind. America's boogeyman is a good-paying gig.

Directors were turned on by my father's ideas, and producers were turned on by money, so a lot of the books were made into films. My father became friends with a well-regarded independent filmmaker named George A. Romero. Romero was the shaggy, rebel auteur who kind of invented the zombie apocalypse with his film *Night of the Living Dead,* who kind of forgot to copyright it, and who, as a result, kind of didn't get rich off it. The makers of *The Walking Dead* will be forever grateful to Romero for being so good at directing and so bad at protecting his intellectual property.

George Romero and my father dug the same kind of comic books: the nasty, bloody ones that were published in the 1950s before a bunch of senators and shrinks teamed up to make childhood boring again. *Tales from the Crypt, The Vault of Horror, The Haunt of Fear.*

Romero and my dad decided to make a film together—*Creepshow*—that would be like one of those horror comics, only in movie form. My dad even played a part in it: He was cast as a man who gets infected with an alien pathogen and begins turning into a plant. They were filming in Pittsburgh, and I guess Dad didn't want to be lonely, so he brought me along, and they stuck me in the film, too. I played a kid who murders his father with a voodoo doll, after Dad takes his comic books away. In the movie my dad is Tom Atkins, who in real life is too affable and easygoing to murder.

The movie was full of big gross-out moments: severed heads, bodies swollen with cockroaches splitting in two, animated corpses dragging their way up out of the muck. Romero hired an artist of assassination to do the special makeup effects: Tom Savini, the same wizard of nasty who crafted the zombies in *Dawn of the Dead*.

Savini wore a black leather motorcycle jacket and motorcycle boots. He had a satanic goatee and arched, Spock-like eyebrows. There was a shelf of books in his trailer full of autopsy photos. He wound up with two jobs on *Creepshow*: doing special makeup effects, and babysitting me. I spent a whole week camped out in his trailer, watching him paint wounds and sculpt claws. He was my first rock star. Everything he said was funny and also, weirdly, true. He had gone to Vietnam, and he told me he was proud of what he accomplished there: not getting himself killed. He thought that revisiting slaughter in film was like therapy, only he got paid for it.

I watched him turn my dad into a swamp thing. He planted moss in my father's eyebrows, attached shaggy brush to his hands, put an artful clump of grass on his tongue. For half a week, I didn't have a dad, I had a garden with eyes. In my memory he smells of the wet soil beneath a heap of autumn leaves, but that's probably my imagination working.

Tom Atkins had to fake-slap me, and Savini painted a hand-shaped bruise on my left cheek. The filming went late that night, and when we left the set, I was starved. My father drove me to a nearby McDonald's. I was overtired and cranked up and hopping up and down, shouting that I wanted a chocolate milk shake, that he *promised* a *milk shake*. At some point my father realized that half a dozen McDonald's employees were staring at us with haunted, accusing looks. I still had that handprint on my face, and he was out at one in the morning to get me a milk shake as . . . what? A bribe not to report him for child abuse? He got out of there before someone could call Child Protective Services on him, and we didn't have McDonald's again until after we left Pittsburgh.

By the time my dad had us heading for home, I knew two things. The first is that I probably had no real future as an actor, and neither did my dad (sorry, Dad). The second is that even if I couldn't act to save a rat's ass, I had nevertheless found my calling, a purpose in my life. I had spent seven solid days watching Tom Savini slaughter people artistically and invent unforgettable, deformed monsters, and that's what I wanted to do, too.

And it is, actually, what I wound up doing.

Which is getting me around to what I wanted to say in this introduction: A child has only two parents, but if you're lucky enough to get to be an artist for a living, ultimately you wind up with a few mothers and fathers. When someone asks a writer "Who's your daddy?" the only honest answer is "That's complicated."

In high school I knew jocks who read every issue of *Sports Illustrated* cover to cover and rockers who pored over each issue of *Rolling Stone* like the devout studying Scripture. Me, I read four years of *Fangoria* magazine. *Fangoria*—*Fango* to the faithful—was a journal dedicated to splatter flicks, pictures like *John Carpenter's The Thing, Wes Craven's Shocker,* and quite a few films with the name *Stephen King* featured in the title. Every issue of *Fango* included centerfolds, just like an issue of *Playboy,* only instead of some babe opening her legs, you had some psychopath opening a head with an ax.

Fango was my guidebook to the all-important sociopolitical debates of the 1980s, such as: Was Freddy Krueger *too* funny? What was the grossest picture ever made? And, crucially, would there ever be a better, nastier, more bone-splitting werewolf transformation than the one in *American Werewolf in London*? (The answers to the first two questions are open to debate—the answer to the third, is, simply, no.)

I was just about impossible to scare, but *American Werewolf* did the next best thing: It stirred in me a sense of dreadful gratitude. It seemed to me that the movie had put its hairy paw on an idea that lurks under the surface of all the truly great horror stories. Namely, that to be a human being is to be a tourist in a cold, unfriendly, and ancient country. Like all tourists we hope for a lark . . . a few laughs, a bit of adventure, a roll in the hay. But it's so easy to get lost. The day ends so quickly, and the roads are so confusing, and there are things out there in the dark with teeth. To survive we might have to show some teeth of our own.

Around the time I started reading *Fangoria,* I also started to write, every day. To me it just seemed like the normal thing to do. After all, when I got home from school and wandered into the house, my mother was always at it, sitting behind her tomato-colored IBM Selectric, making stuff up. My father would be at it, too, hunched close to the screen of his Wang word processor, the most futuristic device he had brought home since the Videodisc player. The screen was the blackest black in the history of black, and the words on the monitor were rendered in green letters the color of toxic radiation in sci-fi films. At dinner the talk was all of make-believe, of characters, settings, twists, and scenarios. I observed my folks at work, listened in on their table talk, and came to a logical conclusion: If you sat by yourself and made things up for a couple hours every day, sooner or later someone would pay you a lot of money for your trouble. Which, as it happened, turned out to be true.

If you Google "How do I write a book?" you'll get a million hits, but here's the dirty secret: It's just math. It's not even hard math—it's first-grade addition. Write three pages a day, every day. In a hundred days, you'll have three hundred pages. Type "The End." Done.

I wrote my first book at fourteen. It was called *Midnight Eats,* and it was about a private academy where the elderly cafeteria ladies chopped up students and fed them to the rest of the kids in school for lunch. They say you are what you eat—I ate *Fango* and wrote something with all the literary merit of a straight-to-video splatter flick.

I don't think anyone managed to read the thing all the way to the end, except possibly my mother. As I said, writing a book is just math. Writing a *good* book, that's something else entirely.

I wanted to learn my craft, and I had not one but two brilliant writers living under the same roof with me—not to mention novelists of all stripes walking through the door every other day. Forty-Seven West Broadway, Bangor, Maine, had to be the world's best unknown writing school, but it was mostly wasted on me, for two good reasons: I was a bad listener and a worse student. Alice, lost in Wonderland, observes that she often gives herself good advice but very rarely takes it. I get that. I heard a lot of great advice as a kid and never took any of it.

Some people are visual learners; some people can glean lots of helpful information from lectures or classroom discussion. Me, everything I ever figured out about writing stories, I learned from books. My brain doesn't move fast enough for conversation, but words on a page will wait for me. Books are patient with slow learners. The rest of the world isn't.

My parents knew I loved to write and wanted me to succeed and understood that sometimes trying to explain things to me was like talking to a dog. Our corgi, Marlowe, could understand a few important words, like "walk" and "eat," but really, that was about it. I can't say I was much more developed. So my folks bought me two books.

My mother got me *Zen in the Art of Writing* by Ray Bradbury, and while the book is full of fine suggestions for unlocking one's creativity, what really turned my head was the *way* it was written. Bradbury's sentences went off like strings of firecrackers erupting on a hot July night. Discovering Bradbury felt a bit like that moment in *The Wizard of Oz* when Dorothy steps out of the barn and into the world just over the rainbow—it was like moving from a black-and-white room into a land where everything is in Technicolor. The medium was the message.

Nowadays I admit I find Bradbury's sentences to be a bit cloying (not every line has to be a clown on a unicycle juggling torches). But at fourteen I needed someone to show me the explosive power of a well-crafted and imaginative phrase. After *Zen in the Art of Writing,* I read nothing but Bradbury for a while: *Dandelion Wine, Fahrenheit 451,* and, best of all, *Something Wicked This Way Comes.* How I loved Dark's carnival of sick, reality-deforming rides, especially that awful carousel at the center, a merry-go-round that spun children into old men. Then there were Bradbury's short stories—everyone knows those short stories—masterpieces of weird fiction that can be read in as few as ten minutes and then never forgotten. There was "A Sound of Thunder," the story of some hunters who pay dearly for the chance to shoot dinosaurs. Or what about "The Fog Horn," Bradbury's tale of a prehistoric creature that falls in love with a lighthouse? His creations were ingenious and dazzling and effortless, and I turned to *Zen in the Art of Writing* over and over to figure out how he did it. And indeed, he had some sturdy, practical tools to offer the student writer. There was one exercise that involved making lists of nouns to generate story ideas. I still use a variation of it to this day (I reworked it into a game of my own called "Elevator Pitch").

My father got me a book by Lawrence Block called *Telling Lies for Fun and Profit,* which collected Block's how-to columns for *Writer's Digest.* I have it still. I dropped my copy into the bath, so it's now swollen and deformed, and the ink is blurred where I underlined long passages, but to me it's as valuable as a signed first edition by Faulkner. What I took from Block was that writing is a trade, like other trades, like carpentry. To demystify the art, he focused in on minutiae, like: What's a great first sentence? How much detail is too much? Why do some shock endings work while others, frankly, suck donkey nuts?

And—I found this especially fascinating—what are the benefits of writing under a pseudonym?

Block was no stranger to pseudonyms. He had a basket of them, had used them to create particular identities for particular works of fiction. Bernard Malamud once observed that a writer's first and most challenging creation is himself; once you've invented yourself, the stories will flow naturally from your persona. I got a charge out of the idea that Block would, when it suited him, throw on a new face and write novels by people who were themselves fictions.

"Oh, yeah," my dad said. "Check out *Such Men Are Dangerous*, the novel Block wrote as Paul Kavanagh. That book is less like a novel, more like getting mugged in an alley." *Such Men Are Dangerous* was the story of an ex-soldier who had done ugly things in the war and come home looking to do some ugly things right here. While it has been decades since I read it, I think my dad's assessment was roughly correct. Bradbury's sentences were firecrackers on a summer night. Kavanagh's were blows from a lead pipe. Larry Block seemed like a real nice guy. Paul Kavanagh didn't.

Around that time I started to wonder who I'd be if I weren't me anymore.

I wrote three other novels in my high-school years. They shared one common artistic thread: They all sucked. Even then, though, I understood that this was normal. Prodigies are almost always tragic figures, who blaze hot for a couple of years and are reduced to cinders by the time they're twenty. Everyone else has to do it the slow way, the hard way, one dull shovel-load of dirt at a time. That slow, hard work rewards a person by building up the mental and emotional muscles, and possibly establishing a firmer foundation on which to build a career. Then, when setbacks come, you're ready for them. After all, you've faced them before.

In college, naturally enough, I began to think about trying to get some of my stories published. I was afraid, though, to submit work under my own name. So far, I knew, I had not written anything worth reading. How would I know when I'd written something good, really good? I worried I might send out a crummy book and someone would publish it anyway, because they saw a chance to make a quick buck on the last name. I was insecure, often gripped by peculiar (and unrealistic) anxieties, and I needed to know, for myself, that when I sold a story, it sold for the right reasons.

So I dropped my last name and began writing as Joe Hill. Why Hill? It was an abbreviated form of my middle name, Hillström—and in retrospect, oh, man, what was I thinking, right? The umlaut is the hardest-rocking unit of punctuation in the English language, and I have one in my name, and I *didn't use it.* My one chance to be metal, and I blew it.

I also thought I'd better avoid writing scary stories, that I should try to find my own material. So I wrote a mess of *New Yorker*–style tales about divorce, raising difficult children, and midlife anxiety. These stories had some good lines here and there and not much else to recommend them. I didn't have much to say about divorce—I'd never been married! Same for raising difficult kids. The only experience I had with difficult kids was being one. And since I was in my mid-twenties, I was spectacularly unqualified to write about midlife breakdowns.

Aside from all that, the real challenge of trying to write a good *New Yorker* story was that I didn't like *New Yorker* stories. In my free time, I was reading fucked-up horror comics by Neil Gaiman and Alan Moore, not tales of middle-class ennui by Updike and Cheever.

At some point, probably about two hundred rejections in, I had a minor revelation. It was true that if I was out there writing as Joseph King, it would be awkward to start banging out horror stories. It would look like I was grabbing at my dad's coattails with both fists. But Joe Hill was just another Joe Schmo. No one knew anything about Hill's father and mother. He could be whatever kind of artist he wanted to be—and what he wanted to be was Tom Savini, on the page.

You get the life you're dealt, and if you're going to write, that's your ink. It's the only ink you get. Mine was just very red.

When I gave myself permission to start writing weird tales of the supernatural, all my problems vanished almost overnight, and before you could say *New York Times* bestseller, I was—*hahahahahaha*, just kidding. I still had piles and piles of shit to write. I churned out another four novels that never went anywhere. There was *Paper Angels*, a third-rate Cormac McCarthy pastiche. There was a young adult fantasy novel, *The Evil Kites of Dr. Lourdes* (no, fuck *YOU*, that's a great title). There was *The Briars*, a confused, unsuccessful effort to write a John D. MacDonald–style thriller about two teenagers on a summer kill spree. The best of them was a J. R. R. Tolkien thing called *The Fear Tree*, which I spent three years on and which became an international bestseller in my wet dreams. In real life it was rejected by every publisher in New York and shanked by every publisher in London. For a final kick in the nuts, it was turned down flat by every publisher in Canada, which is a reminder to us all: No matter how low you go, you can always fall lower still.

(I don't mean it, Canada.)

While I was churning out my train-wreck novels, I was also writing short stories, and over those months (and years—*yikes!*) of writing, good things began to happen. A story about the friendship between a juvenile delinquent and an inflatable boy wound up in a well-regarded anthology of Jewish magical realism, even though I was a goy (the editor didn't mind). A tale about a ghost haunting a small-town movie theater landed in the *High Plains Literary Review*. That doesn't mean much to most people, but for me, getting into the *High Plains Literary Review* (distribution approximately a thousand copies) was like peeling open a chocolate bar and discovering a golden ticket. Some other good shorts followed. I wrote one about a lonely teenage boy who goes Kafka and turns into a giant locust—only to find he prefers it to being human. There was another about a disconnected antique phone that sometimes rang with calls from the dead. Another about the troubled sons of Abraham Van Helsing. And so on. I won a couple of minor literary prizes and landed in a best-of collection. A talent scout at Marvel Comics read one of my stories and gave me the chance to write my own eleven-page Spider-Man story.

It wasn't much, but you know what they say: Enough is as good as a feast. At some point in 2004, not long after it became clear that *The Fear Tree* was going nowhere, I accepted that I didn't have it in me to be a novelist. I had done my best, taken my shot, and washed out. It was okay. More than okay. I had written for Spider-Man, and if I never figured out how to write a good novel, I had at least learned I had it in me to compose a satisfying short story. I wasn't ever going to measure up to my dad, but then I kind of figured that going in. And just because I didn't have a novel in me, that didn't mean I couldn't find myself a job in the world of comic books. Some of my favorite stories were comic books.

I did have enough short pieces for a collection, about a dozen, and decided to put it out there and see if anyone wanted to take a chance on it. I wasn't surprised when it was passed over by bigger publishers, who still prefer novels to collections for sound commercial reasons. I thought I would try the small-press world and in December 2004 got a callback from Peter Crowther, the distinguished gentleman behind PS Publishing, a very small imprint in the east of England. Peter wrote weird tales himself and had been taken with my story "Pop Art," the one about the inflatable boy. He offered to do a small print run of the book, *20th Century Ghosts*, casually doing me a kindness I can't ever repay. But then Pete—and some of the other guys in the small-press world, like Richard Chizmar and Bill Schafer—have done such kindnesses for lots of writers, publishing stuff not because they thought it would make them rich but because they loved it. (Ahem, this is your cue to visit the

Web sites for PS Publishing, Cemetery Dance Publications, and Subterranean Press and do your bit to support an up-and-comer by picking up one of their publications. Go ahead, it'll be good for your bookshelf.)

Pete asked me to write some more short stories for the book, so there'd be some "exclusive," never-published fiction in there. I said okay and started one about a guy who buys a ghost on the Internet. Somehow it got away from me, and 335 pages later I discovered I had a novel in me after all. I titled it *Heart-Shaped Box*.

Boy, it reads like a Stephen King novel. To be fair, I came by it honestly.

I was always a late bloomer, and that first book, *20th Century Ghosts*, came out when I was thirty-three. I'm forty-six now, and will be forty-seven by the time this book is out. The days blast past you at full throttle, man, and leave you breathless.

I had a fear when I started out that people would know I was Stephen King's son, so I put on a mask and pretended I was someone else. But the stories always told the truth, the *true* truth. I think good stories always do. The stories I've written are all the inevitable product of their creative DNA: Bradbury and Block, Savini and Spielberg, Romero and *Fango*, Stan Lee and C. S. Lewis, and most of all, Tabitha and Stephen King.

The unhappy creator finds himself in the shadow of other, bigger artists and resents it. But if you're lucky—and as I've already said, I've had more than my fair share of luck, and please God, let it hold—those other, bigger artists cast a light for you to find your way.

And who knows? Maybe one day you even have the good fortune to work right alongside one of your heroes. I had a chance to write a couple of stories with my father and went for it. It was fun. I hope you like 'em—they're here in this book.

I had some years to wear a mask, but I breathe better now that it's off my face.

And that's enough from me for a while. We've got some riding to do. Come on. Let's go.

Bring on the bad guys.

Joe Hill
Exeter, New Hampshire
September 2018

Throttle
with Stephen King

They rode west from the slaughter, through the painted desert, and did not stop until they were a hundred miles away. Finally, in the early afternoon, they turned in at a diner with a white stucco exterior and pumps on concrete islands out front. The overlapping thunder of their engines shook the plate-glass windows as they rolled by. They drew up together among parked long-haul trucks, on the west side of the building, and there they put down their kickstands and turned off their bikes.

Race Adamson had led them the whole way, his Harley running sometimes as much as a quarter mile ahead of anyone else's. It had been Race's habit to ride out in front ever since he'd returned to them, after two years in the sand. He ran so far in front it often seemed he was daring the rest of them to try and keep up, or maybe he had a mind to simply leave them behind. He hadn't wanted to stop here, but Vince had forced him to. As the diner came into sight, Vince had throttled after Race, blown past him, and then shot his hand left in a gesture the Tribe knew well: *Follow me off the highway.* The Tribe let Vince's hand gesture call it, as they always did. Another thing for Race to dislike about him, probably. The kid had a pocketful of them.

Race was one of the first to park but the last to dismount. He stood astride his bike, slowly stripping off his leather riding gloves, glaring at the others from behind his mirrored sunglasses.

"You ought to have a talk with your boy," Lemmy Chapman said to Vince. Lemmy nodded in Race's direction.

"Not here," Vince said. It could wait until they were back in Vegas. He wanted to put the road behind him. He wanted to lie down in the dark for a while, wanted some time to allow the sick knot in his stomach to abate. Maybe most of all, he wanted to shower. He hadn't gotten any blood on him but felt contaminated all the same and wouldn't be at ease in his own skin until he'd washed off the morning's stink.

He took a step in the direction of the diner, but

Lemmy caught his arm before he could go any farther. "Yes. Here."

Vince looked at the hand on his arm—Lemmy didn't let go; Lemmy of all the men had no fear of him—then glanced toward the kid, who wasn't really a kid at all anymore and hadn't been for years. Race was opening the hardcase over his back tire, fishing through his gear for something.

"What's to talk about? Clarke's gone. So's the money. There's nothing left to do."

"You ought to find out if Race feels the same way. You been assuming the two of you are on the same page, even though these days he spends forty minutes of every hour pissed off at you. Tell you something else, boss. Race brought some of these guys in, and he got a lot of them fired up, talking about how rich they were all going to get on his deal with Clarke. He might not be the only one who needs to hear what's next." He glanced meaningfully at the other men. Vince noticed for the first time that they weren't drifting on toward the diner but hanging around by their bikes, casting looks toward him and Race both. Waiting for something to come to pass.

Vince didn't want to talk. The thought of talk drained him. Lately conversation with Race was like throwing a medicine ball back and forth, a lot of wearying effort, and he didn't feel up to it, not with what they were driving away from.

He went anyway, because Lemmy was almost always right when it came to Tribe preservation. Lemmy had been riding six to Vince's twelve going back to when they'd met in the Mekong Delta and the whole world was *dinky dau*. They had been on the lookout for trip wires and buried mines then. Nothing much had changed in the almost forty years since.

Vince left his bike and crossed to Race, who stood between his Harley and a parked truck, an oil hauler. Race had found what he was hunting for in the hardcase on the back of his bike, a flask sloshing with what looked like tea and wasn't. He drank earlier and earlier, something else Vince didn't like. Race had a pull, wiped his mouth, held it out to Vince. Vince shook his head.

"Tell me," Vince said.

"If we pick up Route 6," Race said, "we could be down in Show Low in three hours. Assuming that pussy rice-burner of yours can keep up."

"What's in Show Low?"

"Clarke's sister."

"Why would we want to see her?"

"For the money. Case you hadn't noticed, we just got fucked out of sixty grand."

"And you think his sister will have it."

"Place to start."

"Let's talk about it back in Vegas. Look at our options there."

"How about we look at 'em now? You see Clarke hanging up the phone when we walked in? I heard a snatch of what he was saying through the door. I think he tried to get his sister, and when he didn't, he left a message with someone who knows her. Now, why do you think he felt a pressing need to reach out and touch that toe-rag as soon as he saw all of us in the driveway?"

To say his good-byes, was Vince's theory, but he didn't tell Race that. "She doesn't have anything to do with this, does she? What's she do? She make crank, too?"

"No. She's a whore."

"Jesus. What a family."

"Look who's talking," Race said.

"What's that mean?" Vince asked. It wasn't the line that bothered him, with its implied insult, so much as Race's mirrored sunglasses, which showed a reflection of Vince himself, sunburned and with a beard full gray, looking puckered, lined, and old.

Race stared down the shimmering road again, and when he spoke, he didn't answer the question. "Sixty grand up in smoke, and you can just shrug it off."

"I didn't shrug anything off. That's what happened. Up in smoke."

Race and Dean Clarke had met in Fallujah—or maybe it had been Tikrit. Clarke a medic specializing in pain management, his treatment of choice being primo dope accompanied by generous helpings of Wyclef Jean. Race's specialties had been driving Humvees and not getting shot. The two of them had remained friends back in the World, and Clarke had come to Race a half a year ago with the idea of setting up a meth lab in Smith Lake. He figured sixty grand would get him started and that he'd be making more than that per month in no time.

"True glass," that had been Clarke's pitch. "None of that cheap green shit, just true glass." Then he'd raised his hand above his head, indicating a monster stack of cash. "Sky's the limit, yo?"

Yo. Vince thought now he should have pulled out the minute he heard that come out of Clarke's mouth. The very second.

But he hadn't. He'd even helped Race out with twenty grand of his own money, in spite of his doubts. Clarke was a slacker-looking guy who bore a passing

resemblance to Kurt Cobain: long blond hair and lay-
ered shirts. He said "yo," he called everyone "man," he
talked about how drugs broke through the oppressive
power of the overmind. Whatever that meant. He surprised and charmed Race with intellectual gifts: plays
by Sartre, mix tapes featuring spoken-word poetry and
reggae dub.

Vince didn't resent Clarke for being an egghead
full of spiritual-revolution talk that came out in some
bullshit half-breed language, part pansy and part
Ebonics. What disconcerted Vince was that when they
met, Clarke already had a stinking case of meth mouth,
his teeth falling out and his gums spotted. Vince didn't
mind making money off the shit but had a knee-jerk
distrust of anyone gamy enough to use it.

And still he put up money, had wanted something to
work out for Race, especially after the way he'd been
run out of the army. And for a while, when Race and
Clarke were hammering out the details, Vince had
even half talked himself into believing it might pay off.
Race seemed, briefly, to have an air of almost cocky
self-assurance, had even bought a car for his girlfriend,
a used Mustang, anticipating the big return on his
investment.

Only the meth lab caught fire, yo? And the whole
thing burned to a shell in the space of ten minutes, the

very first day of operation. The wetbacks who worked inside escaped out the windows and were standing around, burned and sooty, when the fire trucks arrived. Now most of them were in county lockup.

Race had learned about the fire not from Clarke but from Bobby Stone, another friend of his from Iraq, who had driven out to Smith Lake to buy ten grand worth of the mythical true glass but turned around when he saw the smoke and the flashing lights. Race had tried to raise Clarke on the phone but couldn't get him, not that afternoon, not in the evening. By eleven the Tribe was on the highway, headed east to find him.

They had caught Dean Clarke at his cabin in the hills, packing to go. He told them he'd been just about to leave to come see Race, tell him what happened, work out a new plan. He said he was going to pay them all back. He said the money was gone now but there were possibilities, there were contingency plans. He said he was so goddamn fucking sorry. Some of it was lies, and some of it was true, especially the part about being so goddamn fucking sorry, but none of it surprised Vince, not even when Clarke began to cry.

What surprised him—what surprised all of them—was Clarke's girlfriend hiding in the bathroom, dressed in daisy-print panties and a sweatshirt that said CORMAN HIGH VARSITY. All of seventeen and soaring on meth and clutching a little .22 in one hand. She was listening in when Roy Klowes asked Clarke if she was around, said that if Clarke's bitch blew all of them, they could cross two hundred bucks off the debt right there. Roy Klowes had walked into the bathroom, taking his cock out of his pants to have a leak, but the girl had thought he was unzipping for other reasons and opened fire. Her first shot went wide, and her second shot went into the ceiling, because by then Roy was whacking her with his machete, and it was all sliding down the red hole, away from reality and into the territory of bad dream.

"I'm sure he lost some of the money," Race said. "Could be he lost as much as half what we set him up with. But if you think Dean Clarke put the entire sixty grand into that one trailer, I can't help you."

"Maybe he did have some of it tucked away. I'm not saying you're wrong. But I don't see why it would wind up with the sister. Could just as easily be in a mason jar, buried somewhere in his backyard. I'm not going to pick on some pathetic hooker for fun. If we find out she's suddenly come into money, that's a different story."

"I was six months setting this deal up. And I'm not the only one with a lot riding on it."

"Okay. Let's talk about how to make it right in Vegas."

"Talk isn't going to make anything right. Riding is. His sister is in Show Low today, but when she finds out her brother and his little honey got painted all over their ranch—"

"You want to keep your voice down," Vince said.

Lemmy watched them with his arms folded across his chest, a few feet to Vince's left but ready to move if he had to get between them. The others stood in groups of two and three, bristly and road-dirty, wearing leather jackets or denim vests with the gang's patch on them: a skull in an Indian headdress, above the legend THE TRIBE • LIVE ON THE ROAD, DIE ON THE ROAD. They had always been the Tribe, although none of them were Indian, except for Peaches, who claimed to be half Cherokee, except when he felt like saying he was half Spaniard or half Inca. Doc said he could be half Eskimo and half Viking if he wanted—it still added up to all retard.

"The money is gone," Vince said to his son. "The six months, too. *See it.*"

His son stood there, the muscles bunched in his jaw, not speaking. His knuckles white on the flask in his right hand. Looking at him now, Vince was struck with a sudden image of Race at the age of six, face just as dusty as it was now, tooling around the gravel driveway on his green Big Wheel, making revving noises down in his throat. Vince and Mary had laughed and laughed, mostly at the screwed-up look of intensity on their son's face, the kindergarten road warrior. He couldn't find the humor in it now, not two hours after Race had split a man's head open with a shovel. Race had always been fast and had been the first to catch up to Clarke when he tried to run, in the confusion after the girl started shooting. Maybe he hadn't meant to kill him. Race had only hit him the once.

Vince opened his mouth to say something more, but there was nothing more. He turned away, started toward the diner. He hadn't gone three steps, though, when he heard a bottle explode behind him. He turned and saw that Race had thrown the flask into the side of the oil rig, had thrown it exactly in the place Vince had been standing only five seconds before. Throwing it at Vince's shadow maybe.

Whiskey and chunks of glass dribbled down the battered oil tank. Vince glanced up at the side of the tanker and twitched involuntarily at what he saw there. There was a word stenciled on the side, and for an instant he thought it said SLAUGHTERIN. But no. It was LAUGHLIN. What Vince knew about Freud could be summed up in less than twenty words—dainty little white beard, cigar, thought kids wanted to fuck their parents—but you didn't need to know much psychology to recognize a guilty subconscious at work. Vince would've laughed if not for what he saw next.

The trucker was sitting in the cab. His hand hung out the driver's-side window, a cigarette smoldering between two fingers. Midway up his forearm was a faded tattoo, DEATH BEFORE DISHONOR, which made him a vet, something Vince noted in a distracted sort of way and immediately filed away, perhaps for later consideration, perhaps not. He tried to think what the guy might've heard, measure the danger, figure out if there was a pressing need to haul Laughlin from his truck and straighten him out about a thing or two.

Vince was still considering it when the semi rumbled to noisy, stinking life. Laughlin pitched his ciggie into the parking lot and released his air brakes. The stacks belched black diesel smoke, and the truck began to roll, tires crushing gravel. As the tanker moved off, Vince let out a slow breath and felt the tension begin to drain away. He doubted if the guy had heard anything, and what did it matter if he had? No one with any sense would want to get involved in their shitpull. Laughlin must've realized he'd been caught listening in and decided to get while the getting was good.

By the time the eighteen-wheeler eased out onto the two-lane highway, Vince had already turned away, brushing through his crew and making for the diner. It was almost an hour before he saw the truck again.

Vince went to piss—his bladder had been killing him for going on thirty miles—and on his return he passed by the others, sitting in two booths. They were quiet, almost no sound from them at all, aside from the scrape of forks on plates and the clink of glasses being set down. Only Peaches was talking, and that was to himself. Peaches spoke in a whisper and occasionally seemed to flinch, as if surrounded by a cloud of imaginary midges—a dismal, unsettling habit of his. The rest of them occupied their own interior spaces, not seeing one another, staring inwardly at who-knew-what instead. Some of them were probably seeing the bathroom after Roy Klowes had finished chopping up the girl. Others might be remembering Clarke facedown in the dirt beyond the back door, his ass in the air and his pants full of shit and the steel-bladed shovel planted in his skull, the handle sticking in the air. And then there were probably a few wondering if they would be home in time for *American Gladiators* and whether the lottery tickets they'd bought yesterday were winners.

It had been different on the way down to see Clarke. Better. The Tribe had stopped just after sunup at a diner much like this, and while the mood had not been festive, there'd been plenty of bullshit and a certain amount of predictable yuks to go with the coffee and doughnuts. Doc had sat in one booth doing the crossword puzzle, others seated around him, looking over his shoulder and ribbing one another about what an honor it was to sit with a man of such education. Doc had done time, like most of the rest of them, and had a gold tooth in his mouth in place of one that had been whacked out by a cop's nightstick a few years before. But he wore bifocals, and had lean, almost patrician features, and read the paper, and knew things, like the capital of Kenya and the players in the Wars of the Roses. Roy Klowes took a sidelong look at Doc's puzzle and said, "What I need is a crossword with questions about fixing bikes or cruising pussy. Like, what's a four-letter word for what I do to your mama, Doc? I could answer that one."

Doc frowned. "I'd say 'repulse,' but that's seven letters. So I guess my answer would have to be 'gall.'"

"Gall?" Roy asked, scratching his head.

"That's right. You gall her. Means you show up and she wants to spit."

"Yeah, and that's what pisses me off about her. 'Cause I been trying to train her to swaller while I gall her."

And the men just about fell off their stools laughing. They'd been laughing just as hard the next booth over, where Peaches was trying to tell them about why he got his nuts clipped. "What sold me on it was when I saw that I'd only ever have to pay for one vasectomy—which is not something you can say about abortion. There's theoretically no limit there. *None.* Every jizzwad is a potential budget buster. You don't recognize that until you've had to pay for a couple of scrapes and begin to think there might be a better use for your money. Also, relationships aren't ever the same after you've had to flush Junior down the toilet. They just aren't. Voice of experience right here." Peaches didn't need jokes. He was funny enough just saying what was on his mind.

Now Vince moved past the cored-out, red-eyed bunch and took a stool at the counter beside Lemmy.

"What do you think we ought to do about this shit when we get to Vegas?" Vince asked.

"Run away," Lemmy said. "Tell no one we're going. Never look back."

Vince laughed. Lemmy didn't. He lifted his coffee halfway to his lips but didn't drink, only looked at the cup for a few seconds and then put it down.

"Somethin' wrong with that?" Vince asked.

"It ain't the coffee that's wrong."

"You aren't going to tell me you're serious about taking off, are you?"

"We wouldn't be the only ones, buddy," Lemmy said. "What Roy did to that girl in the bathroom?"

"She almost shot him," Vince said, voice low so no one else could hear.

"She wasn't but seventeen."

Vince did not reply, and anyway, no reply was expected.

"Most of these guys have never seen anything that heavy, and I think a bunch—the smart ones—are going to scatter to the four corners of the earth as soon as they can. Find a new purpose for being." Vince laughed again, but Lemmy only glanced at him sidelong. "Listen now, Cap. I killed my brother driving blind drunk when I was eighteen. And when I woke up, I could smell his blood all over me. I tried to kill myself in the Corps to make up for it, but the boys in the black pajamas wouldn't help me. And what I remember mostly about the war is the way my own feet smelled when they got jungle rot. Like carrying a toilet around in my boots. I been in jail, like you, and what was worst wasn't the things I did or saw done. What was worst was the smell on everyone. Armpits and assholes. And that was all bad. But none of it has anything on the Charlie Manson shit we're driving away from. Thing I can't shake loose is how it stank in the place. After it was over. Like being stuck in a closet where someone took a shit. Not enough air, and what there was wasn't any good." He paused, turned on his stool to look sidelong at Vince. "You know what I been thinking about ever since we drove away? Lon Refus moved out to Denver and opened a garage. He sent me a postcard of the Flatirons. I been wondering if he could use an old guy to twist a wrench for him. I been thinking I could get used to the smell of pines."

He was quiet again, then shifted his gaze to look at the other men in their booths. "The half that doesn't take a walk will be looking to get back what they lost, one way or another, and you don't want any part of how they're going to do it. 'Cause there's going to be more of this crazy meth shit. This is just beginning. The tollbooth where you get on the turnpike. There's too much money in it to quit, and everyone who sells it does it, too, and the ones who do it make big fucking messes. The girl who tried to shoot Roy was on it, which is why she tried to kill him, and Roy is on it himself, which is why he had to whack her forty fucking times with his asshole machete. Who the fuck besides a meth-head carries a machete anyhow?"

"Don't get me started on Roy. I'd like to stick Little Boy up his ass and watch the light shoot out his eyes,"

Vince told him, and it was Lemmy's turn to laugh then. Coming up with deranged uses for Little Boy was one of the running jokes between them. Vince said, "Go on. Say your say. You been thinkin' about it the last hour."

"How would you know that?"

"You imagine I don't know what it means when I see you sittin' straight up on your sled?"

Lemmy grunted and said, "Sooner or later the cops are going to land on Roy or one of these other crankies, and they'll take everyone around them down with them. Because Roy and the guys like him aren't smart enough to get rid of the shit they stole from crime scenes. None of them are smart enough not to talk about what they done to their girlfriends. Hell. Half of them are carry-ing rock right now. All I'm saying."

Vince scrubbed a hand along the side of his beard. "You keep talking about the two halves, the half that's going to take off and the half that isn't. You want to tell me which half Race is in?"

Lemmy turned his head and grinned unhappily, showing the chip in his tooth. "You need to ask?"

The truck with LAUGHLIN on the side was laboring uphill when they caught up to it around three in the afternoon.

The highway wound its lazy path up a long grade, through a series of switchbacks. With all the curves, there was no obvious place to pass. Race was out front again. After they departed the diner, he had sped off, increasing his lead on the rest of the Tribe by so much that sometimes Vince lost sight of him altogether. But when they reached the truck, his son was riding the guy's bumper.

The nine of them rode up the hill in the rig's boiling wake. Vince's eyes began to tear and run.

"Fucking truck!" Vince screamed, and Lemmy nodded. Vince's lungs were tight, and his chest hurt from breathing its exhaust, and it was hard to see. *"Get your miserable fat-ass truck out of the way!"* Vince hollered.

It was a surprise, catching up to the truck here. They weren't that far from the diner—twenty miles, no more. LAUGHLIN must've pulled over somewhere else for a while—but there was nowhere else. Possibly he'd parked his rig in the shade of a billboard for a siesta. Or threw a tire and needed to stop and put on a new one. Did it matter? It didn't. Vince wasn't even sure why it was on his mind, but it nagged.

Just past the next bend in the road, Race leaned his Softail Deuce into the lane for oncoming traffic, lowered his head, and accelerated from thirty to seventy. The bike squatted, then *leaped*. He cut in front of the truck as soon as he was ahead of it—slipping back into the right-hand lane just as a pale yellow Lexus blew past, going the other way. The driver of the Lexus pounded her horn, but the *meep-meep* sound of it was almost immediately lost in the overpowering wail of the truck's air horn.

Vince had spotted the Lexus coming and for a moment had been sure he was about to see his son go head-on into it, Race one second, road meat the next. It took a few moments for his heart to come back down out of his throat.

"Fucking psycho!" Vince yelled at Lemmy.

"You mean the guy in the truck?" Lemmy hollered back, as the blast of the air horn finally died away. *"Or Race?"*

"Both!"

By the time the truck swung through the next curve, though, LAUGHLIN seemed to have come to his senses or had finally looked in the mirror and noticed the rest of the Tribe roaring along behind him. He put his hand out the window—that sun-darkened and veiny hand, big-knuckled and blunt-fingered—and waved them by.

Immediately Roy and two others swung out and thundered past. The rest went in pairs. It was nothing to pass once the go-to was clear, the truck laboring along at barely thirty. Vince and Lemmy swept out last, passing just before the next switchback. Vince cast a look up toward the driver on their way by but could see nothing except that dark hand hanging out against the door. Five minutes later they'd left the truck so far behind them that they couldn't hear it anymore.

There followed a stretch of high open desert, sage and saguaro, cliffs off to the right, striped in chalky shades of yellow and red. They were riding into the sun now, pursued by their own lengthening shadows. Houses and a few trailers whipped by as they blew through a sorry excuse for a township. The bikes were strung out across almost half a mile, with Vince and Lemmy riding close to the back. But not far beyond the town, Vince saw the rest of the Tribe bunched up at the side of the road, just before a four-way intersection, the crossing for Route 6.

Beyond the intersection, to the west, the highway they'd been following was torn down to dirt. A diamond-shaped orange sign read CONSTRUCTION NEXT 20 MILES—BE PREPARED TO STOP. In the distance Vince could see dump trucks and a grader. Men worked in clouds of red smoke, the clay stirred up and drifting across the tableland.

He hadn't known there would be roadwork here, because they hadn't come this way. It had been Race's suggestion to return by the back roads, which had suited Vince fine. Driving away from a double homicide, it seemed like a good idea to keep a low profile. Of course, that wasn't why Race had suggested it.

"What?" Vince said, slowing and putting his foot down. As if he didn't already know.

Race pointed away from the construction, down Route 6. "We go south on 6, we can pick up I-40."

"In Show Low," Vince said. "Why does this not surprise me?"

It was Roy Klowes who spoke next. He jerked a thumb toward the dump trucks. "Bitch of a lot better than doing five an hour through that shit for twenty miles. No thank you. I'd rather ride easy and maybe pick up sixty grand along the way. That's my think on it."

"Did it hurt?" Lemmy asked Roy. "Having a thought? I hear it hurts the first time. Like when a chick gets her cherry popped."

"Fuck you, Lemmy," Roy said.

"When I want your think," Vince said, "I'll be sure to ask for it, Roy. But I wouldn't hold your breath."

Race spoke, his voice calm, reasonable. "We get to Show Low, you don't have to stick around. Neither of you. No one's going to hold it against you if you just want to ride on."

So there it was.

Vince looked from face to face. The young men met his gaze. The older ones, the ones who'd been riding with him for decades, did not.

"I'm glad to hear no one will hold it against me," Vince said. "I was worried."

A memory struck him then: riding with his son in a car at night, in the GTO, back in the days he was trying to go straight, be a family man for Mary. The details of the journey were lost now; he couldn't recall where they were coming from or where they'd been going. What he remembered was looking into the rearview mirror at his ten-year-old's dusty, sullen face. They had stopped at a hamburger stand, but the kid didn't want dinner, said he wasn't hungry. The kid would only settle for a Popsicle, then bitched when Vince came back with lime instead of grape. He wouldn't eat it, let the Popsicle melt on the leather. Finally, when they were twenty miles away from the hamburger stand, Race announced that his belly was growling.

Vince had looked into the rearview mirror and said, "You know, just because I'm your father doesn't mean I got to like you." And the boy had stared back, his chin dimpling, struggling not to cry but unwilling to look away. Returning Vince's look with bright, hating eyes. Why had Vince said that? The notion crossed his mind that if he'd known some other way to talk to Race, there would've been no Fallujah and no dishonorable discharge for ditching his squad, taking off in a Humvee while mortars fell; there would've been no Dean Clarke and no meth lab, and the boy would not feel the need to be out front all the time, blasting along at seventy on his hot-shit jackpuppy when the rest of them were doing sixty. It was him the kid was trying to leave behind. He'd been trying all his life.

Vince squinted back the way they had come—and there was that goddamn truck again. He could see it through the trembling waves of heat on the road, so it seemed half mirage, with its towering stacks and silver grille: LAUGHLIN. Or SLAUGHTERIN, if you were feeling Freudian. Vince frowned, distracted for a moment, wondering again how they'd been able to catch up to and pass a guy who'd had almost an hour's lead on them.

When Doc spoke, his voice was almost shy with apology. "Might be the thing to do, boss. Sure would beat twenty miles of dirt bath."

"Well. I wouldn't want any of you to get dirty," Vince said.

And he pushed away from the side of the road, throttled up, and turned left onto 6, leading them away toward Show Low.

Behind him, in the distance, he could hear the truck changing gears, the roar of the engine climbing in volume and force, whining faintly as it thundered across the plain.

The country was red and yellow stone, and they saw no one on the narrow, two-lane road. There was no breakdown lane. They crested a rise, then began to descend into a canyon's slot, following the road as it wound steadily lower. To the left was a battered guardrail, and to the right was an almost sheer face of rock.

For a while Vince rode out front beside Lemmy, but then Lemmy fell back and it was Race partnered beside him, the father and the son riding side by side, the wind rippling Race's movie-star black hair back from his brow. The sun, now on the western side of the sky, burned in the lenses of the kid's shades.

Vince watched him from the corners of his eyes for a moment. Race was sinewy and lean, and even the way he sat on his bike seemed an act of aggression, how he slung it around the curves, tilting to a forty-five-degree angle over the blacktop. Vince envied him his natural athletic grace, and yet at the same time somehow Race managed to make riding a motorcycle look like work. Whereas Vince himself had taken to it because it was the furthest thing from work. He wondered idly if Race was ever really at ease with himself.

Vince heard the grinding thunder of a big engine behind him and took a long, lazy look back over his shoulder just in time to see the truck come bearing down on them. Like a lion breaking cover at a watering hole where a bunch of gazelles were loafing. The Tribe was rolling in bunches, as always, doing maybe forty-five down the switchbacks, and the truck was rushing along at closer to sixty. Vince had time to think, *He's not slowing down,* and then LAUGHLIN slammed through the three running at the back of the pack with an eardrum-stunning crash of steel on steel.

Bikes flew. One Harley was thrown into the rock wall, the rider—John Kidder, sometimes known as Baby John—catapulting off it, tossed into the stone, then rebounding and disappearing under the steel-belted tires of LAUGHLIN's truck. Another rider (*Doc, no, not Doc*) was driven into the left lane. Vince had the briefest glance of Doc's pale and astonished face, mouth opening in an O, the twinkle of the gold tooth he was so proud of. Wobbling out of control, Doc struck the guardrail and went over his handlebars, flung into space. His Harley flipped over after him, the hardcase breaking open and spilling laundry. The truck chewed up the fallen bikes. The big grille seemed to snarl.

Then Vince and Race swung around another hard curve side by side, leaving it all behind.

The blood surged to Vince's heart, and for a moment there was a dangerous pinching in his chest. He had to fight for his next breath. The instant the carnage was out of sight, it was hard to believe it had really happened. Hard to believe the spinning bikes hadn't taken out the speeding truck, too. Yet he had just finished coming around the bend when Doc crashed into the road ahead of them. His bike landed on top of his body with an echoing clang. His clothes came floating after. Doc's sleeveless denim jacket came drifting down last, ballooning open, caught for a moment on an updraft. Over a silhouette of Vietnam in gold thread was the legend WHEN I GET TO HEAVEN, THEY'LL LET ME IN BECAUSE I'VE ALREADY BEEN TO HELL. IRON TRIANGLE 1968. The clothes, the owner of the clothes, and the owner's ride had dropped from the terrace above, falling seventy feet to the highway below.

Vince jerked the handlebars, swerving around the wreck with one boot heel skimming the patched asphalt. His friend of twenty years, Doc Regis, was now a six-letter word for lubricant: "grease." He was face-down, but his teeth were glistening in a slick of blood next to his left ear, the goldie among them. His shins had come out through the backs of his legs, poles of shining red bone poking through his jeans. All this Vince saw in an instant, then wished he could *unsee*. The gag muscles fluttered in his throat, and when he swallowed, there was a burning taste of bile.

Race swung around the other side of the ruin that had been Doc and Doc's bike. He looked sideways at Vince, and while Vince could not see his eyes behind his shades, his face was a rigid, stricken thing, the expression of a small kid up past his bedtime who has walked in on his parents watching a grisly horror movie on DVD.

Vince looked back again and saw the remnants of the Tribe coming around the bend. Just seven now. The truck howled after, swinging around the curve so fast that the long tank it was hauling lurched hard to one side, coming perilously close to tipping, its tires smoking on the blacktop. Then it steadied and bore on, striking Ellis Harbison. Ellis was launched straight up into the air, as if bounced off a diving board. He almost looked funny, pinwheeling his arms against the blue sky—at least until he came down and went under the truck. His ride turned end over end before being swatted entirely aside by the eighteen-wheeler.

Vince caught a jittery glimpse of Dean Carew as the truck caught up to him. The truck butted the rear tire of his bike. Dean highsided and came down hard, rolling at fifty miles an hour along the highway, the asphalt peeling his skin away, his head bashing the road again and again, leaving a series of red punctuation marks on the chalkboard of the pavement.

An instant later the tanker ate Dean's bike, bang, thump, *crunch,* and the lowrider that Dean had still been making payments on exploded, a parachute of flame bursting open beneath the truck. Vince felt a wave of pressure and heat against his back, shoving him forward, threatening to lift him off the seat of his bike. He thought the truck itself would go up, slammed right off the road as the oil tanker detonated in a column of fire. But it didn't. The rig came thundering through the flames, its sides streaked with soot and black smoke belching from its undercarriage but otherwise undamaged, and going faster than ever. Vince knew that Macks were fast—the new ones had a 485 power plant under the hood—but *this* thing . . .

Supercharged? Could you supercharge a goddamn *semi?*

Vince was moving too fast, felt his front tire beginning to slurve about. They were close to the bottom of the slope now, where the road leveled out. Race was a little ahead. In his rearview Vince could see the only other survivors: Lemmy, Peaches, Roy. And the truck was closing in again.

They could beat it on a rise—in a heartbeat—but

now there *were* no rises. Not for the next twenty miles, if his memory was right. It was going to get Peaches next, Peaches who was funniest when he was trying to be serious. Peaches threw a terrified glance back over his shoulder, and Vince knew what he was seeing: a chrome cliff. One that was moving in.

Fucking think of something. Lead them out of this.

It had to be him. Race was still riding okay, but he was on autopilot, face frozen, fixed forward as if he had a sprained neck and was wearing a brace. A thought struck Vince then—terrible but curiously certain—that this was how Race had looked the day in Fallujah that he drove away from the men in his squad, while the mortar rounds dropped around them.

Peaches put on a burst of speed and gained a little on the truck. It blasted its air horn, as if in frustration. Or laughter. Either way, the old Georgia Peach had only gained a stay of execution. Vince could hear the trucker—maybe named Laughlin, maybe a devil from hell—changing gears. Christ, how many forward did he have? A hundred? He started to close the distance. Vince didn't think Peaches would be able to squirt ahead again. That old flathead Beezer of his had given all it had to give. Either the truck would take him or the Beez would blow a head gasket and *then* the truck would take him.

BRONK! BRONK! BRONK-BRONK-BRONK!

Shattering a day that was already shattered beyond repair—but it gave Vince an idea. It depended where they were. He knew this road. He knew them all out here, but he hadn't been this way in years and could not be sure now, on the fly, if they were where he thought they were.

Roy threw something back over his shoulder, something that twinkled in the sun. It struck LAUGHLIN's dirty windshield and flew off. The fucking machete. The truck bellowed on, blowing double streams of black smoke, the driver laying on that horn again—

BRONK-BRONK! BRONK! BRONK-BRONK-BRONK!

—in blasts that sounded weirdly like Morse.

If only . . . Lord, if only . . .

And yes. Up ahead was a sign so filthy it was only barely possible to read it: CUMBA 2.

Cumba. Goddamn Cumba. A played-out little mining town on the side of a hill, a place where there were maybe five slots and one old geezer selling Navajo blankets made in Laos.

Two miles wasn't much time when you were already doing eighty. This would have to be quick, and there would be just one chance.

The others made fun of Vince's sled, but only Race's

ridicule had a keen edge to it. The bike was a rebuilt Kawasaki Vulcan 800 with Cobra pipes and a custom seat. Leather as red as a fire alarm. "The old man's La-Z-Boy," Dean Carew had once called the seat.

"Fuck that," Vince had replied indignantly, and when Peaches, solemn as a preacher, had said, "I'm sure you have," they all broke up.

The Tribe called the Vulcan a rice-burner, of course. Also Vince's Tojo Mojo el Rojo. Doc—Doc who was now spread all over the road behind them—liked to call it Miss Fujiyama. Vince only smiled as though he knew something they didn't. Maybe he even did. He'd had the Vulcan up to one-twenty and had stopped there. Pussied out. Race wouldn't have, but Race was a young man, and young men had to know where things ended. One-twenty had been enough for Vince, but he'd known there was more. Now he would find out how much.

He grasped the throttle and twisted it all the way to the stop.

The Vulcan responded not with a snarl but a cry and almost tore out from under him. He had a blurred glimpse of his son's white face, and then he was past, in the lead, riding the rocket, desert smells packing his nose. Up ahead was a dirty string of asphalt angling off to the left, the road to Cumba. Route 6 went past in a long, lazy curve to the right. Toward Show Low.

Vince looked in his right-hand rearview and saw that the others had bunched and that Peaches still had the shiny side up. Vince thought the truck could have taken Peaches—maybe all the others—but he was laying back a little, knowing as well as Vince did that for the next twenty miles there were no upgrades. Beyond the turnoff to Cumba, the highway was elevated and a guardrail ran along either side of it; Vince thought miserably of cattle in the chute. For the next twenty miles, the road belonged to LAUGHLIN.

Please let this work.

He let off the throttle and began squeezing the handbrake rhythmically. What the four behind him saw (if they were looking) was a short flash . . . a long flash . . . another short flash. Then a pause. Then a repeat. Short . . . long . . . short. It was the truck's air horn that had given him the idea. It only *sounded* like Morse, but what Vince was flashing with his brake light *was* Morse.

It was the letter *R*.

Roy and Peaches might pick it up, Lemmy for sure. And Race? Did they still teach Morse? Had the kid learned it in his war, where squad leaders carried GPS units and bombs were guided around the curve of the world by satellite?

The left turn to Cumba was coming up. Vince had

just time enough to flash *R* one more time. Now he was almost back with the others. He shot his hand left in a gesture the Tribe knew well: *Follow me off the highway.* Laughlin saw it—as Vince had expected—and surged forward. At the same time he did, Vince twisted his throttle again. The Vulcan screamed and leaped forward. He banked right, along the main road. The others followed. But not the truck. LAUGHLIN had already started its turn onto the Cumba spur. If the driver had tried to correct for the main road, he would have rolled his rig.

Vince felt a white throb of elation and reflexively closed his left hand into a triumphant fist. *We did it! We fucking did it! By the time he gets that fat-ass truck turned around, we'll be nine miles from h—*

The thought broke off like a branch as he looked again into his rearview. There were three bikes behind him, not four: Lemmy, Peaches, and Roy.

Vince swiveled to the left, hearing the old bones crackle in his back, knowing what he would see. He saw it. The truck, dragging a huge rooster tail of red dust, its tanker too dirty to shine. But there was shine fifty or so yards in front of it, the gleam of the chromed pipes and engine belonging to a Softail Deuce. Race either did not understand Morse, didn't believe what he was seeing, or hadn't seen at all. Vince remembered the waxy, fixed expression on his son's face and thought this last possibility was most likely. Race had stopped paying attention to the rest of them—had stopped *seeing* them—the moment he understood that LAUGHLIN was not just a truck out of control but one bent on tribal slaughter. He had been just aware enough to spot Vince's hand gesture but had lost all the rest to a kind of tunnel vision. What was that? Panic? Or some animal selfishness? Or were they the same when you came down to it?

Race's Harley slipped behind a low swell of hill. The truck disappeared after it, and then there was only blowing dust. Vince tried to catch his flying thoughts and put them in some coherent order. If his memory was right again—he knew he was asking a lot of it; he hadn't been this way in a couple of years—then the spur road ran through Cumba before veering back to rejoin Highway 6 about nine miles ahead. If Race could stay in front—

Except.

Except, unless things had changed, the road went to hardpan dirt beyond Cumba and was apt to drift across sandy at this time of year. The truck would do okay, but a motorcycle . . .

The chances that Race would survive the last four miles of that nine-mile run weren't good. The chances of his dumping the Deuce and being run over were, on the other hand, excellent.

Images of Race tried to crowd his mind. Race on his Big Wheel: the kindergarten warrior. Race staring at him from the backseat of the GTO, the Popsicle melting, his eyes bright with hate, the lower lip quivering. Race at eighteen, wearing a uniform and a fuck-you smile, both present and accounted for and all squared away.

Last came the image of Race dead on the hard-pan, a smashed doll with only his leathers holding him together.

Vince swept the pictures away. They were no help. The cops wouldn't be either. There *were* no cops, not in Cumba. Someone seeing the semi chasing the bike might call the state police, but the closest statie was apt to be in Show Low, drinking java and eating pie and flirting with the waitress while Travis Tritt played on the Rock-Ola.

There was only them. But that was nothing new.

Vince thrust his hand to the right, then made a fist and patted the air with it. The other three swung over to the side behind him, engines clobbering, the air over their straight-pipes shimmering.

Lemmy pulled up beside him, his face haggard and

cheesy yellow. *"He didn't see the taillight signal!"* he shouted.

"Didn't see or didn't understand!" Vince yelled back. He was trembling. Maybe it was just the bike throbbing under him. *"Comes to the same! Time for Little Boy!"*

For a moment Lemmy didn't understand. Then he twisted around and yanked the straps on his right-hand saddlebag. No fancy plastic hardcase for Lemmy. Lemmy was old-school all the way.

While he was rooting, there was a sudden, gunning roar. That was Roy. Roy had had enough. He wheeled around and shot back east, his shadow now running before him, a scrawny black gantry-man. On the back of his leather vest was a hideous joke: NO RETREAT, NO SURRENDER.

"Come back, Klowes, you dickwad!" Peaches bellowed. His hand slipped from his clutch. The Beezer, still in gear, lurched forward almost over Vince's foot, passed high-octane gas, and stalled. Peaches was almost hurled off but didn't seem to notice. He was still looking back. He shook his fist; his scant gray hair whirled around his long, narrow skull. *"Come back, you chickenshit DICKWAAAAD!"*

Roy didn't come back. Roy didn't even *look* back.

Peaches turned to Vince. Tears streamed down

cheeks sun-flayed by a million rides and ten million beers. In that moment he looked older than the desert he stood on.

"You're stronger'n me, Vince, but I got me a bigger asshole. You rip his head off, I'll be in charge of shittin' down his neck."

"Hurry up!" Vince shouted at Lemmy. *"Hurry up, goddamn you!"*

Just when he thought Lemmy was going to come up empty, his old running buddy straightened with Little Boy in his gloved hand.

The Tribe did not ride with guns. Outlaw motorheads like them never did. They all had records, and any cop in Nevada would be delighted to put one of them away for thirty years on a gun charge. One, or all of them. They carried knives, but knives were no good in this situation; witness what had happened to Roy's machete, which had turned out as useless as the man himself. Except when it came to killing stoned little girls in high-school sweaters, that was.

Little Boy, however, while not strictly legal, was not a gun. And the one cop who'd looked at it ("while searching for drugs"—the pigs were always doing that; it was what they lived for) had given Lemmy a skate when Lemmy explained it was more reliable than a road flare if you broke down at night. Maybe the cop knew what he was looking at, maybe not, but he knew that Lemmy was a veteran. Not just from Lemmy's veteran's license plate, which could have been stolen, but because the cop had been a vet himself. "Au Shau Valley, where the shit smells sweeter," he'd said, and they had both laughed and even ended up bumping fists.

Little Boy was an M84 stun grenade, more popularly known as a flashbang. Lemmy had been carrying it in his saddlebag for maybe five years, always saying it would come in handy someday when the other guys—Vince included—ribbed him about it.

Someday had turned out to be today.

"Will this old son of a bitch still work?" Vince shouted as he hung Little Boy over his handlebars by the strap. It didn't look like a grenade. It looked like a combination thermos bottle and aerosol can. The only grenade-y thing about it was the pull ring duct-taped to the side.

"I don't know! I don't even know how you can—"

Vince had no time to discuss logistics. He had only a vague idea of what the logistics might be anyway. *"I have to ride! That fuck's gonna come out on the other end of the Cumba road! I mean to be there when he does!"*

"And if Race ain't in front of him?" Lemmy asked. They had been shouting until now, all jacked up on adrenaline. It was almost a surprise to hear a nearly normal tone of voice.

"One way or the other," Vince said. "You don't have to come. Either of you. I'll understand if you want to turn back. He's my boy."

"Maybe so," Peaches said, "but it's our Tribe. Was, anyway." He jumped down on the Beezer's kick, and the hot engine rumbled to life. "I'll ride witcha, Cap."

Lemmy just nodded and pointed at the road.

Vince took off.

It wasn't as far as he'd thought: seven miles instead of nine. They met no cars or trucks. The road was deserted, traffic maybe avoiding it because of the construction back the way they'd come. Vince snapped constant glances to his left. For a while he saw red dust rising, the truck dragging half the desert along in its slipstream. Then he lost sight even of its dust, the Cumba spur dropping well out of view behind hills with eroded, chalky sides.

Little Boy swung back and forth on its strap. Army surplus. *Will this old son of a bitch still work?* he'd asked Lemmy, and now realized he could have asked the same question of himself. How long since he'd been tested this way, running dead out, throttle to the max? How long since the whole world came down to only two choices, live pretty or die laughing? And how had his own son, who looked so cool in his new leathers and his mirrored sunglasses, missed such an elementary equation?

Live pretty or die laughing, but don't you run. Don't you fucking run.

Maybe Little Boy would work, maybe it wouldn't, but Vince knew he was going to take his shot, and it made him giddy. If the guy was buttoned up in his cab, it was a lost cause in any case. But he hadn't been buttoned up back at the diner. Back there his hand had been lolling out against the side of the truck. And later, hadn't he waved them ahead from that same open window? Sure. Sure he had.

Seven miles. Five minutes, give or take. Long enough for a lot of memories of his son, whose father had taught him to change oil but never to bait a hook, to gap plugs but never how you told a coin from the Denver mint from one that had been struck in San Francisco. Time to think how Race had pushed for this stupid meth deal and how Vince had gone along even though he knew it was stupid, because it seemed he had something to make up for. Only the time for makeup calls was past. As Vince tore along at eighty-five, bending as low as he could get to cut the wind resistance, a terrible thought crossed his mind, one he inwardly recoiled from but could not blot out—that maybe it would be better for all concerned if LAUGHLIN *did* succeed in running his son down. It wasn't the image of Race lifting a shovel into the air and then bringing it down on a helpless man's head, in a spoiled rage over lost money, although that was bad enough. It was something more. It was the fixed, empty look on the kid's face right before he steered his bike the wrong way, onto the Cumba road. For himself, Vince had not been able to stop looking back at the Tribe, the whole way into the canyon, as some were run down and the others struggled to stay ahead of the big machine. Whereas Race had seemed incapable of turning that stiff neck of his. There was nothing behind him that he needed to see. Maybe never had been.

There came a loud *ka-pow* at Vince's back and a yell he heard even over the wind and the steady blat of the Vulcan's engine: *"Mutha-FUCK!"* He looked in the rearview mirror and saw Peaches falling back. Smoke was boiling from between his pipestem legs, and oil slicked the road behind him in a fan shape that widened as his ride slowed. The Beez had finally blown its head gasket. A wonder it hadn't happened sooner.

Peaches waved them on—not that Vince would have stopped. Because in a way the question of whether Race was redeemable was moot. Vince himself was not redeemable; none of them were. He remembered an Arizona cop who'd once pulled them over and said, "Well, look what the road puked up." And that was what they were: road puke. But those bodies back there had until this afternoon been his running buddies, the only thing he possessed of any value in the world. They'd been Vince's brothers in a way, and Race was his son, and you couldn't drive a man's family to earth and expect to live. You couldn't leave them butchered and expect to ride away. If LAUGHLIN didn't know that, he would.

Soon.

Lemmy couldn't keep up with the Tojo Mojo el Rojo. He fell farther and farther behind. That was all right. Vince was just glad Lemmy still had his six.

Up ahead a sign: WATCH FOR LEFT-ENTERING TRAFFIC. The road coming out of Cumba. It was hardpan dirt, as Vince had feared. He slowed, then stopped, turned off the Vulcan's engine.

Lemmy pulled up beside. There was no guardrail here. Here in this one place, where 6 rejoined the Cumba road, the highway was level with the desert, although not far ahead it began to climb away from the floodplain once more, turning into the cattle chute again.

"Now we wait," Lemmy said, switching his engine off as well.

Vince nodded. He wished he still smoked. He told himself that either Race was still shiny side up and in front of the truck or he wasn't. It was beyond Vince's control. It was true, but it didn't help.

"Maybe he'll find a place to turn off in Cumba," Lemmy said. "An alley or somethin' where the truck can't go."

"I don't think so. Cumba is nothing. A gas station and maybe a couple houses, all stuck right on the side of a fucking hill. That's bad road. At least for Race. No easy way off it." He didn't even try to tell Lemmy about Race's blank, locked-down expression, a look that said he wasn't seeing anything except the road right in front of his bike. Cumba would be a blur and a flash that he registered only after it was well behind him.

"Maybe—" Lemmy began, but Vince held up his hand, silencing him. They cocked their heads to the left.

They heard the truck first, and Vince felt his heart sink. Then, buried in its roar, the bellow of another motor. There was no mistaking the distinctive blast of a Harley running full out.

"He made it!" Lemmy yelled, and raised his hand for a high five. Vince wouldn't give it. Bad luck. And besides, the kid still had to make the turn back onto 6. If he was going to dump, it would be there.

A minute ticked by. The sound of the engines grew louder. A second minute and now the two men could see dust rising over the nearest hills. Then, in a notch between the two closest hills, they saw a flash of sun on chrome. There was just time to glimpse Race, bent almost flat over his handlebars, long hair streaming out behind, and then he was gone again. An instant after he disappeared—surely no more—the truck flashed through the notch, stacks shooting smoke. LAUGHLIN on the side was no longer visible; it had been buried beneath a layer of dust.

Vince hit the Vulcan's starter, and the engine bammed to life. He gunned the throttle, and the frame vibrated.

"Luck, Cap," Lemmy said.

Vince opened his mouth to reply, but in that moment emotion, intense and unexpected, choked off his wind. So instead of speaking, he gave Lemmy a brief, grateful nod before taking off. Lemmy followed. As always, Lemmy had his six.

Vince's mind turned into a computer, trying to figure speed versus distance. It had to be timed just right. He rolled toward the intersection at fifty, dropped it to forty, then twisted the throttle again as Race appeared, the bike swerving around a tumbleweed, actually going airborne on a couple of bumps. The truck was no more than thirty feet behind. When Race neared the Y where the Cumba bypass once more joined the main road, he slowed. He had to slow. The instant he did, LAUGHLIN vaulted forward, eating up the distance between them.

"Jam that motherfuck!" Vince screamed, knowing that Race couldn't hear over the bellow of the truck. He screamed it again anyway: *"JAM that motherfuck! Don't slow down!"*

The trucker planned to slam the Harley in the rear wheel, spinning it out. Race's bike hit the crotch of the intersection and surged, Race leaning far to the left, holding the handlebars only with the tips of his fingers. He looked like a trick rider on a trained mustang. The truck missed the rear fender, its blunt nose lunging into thin air that had held a Harley's back wheel a mere tenth of a second before—but at first Vince thought Race was going to lose it anyway, just spin out.

He didn't. His high-speed arc took him all the way to the far side of Route 6, close enough to the bike-killing shoulder to spume up dust, and then he was scat-gone, gunning down Route 6 toward Show Low.

The truck went out into the desert to make its own turn, rumbling and bouncing, the driver downshifting through the gears fast enough to make the whole rig shudder, the tires churning up a fog of dust that turned the blue sky white. It left a trail of deep tracks and crushed sagebrush before regaining the road and once more setting out after Vince's son.

Vince twisted the left handgrip, and the Vulcan took off. Little Boy swung frantically back and forth on the handlebars. Now came the easy part. It might get Vince killed, but it would be easy compared to the endless minutes he and Lemmy had waited before hearing Race's motor mixed in with LAUGHLIN's.

His window won't be open, you know. Not after he just got done running through all that dust.

That was also out of Vince's control. If the trucker was buttoned up, he'd deal with that when the moment came.

It wouldn't be long.

The truck was doing around sixty. It could go a lot faster, but Vince didn't mean to let him get all the way through those who-knew-how-many gears of his until the Mack hit warp-speed. He was going to end this now for one of them. Probably for himself, an idea he did not shy from. He would at the least buy Race more time; given a lead, Race could easily beat the truck to Show Low. More than just protecting Race, though, there had to be balance to the scales. Vince had never lost so much so fast, four of the Tribe dead on a stretch of road less than half a mile long. You didn't do that to a man's family, he thought again, and then just drive away.

Which was, Vince saw at last, maybe LAUGHLIN's own point, his own primary operating principle—the reason he'd taken them on, in spite of the ten-to-one odds. He had come at them, not knowing or caring if they were armed, picking them off two and three at a time, even though any one of the bikes he'd run down could've sent the truck out of control and rolling, first a Mack and then an oil-stoked fireball. It was madness, but not *incomprehensible* madness. As Vince swung into the left-hand lane and began to close the final distance, the truck's ass-end just ahead on his right, he saw something that seemed not only to sum up this terrible day but to explain it, in simple, perfectly lucid terms. It was a bumper sticker. It was even filthier than the Cumba sign, but still readable.

PROUD PARENT OF A CORMAN HIGH
HONOR ROLL STUDENT!

Vince pulled even with the dust-streaked tanker. In the cab's long driver's-side rearview, he saw something shift. The driver had seen him. In the same second, Vince saw that the window *was* shut, just as he'd feared.

The truck began to slide left, crossing the white line with its outside wheels.

For a moment Vince had a choice: back off or keep going. Then the computer in his head told him the choice was already past; even if he hit the brakes hard enough to risk dumping his ride, the final five feet of the filthy tank would swat him into the guardrail on his left like a fly.

Instead of backing off, he increased speed even as the left lane shrank, the truck forcing him toward that knee-high ribbon of gleaming steel. He yanked the flashbang from the handlebars, breaking the strap. He tore the duct tape away from the pull ring with his teeth, the strap's shredded end spanking his cheek as he did so. The ring began to clatter against Little Boy's perforated barrel. The sun was gone. Vince was flying in the truck's shadow now. The guardrail was less than three feet to his left, the side of the truck three feet to his right and still closing. Vince had reached the plate hitch between the tanker and the cab. Now he could see just the top of Race's head; the rest of him was blocked by the truck's dirty maroon hood. Race was not looking back.

Vince didn't think about the next thing. There was no plan, no strategy. It was just his road-puke self saying fuck you to the world, as he always had. It was,

when you came right down to it, the Tribe's only rai-
son d'être.

As the truck closed in for the killing side-stroke, and
with absolutely nowhere to go, Vince raised his right
hand and shot the truck driver the bird.

He was pulling even with the cab now, the truck
bulking to his right like a filthy mesa. It was the cab that
would take him out.

There was movement from inside: that deeply tanned
arm with its Marine Corps tattoo. The muscle in the arm
bunched as the window slid down into its slot, and Vince
realized that the cab, which should have swatted him already, was staying where it was. The trucker meant to
do it, of course he did, but not until he had replied in
kind. *Maybe we even served in different units together,*
Vince thought. *In the Au Shau Valley, say, where the
shit smells sweeter.* Or maybe he'd been in the sand with
Race—God knew they'd called plenty of old boys back
to fight in the desert. It didn't matter. One war was like
another.

The window was down. The hand came out. It
started to hatch its own bird, then stopped. The driver
had just realized the hand that had given him the finger
wasn't empty. It was curled around something. Vince
didn't give him time to think about it, and he never saw

the trucker's face. All he saw was the tattoo, DEATH BE-FORE DISHONOR. A good thought, and how often did you get a chance to give someone exactly what he wanted?

Vince caught the ring in his teeth, pulled it, heard the fizz of some chemical reaction starting, and tossed Little Boy in through the window. It didn't have to be a fancy half-court shot, not even a lousy pull-up jumper. Just a lob. He was a magician, opening his hands to set free a dove where a moment before there'd been a wadded-up handkerchief.

Now you take me out, Vince thought. *Let's finish this thing right.*

But the truck swerved away from him. Vince was sure it would have come swerving back if there'd been time. That swerve was only reflex, LAUGHLIN trying to get away from a thrown object. But it was enough to save his life, because Little Boy did its thing before the driver could course-correct and drive Vince Adamson off the road.

The cab lit up in a vast white flash, as if God himself had bent down to take a snapshot. Instead of swerving back to the left, LAUGHLIN veered away to the right, first back into the lane of Route 6 bound for Show Low, then beyond. The tractor flayed the guardrail on the right-hand side of the road, striking up a sheet of copper sparks, a shower of fire, a thousand Catherine wheels going off at once. Vince thought madly of July Fourth, Race a child again and sitting in his lap to watch the rockets' red glare, the bombs bursting in air: sky flares shining in his child's delighted, inky eyes.

Then the truck crunched through the guardrail, shredding it as if it were tinfoil. LAUGHLIN nosed over a twenty-foot embankment, into a ravine filled with sand and tumbleweeds. The wheels caught. The truck slued. The big tanker rammed forward into the back of the cab. Vince had shot beyond that point before he could brake to a stop, but Lemmy saw it all: saw the cab and the tanker form a V and then split apart, saw the tanker roll first and the cab a second or two after, saw the tanker burst open and then blow. It went up in a fireball and a greasy pillar of black smoke. The cab rolled past it, over and over, the cube shape turning into a senseless crumple of maroon that sparked hot shards of sun where bare metal had split out in prongs and hooks.

It landed with the driver's window facing up to the sky, about eighty feet away from the pillar of fire that had been its cargo. By then Vince was running back along his own skid mark. He saw the figure that tried to pull itself through the misshapen window. The face turned toward him, except there was no face, only a mask of blood. The driver emerged to the waist before collapsing back inside. One tanned arm—the one with the tattoo—stuck up like a submarine's periscope. The hand dangled limp on the wrist.

Vince stopped at Lemmy's bike, gasping for breath. For a moment he thought he was going to pass out, but he leaned over, put his hands on his knees, and presently felt a little better.

"You got him, Cap." Lemmy's voice was hoarse with emotion.

"We better make sure," Vince said. Although the stiff periscope arm and the hand dangling limp at the end of it suggested that would just be a formality.

"Why not?" Lemmy said. "I gotta take a piss anyway."

"You're not pissing on him, dead or alive," Vince said.

There was an approaching roar: Race's Harley. He pulled up in a showy skid stop, killed the engine, and got off. His face, although dusty, glowed with delight and triumph. Vince hadn't seen Race look that way since the kid was twelve. He had won a dirt-track race in a quarter-midget Vince had built for him, a yellow torpedo with a souped-up Briggs & Stratton engine. Race had come leaping from the cockpit with that exact same expression on his face, right after taking the checkered flag.

He threw his arms around Vince and hugged him. "You did it! You *did* it, Dad! You cooked his fucking ass!"

For a moment Vince allowed the hug. Because it had been so long. And because this was his spoiled son's better angel. Everybody had one; even at his age, and after all he'd seen, Vince believed that. So for a moment he allowed the hug, and relished the warmth of his son's body, and promised himself he would remember it.

Then he put his hands against Race's chest and pushed him away. Hard. Race stumbled backward on his custom snakeskin boots, the expression of love and triumph fading—

No, not fading. *Merging.* Becoming the look Vince had come to know so well: distrust and dislike. *Quit, why don't you? That's not dislike and never was.*

No, not dislike. Hate, bright and glowing.

All squared away, sir, and fuck you.

"What was her name?" Vince asked.

"What?"

"Her name, John." He hadn't called Race by his actual name in years, and there was no one but them to hear it now. Lemmy was sliding down the soft earth of the embankment, toward the crushed metal ball that had been LAUGHLIN's cab, letting them have this tender father-son moment in privacy.

"What's wrong with you?" Pure scorn. But when Vince reached out and tore off those fucking mirror shades, he saw the truth in John "Race" Adamson's eyes. He knew what this was about. Vince was coming in five-by, as they used to say in 'Nam. Did they still say that in Iraq, he wondered, or had it gone the way of Morse code?

"What do you want to do now, John? Go on to Show Low? Roust Clarke's sister for money that isn't there?"

"It could be there." Sulking now. Race gathered himself. "It *is* there. I know Clarke. He trusted that whore."

"And the Tribe? Just . . . what? Forget them? Dean and Ellis and all the others? Doc?"

"They're dead." He eyed his father. "Too slow. And most of them too old." *You, too,* the cool eyes said.

Lemmy was on his way back, his boots puffing up dust. He had something in his hand.

"What was her name?" Vince repeated. "Clarke's girlfriend. What was her name?"

"Fuck's it matter?" Race paused then, struggling to win Vince back, his expression coming as close as it ever did to pleading. "Jesus. Leave it, why don't you? We *won.* We *showed* him."

"You knew Clarke. Knew him in Fallujah, knew him

back here in the World. You were tight. If you knew him, you knew her. What was her name?"

"Janey. Joanie. Something like that."

Vince slapped him. Race blinked, startled. Dropped for a moment back to ten years old. But just for a moment. In another instant the hating look was back, a sick, curdled glare.

"He heard us talking there in that diner parking lot. The trucker," Vince said. Patiently. As if speaking to the child this young man had once been. The young man he'd risked his life to save. Ah, but that had been instinct, and he wouldn't have changed it. It was the one good thing in all this horror. This filth. Not that he'd been the only one operating on filial instinct. "He knew he couldn't take us there, but he couldn't let us go either. So he waited. Bided his time. Let us get ahead of him."

"I have no clue what you're talking about!" Very forceful. Only Race was lying, and they both knew it.

"He knew the road and went after us where the terrain favored him. Like any good soldier."

Yes. And then had pursued them with a single-minded purpose, regardless of the almost certain cost to himself. Laughlin had settled on death before dishonor. Vince knew nothing about him but felt suddenly that he liked him better than he liked his own son. Such a thing should not have been possible, but there it was.

"You're fucked in the head," Race said.

"I don't think so. For all we know, he was going to see her when we crossed his path at the diner. It's what a father might do for a kid he loved. Arrange things so he could look in every now and then. See if she might even want a ride out. Take a chance on something besides the pipe and the rock."

Lemmy rejoined them. "Dead," he said.

Vince nodded.

"This was on the visor." He handed it to Vince. Vince didn't want to look at it, but he did. It was a snapshot of a smiling girl with her hair in a ponytail. She wore a CORMAN HIGH VARSITY sweatshirt, the same one she'd died in. She was sitting on the front bumper of LAUGHLIN, her back resting against the silver grille. She was wearing her daddy's camo cap turned around backward and mock-saluting and struggling not to grin. Saluting who? Laughlin himself, of course. Laughlin had been holding the camera.

"Her name was Jackie Laughlin," Race said. "And she's dead, too, so fuck her."

Lemmy started forward, ready to pull Race off his

bike and feed him his teeth, but Vince held him back with a look. Then he shifted his gaze back to his boy.

"Ride on, son," he said. "Keep the shiny side up."

Race looked at him, not understanding.

"But don't stop in Show Low, because I intend to let the cops know a certain little whore might need protection. I'll tell them some nut killed her brother and she might be next."

"And what are you going to tell them when they ask how you happened to come by that information?"

"Everything," Vince said, his voice calm. Serene, even. "Better get moving. Ride on. It's what you do best. Keeping ahead of that truck on the Cumba road—that was something. I'll give you that. You got a gift for hightailing it. Not much else, but you got that. So hightail your ass out of here."

Race looked at him, unsure and suddenly frightened. But that wouldn't last. He'd get his fuck-you back. It was all he had: some fuck-you attitude, a pair of mirrored sunglasses, and a fast bike.

"Dad—"

"Better go on, son," Lemmy said. "Someone will have seen that smoke by now. There'll be staties here soon."

Race smiled. When he did, a single tear spilled from

his left eye and cut a track through the dust on his face. "Just a couple of old chickenshits," he said.

He went back to his bike. The chains across the insteps of his snakeskin boots jingled—a little foolishly, Vince thought.

Race swung his leg over the seat, started his Harley, and drove away west, toward Show Low. Vince did not expect him to look back and was not disappointed.

They watched him. After a while Lemmy said: "You want to go, Cap?"

"No place *to* go, man. I think I might just sit here for a bit, side of the road."

"Well," Lemmy said. "If you want. I guess I could sit some myself."

They went to the side of the road and sat down cross-legged like old Indians with no blankets to sell and watched the tanker burn in the desert, piling black oil smoke into the blue, unforgiving sky. Some of it drifted back their way, reeking and greasy.

"We can move," Vince said. "If you mind the smell."

Lemmy tipped his head back and inhaled deeply, like a man considering the bouquet of a pricey wine.

"No, I don't mind it. Smells like Vietnam."

Vince nodded.

"Makes me think of them old days," Lemmy said. "When we were almost as fast as we believed we were."

Vince nodded again. "Live pretty—"

"Yep. Or die laughin'."

They said nothing more after that, just sat there, waiting, Vince with the girl's picture in his hand. Every once in a while, he glanced at it, turning it in the sun, considering how young she looked, and how happy.

But mostly he watched the fire.

Dark Carousel

It used to be on postcards: the carousel at the end of the Cape Maggie Pier. It was called the Wild Wheel, and it ran fast—not as fast as a roller coaster but quite a bit faster than the usual carousel for kiddies. The Wheel looked like an immense cupcake, its cupola roof striped in black and green with royal gold trim. After dark it was a jewel box awash in an infernal red glow, like the light inside an oven. Wurlitzer music floated up and down the beach, discordant strains that sounded like a Romanian waltz, something for a nineteenth-century ball attended by Dracula and his icy white brides.

It was the most striking feature of Cape Maggie's run-down, seedy harbor walk. The harbor walk had been run-down and seedy since my grandparents were kids. The air was redolent with the cloying perfume of cotton candy, an odor that doesn't exist in nature and can only be described as "pink" smell. There was always a puddle of vomit on the boardwalk that had to be avoided. There were always soggy bits of popcorn floating in the puke. There were a dozen sit-down restaurants where you could pay too much for fried clams and wait too long to get them. There were always harassed-looking, sunburned grown-ups carrying shrieking, sunburned children, the whole family out for a seaside lark.

On the pier itself, there were the usual stands selling candied apples and hot dogs, booths where you could shoot an air rifle at tin outlaws who popped up from behind tin cacti. There was a great pirate ship that swung back and forth like a pendulum, sailing high out over the sides of the pier and the ocean beyond, while shrill screams carried into the night. I thought of that ride as the SS *Fuck No*. And there was a bouncy house called Bertha's Bounce. The entrance was the face of an obscenely fat woman with glaring eyes and glistening red cheeks. You took your shoes off outside and climbed in over her lolling tongue, between bloated lips. That was where the trouble started, and it was Geri Renshaw and I who started it. After all, there wasn't any rule that big kids, or even teenagers, couldn't play in the bouncy house. If you had a ticket, you could have your three minutes to leap around—and Geri said she wanted to see if it was as much fun as she remembered.

We went in with five little kids, and the music started, a recording of small children with piping voices, singing a highly sanitized version of "Jump Around" by House of Pain. Geri took my hands, and we jumped up and down, bounding about like astronauts on the moon. We lurched this way and that until we crashed into a wall and she pulled me down. When she rolled on top and began to bounce on *me*, she was just goofing, but the gray-haired woman who'd taken our tickets was watching, and she shouted, "NONE OF THAT!" at the top of her lungs and snapped her fingers at us. "OUT! This is a family ride."

"Got that right," Geri said, leaning over me, her breath warm in my face and pink-scented. She had just inhaled a cloud of cotton candy. She was in a tight, striped halter top that left her tanned midriff bare. Her breasts were right in my face in a very lovely way. "This is the kind of ride that makes families, if you don't use protection."

I laughed—I couldn't help it—even though I was embarrassed and my face was burning. Geri was like that. Geri and her brother Jake were always dragging me into situations that excited and discomfited me in equal measure. They led me into things that I regretted in the moment but were later a pleasure to remember. Real sin, I think, produces the same emotions, in the exact opposite order.

As we exited, the ticket collector stared at us the way a person might look at a snake eating a rat, or two beetles fucking.

"Keep your pants on, Bertha," Geri said. "We did."

I grinned like an idiot but still felt bad. Geri and Jake Renshaw would take shit from no man, and no woman either. They relished verbally swatting down the ignorant and the self-righteous: the twerp, the bully, and the Baptist all the same.

Jake was waiting with an arm around Nancy Fairmont's waist when we came reeling across the pier. He had a wax cup of beer in the other hand, and he gave it to me as I walked up. God, it was *good*. That right there might've been the best beer of my life. Salty and cold, the sides of the cup beaded with ice water, and the flavor mixed with the briny tang of the sea air.

It was the tail end of August in 1994, and all of us were eighteen and free, although Jake could've easily passed for almost thirty. To look at Nancy, it was hard to believe she was dating Jake Renshaw, who with his flattop cut and his tattoos looked like trouble (and sometimes was). But then it was hard to picture a kid like me with Geri. Geri and Jake were twins and six feet tall to the inch—which meant they both had two inches on me, something that always bothered me when I had to rise on my toes to give Geri a kiss. They were strong, lean, limber, and blond, and they grew up jumping dirt bikes and doing after-school detentions. Jake had a criminal record. The only reason Geri didn't have one as well, Jake insisted, was that she'd never been caught.

Nancy, on the other hand, wore glasses with lenses as big as tea saucers and went everywhere with a book clutched to her flat chest. Her father was a veterinarian, her mother a librarian. As for me, Paul Whitestone, I longed to have a tattoo and a criminal record of my own, but instead I had an acceptance letter from Dartmouth and a notebook full of one-act plays.

Jake, Geri, and I had made the run to Cape Maggie in Jake Renshaw's 1982 Corvette, a car as sleek as a cruise missile and almost as fast. It was a two-seater, and no one would let us ride in it today the way we did then: Geri in my lap, Jake behind the wheel, and a six-pack of beer behind the stick shift—which we polished off while we were en route. We had come down from Lewiston to meet Nancy, who'd worked on the pier all summer long, selling fried dough. When she finished her shift, the four of us were going to drive nine miles to my parents' summer cottage on Maggie Pond. My parents were home in Lewiston, and we'd have the place to ourselves. It seemed like a good spot to make our final stand against adulthood.

Maybe I felt guilty about offending the ticket lady at Big Bertha, but Nancy was there to clear my conscience. She touched her glasses and said, "Mrs. Gish over there pickets Planned Parenthood every Sunday, with faked-up pictures of dead babies. Which is pretty funny, since her husband owns half the booths on the pier, including Funhouse Funnel Cakes, where I work, and he's tried to cop a feel on just about every girl who ever worked for him."

"Does he, now?" Jake asked. He was grinning, but there was a slow, sly chill in his voice that I knew from experience was a warning that we were wading into dangerous territory.

"Never mind, Jake," Nancy said, and she kissed his cheek. "He only paws high-school girls. I'm too old for him now."

"You ought to point him out sometime," Jake said, and he looked this way and that along the pier, as if scouting for the guy right then and there.

Nancy put her hand on his chin and forcibly turned his head to look at her. "You mean I ought to ruin our night by letting you get arrested and kicked out of the service?" He laughed at her, but suddenly she was cross with him. "You dick around, Jake, and you could do five years. The only reason you aren't there already is the marines took you—I guess because our nation's military-industrial complex can always use more cannon fodder. It's not your job to get even with every creep who ever wandered down the harbor walk."

"It's not your job to make sure I get out of Maine," Jake said, his tone almost mild. "And if I wind up in the state prison, at least I'd get to see you on the weekends."

"I wouldn't visit you," she said.

"Yes you would," he told her, kissing her cheek, and she blushed and looked upset, and we all knew she would. It was embarrassing how tightly she was wrapped around Jake's finger, how badly she wanted to make him happy. I understood exactly how she felt, because I was stuck on Geri just the same way.

Six months before, we had all gone bowling at Lewiston Lanes, something to do to kill a Thursday night. A drunk in the next lane made an obscene moan of appreciation when Geri bent over to get a ball, noisily admiring her rear in her tight jeans. Nancy told him not to be vile, and he replied that she didn't need to worry, no one was going to bother checking out a no-tits cunt like herself. Jake had gently kissed Nancy on the top of her head and then, before she could grab his wrist and pull him back, decked the guy hard enough to shatter his nose and knock him flat.

The only problem was that the drunk and his buddies were all off-duty cops, and in the fracas that followed, Jake was wrestled to the floor and handcuffed, a snub-nosed revolver put to his head. In the trial much was made of the fact that he had a switchblade in his pocket and a prior record of petty vandalism. The drunk—who in court was no longer a drunk but instead a good-looking officer of the law with a wife and four kids—insisted he had called Nancy a "little runt," not a "no-tits cunt." But it hardly mattered what he'd said, because the judge felt that both girls had been provocative in dress and behavior and so presumably had no right to be outraged by a little ribald commentary. The judge told Jake it was jail or military service, and two days later Jake was on his way to Camp Lejeune in North Carolina, his head shaved and everything he owned stuffed into a Nike gym bag.

Now he was back for ten days on leave. The week after next, he'd board a plane at Bangor International Airport and fly to Germany for deployment in Berlin. I wouldn't be there to see him go—by then I'd be moved into my dorm in New Hampshire. Nan was on her way elsewhere as well. After Labor Day she started classes at U of Maine in Orono. Only Geri was going nowhere, staying behind in Lewiston, where she had a job with housekeeping at a Days Inn. Jake had committed the assault, but it often seemed to me that somehow Geri was the one who'd received the prison sentence.

Nan was on break, still had a few hours on her shift to go before she was free. She wanted to blow the smell of fried grease from her hair, so we wandered out toward the end of the pier. A salty, scouring wind sang among the guy wires, snapped the pennants. The wind was blowing hard inland, too, coming in gusts that ripped off hats and slammed doors. Back on shore that wind felt like summer, sultry and sweet with the smell of baked grass and hot tarmac. Out on the end of the pier, the gusts carried a thrilling chill that made your pulse race. Out on the end of the pier, you were in October Country.

We slowed as we approached the Wild Wheel, which had just stopped turning. Geri tugged my hand and pointed at one of the creatures on the carousel. It was a black cat the size of a pony, with a limp mouse in its jaws. The cat's head was turned slightly, so it seemed to be watching us avidly with its bright green glass eyes.

"Oh, hey," Geri said. "That one looks just like me on my first date with Paul."

Nancy clapped a hand over her mouth to stifle her laughter. Geri didn't need to say which of us was the mouse and which was the cat. Nancy had a lovely, helpless laugh that went through her whole tiny frame, doubled her over, and turned her face pink.

"Come on," Geri said. "Let's find our spirit animals." And she let go of my hand and took Nancy's.

The Wurlitzer began to play, a theatrical, whimsical, but also curiously dirgelike melody. Wandering amid the steeds, I looked at the creatures of the Wheel with a mix of fascination and repulsion. It seemed to me a uniquely disquieting collection of grotesqueries. There was a wolf as big as a bicycle, its sculpted, glossy fur a tangled mess of blacks and grays and its eyes as yellow as my beer. One paw was lifted slightly, and its pad was crimson, as if he had trod in blood. A sea serpent uncoiled itself across the outer edge of the carousel, a scaly rope as thick as a tree trunk. It had a shaggy gold mane and a gaping red mouth lined with black fangs. When I leaned in close, I discovered they were real: a mismatched set of shark's teeth, black with age. I walked through a team of white horses, frozen in the act of lunging, tendons straining in their necks, their mouths open as if to scream in anguish or rage. White horses with white eyes, like classical statuary.

"Where the hell you think they got these horses from? Satan's Circus Supplies? Lookat," Jake said, and he gestured at the mouth of one of the horses. It had the black, forked tongue of a snake, lolling out of its mouth.

"They come from Nacogdoches, Texas," came a voice from down on the pier. "They're over a century old. They were salvaged from Cooger's Carousel of Ten Thousand Lights, after a fire burned Cooger's Fun Park to the ground. You can see how that one there was scorched."

The ride operator stood at a control board, to one side of the steps leading up to the merry-go-round. He wore a dress uniform, as if he were an ancient bellboy in some grand Eastern European hotel, a place where aristocrats went to summer with their families. His suit jacket was of green velvet, with two rows of brass buttons down the front and golden epaulets on his shoulders.

He put down a steel thermos and pointed at a horse whose face was blistered on one side, toasted a golden brown, like a marshmallow. The operator's upper lip lifted in a curiously repulsive grin. He had red, plump, vaguely indecent lips, like a young Mick Jagger— unsettling in such an old, shriveled face. "They screamed."

"Who?" I asked.

"The horses," he said. "When the carousel began to burn. A dozen witnesses heard them. They screamed like girls."

My arms prickled with goose bumps. It was a delightfully macabre claim to make.

"I heard they're all salvaged," Nancy said, from somewhere just behind me. She and Geri had circumnavigated the entirety of the carousel, examining the steeds, and were only now returning to us. "There was a piece in the *Portland Press Herald* last year."

"The griffin came from Selznick's in Hungary," said the operator, "after they went bankrupt. The cat was a gift from Manx, who runs Christmasland in Colorado. The sea serpent was carved by Frederick Savage himself, who constructed the most famous carousel of them all, the Golden Gallopers on Brighton Palace Pier, after which the Wild Wheel is modeled. You're one of Mr. Gish's girls, aren't you?"

"Ye-e-sss," said Nancy slowly, perhaps because she didn't quite like the operator's phrasing, the way he called her "one of Mr. Gish's girls." "I work for him at the funnel-cake stand."

"Only the best for Mr. Gish's girls," said the operator. "Would you like to ride a horse that once carried Judy Garland?"

He stepped up onto the carousel and offered Nancy his hand, which she took without hesitation, as if he were a desirable young man asking her to dance and not a creepy old dude with fat, damp lips. He led her to the first in the herd of six horses, and when she put a foot into one golden stirrup, he braced her waist to help her up.

"Judy visited Cooger's in 1940, when she was on an extended tour to support *The Wizard of Oz*. She received a key to the city, sang 'Over the Rainbow' to an adoring crowd, and then rode the Ten Thousand Lights. There's a photo of her in my private office, riding this very horse. There you go, right up. Aren't you lovely?"

"What a crock of shit," Geri said to me as she took my arm. She spoke in a low voice, but not low enough, and I saw the operator twitch. Geri threw her leg over the black cat. "Did anyone famous ride this one?"

"Not yet. But maybe someday you yourself will be a great celebrity! And then for years to come we will be boasting about the day when," the old fellow told her in an exuberant tone. Then he caught my eye and winked and said, "You'll want to drain that beer, son. No drinks on the ride. And alcohol is hardly necessary—the Wild Wheel will provide all the intoxication you could wish for."

I had finished off two cans of the beer in the car on the ride down. My mostly full wax cup was my third. I could've put it down on the planks, but that casual suggestion—*You'll want to drain that beer, son*—seemed like the only sensible thing to do. I swallowed most of a pint in five big swallows, and by the time I crushed the cup and tossed it away into the night, the carousel was already beginning to turn.

I shivered. The beer was so cold I could feel it in my blood. A wave of dizziness rolled over me, and I reached for the closest mount, the big sea serpent with the black teeth. I got a leg over it just as it began to float upward on its rod. Jake hauled himself onto a horse beside Nancy, and Geri laid her head against her cat's neck and purred to it.

We were carried out of sight of the shore and onto the very tip of the pier, where to my left was black sky and blacker sea, roughened with whitecaps. The Wild Wheel accelerated into the bracing, salty air. Waves crashed. I shut my eyes but then had to open them again, right away. For an instant I felt as if I were diving down into the water on my sea serpent. For an instant I felt like I was drowning.

We went round, and I caught a flash of the operator, holding his thermos. When he'd been talking to us, he'd been all smiles. But in that brief glimpse I caught after we started to move, I saw a dead face, expressionless, his eyelids sagging heavily, that swollen mouth compressed into a frown. I thought I saw him digging for something in his pocket—a momentary observation that would end lives before the night was done.

The Wheel went around again and again, faster each time, unspooling its lunatic song into the night as if it were a record on a turntable. By the fourth circuit, I was surprised at how fast we were moving. I could feel the centrifugal force as a sense of weight, right between my eyebrows, and a tugging sensation in my uncomfortably full stomach. I needed to piss. I tried to tell myself I was having a good time, but I'd had too much beer. The bright flecks of the stars whipped past. The sounds of the pier came at us in bursts and were snatched away. I opened my eyes in time to see Jake and Nancy leaning toward each other, across the space between their horses, for a tender if clumsy kiss. Nan laughed, stroking the muscled neck of her ride. Geri remained pressed flat against her giant cat and looked back at me with sleepy, knowing eyes.

The cat turned its head to look back at me, too, and I shut my eyes and shuddered and looked again, and of course it wasn't staring at me.

Our rides rushed us on into the night, rushed us into the darkness in a kind of mad fury, round and round and round, but in the end none of us went anywhere.

For the next three hours, the wind blew us up and down the harbor walk, while Nancy completed her shift. I had already had too much beer and knew it and drank more anyway. When a gust got behind me, it felt dangerously close to swooping me off the ground, as if I were as light as newspaper.

Jake and I banged away at pinball in Mordor's Marvelous Machines for a while. Afterward Geri and I had a walk on the beach that started out romantic—teenage lovers holding hands, looking at the stars—and predictably devolved into our usual giddy game of roughhouse. Geri wound up dragging me by both hands into the water. I staggered in up to my knees and came out with my sneakers squishing, the legs of my jeans soaked and caked in sand. Geri, on the other hand, was wearing flip-flops and had thoughtfully rolled up the cuffs of her Levi's and made it out breathless with laughter and largely unscathed. I warmed myself back up with a pair of hot dogs smothered in bacon and cheese.

At ten-thirty the bars were so full the crowds spilled onto the boardwalk. The road along the harbor was jammed bumper to bumper, and the night resounded with happy shouts and honking horns. But almost everything else around the pier was closing down or already shut. The Bouncy House and the SS *Fuck No* had gone dark an hour before.

By then I was staggering with beer and fairground chow and feeling the first nervous clench of nausea. I was beginning to think that by the time I got Geri to bed, I'd be too tired or maybe too sick to report for action.

Funhouse Funnel Cakes was at the foot of the pier, and when we got there, the electric sign over the order window had been shut off. Nancy used a rag to sweep the cinnamon and powdered sugar from the dented counter, said good night to the girl who'd been working the stand with her, and let herself out the side door and into Jake's arms. She stood on her toes for a lingering kiss, her book under one arm: *All the Pretty Horses* by Cormac McCarthy.

"Want to get another six on our way out of town?" Jake asked me over her shoulder.

The thought turned my stomach, so naturally I said, "We better."

"I'll pay," Nancy said, and led the way to the curb, just about skipping to be free and with her guy, to be eighteen and in love, on a night where it was still seventy degrees at nearly 11:00 P.M. The wind crazed her curly hair, blowing it around her face like seagrass.

We were waiting for a break in traffic when it all began to go wrong.

Nancy smacked herself on the butt—a provocative thing to do, a little out of character, but then she was in high spirits—and fumbled in a pocket for her cash. She frowned. She searched her other pockets. Then she searched them again.

"Shhhhhoooot . . ." she said. "I must've left my money at the stand."

She led us back to Funhouse Funnel Cakes. Her co-worker had shut off the last lights and locked up, but Nancy let herself in and pulled the dangling cord. A fluorescent tube came flickering on with a wasplike buzz. Nancy searched under the counters, checked her pockets again, and looked in her hardcover to see if she'd been using her money as a bookmark. I saw her check the book myself. I'm sure of it.

"What the heck?" Nancy said. "I had a fifty-dollar bill. Fifty dollars! It was so new it looked like no one had ever spent it before. What the frickenfrack did I do with it?" She really did talk that way, like a brainy girl genius in a young-adult novel.

As she spoke, I flashed to a memory of the carousel operator helping her up onto a horse, his hand on her waist and a big smile on those juicy lips of his. Then I remembered catching a glimpse of him as we were spun past on our steeds. He hadn't been smiling then—and he'd been poking some fingers into his front pocket.

"Huh," I said aloud.

"What?" Jake asked.

I looked at Jake's narrow, handsome face, his set chin and mild eyes, and was struck with a sudden premonition of disaster. I shook my head, didn't want to say anything.

"Spill it," Jake said.

I knew better than to reply—but there's something irresistible about lighting a fuse and waiting for it to sizzle down to the charge, just to hear a loud bang. And there was always something exciting about winding up a Renshaw, for much the same reason. It was why I went into the bouncy house with Geri and why I decided to give Jake a straight answer.

"The operator on the carousel. He might've been putting something in his pocket after he helped Nan—"

I didn't get any further.

"That motherfucker," Jake said, and turned on his heel.

"Jake, no," Nancy said.

She grabbed his wrist, but he pulled free and started out along the dark pier.

"Jake!" Nancy called, but he didn't look back.

I trotted to keep up with him.

"Jake," I said, my stomach queer with booze and nerves. "I didn't see anything. Not really. He might've been reaching into his pocket to adjust his balls."

"That motherfucker," Jake repeated. "Had his hands all over her."

The Wild Wheel was dark, its stampeding creatures frozen in midleap. A heavy red velvet rope had been hung across the steps, and the sign that dangled from it said SHH! THE HORSES ARE SLEEPING! DON'T DISTURB THEM!

At the center of the carousel was an inner ring lined with mirrored panels. A glow showed around one of those panels, and from somewhere on the other side you could hear swanky horns and a tinny, crooning voice: Pat Boone, "I Almost Lost My Mind." Someone was at home in the secret cabinet at the heart of the Wild Wheel.

"Hey," Jake said. "Hey, pal!"

"Jake! Forget it!" Nancy said. She was frightened now, scared of what Jake might do. "For all I know, I put my money down for a moment and the wind grabbed it."

None of us believed that.

Geri was the first to step over the red velvet rope. If she was going, I had to follow, although by then I was scared, too. Scared and, if I'm honest, jittery with excitement. I didn't know where this was heading, but I knew the Renshaw twins, and I knew they were getting Nancy's fifty dollars back or getting even—or both.

We wove through the leaping horses. I didn't like their faces in the dark, the way their mouths gaped as if to shriek, the way their eyes seemed to stare blindly at us with terror or rage or madness. Geri reached the mirrored panel with the light leaking out around its edges and rapped her fist against it. "Hey, are you—"

But no sooner had she touched the panel than it swung inward to reveal the little engine room at the center of the Wheel.

It was an octagonal space with walls of cheap plywood. The motor that drove the central pole might've been half a century old, a dull steel block shaped vaguely like a human heart, with a black rubber drive belt at one end. On the far side of the pole was a sorry little camp bed. I didn't see any photographs of Judy Garland, but the wall above the cot was papered in *Playboy* centerfolds.

The operator sat at a folding card table, in a ratty, curiously grand chair. It had curved wooden armrests and horsehair cushions. He was slumped over, using one arm as a pillow, and didn't react as we entered. Pat Boone pitied himself, tunefully, from a little transistor radio on the edge of the table.

I glanced at his face and flinched. His eyelids weren't fully shut, and I could see the slick, gray-tinted whites of his eyes. His fleshy red lips were wet with drool.

The thermos was open nearby. The whole room reeked of motor oil and something else, a stink I couldn't quite identify.

Geri shoved his shoulder. "Hey, jack-off, my friend wants her money back."

His head lolled, but otherwise he didn't stir. Jake crowded into the room behind us, while Nancy stood outside among the horses.

Geri picked up his thermos, had a whiff, and poured it out on the floor. It was wine, a rosé, and it smelled like vinegar.

"He's pissed," she said. "Passed out drunk."

"Guys," I said. "Guys, is he— We sure he's even breathing?"

No one seemed to hear me. Jake pushed past Geri and began to dig around in one of the guy's front pockets. Then, abruptly, he recoiled, yanked his hand back as if he'd been stuck by a needle. At that moment I finally identified the rank odor that had only been partially masked by the aroma of WD-40.

"Pissed is right," Jake said. "Holy fucking shit, he's drenched. Christ, I got piss all over me."

Geri laughed. I didn't. The thought took me then that he was dead. Wasn't that what happened when your heart stopped? You lost control of your bladder?

Jake grimaced and went through the guy's pockets. He dug out a battered leather wallet and a knife with a yellowing ivory handle. Three scrimshaw horses charged across the grip.

"No," Nancy said, entering the room at last. She grabbed Jake's wrist. "Jake, you can't."

"What? I can't take back what he stole?" Jake flipped the wallet open and picked out two wrinkly twenties, all that was in there. He dropped the wallet on the floor.

"I had a *fifty*," Nancy told him. "Brand-new."

"Yeah, that fifty is in the cash register at the liquor store now. Ten bucks is just about exactly what it would've cost for another bottle. Anyway, what are you arguing about? Paul saw him pocket the money."

I hadn't, though. I was no longer sure I'd seen anything more than an old man with a weak bladder adjusting his junk. But I didn't say so, didn't want to argue. I wanted to make sure the old bastard was alive, and then I wanted to go, quickly, before he stirred or anyone else wandered by the carousel. Whatever grubby sense of delight there'd been in this expedition had fled when I caught a whiff of the operator and saw his gray face.

"Is he breathing?" I asked again, and again no one replied.

"Put it back. You'll get in trouble," Nancy said.

"You going to report me to the cops, buddy?" Jake asked the operator.

The operator didn't say anything.

"Didn't think so," Jake said. He turned and took Geri's arm and pushed her toward the door.

"We need to turn him on his side," Nancy said. Her voice was unhappy and shaky with nervousness. "If he's passed out drunk and he vomits, he could choke on it."

"Not our problem," Jake said.

Geri said, "Nan, I bet he's passed out this way a thousand times. If he hasn't died yet, he probably won't die tonight."

"Paul!" Nancy cried, sounding almost hysterical. "Please!"

My insides were knotted up, and I felt as jittery as if I had chugged a pot of coffee. I wanted to leave more than anything and can't explain why I reached for the operator's wrist instead, to search for his pulse.

"He's not dead, asshole," Jake said, but he waited nonetheless.

The operator's pulse was there—raggedy and irregular but measurable. Close up he smelled bad, and not just of urine and booze. There was a cloying odor of caked, rotten blood.

"Paul," Nancy said. "Put him on his bed. On his side."

"Don't do it," Jake said.

I didn't want to, but I didn't think I could live with myself if I found myself reading his obituary in the weekend paper, not after we jacked him for forty bucks. I put my arms under his legs and behind his back and lifted him out of his chair.

I lumbered unsteadily to the camp cot and set him on it. A dark stain soaked the crotch of his green velvet pants, and the smell aggravated my already twitchy stomach. I rolled him onto his side and put a pillow under his head, the way you're supposed to, so if he threw up, it wouldn't go back down his windpipe. He snorted but didn't look around. I circled the room, pulled the cord hanging from the ceiling to switch off the light. On the radio, the Gypsy was telling Pat Boone's fortune. It wasn't good.

I thought we were done, but when I came out, I found Geri getting her own revenge. She'd helped herself to the operator's pocketknife, and she was carving a message into Judy Garland's horse: FUCK YOU. It wasn't poetry, but it made a point.

On the walk back to the boardwalk, Jake tried to hand the forty dollars to Nancy, but she wouldn't accept it. She was too angry with him. He stuck the bills in her pocket, and she took the twenties out and threw them on the pier. Jake had to chase them down before the wind could snatch them away and cast them to the darkness.

When we reached the road, the traffic was already tapering off, although the bars were still doing brisk business. Jake told Nancy he was going to get the car and asked if she would please buy the beer, because obviously they weren't going to have sex now and he was going to need more alcohol to drink away his blues.

This time she took the money. She tried not to smile but couldn't quite help herself. Even I could see that Jake was adorable when he made himself pathetic.

When we took off for my parents' summer cottage, I was in the passenger seat of the Corvette, with Geri on my lap and Nancy squeezed between my hip and the door. They all had bottles of Sam Adams, even Jake, who drove with one nestled between his thighs. I was the only one who wasn't drinking. I could still smell the operator on my hands, an odor that made me think of decay, of cancer. I didn't have the stomach for any more, and when Geri rolled down the window to chuck her bottle out into the night, I was glad for the fresh air. I heard her empty Sam Adams hit with a musical crunch.

We were careless, irresponsible people, but, in our defense, we didn't know it. I'm not at all sure I've made you see the times clearly. In 1994 those Mothers Against Drunk Driving ads were just background noise, and I had never heard of anyone getting a ticket for littering. None of us wore seat belts. It never even crossed my mind.

I'm not sure I have properly shown you Geri or Jake Renshaw either. I've tried to show you they were dangerous—but they weren't immoral. Maybe they even had a stronger sense of morality than most, were more willing to act if they saw someone wronged. When the universe was out of whack, they felt obliged to put it back to rights, even if that meant defacing an antique horse or robbing a drunk. They were entirely indifferent to the consequences to themselves.

Nor were they thoughtless, unimaginative thugs. Nancy and I wouldn't have been with them if they were. Jake could throw knives and walk a tightrope. No one had taught him how to do those things. He just knew. In his last year of high school, after showing no interest in drama for his entire life up until then, he tried out for the Senior Shakespeare. Mr. Cuse cast him as Puck in *A Midsummer Night's Dream,* and damn it, he was *good.* He said his lines as if he'd been speaking in iambic pentameter all his life.

And Geri did voices. She could do Princess Di, and she could do Velma Dinkley. She could do an amazing Steven Tyler from Aerosmith; she could talk like him, sing like him, do his *acka-acka-acka-yow!,* and dance like him, whipping her hair from side to side, hands on her narrow waist.

I thought she was beautiful and gifted enough to be an actress. I said we should go to New York together after I finished college. I'd write plays, and she'd star in them. When I told her this, she laughed it off—and then gave me a look I didn't understand, not then. It was an emotion with which I was not familiar, a feeling no one had ever turned on me before then. I know now it was pity.

There was no moon, and the road grew darker the farther north we traveled. We followed a winding two-lane state highway through marsh and pines. For a while there were streetlights, spaced at quarter-mile intervals. Then there weren't. The wind had been strengthening all evening, and when the gusts blew, they shook the car and sent the cattails in the swamps into furious motion.

We were almost to the mile-and-a-half-long dirt track that led to my parents' cottage and the end of the evening when the Corvette swung around a horseshoe curve and Jake hit the brakes. Hard. The tires shrieked. The back end fishtailed.

"What the fuck is . . . ?" he shouted.

Nancy's face struck the dash and rebounded. Her hardcover, *All the Pretty Horses,* flew out of her hand.

Geri went into the dash, but she rolled as she slid forward and caught it with her shoulder.

A dog looked at us—its green eyes flashed in the headlights—and then it slunk out of the road and lumbered into the trees. If it *was* a dog . . . and not a bear. It certainly looked big enough to be ursine rather than canine. We could hear it crashing through the brush for several seconds after it disappeared.

"Christ," Jake said. "Now *I'm* the one who looks like he pissed himself. I dumped my beer all over my—"

"Shut up," Geri said. "Nan, honey, are you okay?"

Nancy leaned back, her chin lifted, her eyes pointed at the ceiling of the car. She cupped her nose with one hand.

"I smached my node," she said.

Geri twisted around to stretch an arm into the rear of the car. "There's some rags in the back."

I contorted myself to reach past Geri's feet to collect Nancy's book. I grabbed *All the Pretty Horses*—then hesitated, my gaze caught by something else on the carpet. I plucked it off the floor.

Geri settled back into my lap, clutching a ratty Pink Floyd tee.

"Here, use this," she said.

"That's a good shirt," Jake said.

"That's your girlfriend's face, you prick."

"Fair point. Nan, you okay?"

She balled up the T-shirt and held it to her thin, delicate nose, dabbing at blood. With her other hand, she gave a thumbs-up.

I said, "I got your book. Hey . . . um. This was on the floor with it."

I handed her the novel—and a crisp fifty-dollar bill, so clean and new-looking it might've been minted that morning.

Her eyes widened in horror around the bloodstained wad of shirt.

"Un-uh! No! *No!* I looked for it, and it wadn't there!"

"I know," I said. "I saw you look. You must've missed it."

Water quivered in Nancy's eyes, threatening to spill over.

"Hon," Geri said. "Nan. Come on. We all thought he stole your fifty. Honest mistake."

"We can tell that to the cops," I said. "If they show up asking whether we rolled a drunk on the pier. I bet they'll be very understanding."

Geri flashed a look like murder at me, and Nan began to cry, and I immediately regretted saying anything, regretted finding the money at all. I glanced anxiously at Jake—I was ready for an icy glare and some brotherly malice—but he was ignoring the three of us. He stared out the window, peering into the night.

"Anyone want to tell me what the fuck just walked across the road?" he asked.

"Dog, right?" I said, eager to change the subject.

"I didn't see," Geri said, "'cause I was trying not to eat a faceful of dash at the time."

"I never seen a dog like that," Jake said. "Thing was half the size of the car."

"Maybe it was a brown bear."

"Maybe it wad Sasquadge," Nancy said miserably.

We were all silent for a moment, letting that one land—and then we erupted into laughter. Nessie can hang it up. Cryptozoology never came up with a cuter beast than Sasquadge.

Two poles with reflective disks attached to them marked the one-lane dirt road that led to my parents' summer cottage, which sat on the estuarial pool known as Maggie Pond. Jake turned in and rolled down his window at the same time, letting in a warm slipstream of salty air that blew his hair back from his forehead.

The lane was cratered with potholes, some of them a foot deep and a yard across, and Jake had to slow to about ten miles an hour. Weeds hissed against the undercarriage. Rocks pinged.

We had gone a third of a mile when we saw the

branch, a big oak bough across the road. Jake cursed, banged the car into park.

"I god it," Nancy said.

"You stay here," Jake said, but she was already throwing the passenger door open.

"I need to stredge my leds," she said, and tossed the bloody Floyd shirt on the floor of the car as she slammed the door.

We watched her walk into Jake's headlights: cute, fragile little thing in pink sneakers. She hunched at one end of the broken branch, where the splintered, reddish wood shone bright and clean, and she began to tug.

"She ain't gonna be able to move that alone," Jake said.

"She's got it," Geri told him.

"Go help her, Paul," Jake said to me. "It'll make up for you being such a douche a couple minutes ago."

"Oh, shit, man, I wasn't even thinking. . . . I didn't mean to . . ." I said, my head sinking between my shoulders under the weight of my shame.

Out in the road, Nancy managed to turn the eight-foot branch most of the way to one side. She went around to grab the other end, perhaps to try rolling it out of the road and into the ditch.

"Couldn't you just've stuck that fifty under the seat? Nan ain't gonna sleep tonight now. You know she's going to cry her head off as soon as we're alone," Jake said. "And I'm going to be the one who has to deal with it—"

"What's that?" Geri said.

"—not you," Jake went on, as if she hadn't spoken. "You pulled your same old Paul Whitestone magic. You took a good evening, and abra-fuckin'-cadabra—"

"Do you *hear* that?" Geri asked again.

I *felt* it before I heard it. The car shook. I became aware of a sound like an approaching storm front, rain drumming heavily on the earth. It was like being parked alongside a railroad track as a freight train thundered past.

The first of the horses thundered past on the left, so close that one shoulder brushed the driver's-side mirror. Nancy looked up and let go of the branch and made a move like she was going to jump out of the road. She only had a moment, maybe a second or two, and she didn't get far. The horse rode her down, hooves flashing, and Nancy fell beneath them. She was prone in the road when the next horse went over her. I heard her spine crack. Or maybe that was the big tree branch, I don't know.

A third horse flashed past, and a fourth. The first three horses kept going, disappearing past the headlights, into the darkness. The fourth slowed close to Nancy's body. She'd been half dragged and half thrown almost thirty feet from the Corvette, right to the far edge of what the headlights could reveal. The tall white horse lowered its head and seemed to gum Nancy's hair, which was bloody and matted and twitching in the breeze.

Jake screamed. I think he was trying to scream Nancy's name but wasn't able to articulate words. Geri was screaming, too. I wasn't. I couldn't get the breath. I felt as if a horse had run over me also, stamped all the air out of me.

The horse that stood over Nancy had a mangled face, one side pink and flayed as the result of a long-ago burn. Both of its eyes were white, but the one on the ruined side of its head bulged sickeningly from its socket. The tongue that slipped out and lapped Nancy's face wasn't a horse tongue at all. It was as thin and black as a serpent's.

Jake's hand clawed blindly for the latch. He was staring at Nancy, so he didn't see another horse standing alongside the car. None of us did. Jake's door sprang open, and he put his foot on the dirt, and I looked over and had just enough time to shout his name.

The horse alongside the car dipped its powerful neck and clamped its big horsey teeth on Jake's shoulder and snapped its head. Jake was lifted out of the car and hurled into the trunk of a red pine at the side of the road. He struck it as if he'd been fired from a cannon and dropped out of sight into the tangled underbrush.

Geri heaved herself from my lap and into the driver's seat. She grabbed for the door as if she were going to go after him. I got her by the shoulder and hauled her back. At the same moment, the big horse beside the car turned in a clumsy half circle. Its big white rump hit the door and banged it shut on her.

The next I saw Jake, he was pulling himself across the road, into the headlights. I think his back was broken, but I couldn't swear to it. His feet dragged in a useless sort of way behind him. He cast a wild look up at us—at me—and his gaze met mine. I wish it hadn't. I never wanted to see so much terror in anyone's face, so much senseless panic.

The white stallion trotted out after him, lifting its hooves high, as if it were on parade. It caught up to Jake and looked down upon him almost speculatively, then stomped on him, right between his shoulder blades. The force flattened Jake into the dirt. He tried to rise, and the stallion kicked him in the face. It crushed in most of his skull—nose, the ridge of bone above his eyes, a cheekbone—put a red gash right in the middle of his movie-star good looks. The destrier wasn't done with him. As Jake fell, it lowered its muzzle and bit the back of his Levi jacket, pulled him off the ground, and flung him effortlessly into the trees, as if he were a scarecrow stuffed with straw.

Geri didn't know what to do, was fixed in place behind the wheel, her face stricken, her eyes wide. The driver's window was still down, and when the black dog hit the side of the Corvette, its shaggy head barreled right through. It put two paws on the inside of the window and sank its teeth into her left shoulder, tore the shirt from collar to sleeve, mauled the taut, tanned flesh beneath. Its hot breath stank.

She screamed. Her hand found the gearshift, and she launched the Corvette into motion.

The horse that had killed Jake was directly in front of us, and she smashed into it doing twenty miles an hour, cut its legs out from under it. The big horse had to weigh close to twelve hundred pounds, and the front end of the Corvette crumpled. I was slammed into the dash. The horse was thrown across the hood, rolled, legs flailing at the night, turned over, and kicked one hoof through the windshield. It struck Geri in the chest and drove her back into her seat. Safety glass erupted in a spray of chunky blue pebbles, rattled all over the cockpit.

Geri threw the car into reverse and accelerated backward. The big white horse rolled off the hood with a great tumbling crash that shook the roadbed. It hit the dirt lane and hauled itself back up onto its front legs.

Its shattered rear legs trailed uselessly. Geri jammed the car into drive and went straight at it again.

The horse pulled itself out of the way, and we zipped past it, so close that its tail lashed my window. I think that was right around the time Geri drove over Nancy. I only saw Nan in front of the car for an instant before the Corvette thudded and lurched, passing over the obstruction in the road. An oily steam gushed from under the hood.

For one terrible moment, the black dog ran alongside us, its great red tongue lolling out of the side of its mouth. Then we left it behind.

"Geri!" I cried. "Roll up your window!"

"I can't!" she said.

Her voice was thin with strain. Her shoulder had been clawed deep into the muscle, and the front of her shirt was soaked with blood. She drove one-handed.

I reached across her waist and turned the window crank, rolled the glass up for her. We hit a rut, hard, and the top of my skull banged into her jaw. Black pinwheels erupted and whirled and faded before my eyes.

"Slow down!" I yelled. "You'll run us off the road!"

"Can't slow down," she said. "Behind us."

I looked back through the rear window. They pelted after us, their hooves raising a low cloud of white chalk, five figures so pale they were like the ghosts of stallions.

Geri shut her eyes and sagged, lowering her chin almost to her breastbone. We nearly went off the road then, as the Corvette blasted into a hairpin turn. I grabbed the wheel myself and hauled on it, and it still didn't look like we were going to make it. I screamed. That got her attention, drew her up out of her pain. She wrenched at the wheel. The Corvette slung around the corner so hard the back end swished out to one side, throwing rocks. Geri drew a ragged, whistling breath.

"What's wrong?" I asked stupidly—like everything wasn't wrong, like she hadn't just seen her brother and her best friend trampled to death, like there wasn't something impossible coming up behind us in a roar of pounding hooves.

"Can't breathe," she said, and I remembered the hoof coming through the windshield and slugging her in the chest. Broken ribs, had to be.

"We'll get into the house. We'll call for help."

"Can't breathe," she repeated. "*Paul.* They're off the merry-go-round. They're after us because of what we did, aren't they? That's why they killed Jake. That's why they killed Nancy."

It was terrible to hear her say it. I knew it was true, had known from the moment I saw the horse with the burned face. The thought made my head go spinny and light. The thought made me feel like a drunk on a carousel, going around too fast, too hard. When I shut my eyes, it seemed to me I was dangerously close to being thrown right off the great turning wheel of the world.

"We're almost to the house."

"Paul," she said, and for the first time in all the years I'd known her, I saw Geri trying not to cry. "I think there's something broken in my chest. I think I'm smashed up good."

"Turn!" I cried.

The front left headlight had been smashed out, and even though I'd traveled the road to Maggie Pond a thousand times, in the darkness we almost missed the turn to my parents' place. She yanked the wheel, and the Corvette slued through its own smoke. We thudded down a steep gravel incline and swung in front of the house.

It was a two-story white cottage with green shutters and a big screened-in front porch. A single stone stoop led up to the screen door. Safety was eight feet away, on the far side of the porch, through the front door. They couldn't get us inside. I was pretty sure.

No sooner had we stopped than the horses surrounded the car, circling us, tails twitching, shoulders bumping the Corvette. Their hooves threw up dust and obscured our view of the porch.

Now that we were stopped, I could hear the thin, whistling wheeze Geri made each time she drew breath.

She hunched forward, her brow touching the steering wheel, her hand to her breastbone.

"What do we do?" I asked. One of the horses swiped the car hard enough to send it jouncing up and down on its springs.

"Is it because we stole his money?" Geri asked, and drew another thin sip of air. "Or is it because I cut one of the horses?"

"Don't think about it. Let's think about how to get past them into the house."

She went on as if I hadn't spoken. "Or is it just because we needed killing? Is it because there's something wrong with us, Paul? Oh. Oh, my chest."

"Maybe we could turn around, try to get back to the highway," I said, although already I doubted we were going anywhere. Now that we were stopped, I wasn't sure we could get going again. The front end of the car looked like it had met a tree at high speed. The hood was mashed out of shape, and something under the crumpled lid was hissing steadily.

"I've got another idea," she said, and looked at me from behind tangles of her own hair. Her eyes were rueful and bright. "How about I get out of the car and run for the lake? That'll draw them away, and you can get into the house."

"What? No. Geri, *no*. The house is right here. No one else needs to die. The house is *right here*. There's no fucking way you're going to pull some kind of movie bullshit and try to lead them—"

"Maybe they don't want you, Paul," she said. Her chest heaved slowly and steadily, her T-shirt plastered red and wet to her skin. "*You* didn't do anything. *We* did. Maybe they'd let you go."

"What did Nancy do?" I cried.

"She drank the beer," Geri said, as if it were obvious. "We took the money, she spent it, and we all shared the beer—all except for you. Jake stole. I slashed up a horse. What did *you* do? You took the old guy and put him on his side so he wouldn't choke to death."

"You're aren't thinking right. You've lost all kinds of blood, and you saw Jake and Nan get trampled, and you're in shock. They're *horses*. They can't want *revenge*."

"Of course they want revenge," she said. "But maybe not on you. Just listen. I'm too light-headed to argue with you. We have to do it now. I'm going to get out of the car and run to the left, first chance I see. I'll run for the trees and the lake. Maybe I can make it to the float. Horses can swim, but I don't think they could reach me up on the float, and even with my chest fucked up, I think I can paddle out there. When I go, you wait until they've rushed after me, and then you get inside and you call every cop in the state—"

"No," I said. "No."

"Besides," she told me, and one corner of her mouth lifted in a wry smile, "I can still cut a motherfucker."

And she opened her left hand to show me the carousel operator's knife. It rested in the center of her palm, so I could see the scrimshaw, that carving of stampeding horses.

"No," I said. I didn't know any other words. Language had abandoned me.

I reached for the knife, but she closed her fingers around it. I wound up only placing my hand on hers.

"I always thought that stuff about going to New York together was crap," she said. "The stuff about how I was going to be an actress and you were going to be a writer. I always thought it was impossible. But if I don't die, we should give it a shot. It can't be any more impossible than this."

Her hand slipped out of mine. Even now I don't know why I let her go.

A horse wheeled in front of the Corvette and jumped, and his front hooves landed on the hood. The car bounced up and down on its coils. The great white saddle horse glared at us, and his eyes were the color of smoke. A snake's tongue lapped at his wrinkled black gums. He sank onto his haunches, ready to come right through the space where the windshield had been.

"Bye," Geri said, almost softly.

She was out of the car and on her feet and moving before I had time to turn my head.

She ran from the screened-in porch, past the back of the car, heading for the corner of the house and the pines. I could see the lake between the black silhouettes of the tree trunks, faintly luminescent in the night. It wasn't far to the water's edge. Twenty-five yards maybe.

The horse in front of me snapped its head around to watch her flight, then leaped away from the car and followed. Two other horses joined the chase, but Geri was fast, and the brush was close.

She had just made the edge of the woods when the cat vaulted from behind a chest-high screen of bushes. It was the size of a cougar and had paws as big as baseball gloves. One of them batted her hard enough to spin her halfway around. The cat came down on top of her with a strangled yowl that turned into a high-pitched animal scream. I like to think she got the knife into it. I liked to think Geri showed it she had claws of her own.

I ran. I don't remember getting out of the car. I was just out, on my feet, booking it around the ruined front end of the Corvette. I hit the screen door and threw it open and launched myself at the front door beyond. It was locked, of course. The key hung off a rusting nail to the right of the door. I grabbed for it and dropped it and snatched it up. I stabbed it at the lock again and again. I have dreams about that, still—that I am thrusting a key, with a shaking hand, at a lock I must open and which I keep impossibly missing, while something terrible rushes up behind me through the darkness: a horse, or a wolf, or Geri, the lower part of her face clawed off, her throat raked into ribbons. *Hey, babe, be honest: Do you really think I'm pretty enough to be in movies?*

In truth I was probably struggling with the lock for less than ten seconds. When the door opened, I went in so fast my feet caught on the jamb, and I hit the floor hard enough to drive the air out of me. I scrambled on all fours, shouting, making incoherent sobbing noises. I kicked the door shut behind me and curled on my side and wept. I shook as if I'd just been plunged through the ice into freezing water.

It was a minute or two before I brought myself under control and was able to stand. I made my way, shakily, to the door and peered through one of the sidelights.

Five horses watched from the driveway, gathered around the smashed wreck of the Corvette. They studied the house with their eyes of pale poison smoke. Farther up the road, I saw the dog pacing back and forth with a restless, muscular fury. I couldn't tell where the cat had gotten to—but I heard it. At some point in the hours that followed, I heard it yowling angrily in the distance.

I stared at the herd, and they stared back. One of them stood in profile to the house, half a ton of horse. The scars scrawled across his side looked like they might be a decade old, not a few hours, but for all that, they were quite distinct, in silver relief against his fine white hair. Hacked there in the horse's flesh were the words FUCK YOU.

They whinnied together, the pack of them. It sounded like laughter.

I staggered into the kitchen and tried the phone. There was no dial tone, no connection. The line was down. Maybe it was the work of the horses, the creatures that came off the Wild Wheel, but I think it was more likely just the wind. When it gusted liked that out along Maggie Pond, the phone and electric quite often cut out, and as it happened, I had neither that night.

I moved from window to window. The horses watched from the road. Other beasts crashed in the brush, circling the house. I screamed at them to go away. I screamed that I'd kill them, I'd kill all of them. I screamed that we didn't mean it, that none of us meant anything. Only that last bit was true, though, it seems to me now. None of us meant anything.

I passed out on the couch in the living room, and when I woke, to a bright morning—blue skies and every drop of dew glinting with sunlight—the creatures of the Wheel were gone. I didn't dare go out, though. I thought they might be hiding.

It was close on late afternoon when I finally risked the dirt road, and even then I walked with a big kitchen knife in one hand. A woman in a Land Rover rolled slowly by, raising a cloud of dust. I ran after her, screaming for help, and she sped away. Can you blame her?

A state police cruiser collected me fifteen minutes later, was waiting for me where the dirt road met the state highway. I spent three days at Central Maine Medical in Lewiston—not because I'd suffered any great physical injury but to remain under observation after suffering what a clinician described to my parents as a "serious paranoid break from reality."

On the third day, with my parents and our family attorney at my bedside, I admitted to a cop named Follett that the four of us had dropped acid shortly before riding the Wild Wheel. Somewhere on the drive to Maggie Pond, we struck an animal, probably a moose, and Geri and Nan, who were riding without seat belts, were killed instantly. Follett asked who was driving, and the lawyer answered for me, said it had been Jake. I added, in a shaking voice, that I couldn't drive a stick, which was true.

The lawyer told the rest . . . that Jake had dumped the bodies in the lake and fled, probably for Canada, to avoid what almost certainly would've been a life sentence in jail. Our family attorney added that I, too, was a victim—a victim of the drugs Jake had supplied and the wreck he had caused. All I did was nod and agree and sign what they asked me to sign. It was good enough for the cop. He remembered Jake well, had not forgotten the night Jake decked his buddy at Lewiston Lanes.

The Maine State Police and the Warden Service got out on Maggie Pond and dragged for bodies, but nothing was ever recovered. Maggie Pond is, after all, a tidal pool and opens to the sea.

I never went to Dartmouth. I couldn't even leave the house. To step outdoors was as hard for me as it would be to walk on a ledge ten stories above the ground.

It was a month before I looked out my bedroom window one evening and saw one of the horses watching the house from the road. It stood beneath a streetlamp, staring up at me with milky eyes, the left half of its face mottled and withered from ancient burns. After a moment it lowered its head and clopped slowly away.

Geri had thought maybe they didn't want me. Of course they wanted me. I was the one who fingered the carousel operator. I was the one who lit Jake's fuse.

I developed a terror of the night. I was awake at all hours, watching for them—and sometimes I saw them. A couple of the horses one night, the cat another. They were keeping an eye on me. They were waiting for me.

I was institutionalized for ten weeks in the spring of 1995. I got on lithium, and for a while the horses couldn't find me. For a while I was better. I had months of therapy. I began to take walks outside—at first just from the front door to the mailbox and then down the street. Eventually I could go for blocks without a care, as long as it was bright daylight. Dusk, though, still made me short of breath.

In the spring of 1996, with my parents' blessing and my therapist's endorsement, I flew to California and spent two months living with my aunt, crashing in her guest room. She was a bank teller and a devout, practicing, but not overbearing, Methodist, and I think my parents felt I would be safe enough with her. My mother was so proud of me for daring to travel. My father, I believe, was just relieved to get me out of the house, to have a break from my nervous fits and paranoia.

I got a job in a thrift shop. I went on dates. I felt safe and, sometimes, almost content. It was just like normal life. I began seeing an older woman, a preschool teacher who was going prematurely gray and who had a man's husky, rough laugh. One night we met for tea and coffee cake, and I lost track of time, and when we went out, the sky was glazed red with sunset and the dog was there. It had emerged from a nearby park and stood glaring at me, spit dripping from its open jaws. My date saw the dog, too, and gripped my wrist and said, "What the hell is that!" I wrenched my arm free and plunged back into the café, screaming for someone to call the police, screaming that I was going to die.

I had to go back to the hospital. Three months that time, and a cycle of electroshock therapy. While I was in, someone sent me a postcard of the Cape Maggie Pier and the Wild Wheel. There was no message on it, but then the postcard *was* the message.

I had never imagined that the creatures of the Wheel might follow me all the way across the country. It had taken them two months to catch up to me.

In the earliest part of this century, I was accepted to the University of London and flew to the United Kingdom to study urban planning. After I graduated, I stayed there.

134 · FULL THROTTLE

I never did write a play, or even so much as a poem. My literary output has been limited to a few reports for technical journals about dealing with urban pests: pigeons, rats, raccoons. In the field I am sometimes half-jokingly called Mr. Murder. My specialty is developing strategies to wipe out any trace of the animal world from the chrome-and-glass order of the metropolis.

But Mr. Murder is not the kind of moniker that invites romantic interest, and my personal issues—panic attacks, a profound fear of the dark—have left me relatively isolated. I never married. I have no children. I have acquaintances, not friends. Friendships are made in the pub, after hours—and after hours I am safely home, behind a bolted door, in a third-floor apartment, with my books.

I have never seen the horses here. Rationally, I am certain that whatever their powers, they cannot cross three thousand miles of ocean to reach me. I am safe—from them.

Last year, though, I was sent to an urban-planning conference in Brighton. I was to give an afternoon presentation on the Japanese beetle and the dangers it presents to urban forestry. I didn't realize, until the taxi dropped me off, that the hotel was right across from Palace Pier, with its grand carousel turning out on the tip, the wind carrying the hurly-burly song of the

Wurlitzer all up and down the beachfront. I delivered my talk in a conference room with a sick sweat prickling on my forehead and my stomach twisting, then all but fled the room the moment I finished. I could still hear the carousel music inside the hotel, its lunatic lullaby wafting through the imposing lobby. I couldn't go back to London—was scheduled for a panel the following morning—but I could get away from the hotel for a while, and I set out down the beach, until the pier was well behind me.

I had a burger and a pint and another pint, in a beachside place, to steady my nerves. I stayed too long, and when I left and began to walk back toward the hotel along the beach, the sun was touching the horizon. I trekked across cold sand, the salty air snatching at my scarf and hair, going as fast as a man can without breaking into a sprint.

The hotel was in sight before I allowed myself to slow and catch my breath. I had a stitch in my side, and the insides of my lungs were full of icy, abrasive fire.

Something slapped and crashed in the water.

I only saw its tail for a moment, eight feet of it, a glistening black rope, thick as a telephone pole. Its head surfaced, gold and green, like painted armor, its eyes as bright and blind as coins, and then it went under again. I had not seen it in more than twenty years, but I knew the sea serpent of the Wild Wheel at first sight, recognized it in an instant.

They will never be done with me.

I made it back to my hotel room and promptly lost my burger and beer in the toilet. I was sick off and on all night with a chilly sweat and the shakes. I didn't sleep. I couldn't. Every time I shut my eyes, the room would begin to spin, circling in slow revolutions, like a record on a turntable, like a carousel beginning its circuit. Round and round and round I went, round and round, and from a long way off I could hear the music of the Golden Gallopers on the Brighton Palace Pier, the Wurlitzer playing its mad fox-trot to the night, while children screamed, whether with laughter or terror, I could not tell you.

These days it is all the same to me.

Wolverton Station

S aunders saw the first wolf as the train was pulling
in to Wolverton Station.

He glanced up from his *Financial Times* and there it
was, out on the platform, a wolf six feet tall with a scally
cap tucked between his bristly, graying ears. The wolf
stood on his hind legs, wore a trench coat, and held a
briefcase in one paw. A bushy tail whipped impatiently
back and forth, presumably poking out from a hole in
the seat of his pants. The train was still moving, and in
a moment the wolf blinked out of sight.

Saunders laughed, a short, breathless sound that did
not quite convey amusement, and did the reasonable
thing: looked back at his paper. It didn't surprise him,
a wolf waiting on the train platform. The devil would
probably be at the next stop. Saunders thought there was

a good chance the fucking protesters would be parked in every station between London and Liverpool, parading around in costume, hoping someone would point a camera at them and stick them on the telly.

They had staked out his hotel in London, a raggedy-ass pack of a dozen kids, marching back and forth on the sidewalk directly across the street. The management had offered Saunders a room in the rear, so he wouldn't have to see them, but he insisted on a suite up front just so he could look down on them. It was a hell of a lot more entertaining than anything on British TV. He hadn't spotted any wolfmen, but there had been a dude on stilts in an Uncle Sam costume, with a three-foot rubber dong hanging out of his pants. Uncle Sam's features were stern and hateful, but the dong was scrubbed and pink and had some cheerful bounce to it. Slammin' Sammy carried a sign in both hands:

UNCLE SAM PISSES IN A CUP
& WE ENGLISH PAY TO DRINK IT
NO JIMI COFFEE! NO SLAVE CHILDS!

Saunders had a good laugh at that, had enjoyed how it trod the line between righteous anger and mental deficiency. "No slave childs"? What had happened to the legendary British educational system?

The other protesters, a gang of self-important hipsters, were hauling signs of their own. Theirs were a
little less amusing. They showed photos of barefoot,
half-naked black kids, standing by coffee bushes, the
children staring bleakly into the camera, eyes dewing
over with tears, as if they had just felt the foreman's
lash. Saunders had seen it before, too often to really get
angry, to be anything more than irritated, even if those
signs perpetuated an outrageous lie. Jimi Coffee didn't
use kids in the field and never had. In the packing
plants, yes, but not in the fields, and the plants were a
hell of a lot more sanitary than the shantytowns those
kids went home to.

Anyway, Saunders couldn't hate the hot little hipster
girls, in their stomach-baring Che Guevara T-shirts,
or their fashionably scrungy, sandal-wearing boy-
friends. They protested today, but in three years the
hipster girls would be pushing baby carriages, and the
half hour they spent in Jimi Coffee gossiping with their
girlfriends would be the best part of their day. The
scrungy hipster boys would be shaved and chasing jobs
in middle management and would run in to Jimi every
morning on the way to work for their all-important
double shots of espresso, without which they could
not make it through the most boring day of their lives
since the day before. By then, if the hipsters allowed

themselves to think about the time they had picketed to protest the arrival of Jimi Coffee on British shores, it would be with a bemused flush of embarrassment at their own pointless and misplaced idealism.

There had been a dozen of them in front of the hotel the night before and two dozen in front of the flagship store in Covent Garden in the morning, at the grand opening. Not great numbers. Most passersby never so much as glanced at them. The small few who did take note of them always flinched at the sight of Uncle Sam with his rubber prick hanging out, the thing twitching back and forth like the great fleshy pendulum of some perverse, surreal grandfather clock (grandfather cock?). That was all anyone would remember—Uncle Sam's strap-on—not what was being protested. Saunders doubted that the marchers would register as anything more than a single sentence at the end of a minor story buried in the business section of the *Times*. Possibly someone would be quoted about Jimi's business practices, practices Saunders himself had helped to develop.

The way Jimi worked, they found a neighborhood mom-and-pop coffeehouse that was doing good business and opened up across the street. A Jimi franchise could operate at a loss for months—years, if necessary—however long it took to put the competition out of business and claim its customers. And this was looked upon as an outrage, a borderline criminal act, and never mind that the mom-and-pop usually served watery, third-rate instant in thimble-size cups and couldn't be bothered to keep a clean bathroom. As for child labor, the protesters didn't like it but were apparently at peace with children starving because there was no work at all.

Saunders couldn't hate them. He understood their mind-set too well. Once upon a time, he had marched himself . . . marched, smoked weed, danced in his underwear at a Dead concert, and trekked in India. He had gone abroad looking for transcendence, a mantra, *meaning,* and goddamn if he hadn't found it. He had stayed for three weeks in a monastery in the mountains of Kashmir, where the air was sweet and smelled of bamboo and tart orange blossoms. He had walked barefoot on ancient stone, meditated to the ringing drone of the singing bowl, and chanted with all the other potheads who had wound up there. He had given himself over to it all, trying to feel pure, trying to feel love—he even gave himself over to the food, daily servings of a mealy rice that tasted like waterlogged chalk and bowls of what appeared to be curried twigs. And there came a day when at last Saunders received the wisdom he had come looking for.

It was a scrawny, raven-haired kid from Colorado named John Turner who pointed the way toward a higher purpose. No one prayed longer or more intensely than John, who sat through the guided-meditation sessions, stripped to the waist, his ribs showing in his painfully white sides. They were supposed to focus on something beautiful, something that filled them to the brim with happiness. Saunders had tried picturing lotus petals, waterfalls, the ocean, and his San Diego girl-friend naked, without feeling that any of it was quite right. John seemed to get it, though, right away—his long, horsey face shone with rapture. Even his sweat smelled clean and happy. Finally, their third week there, Saunders asked him what he was visualizing.

"Well," Turner said, "he told us to picture some-thin' that filled us with happiness. So I been imaginin' the fuckin' Quarter Pounder with Cheese I'm going to sink my teeth into when I get home. A couple more days of eating sticks and spiced dirt, I think I might be able to visualize a bag of the flavorful motherfuckers right into existence."

Saunders had gone to India in love with a blond-haired girl named Deanie, *The White Album,* and ganja. By the time he got back to San Diego, Deanie was mar-ried to a pharmacist, Paul McCartney was touring with Wings, Saunders had smoked his last-ever joint, and he had a plan. Or not a plan, exactly, but a vision, an *understanding.* Reality had briefly slid aside one of its black, opaque panels, to give him a glimpse of the gears that ticked behind it. Saunders had discovered a universal constant, like gravity or the quantum nature of light. No matter where you went—no matter how ancient the traditions, no matter how grand the history, no matter how awe-inspiring the landscape—there was always a market for a cheap Happy Meal. The Lotus Way might lead to nirvana, but it was a long trip, and when you had a lot of miles to cover, it was just natural to want some drive-thru along the road.

Three years after he left Kashmir, Saunders owned five Burger Kings, and upper management wanted to know why his restaurants turned a profit 65-percent higher than the national average (his trick: set up shop across from skate parks, beaches, and arcades and grill with the windows open, so the kids were smelling it all day). Thirteen years later he was in upper management himself, teaching Dunkin' Donuts how to repel Starbucks (his plan: make 'em look like snobs and outsiders, play up the New England angle, total market saturation).

When Jimi Coffee offered him a seven-figure salary to help the company restructure and take its franchise international, Saunders agreed after mulling it over for less than twenty-four hours. He especially liked the idea of helping Jimi to go global, because it would offer him a chance to travel; he had hardly left the States in the years since India. Maybe he could even get them to open a Jimi Coffee in Kashmir, right across the road from his old monastery. The seekers would probably appreciate the many vegetarian offerings on the Jimi menu, and a vanilla cappuccino would make the sunrise chants a whole lot more palatable. When it came to producing a state of focus, quiet contentment, and inner peace, Zen meditation ran a very distant second to caffeine. Your average suburban white-bread Buddhists could manage without their daily yoga class, but take 'em away from their coffee and they'd be animals in no time, absolute—

Saunders folded back one corner of the paper and took another look at the platform.

The train was yanking itself to a stop at last, in little hitches and jerks. He couldn't see the joker in the wolf suit anymore, had left him well behind. Saunders sat in the frontmost car of the train, the first-class car, and he had a view of one corner of the platform. A metal sign, bolted between two stone pillars, read WOLVERTON STATION. It was a good thing most activists barely had the money for the cardboard, Sharpies, and duct tape they needed to make their protest signs; the last thing Saunders wanted to do was share the otherwise empty first-class car with the crazy son of a bitch dressed like the Big Bad Wolf.

No, thought Saunders. Fuck that. I hope he comes right in and sits down next to me. He can sit there in his asshole wolf suit and lecture me about all the little black kids who suffer under the baking sun in East Africa picking our coffee beans. And then I can tell him we don't let the kids pick and that Jimi Coffee offers full scholarships to ten children from the Third World every year. I can ask him how many kids from the Third World his local mom-and-pop places put through college last year, when they were getting their coffee from an outfit of Samoan slavers, no questions asked.

In his years in management at Burger King, he had earned the nickname "The Woodcutter," because when there was a hatchet job that needed doing, Saunders never shied away from wielding the ax. He had not made his sizable personal fortune (his largest assets being a house on twenty acres in New London, Connecticut, another in the Florida Keys, and a forty-three-foot Sportfisher that ferried him between the two) by avoiding confrontation. He had once fired an eight-months'-pregnant woman, the wife of a close friend, with a two-word text message: YOU'RE TOAST. He had closed packing plants, put hundreds out of work, and had stoically endured being called a soulless cocksucker in Yiddish by a red-faced and shaking old woman who had seen her little chain of kosher coffee shops systematically targeted and taken out by Jimi. But this was, of course, exactly why Jimi hired him—they *needed* a woodcutter, and he had the sharpest hatchet in the forest. Saunders had been all for peace and love in his twenties, and he liked to think he still was, but over the years he had also developed a hankering for the rusty-salt flavor of blood. It was, like coffee itself, an acquired taste.

The train sat for a long time, long enough so that after a while he put down the paper and looked out at the platform again. For the first time since boarding at Euston Station, he was irritated with himself. He should've hired a fucking car. The journey by train had been an impulsive, sentimental act. He had not been in England since the years right after college, had spent two weeks in the UK, on the first leg of the world tour that would eventually dump him in a decaying heap of stone in the breezy mountains of Kashmir. He had come because the Beatles were there; if not for the Beatles, he believed he would've killed himself in his teens, in the bad days after his father had left his mother. He arrived in London with a craving to *feel* the Beatles in some way, a restless need to put his hand against the bricks of the Cavern Club, as if the music they had played there might still resonate in the warm red clay. He rode the rails north, packed into coach, on his feet for hours in the hot stale air, pressed up against an auburn-haired

Edinburgh girl in blue jeans, who he didn't know when the trip began, and who he was half mad for by the time they reached Liverpool. It was maybe the happiest memory of his life, all the reason he needed to go by train now.

Saunders tried never to think about what had happened *after* he got off the train. He and the Edinburgh girl had split up, making a loose plan to meet at the Cavern Club that evening; Saunders had stopped at a mom-and-pop for some fish and chips, but the fish was greasy and spoiled, and he spent the night in a sweat, shaking in a hostel, unable to stand. In the days that followed, there was a continuous sick fizzle in his stomach, as if he had gulped down a cup of especially bitter coffee, and he couldn't go more than half an hour without running for the can. He could not shake the grim conviction that something special had gotten away from him. When he finally made it to the Cavern, the night following, the Edinburgh girl wasn't there—of course she wasn't—and the house band was playing fucking disco. The branch of Jimi Coffee being opened in Liverpool was not actually built on the ruin of the mom-and-pop that had served him rancid fish, but Saunders could pretend.

The platform was lit by fluorescents. He could see nothing of the world beyond. It seemed as if they'd been sitting there for a long time. Although the train was not quite standing still. It rocked now and then on its steel wheels, as if someone were loading something heavy into one of the rear cars. In the distance he heard someone braying, a man's loud, lowing voice, oddly steerlike—*Stop!* he yelled. *Stop it!* Saunders imagined two movers trying to lug an oversize dresser onto the train and being yelled at by a conductor . . . reasonably enough, this wasn't a freight car. A woman's voice rose in a sob of laughter, then faded away. Saunders had half a mind to get up and walk to the back to see what was happening, but then the train jerked forward with a loud bang and began to struggle out of the station.

At the same moment, Saunders heard the door of first class open behind him with a smooth, steely clack.

Well—that's him, he thought, with a certain grim satisfaction. The protester. Saunders didn't look back to confirm it and didn't need to. When he glanced sidelong at the window across the aisle, he could see the dim, blurred reflection of the guy: tall fella with the pointed ears of a German shepherd. Saunders lowered his gaze, fixed it on his newspaper, and pretended to read. Anybody who dressed in a getup like that did it because he wanted to be noticed, was hoping for a reaction. Saunders had no intention of giving him one.

The new arrival in first class started down the aisle,

his breathing loud and strained, what you would expect from a man stuck in a rubber mask. At the last moment, it came to Saunders that it was a mistake to be occupying the window seat. The chair to his left was open and empty, a kind of invitation. He thought of moving, shifting his ass over to the aisle seat. But no, the protester would relish the fear that such a move indicated. Saunders stayed where he was.

Sure enough, the protester took the empty seat beside him, heaving himself down with a heavy sigh of satisfaction. Saunders willed himself not to look over, but his peripheral vision filled in a few details: a wolf mask that covered the entire head, furry gloves, and a bushy tail that was apparently controlled by a hidden wire, because it swung to one side when he sat. Saunders exhaled a thin breath through bared teeth and realized for the first time that he was grinning. It was something he did automatically when he was in for a fight and knew it. His first wife said it made him look like Jack Nicholson with the ax in that movie. She had called Saunders "The Woodcutter," too—initially with coy affection, later when she was being bitchy.

The protester shifted around, getting comfortable, and one hairy-gloved hand brushed Saunders's arm. That casual touch was enough to throw the switch on Saunders's well-practiced rage. He snapped down one corner of the newspaper and opened his mouth to tell Lon fucking Chaney to keep his paws to himself—and then his breath caught in his chest. His lungs seemed to bunch up. He stared. He saw but couldn't make sense of what he was looking at. He tried to see a protester as hard as he could, a protester in a rubber wolf mask and a tan overcoat. He *insisted* on it to himself for a few desperate moments, trying to make the perfectly reasonable notion in his head match the perfectly unreasonable reality beside him. But it wasn't a protester. All the wishing in the world wouldn't make it a protester.

A wolf sat on the seat next to him.

Or if not a wolf, then a creature more wolf than man. He had the body, roughly, of a man, with a broad, wedge-shaped chest that swept down to a sunken stomach and a narrow waist. But he had paws, not hands, wiry gray hair on them. He held a copy of the *Financial Times* himself, and his hooked yellow nails made audible scratching noises as he turned the pages. His nose was literally buried in the paper, a long, bony snout that ended in a wet, black nose. Old, stained fangs protruded over his lower lip. His ears were proud, furry, stiff, his scally cap shoved back between them. One of those ears swiveled toward Saunders, like a satellite dish revolving to lock in a signal.

Saunders looked back at his own paper. It was the only thing he could think to do.

The wolf didn't look at him directly—he remained behind his paper—but he did lean in to him and speak in a gravelly bass. "I hope they bring the dinner trolley through. I could do with a bite. Course, on this line they'll charge you two quid for a plate of lukewarm dog food without blinking."

His breath stank; it was dog breath. Sweat prickled on Saunders's brow and in his armpits, a hot, strange, disagreeable sweat, not at all like the perspiration he worked up jogging on the treadmill. He imagined this sweat as yellow and chemical, a burning carbolic crawling down his sides.

The wolf's snout shriveled, and his black lips wrinkled to show the hooked rows of his teeth. He yawned, and a surprisingly bright red tongue lolled from the opening, and if there had been any doubt in Saunders's mind—there hadn't been, really—that was all for it. In the next moment, he fought with himself, a desperate, terrible struggle, not to issue a soft sob of fear. It was like fighting a sneeze. Sometimes you could hold it in, sometimes you couldn't. Saunders held it in.

"Are you an American?" asked the wolf.

Don't answer. Don't talk! Saunders thought, in a

voice he didn't recognize—it was the shrill, piping voice of panic. But then he did answer, and his tone was his own: level and certain. He even heard himself laugh. "Hah. Got me. 'Scuse, do you mind if I use the bathroom?" As he spoke, he half rose to his feet. He and the wolf were in chairs that faced a spotted Formica table, and he couldn't quite stand all the way up.

"Right," said the wolf. He said it *"Ro-ight,"* had a bit of a Liverpoolian accent. *Liverpudlian,* Saunders corrected himself mentally, randomly. *No, Scouse.* They called it Scouse, which sounded like a disease, something you might die from after being bitten by a wild animal.

The businesswolf turned sideways to allow Saunders by.

Saunders edged past him toward the aisle, leaving behind his briefcase and his eight-hundred-dollar overcoat. He wanted to avoid making contact with the thing, and of course that was impossible—there wasn't enough space to get by without his knees brushing the wolf's. Their legs touched. Saunders's reaction was involuntary, an all-body twitch. He flashed to a memory of sixth-grade biology, prodding the inside of a dead frog with tweezers, touching the nerves and watching the feet kick. It was like that, a steel edge pressed right to the nerves. He could keep the fear out of his voice, but not his body. Saunders believed that one atavistic reaction would be met by another, and the wolf in the suit would lunge, responding to his terror by grabbing him around the waist with his paws, opening his jaws to sink his fangs into Saunders's belly, hollowing him out like a skinned pumpkin: *Trick-or-treat, motherfucker.*

But the wolf in the suit only grunted, low in his throat, and twisted even more to the side to let Saunders past.

Then Saunders was in the aisle. He turned left and began to walk—*walk,* not run—for coach. The first part of his plan was to get to other people. He hadn't worked out the second part of the plan yet. He kept his gaze fixed straight ahead and focused on his breathing, just exactly as he'd been taught in Kashmir, way back down the long and winding road. A smooth *in,* drawn through parted lips. A clean *out,* puffed through his nostrils. *I am not going to be killed and eaten by a wolf on an English train,* he thought, quite clearly. Like the Beatles, he had gone to India as a young man to get himself a mantra and had come home without one. On an unconscious level, though, he supposed he had never stopped yearning to find one, a single statement that resonated with power, hope, and meaning. Now, at sixty-one, he had a mantra he could live by at last: *I am not going to be killed and eaten by a wolf on an English train.*

In and out went his breath, and with every step the door to coach was closer. In eight steps he was there, and he pressed the button that opened the door to the next car. The lights around the button turned from yellow to green, and the door slid back.

He stood looking into coach. The first thing he saw was the blood. A red handprint had been planted in the center of one window and then dragged, to leave a long, muddy-ocher streak across the Plexiglas. A mess of other red smears and splashes made a Jackson Pollock out of a window directly across the aisle. There was a red swipe dragged impossibly down almost the full length of the ceiling.

Saunders saw the blood before he saw the wolves—four in all, sitting in two pairs.

One pair was on the right, in the back. The wolf who sat on the aisle wore a black tracksuit with blue stripes, honoring a soccer team. Saunders thought it might've been Manchester United. The wolf who sat by the window sported a worn white T-shirt advertising an album: WOLFGANG AMADEUS PHOENIX. They were passing something wrapped in a napkin, something brown and circular. A chocolate doughnut, Saunders decided, because that was what he wanted it to be.

The other pair of wolves was on the left, and much closer, only a couple yards from where Saunders stood. They were businesswolves, but less well dressed than the gray wolf in first class. These two wore sagging, wrinkled black suits and standard-issue red ties. One of them was looking at a newspaper, not a *Financial Times* but the *Daily Mail*. His great black furry paws left red prints on the cheap paper. The fur around his mouth was stained red, blood streaked back almost to his eyes.

"Sez Kate Winslet 'as broke up with that bloke of 'ers wot made *American Beyootie*," said the one with the paper.

"Don't look at me," said the other businesswolf. "I didn't 'ave nuthink to do with it."

And they both yapped—playful, puppylike yips.

There was a fifth passenger in the car, a woman, a *human* woman, not a wolf. She was sprawled on her side across one of the seats, so all he could see was her right leg, sticking into the aisle. She wore black stockings, a very bad run in the one that Saunders could see. It was a nice leg, a handsome leg, a young girl's leg. He couldn't see her face and didn't want to. She had lost her heel—it had dropped into the heap of her entrails that were piled in the center of the aisle. Saunders saw those entrails last, a glistening pile of fatty white coils, lightly basted with blood. A string of gut stretched back out of sight in the direction of her abdomen. One of the woman's high heels rested on that mound of intestines, set there like a single black candle on a grotesque birthday cake. He remembered how they had seemed to wait at Wolverton Station forever, the way the train shook now and then as if something were being forcibly loaded into coach. He remembered hearing a woman's sob of laughter and a man yelling orders, *Stop! Stop it!* He had heard it the way he wanted to hear it. He had known what he had wanted to know. Maybe it was always that way for almost everyone.

The businesswolves hadn't noticed him, but the two louts in the back had. The one in the rock T-shirt elbowed Manchester United, and they rolled their eyes meaningfully at each other and lifted their snouts to the air. Tasting the scent of him, Saunders thought.

One of them, Wolfgang Amadeus Phoenix, called out. "'Ey. 'Ey there, mate. Comin' to sit with the lower classes? Goin' to roost with the plebes?"

Manchester United made a choked sound of laughter. He had just had a bite of that glistening chocolate doughnut that he held in the white napkin, and his mouth was full. Only it wasn't a napkin, and it wasn't a doughnut. Saunders was determined to see and hear things as they were, not as he wanted them to be. His life depended on it now. So. See it and know it: It was a piece of liver in a bloodstained hankie. A woman's hankie—he could see the lace trimming at the edges.

Saunders stood in first class, fixed in place, unable to take another step. As if he were a sorcerer who stood within a magical pentagram and to cross the line into coach would be to make himself vulnerable to the demons that waited there. He had forgotten about breathing, no clean in-and-out now, just that feeling of paralysis in the lungs again, a muscular tightening that made it difficult to inhale. He wondered if anyone had ever suffocated to death from fear, had been so afraid to breathe that he'd passed out and died.

The door between cars began to slide shut. Just before it closed, the wolf in the Manchester United tracksuit turned his snout toward the ceiling and uttered a derisive howl.

Saunders backed from the door. He had buried both his parents, and his sister, too, who had died unexpectedly, when she was just twenty-nine, of meningitis; he had been to a dozen stockholder funerals; he had seen a man collapse and die of a heart attack at a Jets game once. But he had never seen anything like guts on the floor, a whole battered train car painted with blood. Yet he did not feel any nausea and did not make a sound, not a single peep. The only physical reaction he was aware of was that his hands had gone to sleep, the fingers cold, tingling with pins and needles. He wanted to sit down.

The door to the bathroom was on his left. He stared at it in a blank, thoughtless kind of way, then pressed the button, popped the door open. An eye-watering smell hit him, a disheartening human reek. The last person through hadn't bothered to flush. Wet, filthy toilet paper stuck to the floor, and the little trash can next to the sink was overflowing. He considered going in there and bolting the door shut. He didn't move, though, and when the bathroom door closed on its own, he was still in the first-class aisle.

That little bathroom was a coffin—a coffin that stank. If he went in there, he understood he would never come out, that he would die in there. Torn apart by the wolves while he sat on the toilet, screaming for help that wasn't going to come. A terrible, lonely, squalid ending, in which he would be separated not just from his life but his dignity. He had no rational explanation for this certainty—how could they get the door open if it was locked?—it was just a thing he knew, the way he knew his birthday or his phone number.

His phone. The thing to do was to call someone, let somebody know (*I am on a train with wolfmen?*) he was in trouble. His cold, dead hands sank to the pockets of his slacks, already knowing that the phone wasn't there. And it wasn't. His phone was in the pocket of his eight-hundred-dollar overcoat—a London Fog overcoat, actually. Everything, even clothing, had, in the last few moments, taken on heightened meaning, seemed significant. His phone was lost in a London Fog. To get to it, he would have to return to his seat and squirm past the businesswolf, something even more impossible than hiding in the bathroom.

There was nothing in his pockets he could use: a few twenty-pound notes, his ticket, a map of the train line. The woodcutter was alone in the deep, dark forest without his ax, without even a Swiss Army knife, not that a Swiss Army knife would do him any good. Saunders was seized by an image of himself knocked flat on his back, the wolf in the scally cap pinning him down, his wretched breath in Saunders's face, and Saunders raking at him frantically with the dull, ridiculous, inch-and-a-half-long blade of a Swiss Army knife. He felt a laugh rise in his throat and choked it back, understood he was quivering on the edge not of hilarity but of panic. Empty pockets, empty head— No. Wait. The map. He jerked the map out of his pocket and unfolded it. It took an effort of will to focus his eyes . . . but whatever his other flaws, Saunders had always had will to spare. He looked for the Liverpool line and began to follow it north from London, wondering about the stop after Wolverton Station, how far it might be.

He spotted Wolverton Station about two-thirds of the

way to Liverpool. Only it wasn't Wolverton Station on the map, it was *Wolverhampton*. He blinked rapidly, as if trying to clear some grit out of his eyes. He supposed it was possible that he had misread the sign at the last stop and that it had *always* been Wolverhampton. Which made the next stop Foxham. Maybe there would be foxes waiting on the platform there. He felt another dangerous, panicky laugh rise in his throat—like bile—and swallowed it down. Laughing now would be as bad as screaming.

He had to insist to himself there would be *people* in Foxham, that if he could get off the train, there was a chance he might live. And on his map, Foxham was barely a quarter inch from the Wolverhampton stop. The train might be almost there, had been rushing along at a hundred-plus miles an hour for at least fifteen minutes (*No. Try three minutes,* said a silky, bemused voice in his mind. *It's only been* **three** *minutes since you noticed that the man sitting beside you wasn't a man at all but some kind of werewolf, and Foxham is still half an hour away. Your body will be room temperature by the time you get there.*)

Saunders had gotten turned around and started, unconsciously, to walk back the way he had come, still staring at his map. At the last moment, he realized he had pulled abreast of the wolf reading the *Finan-*

cial Times. At the sight of the giant dog-faced thing on the periphery of his vision, he felt icy-hot skewers in his chest, needling toward his heart: Saunders, the human pincushion. *You aren't too old for a cardiac arrest, buddy,* he thought—another notion that wouldn't do him any good right now.

Saunders pretended to be lost in the study of his map and kept walking, wandering down to the next row of seats. He looked up, blinking, then settled into a seat on the opposite side of the aisle. He tried to make it look like an absentminded act, a thing done by a man so interested in what he was looking at that he'd forgotten where he was going. He didn't believe that his performance fooled the wolf with the *Financial Times* in the least. Saunders heard him make a deep, woofy-sounding *harrumph* that seemed to express disgust and amusement alike. If he wasn't fooling anyone, Saunders didn't know why he went on playacting interest in his map, except that it felt like the safest thing.

"Did you find the loo?" asked the businesswolf.

"Occupied," Saunders said.

"Right," the wolf said. *Ro-ight.* "You *are* an American."

"Guess you could tell by the accent."

"I knew by the smell of you. You Americans have different accents—your southern accent, your Californiasurfer accent, your Noo Yawk accent." Affecting an atrocious faux-Queens accent as he said it. "But you all smell the same."

Saunders sat very still, facing straight ahead, his pulse thudding in his neck. *I am going to be killed and eaten by a wolf on an English train,* he thought, then realized that somewhere in the last few moments his mantra had turned from a statement of negation to one of affirmation. It came to him that the time for pretend was well past. He folded his map and put it back in his pocket.

"What do we smell like?" Saunders asked.

"Like cheeseburgers," said the wolf, and he barked with laughter. "And entitlement."

I am going to be killed and eaten by a wolf on an English train, Saunders thought again, and for a moment the idea wasn't the worst notion in the world. It was bad, but even worse would be sitting here letting himself be taunted before it happened, taking it with his tail between his legs.

"Fuck you," Saunders said. "We smell like money. Which beats the hell out of stinking like wet dog." His voice shaking just slightly when he said it.

He didn't dare turn his head to look at the wolf directly, but he could watch him from the corner of his eye, and he saw one of those erect, bushy ears rotate toward him, tuning in on his signal.

Then the first-class businesswolf laughed—another harsh woof. "Don't mind me. My portfolio has taken a beating the last couple months. Too many American stocks. It's left me a bit sore, as much at myself as at you lot. It aggravates me that I bought into the whole thing, like everyone else in this blighted country."

"Bought into what whole thing?" Saunders asked. A part of his mind cried out in alarm, *Shut the fuck up! What are you doing? Why are you talking to it?*

Except.

Except the train was slowing, almost imperceptibly. Saunders doubted that under normal circumstances he would've noticed, but now he was attuned to fine details. That was how it worked when your life was measured in seconds: You felt your own breath, were aware of the temperature and weight of the air on your own skin, heard the prickling *tic-tic* of the rain on the windows. The train had hitched, slowed, and hitched again. The night continued to blur past the windows, some rain splatter sprinkling against the glass, but Saunders thought there was a chance they were closing on Foxham, or whatever was next down the tracks. And if the businesswolf was talking to him, then he wasn't attacking.

"The American fairy tale," the wolf said. "You know the one. That we can all be like you. That we should all *want* to be like you. That you can wave your American Tinker Bell dust over our pathetic countries and abracadabra! A McDonald's here and an Urban Outfitters there and England will be just like home. *Your* home. I am honestly humiliated to ever have believed it. You would think a bloke like me, of all people, would know it isn't true. You can stick a Disneyland T-shirt on a wolf, but it's still a wolf."

The train hitched and slowed another degree. When Saunders looked out his window, he could see brick town houses flashing by, some lights on behind a few of the windows, and bare trees tossing in the wind, clawing at the sky. Even the trees were different in England. They were the same varieties you found in the States but subtly unlike American trees, more gnarled and bent, as if twisted by colder, harsher winds.

"Everyone is dead in the other car," Saunders said, feeling curiously removed from himself, from his own voice.

The wolf grunted.

"Why not me?"

The wolf didn't look at him, seemed to be losing interest in the conversation. "This is first class. If you can't get civility here, where can you get it? Besides. I'm wearing a Gieves & Hawkes. This suit set me back five hundred quid. Wouldn't do to stain it. And what's the point of riding first class if you have to chase down your own grub? They bring a trolley through for us." He leafed to the next page of his *Times.* "At least they're supposed to. They're taking their fucking time about it, aren't they?" He paused, then added, "Please pardon my language. The thing about civility—it's hard to maintain when you're barking mad with hunger."

The conductor said something in a choked, wolfish voice on the intercom, but Saunders couldn't hear him over what his own wolf was saying to him and above the roar of blood in his ears. But he didn't need to hear the conductor anyway, because Saunders knew what he was saying. They had arrived at the station at last. The train was slamming ungently to rest. Saunders grabbed the seat in front of him and lurched to his feet. Outside, he had a glimpse of a concrete platform, a brick breezeway, a glowing old-fashioned clock stuck up on the station wall. He began walking swiftly for the front of the car.

"'Ey," laughed the wolf. "Don't you want your coat? Come on back and get it."

Saunders kept walking. He reached the door at the end of the cabin in five long strides and hit the DOOR OPEN button. The wolf barked a last laugh at Saunders's back, and Saunders dared a final glance over his shoulder. The businesswolf was disappearing behind his paper once more.

"Microsoft shares are down," the wolf said, in a tone that somehow combined disappointment with a certain rueful satisfaction. "Nike shares are down. This isn't a recession, you know. This is reality. You people are finding out the actual worth of the things you make: your sneakers, your software, your coffee, your myths. You people are finding out now what it's like when you push too far into the deep, dark woods."

Then Saunders was out the door and on the platform. He had thought it was raining, but what came down was more of a weak, cold mist, a fine-grained moisture suspended in the air. The station exit was across the platform, a flight of stairs to the road below.

He had gone no more than five paces before he heard loud, derisive yipping behind him and looked back to see two wolves descending from coach. Not the wolves in suits but the one in the Wolfgang Amadeus T-shirt and the other dressed for a Manchester United match. Manchester United clapped Wolfgang on the shoulder and jerked his snout in Saunders's direction.

Saunders ran. He had been fast once, on his track team in high school, but that had been fifty years and five thousand Whoppers ago. He didn't need to look back to know they were behind him, loping across the concrete, and that they were faster than him. He reached the staircase and leaped down it, three, four stairs in each step, a kind of controlled falling. His breath screamed in his throat. He heard one of the wolves make a low, purring growl at the top of the stairs. (And how could they be at the top of the stairs already? It wasn't possible that they could've closed so much distance so quickly, it *wasn't*.)

At the bottom of the steps was the line of gates, and the street beyond, and a taxi waiting, a black English taxi straight out of a Hitchcock movie. Saunders picked a gate and ran straight at it. The gates: a row of chrome dividers, with waist-high black Plexiglas shutters between them. You were supposed to stick your ticket into a slot on the top of the chrome dividers and the shutters would swing open, but Saunders wasn't going to fuck with it. When he reached the Plexiglas shutters, he went right over them, in a graceless scramble, followed by a tumble to the ground.

He sprawled onto his stomach, facedown on the rain-spattered concrete. Then he was up again. It was like a skip in a piece of film, so it hardly seemed he had gone down at all. He had never in his life imagined he could recover so quickly from a spill.

Someone yelled behind him. Every set of gates in every train station in the UK had an officer to watch over them and take tickets manually, and Saunders thought this had to be who that was. He could even see him out of the corner of his left eye, a guy in an orange safety vest, white-haired and bearded. Saunders didn't slow down or look over. A joke floated unbidden to his mind: Two hikers in the woods come across a bear. One of them bends over to lace his sneakers. The other hiker says, "Why tie your sneakers? You can't outrun a bear." And the first hiker says, "No shit, asshole. I only need to outrun *you*." Pretty funny. Saunders would remind himself to laugh about it later.

He fell against the back of the taxi, clawed for the door lever, found it, popped it open. He collapsed into the black leather seat.

"Go," he said to the driver. *"Go."*

"Where are we—" said the driver, in the thick accent of western England.

"Town. Into town. I don't know yet, just go. *Please.*"

"Right then," the driver said. The taxi loosened itself from the curb and pushed off down the avenue.

Saunders twisted in his seat to look out the rear window as they left the train station. Manchester United and Wolfgang Amadeus had stopped at the gate. They crowded around the ticket taker, towering over him. Saunders didn't know why the ticket man just stood there staring back at them, why he didn't recoil and run, why they didn't fall on him. The taxi carried him around the corner and out of sight of the station before he could see what happened next.

He sat in the darkness, breathing fast and hard, incredulous at his own survival. His legs shook, the big muscles in his thighs bunching up and uncoiling helplessly. He had not shaken the whole time he was on the train, but now it was as if he had just climbed out of an ice bath.

The cab glided down a long, gradual hill, past hedges and houses, dipping toward the lights of a town. Saunders found one of his hands feeling in his pocket for the cell phone he knew he didn't have.

"Phone," he said, talking to himself. "Damn phone."

"Need a phone?" said the driver. "I'm sure there was one at the station."

Saunders glanced at the back of the driver's head, peering at him in the dark of the car. A big man with long black hair tucked down into the collar of his coat.

"There wasn't time to stop and make a call there. Just take me to someplace with a public phone. Someplace else."

"There's one at the Family Arms. That's only a couple blocks."

"Family Arms? What's that? Pub?" Saunders's voice

cracked, as if he were a fourteen-year-old in the throes of puberty.

"Best'un in town. Also the only'un. But if I'd known that's where you wanted me to drive you, I wouldn't have taken the fare. It's easier walking, see?"

"I'll pay you triple your usual rate. I've got plenty of money. I'm the richest man that's ever sat in this fucking cab."

"Isn't this my lucky day," said the driver. The ignorant country moron had no idea Saunders had just almost been torn apart. "So what happened to your regular chauffeur?"

"What?"

Saunders didn't understand the question; in truth, he hardly registered it, was distracted. They had stopped at a light, and Saunders happened to look out the window. Two teenagers stood necking on the corner. They had a couple dogs with them, who stood at their sides, whisking their tails nervously back and forth, waiting for the kids to get done kissing and start walking again. Only there was something wrong with those two kids. The taxi was moving again before Saunders figured out what it was. Those tails, fretfully whisking from side to side—Saunders hadn't actually spotted the dogs attached to them. He wasn't sure there had been any dogs there at all.

"Where is this?" Saunders asked. "Where am I? Is this Foxham?"

"We isn't anywheres near Foxham, sir. Upper Wolverton, this is," said the driver. "Which is what they call it because 'The Middle of Nowhere' don't sound as good. Edge of the known world, really."

He eased the cab to the end of the next block and swung in at the curb. There was a pub on the corner, big plate-glass windows, bright squares of gold in the darkness, steamed over with condensation on the inside. Even shut into the backseat of the cab, Saunders could hear the noise from within. It sounded like an animal shelter.

A small knot of people loitered outside the front door. A carved and painted wooden sign, bolted to the stone beside the door, showed a crowd of wolves standing on their hind legs gathered around a table. In the center of the table was a great silver platter, with an assortment of pale human arms laid upon it.

"Here you go," said the cabdriver, turning his head to look into the rear. His snout moved close to the glass that separated the front seat from the back and breathed a filmy white mist on it. "You can make your call here, I 'spect. Have to fight your way through a bit of a crowd, I'm afraid." He made a low chuckling sound that Saunders supposed was meant to be laughter, although it sounded more like a dog trying to cough up a hairball.

Saunders did not reply. He sat in the black leather seat, staring at the crowd outside the door of the Family Arms. They were staring back. Some of them were walking toward the cab. Saunders decided not to make any sound when they pulled him out. He had learned in Kashmir how to hold on to silence, and if he was strong, he would only need to hold on to it for about a minute and a half, and then it would be holding on to him.

"Good little mum-and-pop place, this is," his driver told him. "They serve up a right fine dinner in here, they do. And you know what, mate? I think you're just in time for it."

By the Silver Water of Lake Champlain

The robot shuffled *clank–clank* into the pitch-dark of the bedroom, then stood staring down at the humans.

The female human groaned and rolled away and folded a pillow over her head.

"Gail, honey," said the male, licking dry lips. "Mother has a headache. Can you take that noise out of here?"

"I CAN PROVIDE A STIMULATING CUP OF COFFEE," boomed the robot in an emotionless voice.

"Tell her to get out, Raymond," said the female. "My head is exploding."

"Go on, Gail. You can hear Mother isn't herself," said the male.

"YOU ARE INCORRECT. I HAVE SCANNED

HER VITALS," said the robot. "I HAVE IDENTIFIED HER AS SYLVIA LONDON. SHE IS HERSELF."

The robot tilted her head to one side, inquisitively, waiting for more data. The pot on her head fell off and hit the floor with a great steely crash.

Mother sat up screaming. It was a wretched, anguished, inhuman sound, with no words in it, and it frightened the robot so much that for a moment she forgot she was a robot and she was just Gail again. She snatched her pot off the floor and hurried *clangedy-clang-clang* to the relative safety of the hall.

She peeked back into the room. Mother was already lying down, holding the pillow over her head again.

Raymond smiled across the darkness at his daughter.

"Maybe the robot can formulate an antidote for martini poisoning," he whispered, and winked.

The robot winked back.

For a while the robot worked on her prime directive, formulating the antidote that would drive the poison out of Sylvia London's system. The robot stirred orange juice and lemon juice and ice cubes and butter and sugar and dish soap in a coffee mug. The resulting solution foamed and turned a lurid sci-fi green, suggestive of Venusian slime and radiation.

Gail thought the antidote might go down better with some toast and marmalade. Only there was a programming error; the toast burned. Or maybe it was her own crossed wires beginning to smoke, shorting out the subroutines that required her to follow Asimov's laws. With her circuit boards sizzling inside her, Gail began to malfunction. She tipped over chairs with great crashes and pushed books off the kitchen counter onto the floor. It was a terrible thing, but she couldn't help herself.

Gail didn't hear her mother rushing across the room behind her, didn't know she was there until Sylvia jerked the pot off her head and flung it into the enamel sink.

"What are you doing?" she screamed. "What in the name of sweet Mary God? If I hear one more thing crash over, I'll take a hatchet to someone. My own self, maybe."

Gail said nothing, felt silence was safest.

"Get out of here before you burn the house down. My God, the whole kitchen stinks. This toast is ruined. And what did you pour in this goddamn mug?"

"It will cure you," Gail said.

"There isn't no cure for me," her mother said, which was a double negative, but Gail didn't think it wise to correct her. "I wish I had one boy. Boys are quiet. You four girls are like a tree full of sparrows, the shrill way you carry on."

"Ben Quarrel isn't quiet. He never stops talking."

"You ought to go outside. All of you ought to go outside. I don't want to hear any of you again until I have breakfast made."

Gail shuffled toward the living room.

"Take those pots off your feet," her mother said, reaching for the pack of cigarettes on the windowsill.

Gail daintily removed one foot, then the other, from the pots she'd been using for robot boots.

Heather sat at the dining room table, bent over her drawing pad. The twins, Miriam and Mindy, were playing wheelbarrow. Mindy would hoist Miriam up by the ankles and walk her across the room, Miriam clambering along on her hands.

Gail stared over Heather's shoulder at what her older sister was drawing. Then Gail got her kaleidoscope and peered at the drawing through that. It didn't look any better.

She lowered her kaleidoscope and said, "Do you want me to help you with your drawing? I can show you how to draw a cat's nose."

"It isn't a cat."

"Oh. What is it?"

"It's a pony."

"Why is it pink?"

"I like them pink. There should be some that are

pink. That's a better color than most of the regular horse colors."

"I've never seen a horse with ears like that. It would be better if you drew whiskers on it and let it be a cat."

Heather crushed her drawing in one hand and stood up so quickly she knocked over her chair.

In the exact same moment, Mindy wheelbarrowed Miriam into the edge of the coffee table with a great bang. Miriam shrieked and grabbed her head, and Mindy dropped her ankles and Miriam hit the floor so hard the whole house shook.

"GODDAMN IT, WILL YOU STOP THROWING THE GODDAMN CHAIRS AROUND?" screamed their mother, reeling in from the kitchen. "WHY DO YOU ALL HAVE TO THROW THE GODDAMN CHAIRS? WHAT DO I HAVE TO SAY TO MAKE YOU STOP?"

"Heather did it," Gail said.

"I did not!" Heather said. "It was Gail!" She did not view this as a lie. It seemed to her that somehow Gail *had* done it, just by standing there and being ignorant.

Miriam sobbed, clutching her head. Mindy picked up the book about Peter Rabbit and stood there staring into it, idly turning the pages, the young scholar bent to her studies.

Their mother grabbed Heather by the shoulders, squeezing them until her knuckles went white.

"I want you to go outside. All of you. Take your sisters and go away. Go far away. Go down to the lake. Don't come back until you hear me calling."

They spilled into the yard, Heather and Gail and Mindy and Miriam. Miriam wasn't crying anymore. She had stopped crying the moment their mother went back into the kitchen.

Big sister Heather told Miriam and Mindy to sit in the sandbox and play.

"What should *I* do?" Gail asked.

"You could go drown yourself in the lake."

"That sounds fun," Gail said, and skipped away down the hill.

Miriam stood in the sandbox with a little tin shovel and watched her go. Mindy was already burying her own legs in the sand.

It was early and cool. The mist was over the water, and the lake was like battered steel. Gail stood on her father's dock, next to her father's boat, watching the way the pale vapor churned and changed in the dimness. Like being inside a kaleidoscope filled with foggy gray beach glass. She still had her kaleidoscope, patted it in the pocket of her dress. On a sunny day, Gail could see the green slopes on the other side of the water, and she could look up the stony beach, to the north, all the way to Canada, but now she could not see ten feet in front of her.

She followed the narrow ribbon of beach toward the Quarrels' summer place. There was only a yard of rocks and sand between the water and the embankment, less in some places.

Something caught the light, and Gail bent to find a piece of dark green glass that had been rubbed soft by the lake. It was either green glass or an emerald. She discovered a dented silver spoon not two feet away.

Gail turned her head and stared out again at the silvered surface of the lake.

She had an idea a ship had gone down, someone's schooner, not far offshore, and she was discovering the treasure washed in by the tide. A spoon and an emerald couldn't be a coincidence.

She lowered her head and walked along, slower now, on the lookout for more salvage. Soon enough she found a tin cowboy with a tin lasso. She felt a shiver of pleasure, but also sorrow. There had been a child on the boat.

"He's probably dead now," she said to herself, and looked sadly out at the water once more. "Drowned," she decided.

She wished she had a yellow rose to throw into the water.

Gail went on but had trudged hardly three paces when she heard a sound from across the lake, a long, mournful lowing, like a foghorn but also not like one.

She stopped for another look.

The mist smelt of rotting smelt.

The foghorn did not sound again.

An enormous gray boulder rose out of the shallows here, rising right up onto the sand. Some net was snarled around it. After a moment of hesitation, Gail grabbed the net and climbed to the top.

It was a really large boulder, higher than her head. It was curious she'd never noticed it before, but then things looked different in the mist.

Gail stood on the boulder, which was high but also long, sloping away to her right and curling in a crescent out into the water on her left. It was a low ridge of stone marking the line between land and water.

She peered out into the cool, blowing smoke, looking for the rescue ship that had to be out there somewhere, trolling for survivors of the wreck. Maybe it wasn't too late for the little boy. She lifted her kaleidoscope to her eye, counting on its special powers to penetrate the mist and show her where the schooner had gone down.

"What are you doing?" said someone behind her.

Gail looked over her shoulder. It was Joel and Ben Quarrel, both of them barefoot. Ben Quarrel looked just like a little version of his older brother. Both of them were dark-haired and dark-eyed and had surly, almost petulant faces. She liked them both, though. Ben would sometimes spontaneously pretend he was on fire and throw himself down and roll around screaming, and someone would have to put him out. He needed to be put out about once an hour. Joel liked dares, but he would never dare anyone to do anything he wouldn't do himself. He had dared Gail to let a spider crawl on her face, a daddy longlegs, and then, when she wouldn't, he did it. He stuck his tongue out and let the daddy longlegs crawl right over it. She was afraid he would eat it, but he didn't. Joel didn't say much, and he didn't boast, even when he'd done something amazing, like get five skips on a stone.

She assumed they would be married someday. Gail had asked Joel if he thought he'd like that, and he shrugged and said it suited him fine. That was in June, though, and they hadn't talked about their engagement since. Sometimes she thought he'd forgotten.

"What happened to your eye?" she asked.

Joel touched his left eye, which was surrounded by a painful-looking red-and-brown mottling. "I was play-

ing Daredevils of the Sky and fell out of my bunk bed."
He nodded toward the lake. "What's out there?"

"There's a ship sank. They're looking for survivors
now."

Joel grabbed the netting tangled on the boulder,
climbed to the top, and stood next to her, staring out
into the mist.

"What was the name?" he asked.

"The name of what?"

"The ship that sank."

"The *Mary Celeste*."

"How far out?"

"A half a mile," Gail said, and lifted her kaleidoscope to her eye for another look around.

Through the lens the dim water was shattered, again
and again, into a hundred scales of ruby and chrome.

"How do you know?" Joel asked after a bit.

She shrugged. "I found some things that washed up."

"Can I see?" Ben Quarrel asked. He was having
trouble climbing the net to the top of the boulder. He
kept getting halfway, then jumping back down.

She turned to face him and took the soft green glass
out of her pocket.

"This is an emerald," she said. She took out the tin
cowboy. "This is a tin cowboy. The boy this belonged
to probably drowned."

"That's my tin cowboy," Ben said. "I left it yesterday."

"It isn't. It just looks like yours."

Joel glanced over at it. "No. That's his. He's always leaving them on the beach. He hardly has any left."

Gail surrendered the point and tossed the tin cowboy down to Ben, who caught it and lost interest in the sunk schooner. He turned his back to the great boulder and sat in the sand and got his cowboy into a fight with some pebbles. The pebbles kept hitting him and knocking him over. Gail didn't think it was an even match.

"What else do you have?" Joel asked.

"This spoon," Gail said. "It might be silver."

Joel squinted at it, then looked back at the lake.

"Better let me have the telescope," he said. "If there are people out there, we have as good a chance of spotting them as anyone searching for them on a boat."

"That's what I was thinking." She gave him the kaleidoscope.

Joel turned it this way and that, scanning the murk for survivors, his face tense with concentration.

He lowered it at last and opened his mouth to say something. Before he could, the mournful foghorn sounded again. The water quivered. The foghorn sound went on for a long time before trailing sadly away.

"I wonder what that is," Gail said.

"They fire cannons to bring dead bodies to the surface of the water," Joel told her.

"That wasn't a cannon."

"It's loud enough."

He lifted the kaleidoscope to his eye again and looked for a while more. Then he lowered it and pointed at a floating board.

"Look. Part of the boat."

"Maybe it has the name of the boat on it."

Joel sat and rolled his jeans up to his knees. He dropped off the boulder into the water.

"I'll get it," he said.

"I'll help," Gail said, even though he didn't need help. She took off her black shoes and put her socks inside them and slid down the cold, rough stone into the water after him.

The water was up over her knees in two steps, and she didn't go any farther because she was soaking her dress. Joel had the board anyway. He was up to his waist, peering down at it.

"What does it say?" she asked.

"Like you thought. It's the *Mary Celeste*," he said, and held up the board so she could see. There was nothing written on it.

She bit her lip and stared out over the water. "If anyone rescues them, it's going to have to be us. We should make a fire on the beach, so they know which way to swim. What do you think?"

He didn't answer.

"I said, 'What do you think?'" she asked again, but then she saw the look on his face and knew he wasn't going to answer, wasn't even listening. "What's wrong?"

She glanced back over her shoulder to see what he was staring at, his face rigid and his eyes wide.

The boulder they'd been standing on wasn't a boulder. It was a dead animal. It was long, almost as long as two canoes lined end to end. The tail curled out into the water toward them, bobbing on the surface, thick as a fire hose. The head stretched out on the pebbly beach, even thicker, spade-shaped. Between the head and the tail, its body bulked up, thick around as a hippo. It wasn't the mist that stank of rotting fish. It was the animal. Now that she was staring right at the thing, she didn't know how she had ever stood on top of it, imagining it was a rock.

Her chest tingled and crawled, like she had ants under her dress. The ant feeling was in her hair, too. She could see where the animal was torn open, in the place where its throat widened into its torso. Its insides were red and white, like the insides of any fish. There wasn't a lot of blood for such a big hole.

Joel gripped her hand. They stood up to their thighs in the water, staring at the dinosaur, which was as dead now as all the other dinosaurs that had ever walked the earth.

"It's the monster," Joel said, not that it needed to be said.

They had all heard about the monster that lived in the lake. There was always a float in the Fourth of July parade made up to look like a plesiosaur, a papier-mâché creature rising out of papier-mâché waters. In June there'd been an article about the lake creature in the newspaper, and Heather had started to read it aloud at the table, but their father made her stop.

"There isn't anything in the lake. That's for tourists," he'd said then.

"It says a dozen people saw it. It says they hit it with the ferry."

"A dozen people saw a log and got themselves all worked up. There's nothing in this lake but the same fish that are in every other American lake."

"There *could* be a dinosaur," Heather had insisted.

"No. There couldn't. Do you know how many of them there would have to be for a breeding population? People would be seeing them all the time. Now, hush up. You'll scare your sisters. I didn't buy this cottage so the four of you can sit inside and fight all day. If you girls won't go in the lake because you're scared of some dumb-ass American Nessie, I'll throw you in."

Now Joel said, "Don't scream."

It had never crossed Gail's mind to scream, but she nodded to show she was listening.

"I don't want to frighten Ben," Joel told her in a low voice. Joel was shaking so his knees almost knocked. But then the water was very cold.

"What do you think happened to it?" she asked.

"There was that article in the paper about it getting hit by the ferry. Do you remember that article? A while back?"

"Yes. But don't you think it would've washed up weeks ago?"

"I don't think the ferry killed it. But maybe another ship hit it. Maybe it got chewed up in someone's propeller. It obviously doesn't know enough to stay out of the way of boats. It's like when turtles try and cross the highway to lay eggs."

Holding hands, they waded closer to it.

"It smells," Gail said, and lifted the collar of her dress to cover her mouth and nose.

He turned and looked at her, his eyes bright and feverish. "Gail London, we are going to be famous. They will put us in the newspaper. I bet on the front page, with a picture of us sitting on it."

A shiver of excitement coursed through her, and she squeezed his hand. "Do you think they will let us name it?"

"It already has a name. Everyone will call it Champ."

"But maybe they will name the species after us. The *Gailosaurus*."

"That would be naming it after you."

"They could call it a *DinoGail Joelasaurus*. Do you think they'll ask us questions about our discovery?"

"Everyone will interview us. Come on. Let's get out of the water."

They sloshed to the right, toward the tail, bobbing on the surface of the water. Gail had to wade up to her waist again to go around it, then started ashore. When she looked back, she saw Joel standing on the other side of the tail, looking down at it.

"What?" she said.

He reached out gently and put his hand on the tail. He jerked his hand away almost immediately.

"What's it feel like?" she asked.

Even though she'd climbed the net snarled around it and had stood on top of it, she felt in some way she had not touched it yet.

"It's cold," was all he said.

She put her hand on its side. It was as rough as sandpaper and felt like it had just come out of the icebox.

"Poor thing," she said

"I wonder how old it is," he said.

"Millions of years. It's been alone in this lake for millions of years."

Joel said, "It was safe until people put their damn motorboats on the lake. How can it know about motorboats?"

"I bet it had a good life."

"Millions of years alone? That doesn't sound good."

"It had a lake full of fish to eat and miles to swim in and nothing to be afraid of. It saw the dawning of a great nation," Gail told him. "It did the backstroke under the moonlight."

Joel looked at her in surprise. "You're the smartest little girl on this side of the lake. You talk just like you're reading from a book."

"I'm the smartest little girl on *either* side of the lake."

He pushed the tail aside and sloshed past it, and they walked dripping onto the shore. They came around the hind end and found Ben playing with his tin cowpoke, same as they'd left him.

"I'll tell him," Joel said. He crouched and ruffled his little brother's hair. "Do you see that rock behind you?"

Ben didn't look up from his cowboy. "Uh-huh."

"That rock is a dinosaur. Don't be afraid of it. It's dead. It won't hurt anyone."

"Uh-huh," Ben said. He had buried his cowboy up to his tin waist. In a small, shrill voice, he shouted, "Help! Ah'm a-drownin' in this heah quicksand!"

Joel said, "Ben. I'm not playing pretend. It's a *real* dinosaur."

Ben stopped and looked back at it without much interest. "Okay."

He wiggled his figure in the sand and returned to his shrill cowboy voice. "Someone throw me a rope before Ah'm buried alive!"

Joel made a face and stood up.

"He's just useless. The discovery of the century right behind him, and all he wants to do is play with that stupid cowboy."

Then Joel crouched again and said, "*Ben*. It's worth a pile of money. We're all going to be rich. You and me and Gail."

Ben hunched his shoulders and put on a pouty face of his own. He could feel he wasn't going to be allowed to play cowboy anymore. Joel was going to make him think about his dinosaur, whether he liked it or not.

"That's all right. You can have my share of the money."

"I won't hold you to that later," Joel said. "I'm not greedy."

"What's important," Gail said, "is the advancement of scientific progress. That's all we care about."

"All we care about, little guy," Joel said.

Ben thought of something that might save him and end the discussion. He made a sound in his throat, a great roar to indicate a jolting explosion. "The dynamite went off! I'm burnin'!" He flopped onto his back and began to roll desperately around. "Put me out! Put me out!"

No one put him out. Joel stood. "You need to go get a grown-up and tell them we found a dinosaur. Gail and me will stay here and guard it."

Ben stopped moving. He let his mouth loll open. He rolled his eyes up in his head. "I can't. I'm burnt to death."

"You're an idiot," Joel said, tired of trying to sound like an adult. He kicked sand onto Ben's stomach.

Ben flinched, and his face darkened, and he said, "You're the one who is stupid. I hate dinosaurs."

Joel looked like he was getting ready to kick sand in Ben's face, but Gail intervened. She couldn't bear to see Joel lose his dignity and had liked his serious, grown-up voice and the way he'd offered Ben a share of the reward money, without hesitation. Gail dropped to her knees next to the little boy and put a hand on his shoulder.

"Ben? Would you like a brand-new box of those cowboys? Joel says you've lost most of them."

Ben sat up, brushing himself off. "I was going to save up for them. I've got a dime so far."

"If you go and get your dad for us, I'll buy you a whole box of them. Joel and I will buy you a box together."

Ben said, "They've got them for a dollar at Fletcher's. Do you have a dollar?"

"I will after I get the reward."

"What if there isn't no reward?"

"You mean to say what if there isn't *any* reward," Gail told him. "What you just said is a double negative. It means the opposite of what you want things to mean. Now, if there isn't *any* reward, I'll save up until I have a dollar and buy you a box of tin cowboys. I promise."

"You promise."

"That's what I just said. Joel will save with me. Won't you, Joel?"

"I don't want to do anything for this idiot."

"*Joel.*"

"I guess okay," Joel said.

Ben tugged his cowpoke out of the sand and jumped to his feet. "I'll get Dad."

Joel said, "Wait." He touched his black eye, then dropped his hand. "Mom and Dad are sleeping. Dad said don't wake them up until eight-thirty. That's why we came outside. They were up late at the party at the Millers'."

"My parents were, too," Gail said. "My mother has a *beastly* headache."

"At least your mom is awake," Joel said. "Get Mrs. London, Ben."

"Okay," Ben said, and began walking.

"Run," Joel said.

"Okay," Ben said, but he didn't change his pace.

Joel and Gail watched him until he vanished into the streaming mist.

"My dad would just say *he* found it," Joel said, and Gail almost flinched at the ugliness in his voice. "If we show it to my dad first, we won't even get our pictures in the paper."

"We should let him sleep if he's asleep," Gail said.

"That's what I think," Joel said, lowering his head, his voice softening and going awkward. He had shown more emotion than he liked and was embarrassed now.

Gail took his hand, impulsively, because it seemed like the right thing to do.

He gazed at their fingers, laced together, and frowned

in thought, as if she had asked him a question he felt he should know the answer to. He looked up at her.

"I'm glad I found the creature with you. We'll probably be doing interviews about this our whole lives. When we're in our nineties, people will still be asking us about the day we found the monster. I'm sure we'll still like each other even then."

She said, "The first thing we'll say is that it wasn't a monster. It was just a poor thing that was run down by a boat. It's not like it ever ate anyone."

"We don't know what he eats. Lots of people have drowned in this lake. Maybe some of them who drowned didn't really. Maybe he picked his teeth with them."

"We don't even know it's a he."

They let go of each other's hand and turned to look at it, sprawled on the brown, hard beach. From this angle it looked like a boulder again, with some netting across it. Its hide did not glisten like a whaleskin but was dark and dull, a chunk of granite with lichen on it.

She had a thought, looked back at Joel. "Do you think we should get ready to be interviewed?"

"You mean like comb our hair? You don't need to comb your hair. Your hair is beautiful."

His face darkened and he couldn't hold her gaze.

"No," she said. "I mean we don't have anything to

say. We don't know anything about it. I wish we knew how long it is, at least."

"We should count its teeth."

She shivered. The ants-on-skin sensation returned. "I wouldn't like to put my hand in its mouth."

"It's dead. I'm not scared. The scientists are going to count its teeth. They'll probably do that first thing."

Joel's eyes widened.

"A tooth," he said.

"A tooth," she said back, feeling his excitement.

"One for you and one for me. We ought to take a tooth for each of us, to remember it by."

"I won't need a tooth to remember it," she said. "But it's a good idea. I'm going to have mine made into a necklace."

"Me, too. Only a necklace for a boy. Not a pretty one, like for a girl."

Its neck was long and thick and stretched out straight on the sand. If she had come at the animal from this direction, she would've known that it wasn't a rock. It had a shovel-shaped head. Its visible eye was filmed over with some kind of membrane, so it was the color of very cold, very fresh milk. Its mouth was underslung, like a sturgeon's, and hung open. It had very small teeth, lots of them, in slanting double rows.

"Look at 'em," he said, grinning, but with a kind of nervous tremor in his voice. "They'd cut through your arm like a buzz saw."

"Think how many fish they've chopped in two. It probably had to eat twenty fish a day just to keep from starving."

"I don't have a pocketknife," he said. "Do you have anything we can use to pull out a couple teeth?"

She gave him the silver spoon she'd found farther down the beach. He splashed into the water, up to his ankles, crouched by its head, and reached into its mouth with the spoon.

Gail waited, her stomach roiling strangely.

After a moment Joel removed his hand. He still crouched beside it, staring into its face. He put a hand on the creature's neck. He didn't say anything. That filmed-over eye stared up into nothing.

"I don't want to," he said.

"It's all right," she said.

"I thought it would be easy to do, but it doesn't feel like I should do it."

"It's all right. I don't even want one. Not really."

"The roof of his mouth," he said.

"What?"

"The roof of his mouth is just like mine. Ruffled like mine. Or like yours."

He got up and stood for a bit. Joel glanced down at the spoon in his hand and frowned at it, as if he didn't know what it was. He put it in his pocket.

"Maybe they'll give us a tooth," he said. "As part of our reward. It will be better if we don't have to pull it out ourselves."

"Not so sad."

"Yes."

He splashed out of the lake, and they stood looking at the carcass.

"Where's Ben?" Joel asked, glancing off in the direction Ben had run.

"We should at least find out how long it is."

"We'd have to go get a measuring tape, and someone might come along and say they found it instead of us."

"I'm four feet exactly. To the inch. I was last July when my daddy measured me in the doorway. We could measure how many Gails it is."

"Okay."

She lowered herself to her butt and stretched out on the sand, arms squeezed to her sides, ankles together. Joel found a stick and drew a line in the sand, to mark the crown of her skull.

Gail rose, brushed the sand off, and stepped over the line. She lay down flat again, so her heels were touching the mark in the dirt. They went this way down the length of the beach. He had to wade into the lake to pull the tail up onto shore.

"It's a little over four Gails," he said.

"That's sixteen feet."

"Most of it was tail."

"That's some tail. Where *is* Ben?"

They heard high-pitched voices piping through the blowing vapor. Small figures skipped along the beach, coming toward them. Miriam and Mindy sprang through the fog, Ben wandering behind them with no particular urgency. He was eating a piece of toast with jam on it. Strawberry jam was smeared around his lips, on his chin. He always wound up with as much on his face as went into his mouth.

Mindy held Miriam's hand while Miriam jumped in a strange, lunging sort of way.

"Higher!" Mindy commanded. "Higher!"

"What is this?" Joel asked.

"I have a pet balloon. I named her Miriam," Mindy said. "Float, Miriam!"

Miriam threw herself straight up off the ground and came down so heavily that her legs gave way and she sat hard on the beach. She still had Mindy's hand and yanked her down beside her. The two girls sprawled on the damp pebbles, laughing.

Joel looked past them to Ben. "Where is Mrs. London?"

Ben chewed a mouthful of toast. He was chewing it a long time. Finally he swallowed. "She said she'd come see the dinosaur when it isn't so cold out."

"Float, Miriam!" Mindy screamed.

Miriam flopped onto her back with a sigh. "I'm deflating. I'm deflat."

Joel looked at Gail with a mix of frustration and disgust.

Mindy said, "It stinks here."

"Do you believe this?" Joel asked. "She's not coming."

Ben said, "She told me to tell Gail if she wants breakfast to come home. Can we buy my cowboys today?"

"You didn't do what we asked, so you aren't getting anything," Joel told him.

"You didn't say I had to get a grown-up. You just said I had to *tell* a grown-up," Ben said, in a tone of voice that made even Gail want to hit him. "I want my cowboys."

Joel walked past the little girls on the ground and grabbed Ben's shoulder, turned him around. "Bring back a grown-up or I'll drown you."

"You said I could have cowboys."

"Yes. I'll make sure you're buried with them."

He kicked Ben in the ass to get him going. Ben cried out and stumbled and glanced back with a hurt look.

"Bring an adult," Joel said. "Or you'll see how mean I can get."

Ben walked off in a hurry, head down, legs stiff and unbending.

"You know what the problem is?" Joel said.

"Yes."

"No one is going to believe him. Would *you* believe him if he said we were guarding a dinosaur?"

The two little girls were speaking in hushed voices. Gail was about to offer to go to the house and get her mother when their secretive whispering caught her notice. She looked down to find them sitting cross-legged next to the creature's back. Mindy had chalk and was drawing tic-tac-toe on its side.

"What are you doing?" Gail cried, grabbing the chalk. "Have some respect for the dead."

Mindy said, "Give me my chalk."

"You can't draw on this. It's a dinosaur."

Mindy said, "I want my chalk back or I'm telling Mommy."

"They don't even believe us," Joel said. "And they're sitting right next to it. If it was alive, it would've eaten them by now."

Miriam said, "You have to give it back. That's the chalk Daddy bought her. We each got something for a penny. You wanted gum. You could've had chalk. You have to give it back."

"Well, don't draw on the dinosaur."

"I can draw on the dinosaur if I want to. It's everybody's dinosaur," Mindy said.

"It is not. It's ours," Joel said. "We're the ones who discovered it."

Gail said, "You have to draw somewhere else or I won't give you back your chalk."

"I'm telling Mommy. If she has to come down here to make you give it back, she'll scald your heinie," Mindy said.

Gail started to reach out, to hand back the chalk, but Joel caught her arm.

"We're not giving it," he said.

"I'm telling Mother," Mindy said, and got up.

"I'm telling with her," Miriam said. "Mother is going to come and give you heck."

They stomped away into the mist, discussing this latest outrage in chirping tones of disbelief.

"You're the smartest boy on this side of the lake," Gail said.

"*Either* side of the lake," he said.

The mist streamed in off the surface of the water, and Mindy and Miriam walked into it. By some trick of the light, their shadows telescoped, so each girl appeared as a shadow within a larger shadow within a larger shadow. They made long, girl-shaped tunnels in the smoke. They extended away into the vapor, those multiple shadows lined up like a series of dark, featureless matryoshka dolls. Finally they dwindled in on themselves and were claimed by the fishy-smelling fog.

Gail and Joel did not turn back to the dinosaur until Gail's little sisters had vanished entirely. A gull sat on the dead creature, staring at them with beady, avid eyes.

"Get off!" Joel shouted, flapping his hands.

The gull hopped to the sand and crept away in a disgruntled hunch.

"When the sun comes out, it's going to be ripe," Joel said.

"After they take pictures of it, they'll have to refrigerate it."

"Pictures of it with us."

"Yes," she said, and wanted to take his hand again but didn't.

"Do you think they'll bring it to the city?" Gail asked. She meant New York, which was the only city she'd ever been to.

"It depends who buys it from us."

Gail wanted to ask him if he thought his father would let him keep the money but worried the question might put unhappy ideas in his head. Instead she asked, "How much do you think we might get paid?"

"When the ferry hit this thing back in the summer, P. T. Barnum announced he'd pay fifty thousand dollars for it."

"I'd like to sell it to the Museum of Natural History in New York City."

"I think people give things to museums for free. We'd do better with Barnum. I bet he'd throw in lifetime passes to the circus."

Gail didn't reply, because she didn't want to say something that might disappoint him.

He shot her a look. "You don't think it's right."

She said, "We can do what you want."

"We could each buy a house with our half of Barnum's money. You could fill a bathtub with hundred-dollar bills and swim around in it."

Gail didn't say anything.

"It's half yours, you know. Whatever we make!"

She looked at the creature. "Do you really think it might be a million years old? Can you imagine all those years of swimming? Can you imagine swimming under the full moon? I wonder if it missed other dinosaurs.

Do you think it wondered what happened to all the others?"

Joel looked at it for a while. He said, "My mom took me to the Natural History Museum. They had a little castle there with a hundred knights, in a glass case."

"A diorama."

"That's right. That was swell. It looked just like a little world in there. Maybe *they'd* give us lifetime passes."

Her heart lightened. She said, "And then scientists could study it whenever they wanted to."

"Yeah. P. T. Barnum would probably make scientists buy a ticket. He'd show it next to a two-headed goat and a fat woman with a beard, and it wouldn't be special anymore. You ever notice that? Because everything at the circus is special, *nothing* is special? If I could walk on a tightrope, even a little, you'd think I was the most amazing boy you knew. Even if I was only two feet off the ground. But if I walked on a tightrope in the circus and I was only two feet off the ground, people would shout for their money back."

It was the most she had ever heard him say at one go. She wanted to tell him he was already the most amazing boy she knew but felt it might embarrass him.

He reached for her hand, and her heart quickened, but he only wanted the chalk.

He took it from her and began to write on the side of the poor thing. She opened her mouth to say they shouldn't but then closed her mouth when she saw he was writing her name on the pebbly turtle skin. He wrote his name beneath hers.

"In case anyone else tries to say they found it," he told her. Then he said, "Your name ought to be on a plaque here. Our names ought to be together forever. I'm glad I found him with you. There isn't no one I'd rather have been with."

"That's a double negative," she said.

He kissed her. Just on the cheek.

"Yes, dear," he said, like he was forty years old and not ten. He gave her back the chalk.

Joel looked past her, down the beach, into the mist. Gail turned her head to see what he was staring at.

She saw a series of those Russian-doll shadows, collapsing toward them, just like someone folding a telescope shut. They were mother-shaped, flanked by Miriam and Mindy shapes, and Gail opened her mouth to call out, but then that large central shadow suddenly shrank and became Heather. Ben Quarrel was right behind her, looking smug.

Heather stalked out of the mist, her drawing pad under one arm. Coils of blond hair hung in her face. She pursed her lips and blew at them to get them out of her eyes, something she only ever did when she was mad.

"Mother wants to see you. She said right now."

Gail said, "Isn't she coming?"

"She has egg pancake in the oven."

"Go and tell her—"

"Go and tell her yourself. You can give Mindy her chalk before you go."

Mindy held out one hand, palm up.

Miriam sang, *"Gail, Gail, she bosses everyone around. Gail, Gail, she is really stupid."* The melody was just as good as the lyrics.

Gail said to Heather, "We found a dinosaur. You have to run and get Mom. We're going to give it to a museum and be in the paper. Joel and I are going to be in a photo together."

Heather took Gail's ear and twisted it, and Gail screamed. Mindy lunged and grabbed the chalk out of Gail's hand. Miriam wailed in a long, girlish pretend scream, mocking her.

Heather dropped her hand and grabbed the back of Gail's arm between thumb and index finger and twisted. Gail cried out again and struggled to get free. Her hand flailed out and swatted Heather's drawing pad into the sand. Heather didn't give it any mind, her bloodlust up. She began to march her little sister away into the mist.

"I was drawing my *best* pony," Heather said. "I worked on it *really* hard. And Mom wouldn't even look at it because Mindy and Miriam and Ben keep bothering her about your stupid dinosaur. She yelled at me to get you, and I didn't even do anything. I just wanted to draw, and she said if I didn't go get you, she'd take my colored pencils away. The colored pencils! I got! For my birthday!" Twisting the back of Gail's arm for emphasis, until Gail's eyes stung with tears.

Ben Quarrel hurried to keep alongside her. "You better still buy me my cowboys. You promised."

"Mom says you aren't getting any egg pancake," Miriam said. "Because of all the trouble you've caused this morning."

Mindy said, "Gail? Do you mind if I eat the piece of egg pancake that would've been yours?"

Gail looked over her shoulder at Joel. He was already a ghost, twenty feet back in the mist. He had climbed up to sit on the carcass.

"I'll stay right here, Gail!" he shouted. "Don't worry! You've got your name on it! Your name and mine, right together! Everyone is going to know we found it! Just come back as soon as you can! I'll be waiting!"

"All right," she said, her voice wavering with emotion. "I'll be right back, Joel."

"No you won't," Heather said.

Gail stumbled over the rocks, looking back at Joel for as long as she could. Soon he and the animal he sat on were just dim shapes in the fog, which drifted in damp sheets, so white it made Gail think of the veils that brides wore. When he disappeared, she turned away, blinking at tears, her throat tight.

It was farther back to the house than she remembered. The pack of them—four small children and one twelve-year-old—followed the meandering course of the narrow beach, by the silver water of Lake Champlain. Gail looked at her feet, watched the water slop gently over the pebbles.

They continued along the embankment, until they reached the dock, their father's dinghy tied up to it. Heather let go of Gail then, and each of them climbed up onto the pine boards. Gail did not try to run back. It was important to bring their mother, and she thought if she cried hard enough, she could manage it.

The children were halfway across the yard when they heard the foghorn sound again. Only it wasn't a foghorn and it was *close*, somewhere just out of sight in the mist on the lake. It was a long, anguished, bovine sound, a sort of thunderous lowing, loud enough to make the individual droplets of mist quiver in the air. The sound of it brought back the crawling-ants feeling on Gail's scalp and chest. When she looked back at the dock, she saw her father's boat galumphing heavily up and down in the water and banging against the wood, rocking in a sudden wake.

"What was that?" Heather cried out.

Mindy and Miriam held each other, staring with fright at the lake. Ben Quarrel's eyes were wide and his head cocked to one side, listening with a nervous intensity.

Back down the beach, Gail heard Joel shout something. She thought—but she was never sure—that he shouted, "Gail! Come see!" In later years, though, she sometimes had the wretched idea that it had been "God! Help me!"

The mist distorted sound, much as it distorted the light. So when there came a great splash, it was hard to judge the size of the thing making the splashing sound. It was as if a bathtub had been dropped from a great height into the lake. Or a car. It was, anyway, a great splash.

"What was that?" Heather screamed again, holding her stomach as if she had a bellyache.

Gail began to run. She leaped the embankment and hit the beach and fell to her knees. Only the beach was gone. Waves splashed in, foot-high waves like you would see at the ocean, not on Lake Champlain. They drowned the narrow strip of pebbles and sand, running right up to the embankment. She remembered how on the walk back the water had been lapping gently at the shore, leaving room for Heather and Gail to walk side by side without getting their feet wet.

She ran into the cold, blowing vapor, shouting Joel's name. As hard as she ran, she felt she was not going nearly fast enough. She almost ran past the spot where the carcass had been. It wasn't there anymore, and in the mist, with the water surging up around her bare feet, it was hard to tell one stretch of beach from another.

But she spotted Heather's drawing pad, sloshing in on the combers, soaked through, pages tumbling. Gail caught in place and stared out at the plunging waves and tormented water. She had a stitch in her side. Her lungs struggled for air. When the waves drew back, she could see where the carcass had been hauled through the hard dirt, pulled into the water, going home. It looked as if someone had dragged a plow-blade across the beach and into the lake.

"Joel!"

She shouted at the water. She turned and shouted up the embankment, into the trees, toward Joel's house.

"Joel!"

She spun in a circle, shouting his name. She didn't want to look at the lake but wound up turned to face it again anyway. Her throat burned from yelling, and she was beginning to cry again.

"Gail!" Heather called to her. Her voice was shrill with fright. "Come home, Gail! Come home, *right now*!"

"Gail!" yelled Gail's mother.

"Joel!" Gail shouted, thinking this was ridiculous, everyone shouting for everyone else.

The lowing sound came from a long way off. It was mournful and soft.

"Give him back," Gail whispered. "Please give him back."

Heather ran through the mist. She was up on the embankment, not down on the sand, where the water was still piling in, one heavy, cold wave after another. Then Gail's mother was there, too, looking down at her.

"Sweetie," Gail's mother said, her face pale and drawn with alarm. "Come up here, sweetie. Come up here to Mother."

Gail heard her but didn't climb the embankment. Something washed in on the water and caught on her foot. It was Heather's drawing pad, open to one of her ponies. It was a green pony, with a rainbow stripe across it, and red hooves. It was as green as a Christmas tree. Gail didn't know why Heather was always drawing horses that looked so un-horse-like, horses that couldn't be. They were like double negatives, those horses, like dinosaurs, a possibility that canceled itself out in the moment it was expressed.

She fetched the drawing pad out of the water and looked at the green pony with a kind of ringing sickness in her, a feeling like she wanted to throw up. She ripped the pony out and crushed it and threw it into the water. She ripped some other ponies out and threw them, too, and the crushed balls of paper bobbed and floated around her ankles. No one told her to stop, and Heather did not complain when Gail let the pad fall from her hands and back into the lake.

Gail looked out at the water, wanting to hear it again, that soft foghorn sound, and she did, but it was inside her this time, the sound was down deep inside her, a long, wordless cry for things that weren't never going to happen.

Faun

PART ONE: OUR SIDE OF THE DOOR

Fallows Gets His Cat

The first time Stockton spoke of the little door, Fallows was under a baobab tree, waiting on a lion.

"After this, if you're still looking for something to get your pulse going, give Mr. Charn a call. Edwin Charn in Maine. He'll show you the little door." Stockton sipped whiskey and laughed softly. "Bring your checkbook."

The baobab was old, nearly the size of a cottage, and had dry rot. The whole western face of the trunk was cored out. Hemingway Hunts had built the blind right into the ruin of the tree itself: a khaki tent, disguised by fans of tamarind. Inside were cots and a refrigerator with cold beer in it and a good Wi-Fi signal.

Stockton's son, Peter, was asleep in one of the cots, his back to them. He'd celebrated his high-school graduation by killing a black rhinoceros only the day before. Peter had brought along his best friend from boarding school, Christian Swift, but Christian didn't kill anything except time, sketching the animals.

Three slaughtered chickens hung upside down from the branch of a camel thorn, ten yards from the tent. A sticky puddle of blood pooled in the dust beneath. Fallows had an especially clear view of the birds on the night-vision monitors, where they looked like a mass of grotesque, bulging fruits.

The lion was taking his time finding the scent, but then he was elderly, a grandfather. He was the oldest cat Hemingway Hunts had on hand and the healthiest. Most of the other lions had canine distemper, were woozy and feverish, fur coming out in patches, flies at the corners of their eyes. The game master denied it, said they were fine, but Fallows could tell looking at them that they were going down fast.

It had been a bad-luck season on the preserve all around. It wasn't just sick lions. Only a few days before, poachers had rammed a dune buggy through the fence along the northwestern perimeter, took down a hundred feet of chain-link. They roared around, looking for rhino—the horn was worth more by weight than diamonds—but were chased out by private security without killing anything. That was the good news. The bad news was that most of the elephants and some of the giraffe had wandered off through the breach. Hunts had been canceled, money refunded. There'd been shouting matches in the lobby and red-faced men throwing suitcases into the backs of hired Land Rovers.

Fallows, though, was not sorry he'd come. He had, in years before, killed his rhino, his elephant, his leopard, and buffalo. He would get the last of the big five tonight. And in the meantime there'd been good company—Stockton and his boys—and better whiskey, Yamazaki when he wanted it, Laphroaig when he didn't.

Fallows had met Stockton and the boys only a week ago, on the night he arrived at Hosea Kutako International. The Stockton gang were fresh off a BA flight from Toronto. Fallows had flown private from Long Island in the Gulfstream. Fallows never bothered with public aircraft. He had an allergy to standing in line to take off his shoes, and he treated it with liberal applications of money. As they were all arriving in Windhoek at roughly the same time, the resort had sent a G-Class Mercedes to gather them up and bring them west across Namibia.

They'd been in the car for only a few moments before Immanuel Stockton realized he was the very same Tip

Fallows who operated the Fallows Fund, which held a heavy position in Stockton's own pharmaceutical firm.

"Before I was a shareholder, I was a client," Fallows explained. "I proudly served my nation by feeding myself into the woodchipper of a war I still don't understand. I crawled away in shreds and stayed high on your narcotic wonders for close to five years. Personal experience suggested it would be a good investment. No one knows better than I how much a person will pay to escape this shitty world for a while."

He was trying to sound wise, but Stockton gave him an odd, bright, fascinated look and clapped him on the shoulder and said, "I understand more than you might think. When it comes to the luxury goods—cigars, furs, whatever—nothing is worth more than an escape hatch."

By the time they spilled out of the big Mercedes, four hours later, they were all in a jolly mood, and after check-in they took the conversation to the bar. After that, Stockton and Fallows drank together almost every single night, while Peter and Christian horsed around in the pool. When the boy, Christian—he was eighteen but still a boy to Fallows—asked if they could come with him to see him bag his cat, it never even crossed his mind to say no.

"The little door?" Fallows asked now. "The hell's that? Private game reserve?"

"Yes." Stockton nodded sleepily. The smell of Laphroaig exuded from his pores, and his eyes were bloodshot. He'd had a lot to drink. "It's Mr. Charn's private game reserve. Invitation only. But also, the little door is . . . a little door." And he laughed again—almost giggled—very softly.

"Peter says it's expensive," said Christian Swift.

"Ten thousand dollars to look through the door. Ten thousand more to walk on the other side. Two hundred and thirty to hunt there, and you only get the one day. You can bring a trophy back, but it stays with Mr. Charn, at the farmhouse. Those are the rules. And if you don't have your big five, don't even bother sending him an e-mail. Charn doesn't have any patience for amateurs."

"For a quarter a million dollars, you better be hunting unicorn," Fallows said.

Stockton raised his eyebrows. "Close."

Fallows was still staring at him when Christian touched his shoulder with the knuckles of one hand. "Mr. Fallows. Your cat is here."

Christian was all alertness, close by the open flap, gently offering Fallows his big CZ 550. For a moment Fallows had half forgotten what he was doing there. The boy nodded at one of the night-vision monitors. The lion stared into the camera with radioactive green eyes as bright as new-minted coins.

Fallows sank to one knee. The boy crouched beside him, their shoulders touching. They peered through the open flap. In the dark the lion stood beneath the camel thorn. He had turned his great, magnificent head to look at the blind, with eyes that were intelligent and aloof and calmly forgiving. It was the gaze of a king bearing witness to an execution. His own, as the case happened to be.

Fallows had been closer to the old cat, just once, and at the time there'd been a fence between the lion and him. He had studied the grandfather through the chicken wire, staring into those serene golden eyes, and then told the game master he had chosen. Before he walked away, he made the lion a promise, which he now meant to keep.

Christian's breath was shallow and excited, close to Fallows's ear. "It's like he knows. It's like he's ready."

Fallows nodded, as if the boy had spoken some sacred truth, and gently squeezed the trigger.

At the rolling boom of the shot, Peter Stockton woke with a little scream, twisted in his tangle of sheets, and fell out of the cot.

Christian Tears His Shirt

Christian followed the man Fallows out of the tent. The killer crossed the ground in slow, careful steps, always planting his feet just so, like a pallbearer lugging one corner of an invisible coffin. He laughed and smiled easily, but he had attentive, chilly eyes, the color of lead. Those eyes made Christian think, randomly, of the moons around Saturn, airless places where the seas were acid. Peter and his father enjoyed a good shoot, would yell with pleasure when a bullet thwacked into the hide of a crocodile or raised a puff of dust off a buffalo's flank. The way Fallows killed, it was as if he himself were the weapon and the gun was only incidental. Pleasure didn't come into it.

The lion's tail lifted slowly and slapped the dust. Lifted—held in place—and thumped the dust again. The big cat lay toppled on its side.

For a time Fallows sat alone with his lion and the others hung respectfully back. Fallows stroked its wet muzzle and stared into its patient, still face. Perhaps he spoke to it. Christian had overheard Fallows saying to Mr. Stockton that after he got his lion, he might give up hunting, that there was nothing left to go after. Stockton had laughed and said, "What about hunting a man?" Fallows had looked at him with those chilly, distant eyes and said, "Hunted them and been hunted by them and have the wounds to prove it." Peter and Christian had debated, ever since, how many men he'd killed. It delighted Christian to know a no-kidding agent of death.

Some Saan ranch hands materialized out of the night from their own hideaway, and a cheer went up at the sight of the dead lion. One unzipped a canvas cooling bag and dug in the ice for beers. The tail struck the ground again, and Christian imagined he could feel the earth vibrating from the blow. But then Christian had a colorful imagination. Stockton helped Fallows to his feet and handed him an icy Urbock.

Peter pinched his nose. "God. Smells like shit. They ought to groom them before a hunt."

"That's the chickens, dumb-ass," Peter's father said.

The tail rose and fell with a whap.

"Should he shoot it again?" Christian asked. "Is it suffering?"

"No. That's one dead cat," Stockton said. "Never mind the tail. They do that. It's a mindless postmortem spasm."

Christian sank down by the lion's head, sketch pad in hand. He stroked the lion's vast, trembling mane, tentatively at first, then more firmly. He leaned close to one velvety ear, to whisper to it, before it was all the way gone: to say fare thee well. He was only barely sensible of Peter hunkering down beside him and the two older men talking behind them. For the moment he was alone with the lion in the profound stillness between life and death, a separate and solemn kingdom.

"Will you look at this paw?" Peter asked, drawing Christian back to the now. Peter lifted the lion's great limp foreleg, spreading the leathery pads with his thumb.

"Hey there," Fallows said, but Christian wasn't sure who he was talking to.

"Make a hell of a paperweight, wouldn't it?" Peter asked, and growled, and waved the paw at Christian in a lazy swipe.

The paw extruded smooth, sharp hooks of yellowing keratin. A tendon in the foreleg went taut. Christian sprang, throwing his shoulder into Peter's chest. He was fast. The lion was faster. Fallows was faster still. Old, and broken more than once, but fastest of them all.

Fallows hit Peter, who jolted into Christian, and all three of them slammed into the hardpan. Christian felt something snag his shirt, as if the fabric caught on a branch for a moment. Then he was flattened under the other two, and all the breath smashed out of him. Fallows kicked, turning onto his side and rolling the rifle down off his shoulder and into his hands in one fluid motion. The barrel settled into the soft underside of the lion's jaw. The gun went off with a shattering crack that made Christian's ears ring.

Stockton's beer slipped out of his hand and hit the

dirt, where it spouted foam. "Peter? *Peter!* The fuck is wrong with you?"

Peter was the first to struggle out from the pig pile. He left Christian and Fallows sprawled in the dirt, both of them panting for breath, as if they'd collapsed together after a hard sprint. The old soldier groaned exquisitely. Peter stood over them, staring down at the lion in a dazed sort of way and slapping his own bottom to get the dust off his shorts. He remained in a foggy-eyed trance until his father grabbed him by the shoulder and wrenched him around. Mr. Stockton's face was an alarming shade of red, except for a branch of arteries in his brow, which bulged, pale and shiny, in high relief.

"You fuckin' asshole," Peter's father said. "You know what you just did? You just wrecked his fucking trophy. Mr. Fallows paid thirty thousand for that cat, and now there's a hole the size of a golf ball in its face."

"Dad," Peter gasped. His eyes were shiny with shock and grief. "Dad."

"It's not ruined," Fallows said. "Easily fixed by the taxidermist." He stared up into the darkness. "I might be ready for the taxidermist myself."

Peter Stockton looked from Fallows to his father and back again with brimming eyes.

"How you like that, Pete?" Christian said. His own

giddy voice was muffled and distant, as if he had cotton wadding stuffed in his ears. "Mr. Fallows just saved your ass. Lucky for you! That's your best feature."

The Saan bushmen had gone still in the tense aftermath of the gunshot. Now, though, they roared with laughter and erupted into cheers. One of them grabbed Peter by the hands, and another shook a beer and let it foam over the teenager's head. In a moment Peter went from close to tears to crying out in laughter. Stockton gave his son a resentful, furious look—and then his shoulders dropped and he laughed, too.

Christian felt a cool trickle of air on bare skin and peered down, fingering two long slashes in his shirt. The very white chest beneath was unmarked. He laughed and looked at Fallows.

"I'm going to keep this shirt the rest of my life. That's all the trophy I need." He considered for a moment, then said, "Thanks for not letting me get clawed to bits."

"I didn't save anyone. You moved first. You jumped like a deer." Fallows was smiling—but his eyes were thoughtful.

"I don't think so, Mr. Fallows," Christian told him modestly.

"We know what's what around here, Fallows," Stockton said, reaching down with his big hands to squeeze the little man's shoulder. "We know a man when we see one." And he turned his beer over and poured it on Fallows's head, while the Saan whooped it up.

Christian gently collected up his drawing pad from the dust so no one could see what he'd been drawing.

Stockton Repays a Debt

When the bell chimed, Stockton went to the door of the suite and opened it a crack. Fallows was in the hall.

"Come in. Be careful, though. It's dark in here," Stockton warned him.

"What's with the lights?" Fallows asked as he slipped into the room. "Are we attending a presentation or a séance?"

The lights were off and the curtains drawn in Mr. Charn's corner suite on the fourth floor of the Four Seasons, across from the Boston Common. A single lamp shone, on an end table, but the usual lightbulb had been swapped out for one that was tinted red. Stockton had expected the red light. Stockton had seen the Edwin Charn show before.

He opened his mouth to explain—or try to explain, or at least press Fallows to be patient—but Charn spoke first.

"Get used to it, Tip Fallows," came the reedy voice, wavering with age. "If I offer you a spot on my next huntin' party, you'll need to get used to the half-light. What's to be shot on the other side of the little door will be shot at dusk, or not a-t'all.''

Charn sat in a striped easy chair to the left of the love seat. He wore a sprightly yellow bow tie and suspenders that pulled his pants too high. Stockton thought he dressed like the benevolent host of a television program for small children, one where they practiced naming the colors and counting to five.

The boys sat together on the love seat, Peter in a tailored Armani suit, Christian in a blue blazer. Christian didn't come from money, had made it to private school on his wits. Stockton was proud of his son for looking past the other boy's secondhand wardrobe and for quietly accepting Christian's broke, shy, strictly religious foster parents. Of course, Christian was probably the only reason Peter had himself graduated from private school—Stockton was sure Christian let him copy on exams, and he'd probably written more than a few of Peter's papers. That pleased Stockton as well. You looked out for your friends, and they looked out for you. That was the very reason Stockton had insisted on introducing Fallows to Mr. Charn. Fallows had been looking out for Stockton's boy in Africa, three months ago; Stockton took a certain mellow satisfaction in knowing he could pay the man back with interest. To be honest, a trip through the little door was probably worth any number of overweight, intellectually lazy sons.

A birdcage sat on the coffee table, covered with a sheet of red linen. Or maybe it was white linen and only looked red in the horror-house light, Stockton wasn't sure. If Stockton were running the presentation, he would've started with the birdcage, but he wasn't, and Charn wouldn't.

"Thanks for agreeing to meet me, Mr. Charn," Fallows said. "I'm very interested to hear about the little door. Stockton tells me there's nothing like it anywhere in the world."

Charn said, "A-yuh. He's right enough. Thank you for comin' all t'way to Boston. I don't much care to leave Maine. I don't like to leave the door for long, and 'tisn't necessary for me to travel widely to drum up business. Word passes around. The truly curious come to me. I only offer the two hunts a year, and next is on the twentieth of March. Small groups only. Price nonnegotiable."

"I heard about the price. That's most of the reason I came—the sheer entertainment value of hearing what kind of hunt a person could get for a quarter of a million dollars. I can't imagine. I spent forty thousand to kill an elephant and felt I overpaid."

Mr. Charn raised an eyebrow and cast a questioning look at Stockton. "If it's beyond your means, sir, then—"

"He's got the money," Stockton said. "He just needs to see what he'd get for it." He spoke with a certain smooth, confident humor. He had not forgotten how he himself felt when he was in Fallows's boots, recalled his own disgust at the price tag and his icy unwillingness to be conned. The pitch had turned him around, and it would turn Fallows around, too.

"I'm just wondering what I could possibly shoot that would be worth that kind of bread. I hope it's a dinosaur. I read a Ray Bradbury story about that when I was a kid. If that's what you're offering, I promise not to step on any butterflies." Fallows laughed.

Charn didn't. His calm was almost uncanny.

"And if I *do* shoot something—I understand I can't even keep the trophy? All that money and I bring home squat?"

"Your kill will be preserved, mounted, and kept at my farmhouse. It may be viewed by appointment."

"For no additional fee? That's decent of you."

Stockton heard the edge in the old soldier's voice and fought down an urge to put a restraining, comforting hand on Fallows's arm. Charn wouldn't be offended by a brittle tone or a sarcastic implication. Charn had heard it all before. He'd heard it from Stockton himself only three years ago.

"Of course viewing is free, although should you like

to take tea while you're visiting, there is a modest ser-vice charge," Charn said in a blasé tone. "Now I should like to share a short video. It is not professionally pro-duced. I made it myself, quite a while back. Still, I feel it is more than adequate to my needs. The video you are about to see has not been altered in any way. I don't expect you to believe that. In fact, I am sure you will not. That is no matter to me. I will establish its veracity beyond any doubt before you leave this room."

Charn pressed a button on the remote.

The video opened with a view of a white farmhouse against a blue sky on the edge of a field of straw. Titles whisked onto the screen, sliding from left to right.

Charn Estate, Rumford, Maine

They were the sort of titles you could create in-camera if you didn't care that it made your video look like childish junk.

There was a cut to a second-floor bedroom, with homey New England touches. An urn, patterned with blue flowers, stood on the bedside table. A brass bed dressed with a handmade quilt took up most of the space. Stockton had slept in that very bed on his last trip to Rumford—well, not slept. He had lain awake the whole restless night, springs digging into his back through the thin mattress, field mice scuttling frantically in the ceiling. The thought of the day to come had put sleep well out of reach.

New titles swept in, chasing off the previous titles.

4 rustic bedrooms, shared bathroom facilities

"Pretty sure 'rustic' means cold and uncomfortable," Stockton heard his son murmur to Christian. Good Christ, the kid was loud, even when he whispered.

Peter had been too young to go the last time. He wasn't much more mature now, but maybe Christian would keep him in line. Stockton had arranged this meeting to thank Fallows for saving his son. Not for the first time, it crossed his mind he might be even more grateful to Fallows if he *hadn't* saved the fat little nose-picker.

The video jumped to a shot of a small green door—a grown man would have to crawl through it—set at one end of a room on the third floor of the farmhouse. *The door!* Stockton thought, with the passion of a convert heedlessly crying out hallelujah at the sight of a holy relic. The sight of it inspired and delighted him in a way his son never had, not even on the day of his birth.

The ceiling was low on the top floor, and at the far side of the room, opposite the camera, it banked steeply downward, so the far wall was only about three feet high. The room contained a single dusty window with a view of the field outside. A new title swept onto the screen:

the little door is opened for curated hunts twice a year. Charn services cannot guarantee a kll and full payment is required regardless of outcome.

Stockton heard Fallows exhale, a brief, hard snort of disquiet. The old soldier was frowning, three deep wrinkles in his brow, his body language stiff with unease. Up until now, Stockton thought, Fallows had assumed that the little door was the name for a private compound. He had not expected an *actual* little door.

The titles zipped off the screen. Then the camera was outside, on a hillside, in the dusk—or the dawn, who knew? The sun was below the horizon, but only just. The sky was striated with thin crimson clouds, and the rim of the earth was a copper line.

A flight of stone steps descended through high strands of pale, dead-looking grass and disappeared among bare, desolate trees. It didn't resemble the land around Charn's house, and it didn't look at all as if it had been shot at the same time of year. The earlier material had depicted high summer. This was Halloween country.

The next cut took the viewers inside a hunting blind, situated well off the ground, and placed them in the company of two hunters: hefty, silver-haired men dressed in camouflage. The one on the left was recognizable as the CEO of one of the biggest tech outfits. He'd been on the cover of *Forbes* once. The other was a highly regarded lawyer who had defended two presidents. Fallows rocked back on his heels, and some of the tension abandoned his posture. There—he wasn't going to walk out of the room just yet. Nothing reassured a man about an investment like knowing that richer and more powerful men had gone first.

The CEO settled onto a knee, the butt of the gun against his shoulder and about an inch of barrel protruding through the opening in the side of the blind. From here it was possible to see that staircase of rough stone blocks, descending into the valley below. The steps were no more than thirty yards away. At the bottom of the hill, through a screen of wretched trees, it was possible to detect a flash of dark moving waters.

"Hunting is not permitted on the other side of the river," Charn said. "Nor is exploration. Anyone discovered to have crossed the river will have his hunt terminated immediately and will not receive a refund."

"What's over there? State land?" Fallows asked.

"The dolmen," Stockton murmured. "And the sleeper." He spoke without meaning to, and his own tone—reverent, wistful—drew an irritable glance from the other man. Stockton paid him hardly any mind. He had seen her once, from across the water, and some part of him longed to see her again, and some part of him was afraid to go anywhere near.

A flickering light moved into the shot, climbing that distant, crude staircase. It was the figure of a man, holding a torch with a lurid blue flame. He was too far away to see clearly, but he appeared to be wearing baggy, furry pants.

They were coming to it now. The boys on the couch sensed it and leaned forward in anticipation.

The camera zoomed in. The CEO and the lawyer disappeared from the shot, and for a minute the figure on the stairs was an indistinct blot. Then the picture sprang into sharp focus.

Fallows stared at the TV for a long, silent moment and then said, "Who's the asshole in the costume?"

The figure on the steps was hoofed, his legs sleekly furred in a glossy brown coat. His ankles bent backward, close to the hoof, like the ankles of a goat. His torso rose from the flanks of a ram, but it was the bare, grizzled chest of a man. He was naked, except for a stiff-looking vest, faded and worn, patterned in gold paisley. A pair of magnificent spiraled horns curved like conch shells from his curly hair. His torch was a bundle of sticks wired together.

"He's carrying a devil-thorn torch," said Charn. "It crackles and turns green in the presence of . . . menace. But fortunately for our purposes, its range is limited to just a few yards. A Zeiss Victory scope will put you well beyond its reach."

The camera zoomed back out, to include the shoulder and profile of the gunman in the frame.

"Shit," muttered the CEO. "I'm shaking. I'm actually shaking."

The bearded grotesque went still, froze in place on the faraway stone steps. He had the quick, almost instantaneous reactions of a gazelle.

The gun cracked. The faun's head snapped straight back. He tumbled bonelessly, end over end, down three steps, and wound up crumpled in the fetal position.

"Yeah, bitch!" the CEO shouted, and turned to give the famous lawyer a high five. There was the sound of a beer can cracking and fizzing.

"Okay, kids," Fallows said. "This was fun, but now we're done. I'm not getting diddled out of a quarter mil to play paintball with a buncha clowns dressed like extras from *The Lord of the Rings*."

He took one step toward the door, and Stockton moved—not as fast as Fallows had moved in Africa, when he'd saved Peter from getting his face clawed off, but not too slow on the hoof for all that.

"Do you remember what you said the first time we ever sat down together? You told me no one knows better than you how much a person will pay to escape the world for a while. And I said I *knew*. And I do. Give him five more minutes. Please, Tip." And then Stockton nodded at the birdcage. "Besides. Don't you want to see what he's got there?"

Fallows stared at the hand on his arm until Stockton let go. Then he moved his gaze—that look of almost terrifying emptiness—upon Charn. Charn returned the look with a daydreaming calm. At last Fallows shifted his attention back to the TV.

The video cut to a trophy room, back in Charn's Rumford farmhouse. It was decorated like a men's smoking club, with a deep leather couch, a couple of battered leather chairs, and a mahogany liquor cabinet. The wall was crowded with mounted trophies, and as Stockton watched, the CEO—dressed now in flannel pajama bottoms and an ugly Christmas sweater—hung the latest head. The bearded faun gawped stupidly at the room. It joined a little over a dozen other bucks with glossy, curving horns. There was also a trophy that looked at first glance like the head of a white rhino. On closer inspection it more nearly resembled the face of a fat man with four chins and a single, stupid, piggy eye above the tusk of a nose.

"What's that?" Peter whispered.

"Cyclops," Stockton replied softly.

Titles swept across the screen:

> trophies are kept in a climate-controlled room at Charn's.
> Successful hunters may visit with 48hours advance ntice.
> Tea and refreshments provided at small additional charge.

"Mister," Fallows said, "I don't know what kind of asshole you think I am—"

"The kind of asshole who has too much money and too little imagination," Charn said mildly. "I am about to take some of the former and provide you with a bit of the latter, much to your benefit."

"Fuck this," Fallows said again, but Stockton squeezed his arm once more.

Peter looked around. "It wasn't faked. My dad's been."

Christian nodded to the covered birdcage. "Go on and show us, Mr. Charn. You knew anyone who saw that video would figure it was a fake. But people have been paying you scads of money anyway. So there's *something* under that sheet that's worth a quarter of a million dollars."

"Yes," Charn said. "Almost everyone who sees the video thinks of costumes and special effects. In an age of artifice, we recognize reality only when it shows us its claws and gives us a scratch. The whurls have sensitive eyes and ears, and the electric lights of our world cause them exquisite pain—hence the red lightbulb. If you re-move your smartphone from your pocket and attempt to video what you are about to see, I will ask you to leave. It wouldn't be worth the trouble anyway. No one will believe what you recorded, much as you do not believe my video—and you will *never* travel through the little door. Do you understand?"

Fallows didn't reply. Charn looked at him with bland, speculative eyes for a moment, then leaned for-ward and tugged the sheet off the birdcage.

They resembled chipmunks, or maybe very small skunks. They had black, silky fur and brushy tails with silver rings running up them. Their tiny hands were leathery and nimble. One wore a bonnet and sat on an overturned teacup, knitting with toothpicks. The other perched on a battered paperback by Paul Kavanagh and was awkwardly reading one of the little comic strips that came in a roll of Bazooka Joe gum. The tiny square of waxed paper was as large, for the whurl, as a newspaper would've been for Stockton.

Both of the creatures went still as the sheet dropped away. The whurl with the comic strip slowly lowered it to look around.

"Hello, Mehitabel," said Mr. Charn. "Hello, Hutch. We have visitors."

Hutch, the one with the comic, lifted his head, and his pink nose twitched, whiskers trembling.

"Won't you say hello?" Charn asked.

"If I doesn't, will you pokes my beloved with a cigarette again?" said Hutch in a thin, wavering voice. He turned to address Stockton and Fallows. "He tortures us, you know. Charn. If one of us resists him, he tortures the other to force our obedience."

"This torturer," Charn said, "doesn't have to bring you picture stories to read or yarn for your wife."

Hutch flung aside the *Bazooka Joe* strip and jumped to the bars. He looked through them at Christian, who shrank back into the couch. "You, sir! I sees shock in your eyes. Shock at the indecency and cruelty you sees before you! Two intelligent, feeling beings imprisoned by a brute who displays us to wring money out of his fellow sadists for a hunt with no honor! I pleads with you, *run*. Run now. Spread the word that the sleeper may yet awake! Someone may yet revive her with the breath of kings so she may lead us against the poisoner, General Gorm, and free the lands of Palinode at last! Find Slowfoot the faun—oh, I know he lives still but has only lost his way home or been bewitched to forget himself somewise—and tell him the sleeper still waits for him!"

Christian began to laugh, a little hysterically. "Wild! Oh, man. For a minute I didn't get it. It's, like, ventriloquism, right?"

Fallows glanced at the boy and exhaled: a long, slow deflation. "Sure. Pretty good. You've got a little amplifier in the base of the birdcage and someone transmitting in the next room. You had me there for a minute, Mr. Charn."

"We recognize reality only when it shows us its claws and gives us a bite," Charn repeated. "Go on, then. Put your finger in the cage, Mr. Fallows."

Fallows laughed without humor. "I'm not sure I'm up on my shots."

"The whurl is more likely to get sick from you than the other way around."

Fallows eyed Charn for a moment—and then poked a finger into the cage with a brusque, almost careless courage.

Hutch stared at it with golden, fascinated eyes, but it was Mehitabel who sprang, clutched the finger in both of her sinewy little hands, and cried, "For the sleeper! For the empress!" And fastened her teeth on Fallows's finger.

Fallows yanked his hand away with a shout. The sudden force of his reaction knocked Mehitabel onto her back. Hutch helped her up, muttering, "Oh, my dear, my love." She spit the blood on the floor of the cage and shook her fist at Fallows.

Fallows squeezed his hand closed. Blood dripped from between his fingers. He stared into the cage like a man who has been administered a powerful, numbing sedative—a Stockton Pharmaceutical special, perhaps.

"I felt her shouting into my hand," he muttered.

"It's all real, Fallows," Stockton said. "Real enough to sink its teeth into you."

Fallows nodded, once, in a dazed sort of way, without looking from the birdcage.

In a distracted tone, he said, "How much is that deposit again, Mr. Charn?"

Peter Feasts

The men sat up front, and Peter sat in back with Christian. The car glided through a deformed tunnel of whiteness, heavy flakes of snow falling into the headlights. Cell-phone reception sucked. It was a rotten drive. There was nothing to do but talk.

"Tell me about the sleeper," Christian said, like a child asking for a favorite bedtime story.

Peter could never decide if he loved Christian or secretly kind of despised him. There was something almost otherworldly about him, about his shining gold hair and shining joyful eyes, about the easy grace with which he carried himself, and the easy pleasure with which he attacked his studies, and the infuriating skill with which he drew. He even smelled good. They had shared a dorm room for the last four years, and the door was often open, and the room was frequently half full with honor-roll kids and girls in pleated skirts on their way to Vassar, and when Peter stood next to Christian, he felt like a gnome lurking in the shadows a few steps from a blazing torch. Yet Christian adored him, and Peter accepted this somewhat as his due. After all, no one else was going to take Christian to Milan or Athens or Africa—or through the little door.

"That's the other side of the river," Stockton said. "She stays on her side, and we stay on ours."

"But do you have any idea who—what—she is?"

Peter's father unscrewed the cap on an airline-size bottle of Jim Beam. He had cadged it off the flight attendant on the jump from Toronto to Portland, Maine, which was where they'd met up with Fallows. He took a nip.

"You can see her if you go down to the riverbank. She's in a clearing, beneath what you would call a dolmen, which is a little like a prehistoric . . . shed. A stone house with open walls. And there she is . . . this girl, holding a bouquet of flowers."

Peter leaned forward and asked the question Christian wouldn't. "What kind of girl, Dad? The kind of girl who goes to third grade? Or the kind of girl who goes to third base?"

Christian laughed. That was something else Christian got out of his friendship with Peter. Peter got help with his history final; Christian had someone to say the things and do the things a polite boy wouldn't say or do.

"What do you think would happen if someone crossed the river to look at her?" Fallows asked.

"Don't even joke. Remember your smart-ass line about going to shoot a dinosaur?"

"Sure. I said I'd be careful not to step on a butterfly. Because of the story, the Ray—"

"I know the story. Everyone knows the story. Walking across the river? That's stomping on the fucking butterfly. We stay in the hills. We stay on our side of the river."

Stockton abruptly switched on the radio and tuned it to a country-and-western station. Eric Church sang through a thin, grainy layer of static.

Fallows was his father's most interesting friend. Peter wanted to know how he'd killed people in the war. He wanted to know what it was like to sink a knife into someone. Peter had read about soldiers who killed the enemy and then raped their wives and daughters. Peter thought that sounded like a pretty exciting reason to enlist.

He was daydreaming about soldiering when they slowed at a military-style barrier, a mechanical arm lowered across the road at a gap in a ten-foot-high chain-link fence. Fallows rolled down the driver's window. Peter's father leaned across him and saluted the fish-eye lens of a security camera. The barrier went up. The car went on.

"Charn forgot to install a machine-gun nest," Fallows said.

Peter's father finished his bottle of Beam and let it drop onto the floor of the rental car. He burped softly. "You just didn't see it."

They carried their own bags in across a wide porch that stretched around two sides of the house. There was a Mrs. Charn, it turned out: a short, heavy, shuffling woman who didn't make eye contact with them but continuously looked at the floor. The coolest thing about her was the big, gross, red wart below her right eye. It was like a belly button in her face.

She said Mr. Charn wouldn't be home till later but that she would be glad to show them around. Peter hated the way the house smelled, of old paperbacks and dusty drapes and mildew. Some of the floorboards were loose. The doorframes had settled over the centuries (centuries?), and some of them were crooked, and all of them were too low for a twenty-first-century-size man. The bedrooms were on the second floor: small, tidy rooms with lumpy single beds, Shaker furniture, and ornamental chamber pots.

"You *hope* they're ornamental," Stockton said as Peter nudged one with his foot.

"Good one, Mr. Stockton," Christian said.

The more he saw, the more depressed Peter got. The toilet in the upstairs bathroom had a pull chain, and when he lifted the lid, a daddy longlegs crawled out.

"Dad," Peter whispered, in a voice that carried. "This place is a dump."

"You'd think with an income stream of a million dollars a year—" Fallows began.

"The house stays as it is," Mrs. Charn said from directly behind them. If she was disturbed to hear her farmhouse referred to as a dump, one couldn't tell from her voice. "Not a single crooked doorway to be straightened. Not one brick replaced. He doesn't know why the little door opens into t'other place, and he won't change anything for fear 'twon't open into t'other place again.'"

The daddy longlegs crawled across the floor to the toe of one of Peter's Gucci sneakers. He squashed it.

But Peter cheered up when they arrived at the terminus of the tour. A grand table had been set up in the trophy room. The sight of all those decapitated heads gave Peter a funny tickle of sensation in the pit of his stomach. It was a little like the nervous pulse of desire that went through him whenever he was gearing himself up to kiss a girl.

Peter and Christian wandered down the length of one wall and along another, staring into shocked, wondering, dead faces. To a man, all of the bucks sported hipster beards; if you ignored the horns, it was possible to imagine that Mr. Charn had massacred an artisanal chocolate company in Brooklyn. Peter paused at one, a blondie with elfin, feminine features, and reached up to ruffle his hair.

"Looks like we found your real dad, Christian," Peter said. Christian gave him the finger, but he was such a goody-goody that he hid the gesture behind his body so no one else could see.

They studied the cyclops in mute, awed silence for a time and then contemplated a pair of gray-skinned orcs, their ears studded with copper rings, their lolling tongues as purple as eggplants. One of the orc heads was at waist level and Peter surreptitiously mimed face-fucking it. Christian laughed—but he also wiped at a damp brow.

The first course was a pea soup. Even though it looked like something Regan had barfed in *The Exorcist*, it was hot, and salty, and Peter finished his so quickly he felt cheated. The entrée was a leg of lamb, crispy and bubbling with liquid fats. Peter tore off pieces in long, dripping strips—it was just about the best mutton he'd ever had—but Christian only poked at it with his fork. Peter knew from experience that Christian had a nervous, excitable stomach. He threw up easily, always on the first day of school, usually before a big exam.

Mrs. Charn noticed, too. "There's some get that way. They get vertigo here. The more sensitive ones. Especially this close to an equinox."

"I feel like a fly on the edge of a drain," Christian said. He spoke with what sounded like a thickened tongue, sounded like a teenager who's found himself drunk for the first time in his life.

Across the table Fallows held lamb under the table for Mrs. Charn's little dogs, three rat terriers who were scrabbling around his ankles. "You didn't say what Mr. Charn is up to."

"Taxidermist," she said. "Picking up his latest."

"Can I excuse myself?" Christian asked, already shoving back his chair.

He batted through a swinging door. Peter heard him retching in the kitchen. It used to be that the smell of vomit and the sound of someone puking turned his stomach, but after four years of sharing a room with Christian he was inured to it. He helped himself to a second buttery biscuit.

"I had a touchy stomach my first time here, too," Peter's father confessed. He tapped Peter affectionately with one elbow. "He'll feel better after we get where we're going. When the waiting is over. By this time tomorrow, he'll be famished." He looked to the head of the table. "Do save Christian some leftovers, won't you, Mrs. Charn? Even cold faun is better than no faun at all."

Charn Discovers a Snoop

Mr. Edwin Charn let himself in a little before 11:00 P.M., carrying a bell jar under a sheet of white linen. He stomped his boots, and cakes of snow fell off them, and then a floorboard creaked somewhere above, and he went still. He stood at the foot of the stairs and tuned his senses to the farmhouse. It was common to say that one knew a place like the back of one's hand, but in truth Charn knew the Rumford farmhouse quite a bit better than the back of his own hand. He needed only to listen to the hush for a few moments to locate, with an uncanny degree of precision, everyone in the building.

The rackety snore in the rear of his house was the wife. He could picture the way she slept, with her head cocked back and her mouth open, a corner of the sheet bunched up in one fist. Springs creaked in a room on the second floor, off to the right side of the landing. From the heavy *sproing* of it, Charn guessed that would be Stockton. The pharmaceutical man was carrying about sixty pounds more than was healthy. His son, the boy Peter, farted and moaned in his sleep.

Charn cocked his head and thought he heard the soft, light pad of a foot on the staircase leading to the third floor. That couldn't be Fallows, the soldier, who'd been torn apart and put back together in some war or another; Fallows was sinewy and hard but moved with pain. The process of elimination left only Christian, the young man who so resembled an idealistic prince from an inspiring story for young boys.

Charn removed his own boots and climbed the stairs with far more care, bringing the bell jar with him.

Christian was in striped pajamas of a very old-fashioned sort, the kind of thing one of the Darling children might've been wearing on a Christmas Eve in

1904. He was at the far end of the attic. An old sewing table with an iron foot pedal had a spot under the eaves. The moss-colored rug was so old and dusty it was almost the exact shade of the floorboards it covered. The little door—it was like the door to a cupboard—waited at the far end of the room. Charn was silent while the boy turned the brass latch and drew a deep breath and threw it open.

"Just a crawl space," Charn said.

The boy sprang partway up and clouted his head on the plaster ceiling: a satisfying reward for a snoop. He sank back to his knees and twisted around, clutching his head in his hands. Christian's face was flushed with embarrassment, as if Charn had discovered him looking at pornography.

Charn smiled to show the boy he wasn't in trouble. The ceiling was at its highest close to the stairs, but Charn still had to duck to move a few steps closer. He held the bell jar out in front of him with both hands, like a waiter from room service carrying a bedtime snack on a tray.

"I never saw anything except the space behind the walls, until two-thirty A.M. on the night of September twenty-third, 1982. I heard a sound like a goat loose on the third floor, the *trip-trap* of hooves across the planks. I made it into the hall just in time for something to come barreling into me. I thought it was a kid—not a child, you understand, but a baby goat. It struck me in the abdomen with its horns, knocked me over, and kept going. I heard it crash down the stairs and out the front door. Edna—my wife—was afraid to leave the bedroom. When I had my breath back, I went downstairs, doubled over in pain. The front door hung open on a splendid summer night. The high grass rolled like surf under a fat golden moon. Well. I thought p'raps a deer had got into the house somehow, terrified itself, and escaped. But then I was never one to leave the doors open at night, and it struck me peculiar that one would've got all the way up to the third floor. I began to scale the stairs to the attic. I was halfway there when a flash caught my eye. A gold coin it was, with a stag engraven 'pon it, glinting on one of the steps. I have it still. Well. I climbed the rest of the way in a baffled, bemused, half-scairt state. The little door was shut, and I don't know what impulse made me lift the latch. And there, on t'other side. The ruin! The murmur of another world's breeze! That dusk that I think may presage an eternal night. I opened the door every day after that. I kept a calendar. T'other place waited on equinoxes and solstices. On all other days, there was nothing but crawl space back there. I shot my first faun in the spring of 1984, and I brought my kill home with me and was pleased to discover it tasted better than mutton. In 1989 I began the hunts. Since then I've taken down everything from faun to orc, whurl to whizzle, and now my joy is giving other men the opportunity to kill fairy tales themselves, to slaughter the beasts of bedtime stories. Did you know if you eat the heart of a whurl, for a while you can understand the language of squirrels? Not that they have much to say. It's all nuts and fucking. I went bald in my thirties but have recovered my youthful head of hair since I began eating faun. Though I never speak of it to Missus Churn, I fuck like a bull when I'm away. I get to Portland to see their ladies of leisure twice a month, and I've left some walking bowed-legged. Powdered orc horn. Makes Viagra look like an aspirin." He winked. "Go to bed, young fellow. Tomorrow you will see your companions strike down daydreams in the flesh."

Christian nodded obediently and pushed the little door shut. He walked on bare feet, with head down, toward the stairs. But then, just as he crossed by Charn, he looked back, at the bell jar covered in the linen sheet, the same sheet that had previously covered the birdcage.

"Mr. Charn? What's that?" he asked.

Charn stepped forward into the moonlight, set the jar on the sewing desk. He slipped the linen cloth off it, folded the sheet over one arm. "This room is rather bare, isn't it? I thought it needed something to liven it up."

Christian bent to look into the jar. Two whurls had been stuffed and dramatically posed. One stood on an artfully positioned tree branch, holding a sword as long as Christian's pinkie and baring his teeth in a fanged roar. The other, in a green cape, huddled beneath the branch, eyes narrowed in sly thought: a conspirator preparing to spring.

"Good old Hutch," Charn said "Good old Mehitabel."

PART TWO: *THEIR* SIDE OF THE DOOR

Stockton Wishes for Better Company

Peter was in a pissy mood in the morning. He had forgotten to pack his tactical knife, an MTech with a pistol grip, and he bitched and moaned and stomped around in his bedroom, tossing the contents of his duffel, sure it had to be in there somewhere, until Stockton told him to give it a fucking rest or he could stay behind on earth with the old ladies.

When they assembled in the attic after coffee and pancakes, they were in autumnal camo, beiges and murky greens. They all had guns, except for Christian, who was armed only with his sketch pad. He was fully recovered from the previous evening's queasy spell, and now his eyes shone with happiness. He looked from man to man as if it were Christmas morning, and he was bursting with feelings of good fellowship. Stockton wondered if you could get a headache from spending too much time with someone so cheerful. Too much uncontrolled optimism ought to be prohibited; people needed to be protected from it, like secondhand smoke. To soften the dull throb of pain behind his eyes, it was necessary to unscrew the lid of his thermos and have a sip of coffee, liberally punched up with some Irish Cream.

Charn was the last to join them and today looked nothing like the host of a program for children on public television. With his Marlin 336 over his shoulder, he carried himself with the casually assertive bearing of the seasoned, lifelong hunter.

"One amongst you was too eager to wait for morning and tried the door last night," Charn said, looking around at them. Christian blushed, and Charn smiled indulgently. "Would you care to give it another go, young Mr. Swift?"

Christian sank to one knee by the little door. He held the latch for a single dramatic moment—and then pulled it open.

Dead leaves blew across the wooden floor, carrying with them the scent of fall. Christian stared into the gloaming on the other side for the time it took to draw a single breath and then crawled through. The gay, bright-as-brass tinkle of his laughter echoed strangely from the far side. Stockton tipped back his thermos and had another swallow.

Peter Yearns for Action

Peter followed Christian through, across the dusty attic floorboards, onto cold, bare earth and then out from under a low ledge of rock.

He rose and found himself in a clearing on the side of a hill, a natural amphitheater overgrown with pale grass. He turned in a complete circle, looking around. Boulders capped in moss had been scattered helter-skelter around the glade. It took a moment of study to recognize they had been deliberately positioned, creating a semicircle, like teeth in the lower jaw of some enormous antediluvian brute. A single dead-looking tree, deformed and hunched, cast wild branches out over the ruin. Ruin of what? Some place of cruel worship, perhaps. Or maybe just the equivalent of a scenic turnoff. Who could say? Not Peter Stockton.

His father's hand fell onto his shoulder. The wind hissed through the blades of grass.

"Listen," his father said, and Peter inclined his head. After a moment his eyes widened.

The grass whispered, *"poison, poison, poison, poison."*

"It's murder-weed," his dad told him. "It says that whenever the wind blows and men are about."

The sky above them was the dull color of a blood-stained bedsheet.

Peter looked back at the door as Mr. Fallows pulled his way out of one world and into the other. On this side the doorframe was made of rough stone and the door itself was built into the slope of the hill, which rose steeply away above that rock ledge. Charn crawled through last and closed the door behind him.

"Regard your watches," Charn said. "I make it 5:40 A.M. By 5:40 P.M. we must be on our way back. If you open that door one minute after midnight, you will find naught but a slab of rock. Oh, and then you are in for it. In our world the door opens every three months. But three months there is *nine* months *here.* You must wait the term of a woman's pregnancy before it will open again, on the summer solstice, June twenty-first. And in case you can't do the math . . . *yes.* It has been thirty-seven years since I first opened the door in our world. But it has been one hundred and *eleven* years here."

"A century of twilight," Christian said, with a prickle of delight.

"A century of shadows," Peter replied, in a tone of hushed awe.

Charn talked over them. "I speak from terrifying personal experience: You do not want to risk being caught here. I spent most of 1985 in this world, was hunted by fauns, betrayed by whurls, and forced to strike a vile bargain with a golem in the service of General Gorm the Obese. It was always twilight, nine months of shadows fighting shadows. If we are separated and you do not find your way back here, you *will* be left."

God, he loved to talk, Peter thought. It seemed to Peter that Charn's true calling was not *hunting* but *lecturing.*

They followed Charn down the meandering flight of rough stone steps. The branches of dead trees creaked and rustled, and ancient leaves blew around their ankles.

Once they all stopped at the sound of a great distant lowing.

"Ogre?" Peter's father asked.

Charn nodded. The groan came again, a sound of aching despair. "Mating season," Charn said, and chuckled indulgently.

Peter's rifle thudded and banged against his back, and once the barrel caught on a branch. Mr. Fallows offered to carry it for him. His voice did not quite disguise an edge. For himself Peter was relieved to get it off his back. He felt he was already carrying too much. He hated hunting for the most part. There was too much waiting around, and his father wouldn't let him bring his phone. Shooting things was fun, but often hours went by and *nothiiiiiiing* happened. He sent a mental prayer up to whatever barbaric gods ruled this world for a good quick piece of slaughter before he himself dropped dead, of boredom.

Christian Longs for Night

They went down and down. Christian heard the rushing of water in the distance and shivered with delight, as if he were already up to his waist in the frigid stream.

Charn led them off the steps and into the woods. A yard from the path, he touched a black silk ribbon hanging from a low branch. He nodded meaningfully and walked on into the poisoned forest. They followed a trail of the discreet ribbons for not quite half a mile and at last arrived upon the blind, set twenty feet off the ground. It was a shed resting on cross-planks in the boughs of a tree that resembled but was not an oak. A mossy rope ladder had been draped up out of reach on a high branch. Charn dropped it with the help of a long forked stick.

There were a couple camp chairs in the blind, and a wooden shelf holding some dusty glasses, and a dirty-looking paperback called *$20 Lust* if someone wanted something to read. A wide slot, about a foot high and three feet across, faced downhill. Through the trees it was just possible to see the flash of black water below.

Charn was the last up the ladder, and he only stuck his head and shoulders through the trap.

"I built this blind in 2005 and haven't shot from here since 2010. As every year of ours is three of theirs, I think it safe to assume none of them will be on their guard should they pass near. From here you can sight on the stairs and also pick off anyone moving along the footpath beside the river. I must be out to check the condition of my other blinds and to place a few snares for whurls. With luck I will have some new prizes to replace Mehitabel and Hutch before we exit this world. If I hear a shot, I will return at a brisk pace, and you need have no fear of shooting me in the half-light. I know what you can see from this blind and have no intention of crossing into your field of fire. Watch for faun! They are plentiful, and you are sure to see some before long. Remember, there are no laws here against taking down a doe or a young'un, and the meat is just as tender—but we only mount the bucks as trophies!"

He lifted two fingers in a wry salute and descended, gently dropping the trap shut behind him.

Christian had settled in one of the camp chairs with

his drawing pad but leaped up to study a cobweb in a high shadowed corner. The spider had spun a few words into the web:

FREE BED FOR FLYS

Christian whispered in a breathless voice for Peter to come look. Peter studied it for a moment, then said, "I don't think that's how you spell flies."

Stockton dropped into a camp chair, unbuttoned one of the snap pockets on the front of his camos, and produced a small canteen. He had a sip of coffee and sighed and offered it to Fallows. The other man shook his head.

"Hard to believe it's real," Christian said, turning his drawing pad to a new page and idly beginning to sketch. "That I'm not dreaming this."

"What time do you think it is? Almost night or almost day?" Stockton asked.

Christian said, "Maybe it hasn't made up its mind. Maybe it could still go either way."

"What do you want it to be?" Fallows asked.

"Night for sure! I bet the best things come out at night. The real monsters. Be great to bring back a werewolf head for the wall."

Peter guffawed. He took his rifle back from Fallows and flung himself onto the floor.

"Let's hope we don't see a werewolf," Stockton said over the rim of his thermos. "After what we spent to get here, we didn't have much left over for silver bullets."

Fallows Prepares

One hour went by, then another. Christian and Peter ate sandwiches. Stockton sagged in his camp chair, drinking Irish coffee, looking sleepy and content. Fallows waited by the open window, staring into the night. His pulse beat rapidly and lightly, a feeling of anxiety and excitement in him that made him think of waiting in line for a roller coaster. Fallows always felt this way before a kill.

"I'd like to see her," Christian said. "The sleeper. Hey, Mr. Stockton. You never said. Is she a *little* girl or like, a grown-up girl?"

"Well, I've only seen her from a distance, but I'd say—"

Fallows reached back with one hand in a gesture that called for silence. Peter stiffened, staring through the slot that faced the slope below. Without looking back, Fallows beckoned Christian to join them at the window.

Three figures mounted the steps. One of them, the tallest, held a torch that blazed with blue fire. Ram's horns rose from either side of his skull, and he walked with his hand on the shoulder of his kid, a child in a loose, flapping vest, with fuzzed budding horns of his own. The doe was close behind them, carrying a basket.

"It's all yours, Peter," Fallows whispered. "I loaded your gun myself."

"Nail the big one," Stockton said.

Peter stared out at the targets with inquisitive, thoughtful eyes. "If I shoot the kid, they'll stop to look after him, and we can nail all three."

"Oh, that's thinking," Stockton said. "You got a good head on your shoulders. And in a minute you're going to have an even better one for Charn's wall."

"Do it," Christian said.

Peter pulled the trigger.

The Hunter Racks Up His First Kills

The gun made an unsatisfying *clack*.

Frustrated and confused, Peter threw back the bolt. The rifle was empty.

"Fucking thing," Peter said. Behind him a chair fell over. "Mr. Fallows, this isn't loaded."

He looked back over his shoulder. His face darkened, then went pale, and Christian tore his gaze away from the fauns to look for himself.

Peter's father had toppled over in his chair, the black rubber handle of a combat knife in his chest. His red, heavy, souse's face was perplexed, a man reading a bank statement that suggests somehow, impossibly, his savings have been wiped out. Christian had a distant, distracted thought, that it was the knife Peter had been unable to find in the morning.

Peter stared at his father. "Dad?"

Fallows stood over Stockton, his back to the boys. He was tugging Stockton's rifle off the dying man's shoulder. Stockton didn't make a sound, didn't gasp, didn't cry out. His eyes strained from his head.

Peter lunged past Christian and grabbed for Fallows's big CZ 550, which was leaning against the wall. His fingers were stiff and clumsy with shock, and he only knocked it over.

Fallows couldn't pull Stockton's rifle away from him. The strap was still snagged over his shoulder, and Stockton himself was clutching the butt, in a last, failing effort to resist.

Fallows glanced back at the boys.

"Don't, Peter," he said.

Peter finally grabbed the CZ. He slid open the bolt to make sure it was loaded. It was.

Fallows stepped over Stockton and turned to face them. Stockton still had the strap of the rifle over his shoulder and was clutching the butt, but Fallows had one hand under the muzzle and a finger on the trigger and the barrel pointed at Peter.

"Stop," he said again, his voice almost toneless.

Peter fired. From so close the *blam* of the gun was deafening, a great roar followed by a deadening whine. A chunk of blazing-white wood exploded from the tree trunk to the right and just behind Fallows. As the splinters flew past him, Fallows slapped Stockton's hand away and squeezed the trigger of his gun. Peter's head snapped back, and his mouth dropped open in an expression that had been common to him in life: a look of dim-witted bewilderment. The red-and-black hole above his left eyebrow was big enough to insert two fingers into.

Christian heard someone screaming, but there was no one left alive in the blind except for Fallows and himself. After a few moments, he realized he was the one making all the noise. He'd dropped his sketch pad and held up both hands to protect his face. He didn't know what he said or promised, couldn't hear himself through the ringing in his ears.

The trapdoor rose about a foot, and Charn looked in on them. Fallows wrenched the rifle free from Stockton at last and turned the barrel around to point it at the old man. Charn fell, just as quickly, the trapdoor slamming behind him. Christian heard a leafy crunch as the tall man hit the ground below.

Without a look back, Fallows flung open the trap-door, dropped through it, and was gone.

Christian in Flight

It was a long while before Christian moved. Or at least he felt it was a long while. In that half-lit world, the passage of minutes was difficult to judge. Christian did not own a watch and had left his phone, by command, in the other world. He knew only that he'd had time to dampen his crotch and then time for that dampness to grow cold.

He trembled in convulsive bursts. He lifted his head and peered through the lookout. The fauns had long disappeared from the steps. The hill was silent in the gloaming.

It came to him, with a sudden, sickened urgency, that he had to get back to the little door. He picked up his sketchbook, hardly thinking why—because it was his, because it had his drawings in it—and crawled across the plank floor of the blind. He hesitated beside the corpse of Mr. Stockton. The big man stared at the ceiling with wide, startled eyes. His thermos lay close to hand. The coffee had spilled out and soaked into the floorboards. Christian thought he should take the knife and he tried to pull it out of Stockton's chest, but it was buried too deep, the blade jammed between two ribs. The effort made him sob. Then he thought he should crawl back to Peter and pull the CZ 550 out of his hands, but he couldn't bear to look at the hole in Peter's forehead. In the end he left the blind as he had come, unarmed.

He made his unsteady way down the rope ladder. It had been easy going up. It was much harder going down, because his legs were shaking.

When he was on the ground, Christian scanned the gloom and then began to move across the face of the hill, toward the flight of rough stone steps. A black silk ribbon caught his eye, and he knew he was not turned around.

He had hiked far enough to work up a good sweat when he heard shouts and a sound like a herd of ponies running through the trees. Not a dozen feet away, he saw a pair of fauns dart through the shadows. One carried a curved blade. The other had what looked like a throwing bolas, a mass of hanging leather straps with stones tied at the ends.

The faun with the scimitar leaped a fallen trunk, scrambled with the vitality of a stag up the hill, and bounded out of sight. The one with the bolas followed for a few yards—then caught himself and looked down the hill, fixing his gaze on Christian. The faun's leathery, scarred face was set in an expression of haughty contempt. Christian screamed and fled down the slope.

The trunk of a tree rose out of the darkness, and Christian slammed into it, was spun halfway around, lost his footing, and fell. He rolled. His shoulder struck a sharp stone, and he was spun again, continuing to tumble down the incline, picking up speed. Once it seemed his whole body left the ground in a spray of dead leaves. At last he struck hard against another tree and was jolted to a stop against it. He found himself in the bracken at the bottom of the hill. Just beyond the ferns was a mossy path and the river.

Christian was too afraid to pause and consider how badly he might've been hurt. He looked up the hill and saw the faun glaring down at him from fifty feet away. Or at least that's what he thought he saw. It might've been a gaunt and hunched tree, or a rock. He was mad with fear. He sprang to his feet and ran limping on, breath whining. His left side throbbed with pain, and he had twisted his ankle coming down the hill. He'd lost his sketch pad somewhere.

The lanky boy followed the path downstream. It was a wide river, as wide as a four-lane highway but, at a glance, not terribly deep. The water rushed and foamed over a bed of rock, spilling into dark basins before hurrying on. In the blind their shared body heat had created a certain stuffy warmth, but down by the river it was cold enough for Christian to see his own breath.

A horn sounded somewhere far off, a hunting horn of some sort, a long, bellowing cry. He cast a wild look back and staggered. Torches burned in the almost-night, a dozen distant blue flames flickering along the mazy staircases that climbed the hills. It came to Christian there might be dozens of parties of fauns in the hills, hunting the men. Hunting him.

He ran on.

A hundred yards along, his right foot struck a stone, and he went down on hands and knees.

For a while he remained on all fours, gasping. Then, with a start of surprise, he saw a fox on the far side of the water, watching him with avid, humorous eyes. They gazed at each other for the length of time it took to draw a breath. Then the fox bayed at the night.

"Man!" the fox cried. "Man is here! A Son of Cain! Slay him! Come and slay him and I will lap his blood!"

Christian sobbed and scrambled away. He ran until he was dizzy and seeing lights, the world throbbing and fading, throbbing and fading. He slowed, his legs shaking, and then shouted in alarm. The light he'd been seeing at the edge of his vision, a wavering blue glow, was a torch. A man stood on the hill, a black shape against a blacker background. He held the torch in his right hand. In his left was a gun.

Christian acted without thought. Because the man was on his right, Christian swerved to the left and crashed into the river. It was deeper than it looked. In three lunging steps, he was up to his knees. In moments he had lost all sensation in his feet.

He ran on, and the ground dropped away, and he plunged in up to his crotch and cried out at the shock of the cold. His breath was fast and short. A few desperate steps later, he fell and all but went under. He struggled against the current, had not expected it to be so strong.

The boy was halfway across when he saw the dolmen. A plate of gray stone, as big as the roof of a garage, stood on six tilting, crooked rocks. Beneath the roof of gray stone, in the center of the covered area, was an ancient, uneven altar stone, with a girl in a white nightdress sleeping peacefully upon it. The sight of her terrified him, but fear of his pursuers drove him on. Fallows had moved out from beneath the darkness of the trees. He was already up to his ankles in the river, having removed his shoes before stepping into the water. While the boy had stumbled, sunk, and half drowned, somehow Fallows knew just where to step so he was never more than shin-deep.

The water along the bank was hip-high, and Christian grabbed at handfuls of slippery grass to pull himself up. The murder-weed hissed *"poison, poison!"* at him and came out in clumps and dropped him back into the river, and he went up to his neck and exploded into sobs of frustration. He threw himself at the bank again and kicked and squirmed in the dirt like an animal—a pig, trying to struggle out of a mire—and floundered onto dry land. He did not pause but ran beneath the dolmen.

It was at the edge of a grassy meadow, the nearest line of trees hundreds of feet away, and Christian understood that if he tried to make it to the forest, Fallows would easily pick him off with the rifle. Also, he was shaking and exhausted. He thought desperately he might hide and reason with Fallows. He had never shot a thing. He was an innocent in this. He felt sure that Fallows had killed the others as much for what they had done as for what they had intended to do. The unfairness of it raked at him. Fallows had killed, too. The lion!

He ducked behind one of the standing stones and sat and hugged his knees to his chest and tried not to sob.

From his ridiculous hiding place, Christian could see the child. Her golden hair was shoulder length and looked recently brushed. She held a bouquet of buttercups and Queen Anne's lace to her chest. Everything Christian had seen in this place was dead or dying, but those flowers looked as fresh as if they'd just been picked. She might've been nine and had the sweet pink complexion of health.

Firelight cast a shifting blue glow across the dolmen as Fallows approached.

"Have you ever seen a more trusting face?" Fallows asked softly.

He stepped into view, the gun in one hand, the torch in the other. He had collected Christian's drawing pad and carried it under one arm. He did not look at Christian but instead sat on the edge of the stone, beside the sleeper. He gazed upon her like one inspired.

Fallows set down the sketchbook. From inside his camouflage coat, he produced a small glass bottle, and another, and a third. There were five in all. He unscrewed the black top of the first and held it to the little girl's lips, although it was empty, or seemed empty.

"This world's been holding its breath for a long time, Christian," Fallows said. "But now it can breathe again." He unscrewed the next and raised it to her mouth.

"Breath?" the boy whispered.

"The breath of kings," Fallows agreed, with a mild nod. "Their dying breaths. Breath of the lion and the elephant, the leopard and the buffalo, and the great rhino. It will counteract the work of the poisoner, General Gorm, and wake her and wake the world with it."

When he had emptied all the empty bottles, he sighed

and stretched his legs. "How I hate shoes. God save my kind from shoes. And those awful prosthetic feet!"

Christian dropped his gaze to the black, shining, bony hooves at the end of Fallows's ankles. He tried to scream again but was all screamed out.

Fallows saw him recoil, and the faintest smile twitched at his lips. "I had to shatter my own ankles— smash and reset them, you know. When I first came to your world. Later I had them broken and rebuilt again, by a doctor who was offered a million dollars to keep my secret and was paid in lead to confirm his silence." Fallows brushed back his curly hair and touched the tip of one pink ear. "Thank goodness I am not a Mountain Faun but only a mere faun of the plains! The Mountain Faun have ears just like the deer of your world, whereas we simple country faun have the ears of men. Though I would have gladly cut my ears off for her if it had been necessary. I would have cut my heart out and offered it to her slippery and red and beating in my own hands."

Fallows rose and took a step toward him. The torch, which he had never set aside, shifted from blue to a lurid, polluted emerald. Sparks began to fall from the flames.

"I don't need my torch," Fallows said, "to know what you are. And I didn't need to see your sketches to know your heart."

He tossed the sketchbook at Christian's feet.

Christian looked down at a drawing of severed heads on sticks: a lion, a zebra, a girl, a man, a child. The breeze caught the pages and leafed through them idly. Drawings of guns. Drawings of slaughter. Christian's stunned, frightened gaze shifted to the torch.

"Why is it changing color? I'm not a menace!"

"Charn doesn't know much about devil-thorn. It doesn't change color in the presence of *menace* but of *wickedness*."

"I never killed anything!" Christian said.

"No. You only laughed while other men killed. Who is worse, Christian, the sadist who serves his true nature honestly or the ordinary man who does nothing to stop him?"

"*You* killed! You went to Africa to kill a lion!"

"I went to Africa to free as many of my empress's friends as I could, and so I did, after putting a little money in the right hands. A dozen elephants and two dozen giraffes. The lions I infected with one of your unclean world's many diseases, to give them their dignity and release. As for the grandfather I shot, he was ready to walk the tall grass in the savanna of ghosts. I asked his forgiveness the day before the hunt, and he gave it. You spoke to him, too—after I shot him. Do you remember what you said as he bled out?"

Christian's face shriveled with emotion, and his eyes stung terribly.

"You asked him how it felt to die. He tried to show you, Christian, and he almost did it. How I wish you hadn't escaped him. It would've saved me an ugly bit of work here."

"I'm sorry!" Christian cried.

"Aye," Fallows said. "Aren't we both?"

He lowered the barrel of the gun. The steel kissed Christian's right temple.

"Wait, I—" Christian shrieked.

His voice was lost to the rolling sound of thunder.

The Sleeper Awakes

After, Fallows sat by the girl to wait. For a long time, nothing happened. Fauns crept close to the dolmen but stayed respectfully outside the circle, looking in. The oldest of them, Forgiveknot, an elderly faun with a rippling scar across his leathern face, began to sing. He sang Fallows's old name, the name he had left behind in this world when he fled through the little door with the last of the empress's treasures, to find the breath of kings and return her to life.

The light had taken on a faint, pearly glow when the girl yawned and rubbed one fist in a sleepy eye. She looked up, her eyes fogged with drowsiness, and her gaze found Fallows. For a moment she didn't recognize him, her brow creased with puzzlement. Then she did, and she laughed.

"Oh, Slowfoot," she said. "You've gone and grown up without me! And you have lost your proud horns! Oh, my darling. Oh, my old playmate!"

By the time Fallows had shed his human clothes and Forgiveknot was cutting his hair with a wide-bladed knife, she was sitting on the edge of the stone altar, swinging her feet above the grass, as the fauns formed a line to kneel before her, and bow their heads, and receive her blessing.

A World Awakes with Her

For the third time, Charn gritted his teeth to keep from passing out. When the woozy feeling passed, he went on, crawling arm over arm, staying down. He went slowly, crossing no more than ten yards in a single hour. His left ankle was broken—badly. It shattered when he fell from the blind, and it had been a narrow thing giving Fallows the slip.

There were six fauns in the circle of worship, set there to cut off any escape through the little door. But Charn still had a gun. He had methodically worked his way higher, avoiding the murder-weed that would whisper if it saw him—*"poison! poison!"*—moving so slowly that the crackle of dead leaves beneath him was all but imperceptible, even to the sharp ears of the fauns. There was a shelf of rock, jutting out over the clearing. It was accessible only from one side, as the slope on the other side was too steep and the earth too loose. Nor could it easily be approached from the crag above. For an armed man on this outcropping, though, firing into the clearing would be like shooting faun in a barrel.

Whether he ought to open fire . . . well, that was another question. The faun war party might yet be led away. The boy Christian could still make a convenient appearance and draw them off. On the other hand, if the numbers below swelled, perhaps it was best to simply slink away. He had survived in this world for nine months once before, and he knew a golem who would make a deal. General Gorm the Obese always had work for a bad man with a gun.

Charn pulled himself behind a rotting log and swiped the sweat from his brow. A single lightning-struck tree, like a beech, loomed over him, partially cored out. Below him some brush rustled at the edge of the clearing, and the one named Forgiveknot slipped into the glade, bolas hanging from his belt. Charn knew him well. He'd misjudged a shot at the old faun years before and given him that scar across the face. He smiled grimly. He so hated to miss.

The sight of him made up Charn's mind: kill them now, before any more showed up. He slipped the Remington off his shoulder and rested the barrel on the log. He put the front sight on Forgiveknot.

Something clattered in the dead tree over him. There was a chittering and a rustle.

"Assassin!" cried a whurl gazing down at Charn from one branch of the blasted tree. "Save yourselves! A Son of Cain is here to kill you all!"

Charn rolled and swung the barrel up. His sights found the whurl, and he pulled the trigger, and the gun made a flat, tinny click. For a moment he just stared at the old Remington in a kind of blank bewilderment. It was loaded—he had put in a fresh cartridge himself only a few minutes before. A misfire? He didn't believe it. He cleaned and oiled the gun once a month, whether he used it or not.

He was still trying to come to grips with that awful, dead click when the loop of rope fell. It caught him around the face, and Charn sat up, and as he did, it dropped around his neck and tightened. The lasso *yanked.* The rope choked off his air, and it jerked him back, over the rotten log and over the edge. He spun as he fell. He hit the earth with enough force to drive all the air out of him. Ribs broke. Pain screamed in his shattered ankle. A thousand black specks wheeled around him, like midges, only they were in his head.

He sprawled on the ground, ten feet from his little door. As his vision cleared, it seemed the sky was lighter, almost lemon-colored. He could see fair clouds in the distance.

His right hand fumbled for the rifle, but just as his shaking fingers scraped the butt, whoever held the other end dragged him away. Charn choked, tried to force his fingers under the rope and couldn't. He rolled and kicked as he was dragged and wound up on his belly, beneath the single corrupted, dead tree that leaned out over the whole natural amphitheater.

"Rifle wouldn't do you any good anyway," Fallows said from above him. Charn stared at his black hooves. "I took the firing pin out last night, while you were upstairs with Christian."

The tension on the line slackened, and Charn was able to loosen the noose a few centimeters and capture a breath. He stared up at Fallows. His skull was shaved clean to show the stumps of two horns, long since sawed off, and he was backlit by a sky the reddish gold of new-minted copper.

A little girl stood beside Fallows, holding his hand. She looked gravely down at Charn—the stern, cool, appraising look of a queen.

"It's come for you, Mr. Charn," the little girl said. "It's found you out at last."

"What?" Charn asked. "What's come?"

He was confused and frightened and desperately wanted to know.

Fallows cast one end of the rope over a bough of the overhanging tree.

"Daylight," the girl said, and with that, Fallows hoisted Charn kicking into the air.

Late Returns

When my parents went, they went together.

My father wrote a couple letters first. He wrote one for the Kingsward PD. His vision was very poor—he'd been legally blind for three years—and the letter was brief, composed in a hardly legible scrawl. It informed police that they would find two bodies in a blue Cadillac, parked in the garage, at his home on Keane Street. My mother had been able to look after my father until three months before, but she had received a diagnosis of progressive dementia, and her condition was worsening fast. They both feared leaving their only son with the burden of their long-term care and had decided to act before the power to choose was taken away from them. My father sincerely apologized for "any mess and any stress" their choice caused.

He wrote another letter for me. He said he was sorry about his shitty handwriting, but I knew about his eyes, and "Mom is worried she'll get too emotional if she tries to write this." She had told him that she wanted to die before she forgot the people who made her life worth living. She asked him to assist her suicide, and he admitted to her that he'd been ready to "get this shit over with" for a couple years. He was only sticking around because he couldn't bear the thought of leaving her on her own.

My father said I'd been a damn good kid. He said I was the best part of his life and that my mom felt the same. He asked me not to be angry at them—as if I ever could be. He said he hoped I understood. They'd never wanted to hang on for the sake of hanging on.

"I've said it a thousand times, but I still believe some words never lose their power, no matter how many times they're repeated. So: I love you, Johnnie. Mom loves you, too. Don't be unhappy for too long. The child outliving the parents is the only happy story us human beings get."

He stamped both envelopes, put them in his mailbox, and snapped the red tin flag up. Then he went into the garage, where my mother was waiting for him in the passenger seat of the Caddy. The car ran until it was out of gas and the battery died. The car was old enough to still have a tape deck, and they went down listening to

Portrait of Joan Baez. In my mind my mother's head is on my father's chest and he has an arm around her, but I don't know if that's how they were found. I was in Chicago, driving a semi for Walmart, when the police entered the garage. The last time I saw my parents was in the morgue. The suffocation had turned their faces the color of eggplants. That's the last look at them I ever had.

The shipping and logistics company I was working for fired my ass. When the cops called my cell, I turned the truck straight around without delivering my freight. A couple midwestern Walmarts didn't get red grapes for their produce section, and my supervisor went batshit and told me to take a walk.

My folks got to die the way they wanted, and they lived the same way. It didn't look like they had so much from the outside: a one-floor ranch in a New Hampshire podunk, a twenty-year-old Caddy, and a heap of debt. Before they retired together, my mother taught yoga and my father was a long-haul trucker. They didn't get rich, they didn't get famous, and they lived in their house for twenty-five years before they could say they owned it.

But she read to him while he cooked, and he read to her while she folded clothes. They did a thousand-piece jigsaw puzzle every weekend and the *New York Times* crossword every day. They smoked prodigious amounts of weed, including sharing a spliff in the car before they gassed themselves. My mother had memorably whipped up a pot-laced stuffing one Thanksgiving when I was nineteen that made me awesomely sick. I was never able to pick up the pot habit, a failing they accepted with a certain amused resignation.

My father umped over a thousand Little League games. My mother volunteered for Bernie Sanders, Ralph Nader, and George McGovern. No one has ever worked harder or with more optimism for so many lost causes. I told her she was allergic to winners, and my dad shouted, "Hey! Don't knock it! If she wasn't, I'd never have stood a chance!" They held hands on walks.

And they both loved the library. When I was little, we took family trips there every Sunday afternoon. The first Christmas present I remember receiving was a shiny blue wallet with showy stitching, my library card tucked in to it.

For some reason whenever I think about our weekend library visits, it's always the first snow of the year. My dad sits at one of the scarred wooden tables in the periodicals room, reading the *Atlantic* by the light of a green-shaded lamp, beneath a stained-glass window that shows a monk inking an illustrated manuscript. My mother leads me to the children's library, where there are oversize couches in bright primary colors, and sets me loose. When I need her, she will be reading Dorothy Sayers under the giant plastic statue of an owl in bifocals.

It was an important place for them. My parents met in a library. In a sense. My mother lived in the nearby town of Fever Creek, in a little brick vicarage, her step-father being a humorless, neurotic Anglican priest. My dad wound up spending a summer down the Creek, working in his uncle's scrapyard. They met waiting for the library's Bookmobile, which did a weekly swing through Fever Creek. At that time you could borrow LPs as well as books—it was the Summer of Love, after all—and my not-yet-parents had an argument when they both grabbed for the lone copy of *Portrait of Joan Baez* at the same time. They reached a truce when she said that if he let her take it out, he could come by the vicarage to listen to it anytime he liked. They listened to *Joan Baez* together all summer long, at first on the floor of her bedroom and later up in the bed itself.

I didn't actually mean to become a librarian. When I walked in there, five weeks after I buried my parents, I didn't have anything in mind beyond returning a grotesquely overdue book.

My parents had left behind a teetering pile of unpaid medical bills and still owed a hundred thousand dollars on the loan they took out to put me through college. Wasted money. I'd netted a bachelor's in English at Boston University, but it had done less for me, in strictly financial terms, than the eight-week course that earned me a commercial driver's license.

I had no job, about twelve hundred dollars to my name, and there was no insurance payout coming, not in the wake of what amounted to a murder-suicide. My father's lawyer, Neil Belluck, suggested that my best option was to get rid of anything I didn't absolutely have to keep for myself and sell the house. If I were lucky, it would pay their outstanding bills and leave me with enough to float on until I booked a job with another shipping company.

So I propped open the doors, bought a couple of boxes of heavy-duty garbage bags, rented a steam vacuum, and went to work. My parents had let the place go in the last year of their lives. It got away from them, and I hadn't wanted to see it: the dust on everything, the mouse droppings in the carpet, half the lightbulbs out, and mold spotting the wallpaper in the dark hallway between the living room and the master bedroom. The house smelled like Bengay and abandonment. It came to me that in the last year I had abandoned them. I was glad to get rid of their stuff. Everything I unloaded was one less thing to remind me of their last unhappy months, facing blindness and dementia alone, making up their minds to take one final ride in the Caddy together, to drive away from their troubles without ever leaving the garage. I brought musty comforters and piles of dresses to Goodwill. I put the couch out in the yard with a cardboard FREE sign on it. No one wanted it, but I left it out there. It rotted in the rain.

I stuck a broom under the bed to get at the dust bunnies and swept out a pair of my dad's jockeys and one of my mother's shoe boxes. I took a peek in the box, expecting to find a pair of heels, and was stunned to discover that it contained nearly two thousand dollars in unpaid parking and speeding tickets—there was an unpaid parking violation from the City of Boston that dated to *1993*. There was also an unpaid dentist bill from 2004, a VHS copy of *When Harry Met Sally . . .* from Blockbuster Video, and a paperback titled *Another Marvelous Thing*. I didn't understand how the book connected to the other items until I flipped open the back cover. It was a library book, and I knew at first glance that my mother had borrowed it in the last century and never got around to returning it. There was a lending card in the back, tucked into a stiff beige pocket, stamped with a return date. A relic from that ancient, fabled era before Facebook. At a dime a day, we probably owed the library our whole house. Or at least the cost of a replacement book.

The dentist my mother had stiffed retired in 2011 and now lived in Arizona. The local Blockbuster had long since been replaced by a cell-phone dealership. I figured my mom was off the hook for the parking tickets; you couldn't try a dead woman. That left the book. I stuck *Another Marvelous Thing* into the pocket of my baggy army jacket and got moving.

It was the end of September but still felt like summer. Moths batted at the old-fashioned wrought-iron lampposts on the street corners. A trio of accordion players in striped shirts and suspenders entertained a sparse audience on the town green. Kids out with their parents crowded the patio tables at the ice-cream parlor. If you ignored the cars, it might've been 1929. The walk to the library was the first time I had not felt ugly with grief in weeks. It felt like I'd been paroled.

I climbed the white marble steps into the dramatic atrium of the library, beneath a copper dome eighty feet overhead. My steps echoed. I couldn't remember when I'd last been in the place and regretted that it'd been so long. It had the soaring, tranquil grandeur of a cathedral, but, better than incense, it smelled like books.

I approached the great rosewood desk, looking for

the slot to drop my book into, but there wasn't one. Instead a sign on the desk read ALL RETURNS MUST BE SCANNED IN. There was a black laser scanner next to it with a pistol grip, just like you'd see at the supermarket checkout. I approached, thinking I would pretend to scan it and run—but the old lady behind the desk held out one quavering hand, gesturing for me to wait. Her other hand clutched a phone to her ear. She tapped one finger against the scanner and then drew her nail across her neck in a throat-cutting gesture. Broken. I thought maybe when she was free, I'd ask about renewing my library card—and wait for an opportunity to drop my mother's late return behind the desk when no one was watching. I didn't want to discuss her late fees and wanted even less to discuss her death.

I cooled my black Converse All-Stars next to a display showcasing local authors. The offerings included a crudely illustrated picture book about a rabid-looking koala, titled *I Can't Eat That,* and the self-published memoir of a woman who claimed she'd been abducted by aliens and taught the language of dolphins, leading, ultimately, to her legal struggle to marry a porpoise. I wish I were making that up. The centerpiece, of course, were the Brad Dolan novels, Kingsward's favorite son. I had met him once—he came to speak to my eighth-grade class. I had adored his old-fashioned mustache and bushy eyebrows and the rumble of his voice, and that he wore a plaid overcoat with a cape. I'd also been a little frightened of him—he stared out upon the classroom with eyes that never seemed to blink, studying us a bit like a general surveying a map of enemy territory.

Shortly afterward I had zipped through all thirteen of his books, sometimes cramming my hand in my mouth to stifle giggles if I happened to be reading in class. You know the books, with their exclamation points in the titles. There was *Die Laughing!*, the Vietnam novel about a chemical weapon unleashed by the U.S. Air Force that causes people to laugh hysterically until they keel over and for which the only cure is sex; there was *Presto!*, about a world where magical wands are protected by the Second Amendment and our hero is searching for the man who sawed his wife in half; and *Salute!*, in which Ronald Reagan wins the presidency with his running mate, Bonzo, a descendant of the monkey who starred in Reagan's hit *Bedtime for Bonzo.* Are the books less funny when you know that Dolan himself was a suicide? I don't think so, but I admit those stories carry a certain piquant sadness to them now. It's like eating cotton candy with a broken tooth in your mouth: You get sweetness, but also the ache. A cloud of sugar, but also blood.

"No, Mr. Gallagher, we can't bring it out to you," said the old lady on the telephone. "I can hold the Bill O'Reilly for you here at the desk, but if you come in, you will have to return the books you already have." She was a hobbit of a woman, with a small square face beneath silver bangs. She met my gaze with dark blue, sorrowful eyes and slowly shook her head. The voice on the other end of the line squawked indignantly. "I'm sorry, darling, I don't like it either. The Bookmobile is off the road indefinitely, and even if it weren't, Mr. Hennessy no longer works for the public library. His license has been revoked. . . . Yes. That's what I said. . . . Yes, and his library card! And Mr. Hennessy was the only one qualified to drive the old—"

There was a high-pitched shout from the other end, and the librarian flinched as Mr. Gallagher banged the phone down.

"Another satisfied customer," I said.

She gave me a resigned look. "That's Mr. Gallagher at the Serenity Apartments. The only thing he wants to read is Bill-O and Ann Coulter, large-print editions, and goodness help us if we can't bring him the book he's after. He wants to know what we do with all the tax money we drain from the town budget. I'd like to tell him it pays for our subscription to *Socialist Weekly*."

"I didn't know you deliver," I said. "Do you do pizza, too?"

"We don't deliver *anything* now, darling," she said. "The brand-new Bookmobile is a total heartbreaking wreck and—"

"Why do people keep calling it the brand-*new* Bookmobile?" a man yelled through a door that opened into a rear office. "Why don't they call it the less-*old* Bookmobile? It's been on the road since 2010, Daphne. It's not old enough to be tried as an adult for its crimes, but it's getting there."

Daphne rolled her eyes. "The new*ish* Bookmobile is guilty of nothing. I can't say the same for that hapless, feckless drunk you hired to drive it. Men like Sam Hennessy make me think the death penalty wasn't such a bad idea."

The man in the back room called, "He wrecked a truck, he didn't kill a child—thank God. And in my defense, Sam had all the necessary qualifications: He had the right kind of license, and he was cheap."

"What kind of license are we talking about?" I heard myself ask. "Class B?"

A rolling office chair squeaked, and the man in the back room glided into view. He was of indeterminate age. He might've been seventy-five or fifty-five. His silver hair had a few threads of gold in it, and he had the striking blue eyes of an aged model, the sort of rugged gent who can be found paddling a canoe through the middle of a Viagra ad. The tie was undone. The suit was tweed, gently worn in at the elbows and knees.

"That's right," he said.

"I've got a Class B. If there's a *less*-old Bookmobile, does that mean there's also a *more*-old Bookmobile?"

"An antique!" the librarian announced.

"Not quite, Daphne," said the man in tweed. "Though it's true we only take it out for the Fourth of July parade these days."

"It's an antique," Daphne repeated.

Tweed scratched his throat, leaning back in his chair to study me from around the door. "You're a commercial trucker?"

"I was," I said. "I'm taking the fall off to deal with some family business. What kind of truck are we talking about?"

"Wanna see it?" said the man in tweed.

What does it run on?" I asked after I'd stared at it for a few moments. "Unleaded? Or bong water?"

Ralph Tanner contentedly mouthed the stem of his Liverpool pipe. "It got pulled over once. The cop said he wanted to arrest whoever painted it for disturbing his peace. The chief of police tells people he has a solemn duty to impound drug paraphernalia and that's why he keeps it locked up in this carriage house."

The library shared a vast expanse of parking lot with the town office, the rec department, and an old carriage house. This last hadn't kept horses in almost a century, but it still smelled like them. It was a rickety, barnlike structure with gaps between some of the planks and pigeons cooing in the rafters. Public Works kept the street sweeper and a little golf-cart-size plow for the sidewalks and parking lots in there. The older Bookmobile was parked at the back.

It was a modified panel truck on a 1963 International Harvester chassis, a three-axle twelve-wheeler. The sides had been painted with a garish psychedelic mural. Over on the passenger side, Mark Twain's head opened like a teapot and a rainbow-colored Mississippi River frothed out. Huck and Jim and the hookah-smoking caterpillar from *Alice in Wonderland* rode a raft toward the back end. The caterpillar blew a long thread of smoke that billowed around the corner to become an ocean roiling over the rear bumper. Moby-Dick erupted from the waves with Ahab bound to his side and harpooning him in the eye. The *Nautilus* lurked in the garish depths. A gush of ocean foam melted into clouds drifting across the driver's side of the truck. The rain poured down onto

Sherlock Holmes, who did not see Mary Poppins sailing through the thunderheads above.

"Who did you say drove it back in the day? Cheech or Chong?" I asked. Then I gave Ralph Tanner the side eye. "Or was it you?"

He laughed. "I'm afraid I sat the sixties out. The Age of Aquarius was something that happened to other people while I was watching *Gilligan's Island.* I missed out on disco, too. Never owned a single pair of bell-bottoms. Instead I wore bow ties, lived in Toronto, and worked on a groundbreaking dissertation about Blake, which my thesis adviser returned to me with a can of lighter fluid. I wish my twenties *had* looked a little more like this. Peek inside?"

He gestured to the door into the rear. When I opened it, two rusty corrugated steps unfolded, ushering me into the Bookmobile.

The steel shelves were bare, and a veil of cobweb hung from one of the ceiling's fluorescent lights. I was surprised to see a handsome mahogany desk with a dark leather surface, bolted to the floor behind the cab. A runner carpet, the color of chocolate, ran up the middle. I smoothed one palm along a cold steel shelf, and my hand came up wearing a mitten of dust.

"This did for forty years," he said from just behind

me. "I suppose it could do for a few more. If we had a driver."

I already knew I wanted the job. I had known before I was sure there even *was* a job. There was the practical side: I was out of work, and a low-paying job was better than none. Besides, whatever hours they were offering, it had to be substantially less than I would've worked if I were back behind the wheel of a long-haul rig, where sometimes I might be on the road for ten or twelve days without returning home.

In truth, though, the practical side didn't cross my mind until later. I was spending all day every day in the place where my parents had died and felt, from that first instant, that they'd sent me a set of wheels to escape in—like sending a truck to take me away from the world's most joyless and dismal summer camp. *Your ride is here,* I thought, and my arms pebbled with gooseflesh. I could not help thinking that my mother had specifically avoided returning *Another Marvelous Thing* so I'd have to return it for her and in such a way be led back to the place where her story with my father began.

"What'd you say happened to your last guy?" I asked.

"I didn't," Ralph said. He twitched his mouth back and forth to move his still-unlit Liverpool pipe to the other corner of his mouth. "A local fellow, Sam Hennessy, got out of full-time trucking to focus on the two things he loved best, reading and making homebrew. He kept his Class B valid and offered to drive the new Bookmobile, just for something to do. Alas, Sam didn't only enjoy *making* homebrew. He relished drinking it as well and took to enjoying a few on his lunch break. Well, he was out a month ago in our newish Bookmobile and began to worry he was a little crocked. He decided he could use some coffee and turned in to the nearest McDonald's. And I do mean right into it. He put the front end straight through the wall and into a booth. No one sitting there, thank God. When you think of all the kids that eat in McDonald's." He shuddered, then asked if I wanted to look in the cab.

On the walk around the front, he pointed to a panel on the side of the truck. There was a diesel generator behind it that ran the lights and the heat in the book car. "The nearly new Bookmobile had a pair of computers for the patrons, but I wonder if tablets could serve the same function. Checking out the books is easy enough—it's done through an app on your phone." He had started to sketch the job out for me as if I'd already put in my application.

I climbed onto the running board and peered into the front seat. The gearshift protruding from the center of the floor was as long as a gentleman's cane, with a polished walnut ball on the top. Dead leaves had drifted onto the floor. The radio looked like it was AM only.

"What do you think?" he asked.

I opened the door, turned around, and sat in the driver's seat with my feet hanging out.

"Are you asking what I think of the truck? Or what I think of the job?"

He pushed his thumb down into the bowl of his pipe and lit it with a match from a small box, took some time drawing on it to get it going. Finally he tipped his head back and blew gray smoke out of the corner of his mouth. "You ever hear the one about the guy who went to England and came back complaining about the meals? Not only was the food awful, but there was so little of it! That's kind of like the pay we're offering and the hours we can guarantee. It's not even close to a full-time job. Six hours on Tuesday and Thursday, eight on Wednesday. And the money? You could make much more driving a school bus."

"But then I'd have to get up before dawn. No thanks. Besides, like I said—I have some family affairs to deal with here."

"Yuh," he said, and his gaze was kind and sensitive, and I wondered if he knew. Kingsward is a big town, fourth-biggest in the state—but still not that big when you come down to it. "Can you pass a background check, Mister—?"

"John. John Davies. I think I'd squeak by. I had five years on the road for Winchester Trucking and never put a single one through the wall of a fast-food restaurant. Am I qualified, though? Wouldn't I need to have a degree in, like, the library sciences? The library arts?"

"Sam Hennessy didn't have a degree. Loren Hayes, who drove this very Bookmobile for almost thirty years, worked in a technical library for the air force before he came to us, but he never acquired any formal certification." Ralph lifted his eyebrows and cast his gaze lovingly over the truck. "Won't he be surprised to see this old thing on the road again."

"He's still knocking around?"

"Oh, yuh. He's at Serenity Apartments, same as our friend Mr. Gallagher, who'll read anything and everything as long as it was written by someone who works at Fox News." Ralph thought for a bit, then said, "Loren loved this truck. Handed me the keys and gave it up for good in 2009." Ralph turned a wry, wistful look upon me. "We were getting ready to retire it, and he decided to retire with it. He had a bad experience behind the wheel and scared the hell out of himself. He was driving around and suddenly didn't know where he was anymore. There'd been other disconcerting moments before that. He'd tell me someone who'd been dead for ten years had asked him about a book, that kind of thing."

"Ah, that's too bad," I replied, thinking about my mother, about dementia. "You positive he'd still know it if he saw it?"

Ralph returned my gaze with a blank stare. "Hm? Oh, yes. I'm afraid I've given you the wrong impression. Loren can be forgetful, but no more so than anyone else his age. He's still sharp enough to beat me at rummy. We play the last Thursday of every month, and I usually lose to him. No, he's still all there."

"But . . . you said he was driving into town and didn't know where he was?"

"Yes," Ralph said. "He was very badly shaken. He couldn't tell if it was 1965 or 1975 or what. Every block looked like a different decade to him. He was worried he wouldn't be able to find his way home to the twenty-first century." He looked at his watch and said, "I should get back to the library. My coffee break has been long enough. You'll e-mail me with your details? My address is on the library Web site. I look forward to continuing our conversation very soon."

I followed him out, waited while he locked the carriage house, and said good night. I stood there and watched him go, blue smoke spilling from his pipe and mingling with the blue fog that had started to drift out of the trees. The night had turned clammy while we were inside.

He'd disappeared back into the library before I realized I still had *Another Marvelous Thing* in my coat pocket.

I probably saw a few without recognizing them for what they were—the ghosts. That's what I thought they were at first. Now I know better.

Late returns . . . that was Loren's term for them, although I wouldn't hear it for months, wouldn't meet him until a chilled, soggy day just after Christmas.

Once when I'd been driving the old Bookmobile for no more than a few weeks, I saw a little girl walking with her mother. The little girl wore a pair of Mickey Mouse ears and was skipping, jumping in shallow puddles left by a recent rain. Her mother had a flowered kerchief over her hair and carried a paper sack with twine handles. The sack said WOOLWORTH'S on the side. I remember thinking that odd, because there'd been a Woolworth's in downtown Kingsward when I was a child, but it had been closed since 1990. When I pulled up to a stop sign, I looked for them in the passenger-side mirror, but they were gone. Were they late returns? I don't know.

Another time two shrunken old ladies, sisters, entered the truck at St. Michael's Rest, one of the old-folks' homes on my Tuesday schedule. They browsed without speaking to me. Instead they talked about Ted Kennedy and the accident at Chappaquiddick. "The men in that family is all whoremasters," said one of the women, and the other replied, "What does that have to do with going off the road?" It was only after they were gone that it seemed to me they'd been speaking in the present tense, as if Chappaquiddick had only just happened, as if Ted Kennedy were still alive.

It was early November, the first time it happened, and I *knew* it. The first time I encountered someone who had *slipped forward,* who climbed up into the truck from a different *when.*

On Thursdays my route took me through West Fever, a miserable tick of a town burrowed into one side of the county. It contains a bit of pastureland and a lot more marsh, a few gas stations, and a single shopping center known locally as the Man Mall. In the Man Mall there's a shop that sells fireworks, another that sells guns, a liquor store, a tattoo parlor, and an adult-toy shop with a peep show in the back. With forty dollars in your pocket, you can hit the Man Mall on a Friday night, get shitfaced, get blown by a stripper, get her name tattooed on your arm, celebrate by launching a bottle rocket over the interstate, and pick up a .38 so you'll have an easy way to kill yourself in the morning.

The Man Mall shares two acres of unpaved parking lot with a shabby, sprawling two-story efficiency-apartment complex. A fair number of single mothers with small children and some elderly dissolute drunks called the place . . . well, not home. I'm sure no one there viewed it as home. If you were staying at the efficiencies, home was somewhere you'd left or somewhere you were going in the indeterminate future. It was little more than a neglected, shabby motel with long-term guests, and everyone there was just making do until they got to something better. Some of the tenants had been making do for years.

I saw him—the late return—as I swung in: a guy in a red flannel coat and a checked hat with earflaps framing cheeks chapped pink from the cold. He raised a gloved hand, and I waved reflexively back and didn't give him another thought. It was cold and wet, and the lot was hazed over with a filthy mist. It was ten in the morning and looked like twilight.

I pressed and held the red button on the dash until the generator chunked noisily to life, then got out and went around back to unlock the rear door. The man in the earflaps met me at the steps. He had a quizzical smile on his face.

"Where's the other guy? Sick?" he asked, his breath puffing from his lips in clouds.

"Mr. Hennessy? He had a little bang-up. He's off the road."

"I wondered what was up," he said. "Feels like I haven't seen the Bookmobile in half a century." I thought that was funny, that he hadn't noticed the difference between the old Bookmobile and the other one, the one Hennessy had driven into a McDonald's. I didn't say anything about it, though, just opened the rear door and led him in.

The heaters roared. The lights buzzed. Earflaps shuffled in past me while I held the door and stared back toward the efficiencies. There was usually a herd of sinewy, haunted-looking mothers waiting with their children to stampede the Bookmobile. But today no one emerged. The cold, grimy mist billowed along the concrete walkways facing the building. It looked like a set in a movie about the apocalypse. I climbed up the steps and closed the door behind me.

"I hope I'm not in too much trouble." He slipped a sun-faded, cranberry-colored hardback out of one pocket: *Tunnel in the Sky* by Robert Heinlein. "I'm *way* overdue. But hey, it's not my fault! If I could get to the library, I wouldn't need you!"

"If you and everyone like you could get to the library, I wouldn't have a job. I think that makes us even," I said. "Don't worry about the late fees. We're forgiving penalties for all Bookmobile patrons, since we were off the road for a while."

"Hot-diggity," he said, like a freckled farm boy in an episode of *The Andy Griffith Show*. "Not that I'd mind if I did have to cough up a few pennies for the late return. This one was worth it. I wish I had another just like it."

"Oh, sure," I said. "I love those old Heinleins, too."

He turned and let his gaze drift across the shelves, smiling to himself. "That one did just what I want a story to do. I like a story that doesn't mess around too much. That starts right away, sticks the hero in a good, rotten, messed-up fix from the first paragraph, and then lets him wriggle awhile. I spend all week behind the counter in the hardware store. When I sit down with a book, I want to try someone else's life on for a bit, some other life I'm never going to have myself. That's why I like to read about trolls and cops and celebrities. Also, I want 'em to say clever things, because in my mind I'm the one saying it."

"But not too clever. Or it breaks the illusion."

"That's right. Find a guy with an interesting life and then deal him a bad hand so I can see how he snaps back. And while we're at it, I want to head somewhere I'm never going to go myself, like Moscow or Mars or the twenty-first century. NASA isn't hiring, and I can't afford transatlantic tickets. I'm so strapped these days, it's just as well for me the library card is free."

"You're never going to go to the twenty-first century?" I asked. I didn't think he knew what he'd just said, but he took the question straight.

"Well, I'm sixty-six now, so you do the math," he said. "I guess it's technically possible, but I'd be a hundred and two! If you told me in 1944 that I was going to have another twenty, thirty years, I would've fell down on my knees and kissed your feet with happiness. At the time I had half of Japan trying to drop airplanes on me. Seems greedy to hope for thirty more."

The sum of my entire reaction to this earnest statement was a light tingling along the scalp, a little shiver of pleasure and interest. I didn't believe for an instant he was having me on, but the thought struck me that maybe he was mentally infirm. He wouldn't be the only older guy who lived in the efficiencies and had trouble sorting fantasy from reality. Even his choice of words—"hot-diggity," "shoot"—gave him a childlike aspect, suggested a boy's mind in a man's body.

"It's 2019," I said, slowly, more to see how he would react than anything else. "It's the future already."

"In which book?" he said, scanning the shelves. "I do like a good time-travel novel. Although really what I want is more good rockets-and-ray-guns stuff."

I paused, then said, "There are a couple Brad Dolan novels about men coming unmoored in time. But they're not like Heinlein. It's more . . . what? Literary?"

"Brad Dolan?" the man in the earflaps said. "He used to deliver my papers! Or his mother did anyhow. He slept in the passenger seat most mornings. That was a while ago." His smile took on a fretful quality, and he rubbed the back of his neck. "He's over *there* now. They grow up fast, huh? Seems like ten minutes ago he was lugging a canvas sack full of newspapers. Now he's got an M16 over one shoulder and he's tramping through the mud. It's Korea all over again. I don't know what we did there, and I can't tell what we're doing in Vietnam either. We got enough trouble here. Men with hair down to their butts and church half empty and girls walking around in skirts so short I feel like I ought to run and get them an overcoat. Tell the truth, I'm not entirely sure about the messages you're sending with the Bookmobile done up like it is. I can't tell if you're peddling books or Mary Jane."

I laughed but then trailed off, uncertainly, when he cocked a quizzical eyebrow at me and offered me a polite but slightly stiff smile. It was a look that said he didn't think it was any laughing matter but in the interests of our getting along he would take the subject no further.

I studied him while he studied the shelves. My scalp was still crawling strangely, but other than that I felt fine. If he was playing a game with me, he was playing hard, completely committed to the performance. But I didn't think it was an act. The possibility that someone from the mid-sixties had shown up to return an overdue book, and maybe get something new to read, did not have the effect on me you might think. I wasn't frightened, not at any time. I wasn't alarmed. I felt something closer to gratitude and also . . . bemusement. In the older, truer sense of that word, which once meant a sweet perplexity.

I had a thought then—a little tug of curiosity—and acted before the idea even had time to settle.

"You liked *Tunnel in the Sky*, huh? I've got something for you. Have you tried *The Hunger Games*?" As I spoke, I slipped *The Hunger Games* off the YA shelf and held it out to him.

He peered down at it—a slick black paperback that had a gold bird embossed on the cover—with a puzzled half smile on his face. He lifted two fingers to his left temple. "No, I missed that one. Is that Heinlein or . . . excuse me. That book does something funny to my eyes."

I looked down at it. Just a trade paperback. I looked back. He had an expression of concentration mingled with faint anxiety, and the tip of his tongue flicked out to touch his lips. Then he reached out and gently took the paperback from me . . . and his face relaxed. He smiled.

"I've been shoveling out my sister's walkway all morning. I guess I'm a little punchy," he told me. "And more snow coming this weekend." He shook his head but smiled down at the book. "Well, this looks like the thing." He read out the shout line on the cover: "'*In the future, the only thing more lethal than the games . . . is love!*'"

I looked at the book myself, and for a moment my vision darkened and my head went woozy, as if I had stood up too fast.

He was still holding *The Hunger Games,* although it took a moment for me to recognize it. It remained a black paperback, but the cover now showed a girl in a clinging flame-colored sci-fi gown preparing to shoot an arrow from some kind of mechanical, laser-guided bow. Her face was drawn in an expression of terror while her eyes flashed with righteous fury. She crouched in a Dagobah-like forest of psychedelic-colored trees. It was the cover of a pulp sci-fi novel from the early sixties, right down to the price tag in the upper left corner: 35¢. I know something about the famous pulp artists of the era, and I think it was a Victor Kalin, although I find it hard to tell him from Mitchell Hooks. Google 'em—you'll get the idea. It had the battered look of a paperback that has passed through quite a few hands, most of them clumsy and in a hurry.

Something sharp twinged in my head, behind my eye. It was as if someone was pressing their thumbs into my temples. Earflaps looked at me with some concern.

"You okay, mac?" he said.

I didn't answer. Instead I said, "Can I see that?" and took the book back from him.

It was a 35¢ paperback when I looked down at the cover. But when I turned it over to read the back, I found myself looking down at a black trade paperback, the one I recognized from my own time. I flipped to the cover again. Black, smooth, glossy, with a golden brooch printed on it and a bird on the brooch. Then I lifted my face and looked at Earflaps. His gaze had drifted away from me, was floating across the books on the top shelf.

"I can't see some of them," he said in a casual tone of voice. "They go all funny when I try to read the titles. The words swim away when I try to concentrate on them. Some of them anyhow. *A Tree Grows in Brook-lyn* is all right. So's the Narnia books. But the ones in between"—he was staring at the Harry Potter novels—"I can't see them right. Mister, am I having a stroke?"

"I don't think so," I said.

He sighed and looked at me and smiled and put one

palm to his left temple. "I ought to take my book and go. I think I need to lie down."

"Let me get you checked out," I said.

I sat behind the mahogany desk, and he produced his library card: Fred Mueller, 46 Gilead Road. There was a borrower number (1919) but no barcode to scan with my phone. Which was just as well—when I picked up my smartphone, the screen was completely black and the white circle was spinning around and around, as if it had just crashed and was trying to reload.

Mueller didn't seem to notice the phone. His gaze passed the gadget in my hand without catching upon it. Here was the very embodiment of the future, the twenty-first century made solid in the form of an iPhone Plus, so much more beautiful and science-fictional than anything in Heinlein, than anything on the original *Star Trek*—and it might've been a pencil for all he cared. His indifference didn't surprise me, though. He couldn't see the Harry Potter books either, and I thought I knew why. They didn't belong in his *when,* hadn't happened yet. He *could* see *The Hunger Games,* and I thought I understood that, too. It didn't belong in his *when* either—not until I handed it to him. Once it was in his hands, he saw it as he needed to see it, to accept it. It took a form he could understand, that wouldn't trouble him.

I'm probably wrong to suggest I understood this all right away. I was more like the blind man holding on to the elephant's knee, dimly beginning to suspect he had his hands on an animal instead of a tree trunk. It didn't all make sense in the moment, but I instinctively felt that there was a logic to the situation that might yet be revealed.

"Don't you need to stamp it?" he asked, putting his hand on the paperback and turning it to face me.

And there was that pulp cover again that I'm almost sure was painted by Victor Kalin, although if you look at Kalin's Web site showcasing his fifties- and sixties-era paperbacks, you won't find it there. How could you? *The Hunger Games* was published in 2008. By then Fred Mueller had been dead for almost half a century. He dropped dead in January of 1965, suffered a fatal heart attack while shoveling his sister's walkway—as you have almost certainly guessed by now, I read about it on my phone that evening, the phone he couldn't see. He'd won the Distinguished Service Medal in the Surigao Strait, during some of the fiercest fighting of the Pacific war. He was survived by a son, who, according to the obituary, was a math student in Cambridge, England.

Fred put his Heinlein on the table, took his vintage copy of *The Hunger Games*, and moved toward the exit, a door in the side of the library car. He had his hand on the latch when he hesitated and glanced back at me. He smiled uneasily. I thought he looked a little waxy, and there was a bead of sweat crawling from his left temple.

"Hey," he said. "Can I ask you a funny question?"

"Sure," I said.

"Anyone ever ask you if you're a ghost?" he said, and laughed, and touched his forehead as if he were feeling a touch woozy again.

"I was wondering the same thing about you," I said, and laughed with him.

No sooner had he stepped out and closed the door than a fist rapped against it. I came around the desk and threw it open and stared down at a knot of mothers and small children with snot-crusted upper lips. The sky was so blue it hurt to look at it. In the time I was talking to Fred Mueller, borrower number 1919 of Gilead Road, West Fever, that low, filthy, cold mist had dried out and burned off entirely.

I craned my neck, peering over the small crowd, looking across the vast parking lot of gravel and potholes, but there was no sight of Mr. Mueller and his hat with the giant earflaps.

I couldn't say I was surprised.

It was only four in the afternoon when I returned the Bookmobile to the lot between the library and Parks & Rec, but it was already dark and smelled like snow. I walked half a block to a local coffee chain, got a coffee, and sat with my phone, reading about Fred Mueller and then Fred Mueller's son. His kid, who'd been in his early twenties when his father died, was in his seventies now, had retired to Hawaii. In the 1970s he had come up with a protocol allowing computers to talk to each other over phone lines. He was one of about a dozen guys who could claim to be the father of the Internet. His virtuosity with electronics had made him a minor celebrity in geek circles. He'd done a cameo on *Star Trek: The Next Generation*, been name-checked in a William Gibson novel, was the basis for a scientist character in one of the James Cameron flicks. I visited his Web page and broke into a nasty sweat. The bio photo showed a stringy old man with a patchy beard standing with a surfboard under a palm tree. He wore board shorts . . . and a *Hunger Games* T-shirt. In a FAQ it was listed as a favorite book. He'd even been a consultant on the film. He'd been a consultant on a lot of sci-fi films.

I wondered if he'd read it before it was published. I wondered if he'd read it before the author, Suzanne Collins, had been born. That thought made me clammy.

My next thought gave me an outright chill. What, I wondered, would've happened if I'd given Mr. Mueller a book about 9/11 instead? Could he have stopped it?

I did not wonder if it had happened. I did not need to wonder. I had his late return in the pocket of my coat: that scuffed cranberry-colored hardcover of *Tunnel in the Sky*. Fred Mueller's name was the last entry on the borrower card in the back. The return-by stamp said 1/13/65, and he had dropped dead on January 17 of that year, just four days later.

Did he finish reading *The Hunger Games* before his heart gave out? I hoped so. For me, a lifelong bookworm, there was nothing quite so awful as the thought of dying fifty pages from the end of a good novel.

"If I sit down with you, will I be derailing an important train of thought?" Ralph Tanner asked from over my left shoulder.

"That train isn't going anywhere. It's just sitting on the tracks," I said, looking around.

He had his unlit pipe in one hand and a coffee in the other. If I'd given it the slightest thought, I might've expected I'd run into him. It was time for his evening pipe and his last hit of caffeine, and the café was just a short walk from the library.

"How's bookslinging treating you?" he asked, settling onto a stool beside me.

I considered his half smile and his pale, watchful eyes and had an unexpected, jolting thought: *He knows.* I remembered that first conversation and my sudden impression that he knew about my parents but was too polite to broach the subject. In time I came to feel it was characteristic of Ralph Tanner to always know a little more than he let on, to hold his hand so close to the vest you could hardly tell he had cards to play at all.

"Not too bad," I said. "A guy returned an overdue copy of *Tunnel in the Sky* by Robert Heinlein."

"Ah! The juveniles. Quite a bit better than Heinlein's work for adults, in my opinion."

"It was very late. He took it out in December 1964. He would've returned it sooner, but he died in January 1965, and that kept him and his book out of circulation for a while."

"Ah," Ralph said, and he smiled and sipped his coffee and looked away. "One of *them*."

I turned my own coffee cup around and around with my fingertips. "So this isn't new?"

"It happened to Loren Hayes from time to time. I told you that, although I admit I was happy to let you think his encounters with the dead were strictly imaginary. At first it was just once, maybe twice a year. Toward the end it happened more frequently."

"That why he gave it up?"

Ralph nodded, slowly, not looking at me. "He thought . . . when he was young, and his concentration was sharper, he could mostly hold the Bookmobile *here*, in the present, where it belongs. But as he got older and his attention started to drift, the Bookmobile began to find its way into the past more frequently. More and more of his customers were . . . well, like whoever you met today. He calls them late returns." He had another taste of his coffee and spoke with no urgency. We might've been discussing the Bookmobile's tendency to drip oil or the way the heating system smelled like old shoes. "In one sense, you know, it's perfectly unremarkable. It's quite common to enter a library and find yourself in conversation with the dead. The best minds of generations long gone crowd every bookshelf. They wait there to be noticed, to be addressed, and to reply in turn. In the library the dead meet the living on collegial terms as a matter of course, every day."

"Nice analogy, but this wasn't a metaphorical encounter with a long-gone mind. His coat was wet. I could smell it. Smelled like a sheep. And I don't think he was dead— No, wait. I mean I *know* he was dead. He's been dead for fifty years. But while he was in the Bookmobile, he was—"

"'*I dreamed I saw Joe Hill last night, alive as you and me,*'" Ralph sang, and I shuddered. Joan Baez had

316 • FULL THROTTLE

sung that song. When it came on, my parents always sang along with her.

"He borrowed a book, and I think—I can't know this—but I *think* he took it back with him. *The Hunger Games.* Jesus. I gave him a book that didn't come out until fifty years after he died."

I was surprised when Ralph's mouth widened in a great grin. "Wonderful. Good man."

"Good man? What if I fucked up—excuse me, *messed* up—the space-time continuum? Like, what if now John Lennon doesn't get shot?"

"That would be wonderful, too, don't you think?"

"Yes, but—*obviously.* But you know what I'm talking about. The butterfly effect." He was smiling at me in a way I found mildly maddening. "What would've happened if I gave him a book about the Columbine massacre?"

"Did he ask for a book about school shootings?"

"No."

"Well, there you go, then." He must've seen the frustration in my face, because he softened a little, bumped his shoulder against mine in an avuncular sort of way. "Loren Hayes, who you should meet, thought they could only find their way to the Bookmobile at the end of their story and that they could only borrow books that wouldn't hurt them. That wouldn't scratch time's record. This guy you met today. Did he have trouble seeing the books?"

I nodded. My arms were crawling with goose bumps. Meeting the man from 1965 had been less uncanny than this calm, reasonable conversation about it over coffee with my employer.

"He could only take one that wouldn't threaten anything, and even then it had to be one that was right for him. When you consider that . . . *well.* Just imagine if you lived in the fifties and liked the twists in Agatha Christie novels. Now imagine that right before you died, you had a chance to read *Gone Girl.* You'd die for sure—of happiness. For all we know, that's what happened to the man you saw today!"

"Don't say that," I objected, flinching. "That's awful."

"I can think of worse ways to go than with a good book in my hand. Especially if it was one I had no right to ever read, because it wasn't going to be published until after I was dead. If you don't quit on me, you'll see others, now and then. And you won't be able to give them anything that hurts them."

"But what if I give them something that changes history?"

"How would you know?" he asked me, smiling again. "Maybe you did! Maybe this crap is all your fault!" He looked around the café—customers on their smartphones, a checkout girl ringing up coffees on a tablet computer—and back to me, and he looked pleased with himself. "The history you have is the only history you know. Besides. People come to the library to improve themselves or to be entertained or to discover something new about the world. How can that be bad? I believe that the late returns who visit the old Bookmobile are just having themselves a little literary dessert before the restaurant kicks them out."

"So it's like, what? A reward from God for living a good life?"

"Why can't it be a reward from the library," he said, "for returning overdue books in spite of the inconvenience of being dead? Are you going to quit?"

"No," I said, and heard a faintly peevish tone in my own voice. "I'm listening to a Michael Koryta novel on audio, and I can only concentrate on it while I'm driving."

He laughed. "I hope you didn't pay for it. The library has an excellent audiobook collection." He stood up with his pipe. "I have to step out now. They quite sensibly won't let me smoke inside. Why don't you come play rummy with Loren and me? I'm sure you'd have a lot to talk about."

He started toward the door.

"Mr. Tanner?" I asked.

He looked back, his hand on the handle.

"Did *you* ever think of driving the Bookmobile yourself? To see who turns up?"

He smiled. "I don't have my Class B license. Big trucks scare me. Good night, John."

For the next ten days, I drove around hunched over the steering wheel, scanning the sidewalks for anyone who looked like they had stumbled out of a black-and-white movie. I could not have been more anxious or more alert if the Bookmobile had been loaded with crates of sweating TNT.

It was hard to control the temperature in the cab. The heat came on full blast, smelling like old socks, and soon I'd be tacky with sweat, my shirt sticking to my sides. But if I turned it off, the temperature would plummet in a handful of minutes, and soon it would be so cold that my toes went numb in their shoes and my sweat froze against my skin. My thoughts ran the same way, hot and cold, careening between eagerness and anxiety, between hoping I would see someone who didn't belong in my time and dreading it.

Thing is, nothing happened, and after another couple weeks of making my rounds I realized that nothing was *going* to happen and it took the heart out of me. Not all at once. It snuck up on me, an emotion stronger than simple disappointment, a numb, dull lethargy. At the time I blamed my depression on what had happened when I tried to clean out the garage, but looking back, I can see I was going down hard even before then.

I'd finished cleaning out the master bedroom and my mother's home office. Boots and scarves went to Goodwill. I emptied a filing cabinet, shredded what wasn't important, collected together what mattered into a pile to deal with later. I filled trash bags and recycling bins.

Finally, on a brilliant Sunday morning, I decided to have a look in the garage. The whole house was flooded with sunshine, and brightness glinted off the shriveled islands of snow under the trees. On a day so full of light, I felt I was ready to tackle the place where my parents had died.

Only in the garage, the sunlight hit the grimy, cobwebby windows and turned to dull milk. Although the Caddy was gone, towed away by the cops, the plaster ceiling was black from exhaust. I drew a breath and reeled back out, gagging at a stink of exhaust and rank meat. I am now reasonably sure that odor was mostly in my mind, but so what? Imaginary or not, it made me feel I was going to be sick every time I inhaled.

I forced myself back in there with a rag tied over my mouth and ran the automatic garage-door opener. The motor thrummed, but the door rose only a quarter of an inch before making a banging noise and refusing to rise any further. It was bolted shut. I struggled with the bolts, but it seemed to me they had impossibly rusted in place, and I couldn't force them free. I turned in a circle, looking for something I could hammer against the bolts to free them up, and that's when I saw one of my father's blue, flat-soled boat shoes. Perhaps it had dropped off his foot when the EMTs pulled him out from behind the driver's seat. I picked it up, and a spider crawled out onto the back of my hand. I shouted and threw it, shook the spider off my knuckles, and got the fuck out of there. That was enough for me.

After that I stopped working on the house. I had found the old Sega in the living-room closet. I hooked it up and played NBA Jam, sometimes for five, six hours straight. I played Sonic the Hedgehog 2 until I made it to the end. I played in the dark while headaches intensified to migraines. Then I played some more. When I was fed up with gaming, I watched whatever was on TV: reality shows, cable news, I wasn't picky. I felt like I was recovering from a stomach bug—only I never actually recovered.

I'd always been a reader, but I lacked the mental energy to force my way through a book. Everything looked too long. Every page had too many words on it. In that whole stretch, I read just a single novel, Laurie

Colwin's *Another Marvelous Thing,* and then only because it was so short it could be read in one sitting, and only because she didn't clutter up the page with a whole mess of words. It was about a young woman, just married, just pregnant, who falls in love with and has an affair with a much, much older man for reasons she hardly understands herself. You hear about a woman sleeping around on her husband, you're automatically inclined to be judgmental. But everyone in the book was kind, everyone wanted the best for one another. In the end it seemed to me it was really about one generation saying good-bye to another, and I had an ugly cry about it on the couch. It made me glad to think my mother had carried such a happy, romantic heart in her.

I had meant to read it and slip it into the returns pile at the library, but I wound up just putting it back in the shoe box with my mother's unpaid parking tickets. By the time I was done reading it, that book felt like it belonged to me.

I only ever left the house to drive the Bookmobile, and I went through my routes automatically, hardly seeing the people who entered the book car to find something to read. The next time I met someone who was dead—the next time a Late Return paid me a visit—I barely saw her face until she began to weep.

She'd entered after a small parade of children and

their mothers had worked their way through the car in a noisy, milling line. I was in Quince, a country hamlet south of Kingsward, parked in the lot between an elementary school and a baseball field. The field was churned to frozen mud and smelled like thawing dog shit. The day was like my mood: hazy, buried under a low mass of icy cloud. At some point I became aware there was a single woman in the car, a skinny little thing in a salt-and-pepper man's overcoat that was three times too big for her. I ignored her and went on scanning in returned books until I heard her take a small gasping breath. She clutched a battered reddish book with a brown binding, open to the back. Her delicate nose was bright red from weeping. She looked at me and smiled weakly and wiped at the tears on her face.

"Carry on," she said in a chipper tone. "Just my allergies."

"What are you allergic to?" I asked.

"Oh," she said, and looked up at the ceiling while the tears streamed down her pretty, pale face. "Sadness, mostly. Also lavender and bee stings, but mostly I'm allergic to feeling miserable, and when I am, this always happens to me."

I picked up the box of Kleenex on the desk, got up, and came around to offer her one. "I hope this isn't because we're missing the book you want."

She laughed—a miserable-grateful kind of sound—and snatched a tissue. She gave her nose a great honk. "No. Plenty to read here. I was thinking I've never read Sherlock Holmes and that maybe a few nice little mysteries in an English accent would go well with tea and Nilla wafers this afternoon. I looked in the back and saw my son's name. Of course he took this book out. I think I even remember him reading it one weekend when he was home sick."

She opened *The Adventures of Sherlock Holmes* to show me the cardboard sleeve in the back, with the borrower's card stuck into it, and the skin on the nape of my neck crawled. That was when I knew she was one of them, a Late Return. Because those cards aren't in modern library books. They've been replaced by bar codes.

There were half a dozen names written in pencil on the borrower's card. The first was Brad Dolan, 4/13/59. She shifted the card, and her fingernail pointed to the name Brad Dolan again, lower down: 11/28/60. I felt as if I had drunk down a whole glass of ice water, in a hurry. My insides went ill and cold. One of Brad Dolan's last great novels had been called *Investigations!* about a detective named Sheldon Whoms who deduces impossible facts from minor clues—looking at a woman's chewed fingernails, Whoms determines that she had her first period at eleven and once owned a cat named Aspirin. I vaguely recalled Dolan telling my eighth-grade class that he'd always loved the Sherlock Holmes stories because they told a comforting lie: that the world made sense and that effect followed cause. In contrast, Vietnam had taught him that the army would napalm naked children to stop a political ideology based on people sharing what they have with one another. He said why they would do such a thing was a mystery that no detective, no matter how brilliant, could fathom.

I knew she had wandered into the Bookmobile from the past—knew from that icy chill sinking through my insides—but to be sure, I asked to see the book. She gave it to me, and I turned slightly away and closed it.

When it had been in her hands, it was an old, almost featureless hardcover, with a fraying binding. When it was in mine, it was a lurid crimson paperback that depicted Benedict Cumberbatch and Martin Freeman dashing across a red, impressionistic background. *A Study in Scarlet*, with an introduction by Steven Moffat.

"Brad Dolan?" I said. "I feel like I know his name."

"Maybe he used to deliver your paper," she said, and laughed.

"Maybe *you* used to deliver it," I said. "While he slept in the passenger seat."

I turned and handed the book back to her. By the time she took it, it was a battered brownish red hardcover again, with a gold Meerschaum pipe stamped on the front. She smiled, her face blotchy from crying.

"Thanks for the tissue," she said. "I'm so sorry."

"What's he doing these days? Your son?"

"He's over there," she said. "He volunteered. His father died in Korea and . . . he wanted to do his bit. He's very brave." She smiled a moment longer, and then her face wrinkled and she put a hand over her eyes and her shoulders began to twitch. She took short, gasping breaths. "I'm sorry. I'm so sorry. I haven't done this before."

I put a hand on her back and let her bump her head against my shoulder. In her time maybe men could casually hug strange crying women, but a hand lightly resting between her shoulder blades was all I felt comfortable with. "What haven't you done before? Cry? First time? It does pass, usually when your eyes start to feel sore."

She laughed again. "Oh, I cry plenty. It's just my first time in a public place, except church, and no one minds if I cry there. I'm all one tender spot these days. Like a bruise, only it's my whole body. Everything makes me feel weak and weepy. I haven't had a letter from him in two months. That's the longest it's ever been. I sit in the front room tingling all over, watching for the postman. It's like I'm holding my breath, but for hours. Then the postman comes, and there's no letter."

I'm all one tender spot these days, she had said. Something about that line gave me a twinge of anxiety. Fred Mueller had shown up to take out one last good science-fiction novel in the week before he fell dead in his sister's front yard. Ralph seemed to think that was part of it—that the Late Returns could find their way to the Bookmobile only when they were close to the end. I recollected something else now from that day in eighth grade when Brad Dolan came to talk at my school. He'd mentioned that his mother had died alone, of uterine cancer, while he was trying not to get killed in Vietnam. He said it was the great regret of his life: that he had to go get rich after she was dead, when his money couldn't do her any good. She had wanted to go to Paris, or at least Fort Lauderdale, but she'd never left New England. She never had a vacation. She never owned a car or a new coat, since she always shopped for her clothes at the Salvation Army. She gave 10 percent of her salary every year to her church, and later, after she was dead, it turned out the priest who ran the place molested little boys and had drunk away most of the church's savings.

"Is he going to come home?" she asked, and looked up at me, smiling weakly.

My insides flopped, like a fish hauled up onto a dock.

I turned away from her. I didn't want her to see my expression.

"I . . . I believe he will, Mrs. Dolan. I'm sure of it. You can have faith in that."

She said, "I'm trying. Though I feel more and more like a little girl who's overheard there's no Father Christmas. Have you seen the films on Cronkite? Have you seen what's happening over there? I want to believe he'll come back and he'll still be himself. Just as good. Just as kind. Not broken inside. I pray every day that I'll die before him. That's the only happy ending us humans can have, isn't it? For the parent to die before the child?"

If she hadn't said that, in precisely that way, I wouldn't have done it. But I had read a line almost exactly like that only five months before, in my father's final letter.

Ralph was sure I couldn't give them anything that would hurt them. But then Ralph couldn't drive the old Bookmobile and he'd never met any of the Late Returns.

I reached for Dolan's first novel, *Die Laughing!* It was the movie edition, the one with Tom Hanks and Zachary Quinto on the cover, but when I turned and put it in her hand, it was a first edition. No . . . even that is not quite right. It was someone's idea of what the first edition could've been. The SF pulp artist Frank Kelly Freas had done the original cover, and he'd done this one, too, which showed a sweating GI laughing maniacally while he rode his M16 like a child's wooden pony. The actual cover (I looked it up later) was all but identical, except with another soldier in the background, weeping with laughter while he juggled grenades.

She stared down at the thin, raggedy book in her hands (25¢ ACE PAPERBACK across the cover and "War is no laughing matter . . . except when it is!"). Then her gaze found the author's name and snapped back up at me.

"What is this? A joke?"

I didn't answer right away. I wasn't sure what to say. She searched my face with a rigid smile that expressed no humor at all.

"Take it home," I said. "It's good. One of his best."

She gave it another searching look. When she glanced back at me, her smile had become thin indeed. "I suppose there's some humor in finding a book by a writer who shares my son's name, but I also feel a little like you're making fun. Maybe I asked for it, getting emotional over Sherlock Holmes. Still. Not a nice thing to do, mister." She dropped the book and turned to leave.

"Ma'am," I said quietly. "I'm not making fun. Don't go yet. Wait a moment."

She hesitated with her hand on the latch. She was very pale.

"Your son is going to make it home and write a whole pile of novels. That's the first of them. If you try and look at it now, your eyes will go funny, because *Die Laughing!* hasn't been published yet. I'm not sure when it came out—1970, maybe? Go ahead. Look at it."

She lowered her chin and stared at the book on the floor, a slick trade paperback with Tom Hanks's stern, grieving face on the cover and Zachary Quinto in the background, on his knees, laughing convulsively with blood all over his hands.

"Oooh," she said, and put a hand to her left temple and swayed and shut her eyes. "It makes me motion sick." When she looked at me again, her lips were color-less and she was beginning to tremble. "What are you doing to me? Did you . . . I don't know, give me dope? I've heard you can put LSD right against someone's skin and make them ill."

"No, ma'am." I picked up the book and handed it to her. When she looked at it again, it was the Freas cover once more. She exhaled slowly. "When you're not hold-ing it, it slides out of your time and back toward mine. That's why it makes you motion sick to look at it. But as long as you're holding it, it'll stay frozen in your time, and then it's safe to read." I flashed to a sudden memory of reading the book myself in eighth grade and said, "I think he dedicated it to you. I'm not sure. Look."

She folded back the cover, and there it was:

To Lynn Dolan, without whom this book wouldn't have been possible

But I had forgotten what was below the dedication:

(1926–1966)

Now it was my turn to feel motion sick. "Oh, Jesus. I'm sorry. I forgot—I haven't read it since I was in junior high school—"

When she lifted her chin, though, she no longer looked afraid but instead stricken with wonder. She was heartbreakingly beautiful, with her fine delicate features and great dark eyes. I could've just about fallen in love with her, if she weren't more than fifty years dead.

"It's real," she whispered. "It's not a bad joke. My son writes this in a few years, doesn't he?"

"Yes. Mrs. Dolan . . . I'm so sorry . . . I shouldn't have . . ."

"But you should have, and you did, and this is how I know you aren't being cruel. I'm quite aware this is the last year of my life," she said, and her lips moved in the slightest smile. "I've known for a few weeks. That's what I can't stand. Not hearing from him, and knowing I might never find out if he makes it back. How do you—" She pursed her lips.

"When I left this morning," I said, "to do my rounds in the Bookmobile, it was December 2019. But sometimes this happens. People from the past show up to borrow books. I met a guy named Fred Mueller—"

"Fred Mueller!" she cried. "That's a name I haven't heard in a while. From West Fever. Poor man."

"Yes. He turned up in my Bookmobile a few weeks ago, and I gave him a book that won't be out for a while. I hope he liked it. I'm pretty sure it was his kind of thing."

"A few weeks ago?" she said. "He died ten months back. I was going to write Brad and tell him, then thought better. I only send him good news from home. Every day over there could be his last, I don't want him to have a head full of rotten . . ." But then she fell silent and looked down at the paperback in her hands again. She peeked inside and flinched. "I can't read the copyright. The numbers jump out of sight when I try to focus on them." She leafed through some of the other pages. "But I can read the rest." Then she gave me a bright, curious look. "*Can* I read the rest? You're going to let me borrow it?"

"As long as you've got a library card," I said, and she

laughed. "I think you have one to return? One that's past due? That's part of how this seems to work."

"Oh! Yes," she said. She opened a black velvet flap on her purse and plucked out a copy of *Valley of the Dolls*. Her cheeks pinked up just slightly. "What trash," she said, and burbled softly with embarrassed amusement.

"So pretty great, huh?" I asked, and her giggle turned to a shout of laughter.

I led her back to the desk. She followed on unsteady legs, glancing here and there.

"I see it now," she said. "The books. Some of them are all right. But most of them are . . . shivering. Like they're cold. And it's hard to read the names on the bindings." She laughed again, but it was a nervous, unhappy titter. "This isn't happening, is it? I'm on the couch. I've been taking pills for my . . . well, I've had some discomfort. I must've passed out, and now I'm imagining this."

"Can you talk to a doctor?" I asked. "About your condition?"

When she replied, it was a one-word whisper: "No."

"It might not be too late, and it would mean everything to Brad Dolan if he could come home to his mother."

The muscles at the corners of her jaw tightened, and it came to me that this small, frail, pretty woman was harder—tougher—than she'd seemed at first. "It would mean everything to me to be there when he does. But I don't get to have that. I worked eight years on the cancer ward in Kingsward Hospital. I know the best-case scenario. I'm living it. Has treatment improved any in your time?"

"I think so," I said.

"Well, then. I'm sorry I can't hold on for fifty years. How's my son doing in the next century?"

I felt a drafty, hollow feeling in my chest, but I think I was able to keep my face all but expressionless when I replied, "He's never been more popular. They teach him. There have been movies based on the books."

"Do I have grandchildren?"

I said, "Truthfully, I don't know. I love his novels, but it's not like I've ever Googled him."

"Goo-gilled?"

"Oh. Uh. Looked him up. Google is like a twenty-first-century encyclopedia."

"And he's *in* it? He's in the Google?"

"You bet."

She looked very pleased at that. "My kid! Right there in the Google." She considered me for a moment. "How is this happening? *If* it's happening. I still expect to wake up on the couch any minute now. I doze off all the time these days. I get tired so easily."

"It's happening, but I couldn't tell you how it's possible."

"And you're not an envoy from the Lord? You're not an angel?"

"Nope. Just a librarian."

"Ah, well," she said. "That's close enough for me."

And before I stamped her card, she leaned across my desk and kissed my cheek.

It was dark and snowing briskly the night I knocked on a door marked 309 at Serenity Apartments. Voices murmured. Chair legs scraped across the floor. The door opened, and Ralph Tanner peered out at me. He had on a blue cardigan and a blue collared shirt and steel-colored denims—I assumed this was his idea of dressing down.

"What's the password?" he asked.

I lifted the bottle in my right hand. There was a silver bow on the neck. "I brought bourbon?"

"Right the first time," he said, and let me in.

He led me into a large room that served as kitchen, living area, and bedroom all at once. It was, I imagined, not so different from one of the efficiency apartments in West Fever, although of a better class. The TV was tuned to MSNBC, the volume turned down. Rachel Maddow, looking good in a close-cut jacket, spoke sincerely into the camera. In front of it, two old men sat at a table that looked as if it had been nailed together out of driftwood. One of them I recognized. His name was Terry Gallagher, and that evening he wore a floppy-brimmed fishing hat with a LOCK HER UP pin on it. I saw Gallagher every Thursday morning when I brought the Bookmobile around to Serenity Apartments. He would scuffle slowly through the library car, grousing at books by bleeding-heart lefties like Michael Moore, Elizabeth Warren, and Dr. Seuss, then check out something by Laura Ingraham. The other guy at the table I had never met. Loren Hayes was riding a bulky, electrically powered wheelchair and had an oxygen tube in his nose. He shot me a wary look with bloodshot eyes.

He had a big, craggy face with somewhat comical, oversize features. He was heavily overweight, but even still his head was too big for his body, an effect amplified by the great oily black sweep of his hair, which he combed Ronald Reagan style. His white T-shirt, which showed Ian McKellen standing in front of a gay-pride flag, clung to the bulge of his stomach and his sagging bosom. (Across the top it read GANDALF IS GAY, AND IF YOU DON'T LIKE IT, YOU'RE PROBABLY AN ORC.)

"What are we playing?" I asked as I sat down. Ralph took the bourbon off my hands, unscrewed the top, and poured an inch into a quartet of chipped mugs and plastic cups.

"An old, well-loved game," Gallagher called. "Put on MSNBC and see how long Terry Gallagher can sit there before he loses his goddamned mind. It's like putting a lobster into a pot of cold water and turning on the heat. They want to see how long I can take it before I start leaping to escape."

"Someone open the window," Loren Hayes said. "We're on the third floor. Maybe he'll leap that way."

Ralph sat down with us. "How about Hearts? There's four of us, we've got just the right number. Come on now, Mr. Gallagher. We turned the sound off for you. The bad woman can't hurt you. We'll keep you safe from all her reason and science and compassion."

"Just keep your back turned," Loren Hayes added. "If you look at her, there's the very real possibility you might catch a glimpse of empathy and it'll give you a sour tummy."

Gallagher shot me a pleading gaze. "They've got me outvoted two to one. Any chance you'll throw your support behind Fox? We're missing Tucker."

"I met a woman last week who got all her news from Walter Cronkite," I said. "Boy, they sure don't make 'em like him anymore, do they?"

The table was silent while Ralph dealt. Gallagher looked from me to Loren Hayes and back. Loren fanned his cards out and gave them a long, silent study.

I said, "Mr. Hayes, you know we've got a wheelchair-ramp attachment for the Bookmobile."

"Oh, yeah? Where'd that come from? That's new," Hayes said. "We never had that when I was driving."

"We lifted it off the newer Bookmobile," Ralph said. "The one that was damaged."

"If you're ever in the mood for something to read—" I began.

"If I'm in the mood for something to read, I'll order it online," Hayes said. "I don't think I'd want to borrow from the Bookmobile. You might try to offer me a novel that won't come out for another ten years, and I'd be faced with the very strong possibility this old basstid is going to outlive me." Nodding at Gallagher.

We played a couple of tricks without speaking.

"Did you ever change anything?" I asked. "Did you ever *try* to change anything?"

"Like what?" Hayes asked.

"Give someone a book about John Lennon's life and death to see if they could stop the assassination?"

"If I gave someone a book about John Lennon's assassination," Hayes said, "and they stopped it, then how would I give them a book about John Lennon's assassination?"

"Different . . . timelines? Parallel universes?"

"In a parallel universe, you didn't take the queen of spades. But in this reality you just ate thirteen points," Hayes said, and dropped the queen on me. "Whoever you want to save, Mr. Davies, they can't be saved. I've tried."

"Then what's the point?" I asked. "What's the point of being able to reach back in time if you can't do any good?"

"Who said you can't do any good? Did I say that? I just said you can't save them."

"Save who?" I asked. I felt a little winded. I'd had a single swallow of bourbon, and it was in my stomach like a thimbleful of battery acid.

"Whoever they are," he said, and met my gaze. One of his eyes was filmed lightly with cataract. "I tried. I thought I could smuggle a letter back to the past and save my best friend in the world, Alex Sommers. This was 1991, and Alex was in hospice. Alex caught himself a fatal case of what was going around among my people then, and he slunk off to die, shunned and forgotten, despised by his ultra-Christian family for being a faggot and feared by his friends who worried they might catch it off him if he started to cough. I thought I could stop it from ever happening." His voice roughened, and he dropped his cards.

"That's enough of this," Gallagher said. He took Hayes's hand and glared at me. "Who the fuck are you? Come in here and ruin our game of cards."

Ralph Tanner spoke very softly. "Mr. Davies has also lost people. And only wants to do the right thing. But he's dealing with something only Loren really understands." It was the first I was sure Ralph knew about my parents. He had known right from the start, I suppose. Like I said, Kingsward is a big town, but not big enough for secrets.

Hayes said, "I wrote a letter. I had it all ready to go. I had stamps from different time periods, because you don't know where they'll come from. I had some from the early sixties, some from the mid-eighties, and everything in between. One day a woman climbs on, buxom redhead. Glasses. Very strict, stern, right-wing dominatrix type. Gallagher, you woulda had a stroke. You would've been almost as hot for her as you were for them to impeach Clinton. We got to talking, and she wondered aloud if the terrorists were going to kill the Jewish athletes in Munich, and that was how I knew she was one of them, a Late Return. She liked legal thrillers, so I got her a Scott Turow that wouldn't be published for another twenty years. Then I asked if she'd post a letter. She looked at the envelope and laughed and rubbed her eyes. I slipped the letter in the back of her book. Well. I went back to my time. She went back to hers. In her time, 1972, she was a paralegal having an office romance, and her ex-husband shotgunned her and her lover both. In my time Alex Sommers weighed about ninety pounds and was black all over with Kaposi's sarcoma. I couldn't figure what went wrong. I tried to talk to him about it. I asked him if he got a letter when he was ten years old from someone he didn't know, and he went paler than his sheets. He said he read the part about being gay and tore it up. He said he vomited for days afterward. Not just because of what it said but because trying to read it had made him sick. He said the words kept swimming away when he tried to look at them. Later he decided he was mental and had hallucinated the whole thing. He thought his subconscious was trying to find some way to make him accept that he was gay and came up with an imaginary letter. He remembered some stuff about sickness but assumed that was just his guilt talking. He had a lot of guilt back then. Anyway. I couldn't change it." Hayes's bloodshot eyes were damp.

I knew that Ralph and Gallagher had heard some of this before. I could tell from how Ralph stared mildly down at his cards, refusing to make eye contact. I could tell from the way Gallagher glared at me with a kind of naked hatred. I liked him better for his hate. It was born from the love of a comrade.

"There you go," Gallagher said. "Get what you wanted?"

"I'm sorry you couldn't do him any good," I said.

Ralph said, "But he did."

"I don't know about that," Hayes said.

"He did," Ralph repeated. "You said Alex had a lot of guilt as a kid. Enough to kill himself? Maybe. Plenty of young gay men do and did, especially then. But the letter was the living proof that he had a future where someone cared about him. He got that much, even if you couldn't prevent him from contracting a tragic illness, and it was a reason to carry on with his life." He fell back to the study of his cards. "Then there was the Harry Potter situation. I think that's particularly illustrative of the good you've done, Loren."

"Good I've done," Hayes said scornfully.

"What was the Harry Potter situation?" I asked, although I already had an idea.

Loren Hayes took a long, measuring look at Terry Gallagher, then lowered his head and told it. "The last year I drove the Bookmobile was 2009. At that time I had a Monday stop at the hospital. Sometimes a few of the kids from the cancer ward would march out, if they were having a good day, for a poke around. There was a girl who stalked in one day in wizard robes, absolutely furious, shouting that goldarn it, J. K. Rowling had ended the frickin' book on a frickin' cliff-hanger, and she was going to die before she knew how it all came out. And she threw a copy of the second-to-last Harry Potter at me. Well, the final Potter book hadn't come out in her time, but it had in mine. She wanted magic. I gave her some."

"That kid finished the series before J. K. Rowling did," Ralph said with a raised eyebrow. "After she passed away, someone in her family thoughtfully returned her library books. I recognized *Harry Potter and the Deathly Hallows* right off as something that didn't exist yet, and I set it aside, put it out of circulation. After reading it myself, of course. While I am not utterly without self-control, I'm also not a masochist, and I very much wanted to know about Snape."

"What's your angle?" I asked Terry Gallagher. "You've heard all this crap before, I take it. And you believe it?"

Gallagher gave me a dismal, harried, out-of-sorts look. "Who do you think returned *The Deathly Hallows* to the library? My daughter was too distraught to do anything after Chloë died, so I did it for her. My grandkid loved those books." He paused, tugged at one corner of his bushy white mustache. "I read it to her, the last one. When she was too weak to pick up the book. I wanted to know how it came out, too."

"I've thought about this for decades," Hayes said. "Tried to make sense of it. I know this much: The people who show up in the Bookmobile from other eras are there because they're yearning for something. Yearning is the only thing that can reach across time that way. You can't give them something they don't *need*. Terry's granddaughter *needed* to know if Snape was a bad guy or not. She didn't need to know about all the shit that was going to happen after she passed. Assassinations and natural disasters and terrorism. She had a story to finish before her own story was finished. That's what she was there for. That's what I could do for her."

Ralph said, "It's how the library has always worked. People aren't there to get the books *you* want them to read."

"What I wonder," Terry Gallagher said, "is if there's a movie theater somewhere that plays pictures that haven't come out yet. Or if there's a cable channel that plays TV shows that haven't yet been released. For people who need to know. Maybe there is. Maybe the universe is kinder than we thought."

I said, "Mr. Gallagher, I see a lot of you. You're one of my steadiest customers. You aren't scared that one of these days you'll climb up there and I'll offer *you* something that hasn't come out yet?"

"I'm counting on it," Gallagher said. "If that ever happens, I'll know I have one good read left and to get my affairs in order." He seemed quite calm at the thought.

Ralph dealt a fresh hand. "And what book from the future are you hoping to read, Mr. Gallagher?"

Gallagher lifted his chin and stared at the ceiling for a moment.

"*The Art of the Presidency: How I Won My Third Term* by Donald J. Trump," he announced.

"That ever happens," Hayes said, "it'll prove the universe don't actually give a fuck."

The second week in January, Lynn Dolan paid me another visit.

She was through the door and across the library car before I had time to stand up. The sight of her gave me a nasty turn. She had lost ten pounds, and her neck and brow glowed with an oily film of sweat. I could feel the heat coming off her, even with the desk between us. I could smell blood, too, a faint rankness clinging to her woolen coat.

"I want the rest," she said. "I need the rest. Please. My son's books."

The door creaked slowly shut behind her. In my time it was raining, a dismal, cold, January drizzle, turning the snow to slush, dirt to mud, and parking lots to shallow swimming pools. But for an instant I glimpsed big fat flakes of falling snow outside, and a black late-1950s car rolling by out on the street, and I had a wild moment of wondering if I could push by her and escape into the past.

But she was leaning over me, feverish and weak, her pupils very small and her lips dry and cracked. I came around the desk and touched her arm.

"Sit," I said. "Please sit."

She tottered to my chair and eased herself down.

"Should you be out of bed?" I asked.

She wiped one hand over her damp cheek, then hugged herself. "I'm fine."

"The hell you are."

"All right, I'm not. I'm dying. You already know I'm dying. But I want my son's books, and you can give them to me. You're from the future. I want to read all my son's stories." Her eyes were bright and shiny and full of water, but she did not cry. The corner of her mouth twitched in something close to a smile. "He's so funny. He was always so funny." Then, after a pause, "He shouldn't be over there. None of our boys should be. It's a bad war. That book of his made me laugh, but it also made me sick." Then she smiled again. "He got the clap, didn't he? Is that why he's not writing me?"

We had swapped positions. She sat behind my desk as if she were the librarian, and I stood on the other side as if I were the one looking for a story.

"I think it might be," I said. "He wasn't sure how to talk to you about what he was seeing there. He started writing the book to explain. In your time he's probably just started."

"Yes," she said, in a strange, stiff way. "Almost certainly."

I turned to the fiction shelf. We had his entire collection in stock. Because he was a local guy, there was always a steady demand. I ran my finger along the spines, then hesitated.

Without looking at her, I said, "What are you going to do with them when you're done?" My scalp was crawling strangely, the way it had when I met that first Late Return, Fred Mueller. I was troubled by her odd tone of voice when she agreed that yes, her son had almost certainly started writing his first novel over there on the other side of the world.

She didn't reply.

When I looked at her, her chest was rising and falling and her damp eyes were shining with triumph.

"What do you think I did with it?" she asked. "My boy needs a reason to go on."

I went all ice water inside.

"You can't *send* him his own books," I told her. "The ones he hasn't written yet."

"Maybe if I don't," she said, "he won't write them. Have you ever thought that?"

"No. *No.* If he just copies the books I send back in time with you, then who wrote them in the first place?"

"My son. He wrote them before, and he'll write them again. So I can read them and then pass them on to him."

I'd had three glasses of bourbon that night with Terry Gallagher, Loren Hayes, and Ralph Tanner, but I felt more woozy standing there cold sober in the library car with the dead woman.

"I don't think that's how time is supposed to work," I said.

She said, "It works however you say it works. His books exist. They exist now, whether I get to read them or I don't. So that's all you have to decide, mister. Do I get to have this last good thing in my life or not? Do I get to have another marvelous thing, or are you going to—"

"What?" I said. "What did you say?" I was suddenly as sweaty as she was and felt maybe half as sick.

"Do I get to go out on a good note?" she said patiently. "Or not? Because you decide, mister. I can have the last days of my life the way I want them, with my son at my side, in his stories if not in the flesh. Are you going to be the guy who says no?"

I wasn't going to be the guy who said no. I turned away, reached up onto the shelf, and lifted the whole stack down.

Brad Dolan dedicated his last book to his mother, too. The dedication reads:

> *One more for my mother, without whom I would not ever have written a word*

You could go crazy trying to figure out what that means. But I don't have to. Because in June, five months after the last time I saw Lynn Dolan, I received a letter from a dead man, a letter from the past.

It had been mailed care of the Kingsward Public Library and addressed to "The Current Driver Of The Bookmobile." A law firm that represented the estate of Brad Dolan had been sitting on it ever since Dolan's suicide by handgun in 1997, shortly after the publication of his final book. His will had specified the date on which to place it in the post.

Dear Sir,

I have wondered about you for most of my adult life: who you are, how you managed to slip through time in the Kingsward Public Library's Bookmobile, what your life has been like. I know nothing about you for certain except that you are kind. Maybe nothing else matters.

That said, I am sure we have met. I am careful to visit every eighth-grade class at Kingsward Junior High, and I think it highly likely that I have gaped at you through my bifocals and you have gaped back, probably while picking your nose, from across your desk, wondering when I'll stop talking so you can go to lunch.

On the sunny fall morning on which I write this note—I can see fat chipmunks outside my window, frisking after one another, caught up in their torrid rodent romances—you are probably in your mid-teens. By the time you read it, however, you will be close to thirty. See, you are not the only one who can stretch the rubber band of time and shoot it in someone's eye.

It is possible you are anxious about my death. Perhaps you wonder if I killed myself after I wrote my last book because I had no more books from the future to copy. Did I copy them, line for line, over the years, spacing the publications for maximum commercial impact? Beginning with that first one, which I received in the Da Nang province in 1966, shortly before I received notice of my mother's death? Did I come home and discover twelve more novels in a cardboard suitcase in the front closet? Did I study their titles and covers with a dry mouth and my heart beating tremulously and then burn them in my fireplace without reading them? Does it matter? I had my life. The books have theirs. But when I put a pistol in my mouth, a few days or a few hours from now—I'm still making up my mind about it—it will not be because I ran out of things to write. It will be because I miss my mother, and because I broke my back in a motorcycle accident in 1975 and the pain is rotten, and because I shot an unarmed woman in the throat in Vietnam and have never forgiven myself for it. She was hiding under a blanket in a dark room, and when I poked the blanket, she rose, screaming, and I killed her. Upon seeing the body, my sergeant put a grenade in her hand and said he'd file papers to see I got a medal. I have been a war hero ever since. That is why I did not write to my mother for three months: not the clap, as I have said elsewhere. This is why I wrote fiction for thirty years: because I could not bear the truth.

Or at least I could not bear <u>most</u> of the truth. Once my mother was dying and a man was kind to her. That is a truth that has kept me going well past my time.

I have the gun, and I have tested the feel of the barrel in my mouth, but I haven't pulled the trigger yet. I go for a walk every day. Sometimes I walk down to the park, where the Bookmobile stops on Thursday mornings. A little part of me is hanging on to see if we may yet have a word with each other. Also, I would like to know what Philip Roth is going to publish after my death. Isn't that what keeps so many of us hanging on past our <u>Return-By</u> date? We can't help wishing for one more lovely story.

I hope you are well. I wish you a lifetime of happy reading, free from guilt. See you around sometime?

Best,

Brad Dolan

On a dry afternoon in midsummer, with the insects producing a drowsy, throbbing hum in the trees, I opened the side door to the garage and then wrestled with the locks on the automatic door until at last I was finally able to set them free and roll the door up. The air that blew into the concrete-floored room smelled sweetly of fresh-cut grass and my mother's roses, and I had a happy, quiet afternoon of sweeping and bagging up garbage. I connected my phone to a Bluetooth speaker and played Joan Baez. A strong, sweet, hopeful voice from the past kept me company in the garage, 1965 echoing into the twenty-first century. The past is always close, so close you can sing along with it, anytime you like.

I found some boxes I thought I could send on to the library—a crate of my dad's old *Rolling Stones*, a box of Danny Dunn young-adult novels I had loved as a boy—and it came to me I ought to grab my mother's overdue Laurie Colwin and return that, too. Only when I went looking for it, I couldn't find it. I tossed the whole house, hunting for it, but it's not there. It has vanished to elsewhere.

It made me think maybe my mother will return it sometime soon. I am ready to see her. I have a couple books I think she'd like. I have a couple Philip Roths set aside, too, just in case. You never know who will turn up at the Bookmobile. I'm always ready to see *Another Marvelous Thing.*

Are you?

All I Care About Is You

Limitation makes for power. The strength of the genie comes of his being confined in a bottle.

—RICHARD WILBUR

1.

She grabs the brake and power-drifts the Monowheel to a stop for a red light, just before the overpass that spans the distance between bad and worse.

Iris doesn't want to look up at the Spoke and can't help herself. The habit of longing is hard to quit, and there's a particularly good view of it from this corner. She knows by now that certain things are out of reach, but her *blood* doesn't seem to know it. When she allows herself to remember the promises her father made a year ago, her blood seems to *throb* inside her with excitement. Pitiful.

She finds herself staring up at it, that jagged scepter of steel and blued chrome lancing the dingy clouds, and hates herself a little. *Let that go,* she tells herself with a certain contempt, and forces herself to look away from the Spoke, to stare blindly ahead. Her idiot heart is beating too fast.

Iris doesn't notice the not-alive, not-dead boy watching her from the corner. She never notices him.

He *always* notices her. He knows where she's been and where she's going. He knows better than she knows herself.

2.

"Got you something," her father says. "Close your eyes."

Iris does as she's told. She holds her breath, too. And there it is again, that thrill in the blood. Hope—stupid, childish hope—fills her like a trembling, fragile soap bubble, effervescent and weightless. It feels like it would be a terrible jinx to even allow herself to think the word: "Hideware."

She isn't going to the top of the Spoke tonight, she knows that. She isn't going to be drinking Sparklefroth with her friends on the top of the world. But maybe the old man has a trick up his sleeve. Maybe he had a couple tokens socked away for an important day. Maybe the former Resurrection Man has one more miracle to work. Her blood believes that all these things might be possible.

He sets something heavy in her lap, something far too heavy to be Hideware. That fantastic bubble of hope pops and collapses inside her.

"Okay," he says. "You c-can look."

His stammer disturbs her. He didn't stammer BEFORE, didn't stammer when he was still with her mother and still in the Murdergame. She opens her eyes.

He didn't even wrap it. It's something the size of a bowling ball, shoved in a crinkly bag. She peels the sack open and looks down at a cloudy emerald globe.

"Crystal ball?" she asks. "Oh, Daddy, I always wanted to know my future."

What tripe. She doesn't have a future—not one worth thinking about.

The old man leans forward on his bench, hands clasped between his knees so they won't tremble. They didn't tremble BEFORE either. He sucks a liquid breath through the plastic tubing up his nose. The respirator pumps and hisses. "There's a m-mermaid in there. You've wanted one since you were small."

She wanted a lot of things when she was small. She wanted Microwing shoes so she could run six inches off the ground. She wanted gills for swimming in the underground lagoons. She wanted whatever Amy Pasquale and Joyce Brilliant got for their birthdays, and her parents always saw that it was so, but that was BEFORE.

Something swishes, takes a slow turn in the center of the spinach-colored sludge, then drifts to the glass to gaze up at her. She is so repulsed by the sight she almost shoves the sphere out of her lap.

"Wow," she says. "*Wow.* I love it. I really did always want one."

He bows his head and squeezes his eyes shut. A tingle of shock prickles across her chest. He's about to cry.

"I know it isn't what you wanted. What we t-t-talked about," he says.

She reaches across the table and clasps his hand, feels like she might start to cry herself. "It's perfect."

Only she's wrong. He wasn't struggling against tears. He was fighting a yawn. He surrenders to it, covers his mouth with the back of his free hand. He doesn't seem to have heard her.

"I wish we could've done all the things we talked about. The S-Sp-Spuh-Spoke. R-Ride in a big buh-b-bubble together. These fuckin' medical Clockworks, kid. They're like hyenas pulling apart the corpse for the last goodies. The medical Clockworks ate your b-birthday c-cake this year, kiddo. We'll see if I can't do a little better for you next year." He shakes his head in a good humored way. "I have to c-c-crap out for a while. A man c-can only take so much excitement when he's g-got half a working heart." He opens his eyes to a sleepy squint. "You know about m-mermaids. When they fall in love, they sing. Which I understand. Same thing happened to me."

"It did?" she asks.

"After you were b-born"—he turns sideways, stretches himself out on the bench, struggles with another yawn—"I sang to you every night. Sang until I was all sung out." He shuts his eyes, head pillowed on a pile of grubby laundry. "*Happy birthday to you. Happy b-birthday to you. Happy b-b-b-buh-birthday, sweet Iris. Hap-p-puh-p-p—*" He inhales, a wet, clogged, struggling sound, and begins to cough. He thumps his chest a few times, turns his face away from her, shrugs, and sighs.

He is asleep by the time Iris reaches the top of the ladder, climbing out of his pod and leaving him behind.

She shuts the hatch, one of eight thousand in the great, dim, clammy, cavernous hive. The air smells of old pipes and urine.

Iris left her Monowheel next to her father's pod on a

mag-lock, because here in the Hives anything that isn't bolted down will vanish the moment you take your eyes off it. She climbs up onto the big red leather seat of her 'wheel and flips the ignition four or five times before realizing it isn't going to start. Her first thought is that somehow the battery has gone dead. But it hasn't gone dead. It's just gone. Someone yanked it out of the vapor-drive and strolled off with it.

"Happy birthday to me," she sings, a little off-key.

3.

A cannon-train approaches, making that cannon-train sound, a whispery whistle that builds and builds until suddenly it passes below her with a concussive blast. Iris loves the way it hits her, loves to be struck through by the shriek and boom, so all the breath is slammed from her body. Not for the first time, she wonders what would be left of her if she jumped off the stone balustrade. Iris fantasizes about being pulverized into a fine, warm spray and raining gently upon her rotten, selfish mother and sorry, hopeless father, wetting their faces in red tears.

She sits on the balustrade, swinging her feet over the drop, the smooth green ball of sludge resting in her lap. There'll be another train in a few minutes.

When she looks into her poisoned crystal ball, it isn't the future she sees but the past. This time last year, she was fifteen, with fifteen of her best friends, fifteen hundred feet underground in the Furnace Club. Magma bubbled beneath the BluDiamond floor. They all traipsed barefoot to feel the warmth of it, guttering streams of liquid gold not half an inch from their heels. The waiter was a floating Clockwork named Bub, a polished copper globe who hovered here and there, opening the bright lid of his head to offer each new course. In the throbbing red light, the faces of the other girls glowed with sweat and excitement, and their laughter echoed off the warm rock walls. They looked as roasted as the piglets they were served for the main course.

Her friends were all drunk on one another by the end of it, and there was a lot of hugging and smooching. They said it was the best birthday party ever. Iris got carried away by all the good feeling and promised them next year would be even better. She said they would ride the elevator to the top of the Spoke to see the stars—the ACTUAL stars—above the cloudscape. They would drink Sparklefroth and electrocute one another with happiness. They would take the long, dreamy plunge back to earth together in Drop Bubbles. And after, they would all mask themselves in Hideware and go down into the Carnival District—which was forbidden to anyone under sixteen—and everyone who saw them in their expensive new faces would fall in love with them.

Something stirs in the cloudy green globe. The mermaid looms up from the mucus-hued shadows and boggles out at her. The girl-fish is little more than a grotesque pink slug with a face and waving, mossy-green hair.

"You might want to do something adorable," she says, "while you've got the chance."

A black string of poop squirts from a hole above her tail fin. The mermaid gawps, as if astonished by the functions of her own body.

A hoop of eldritch jade light flares in her right eye, half blinding her, signaling an incoming message. She pinches her thumb and index finger together, as if squeezing a bug to death. Words appear in fey emerald letters, seeming to hover three feet from her face, a trick of the messaging lens that she puts in her eye first thing every morning, even before she brushes her teeth.

JOYCE B: WE HAVE PLANS FOR YOU.
AMY P: EVIL PLANS.
JOYCE B: WE'RE GETTING YOU INTO THE CARNIVALS TONIGHT. IT HAS BEEN OR-DAINED.

Iris shuts her eyes, rests her forehead against the cool glass of the aquaglobe.

"Can't," she says, squeezing her thumb and index finger together to SEND.

JOYCE B: DON'T MAKE US FORCE YOU INTO A SACK & DRAG YOU OUT KICKING & SCREAMING.
AMY P: IN A SACK. KICKING. SCREAMING.

Iris says, "My mom's new guy is off work in an hour, and Mom wants me home for cake and presents. I guess they got me some big-deal gift that won't wait."

This is a lie. Iris will decide what the big-deal gift was later. It will have to be something that could only be used once, something no one can prove she didn't get. Maybe she will tell her friends she went on a hallucication to the lunar surface and spent the night in Archimedes Station, playing Moon Quidditch with the Archimedes Owls.

JOYCE B's reply appears in lurid fire: HIDE-WARE??? DO YOU THINK YOUR MOM GOT YOU A NEW FACE?

Iris opens her mouth, closes it, opens it again. "We won't know until I unwrap it, will we?"

The moment it's out of her mouth, she doesn't know why she said it, wishes she could unSEND.

No. She knows why she said it. Because it feels good to act like she's still one of them. That she has everything they have and always will. That she isn't falling behind.

AMY P: I HOPE YOU GOT AN "OPHELIA" BECAUSE IT WILL MAKE JOYCE JEALOUS AND I LIKE TO WATCH JOYCE FAKE-SMILE AT PEOPLE WHEN SHE'S MISERABLE.

The Ophelia has been out for just two months and might've been too expensive even when her father was making tokens by the shovel-load in the Murdergame.

"It probably won't be the Ophelia," Iris says, then immediately wishes she could rephrase.

JOYCE B: THERE'S NOTHING WRONG WITH A BASIC "GIRL NEXT DOOR." THAT'S WHAT AMY HAS AND I'M NOT EMBARRASSED TO GO OUT WITH HER. I'M NOT PROUD, BUT I'M NOT EMBARRASSED.

AMY P: WHATEVER IT IS, YOU'RE FREE BY 2100, BECAUSE YOUR MOM ALREADY SAID YOU'LL MEET US AT THE SOUTH ENTRANCE TO THE CARNIVALS. I MES-

SAGED WITH HER THIS MORNING. SO GO
HOME AND SCARF CAKE AND UNWRAP
YOUR SEXY NEW FACE AND GET READY
TO MEET US.

JOYCE B: IF YOU DO GET AN "OPHELIA,"
I WANT TO WEAR IT FOR AT LEAST A
LITTLE WHILE, BECAUSE I COULDN'T
BEAR IT IF YOU WERE MORE AMAZING
THAN ME.

"I could never be more amazing than you," Iris says,
and Joyce and Amy disconnect.

Below her another cannon-train booms past.

4.

The disaster happens two-thirds of the way across the
overpass.

The Monowheel is lightweight but big, bigger than
she is, and walking it home is awkward business. It's
a drunken giant who keeps leaning on her or trying
to sit down in the road. She leans in to guide it with a
hand on the control stick, her other hand clutching the
aquaball to her side. The overpass has a gentle arch to it
and the 'wheel wants to speed up as soon as she's on the
downward slope. She jogs to keep up with it, huffing for

breath. It tilts toward her. The inner chrome hoop bangs her head. She makes a little sound of pain, lifts her free hand to press a palm to the hurt place, only to remember she doesn't have a free hand. The aquaball slips free and strikes the sidewalk with a glassy crack!

Good, she thinks. *Smash.*

But it doesn't smash, it *rolls,* with a grinding, droning kind of music, weaving this way and that, hopping the curb and trundling into the road. A vapordrive hansom cab on gold razorwheels whines shrilly along the cross street, and the aquaball disappears beneath it. Iris tenses, with a certain pleasure, anticipating the crunch and the loud splash. But when the hansom flashes past, the murky green globe is impossibly still rolling, undamaged, along the far sidewalk. Iris has never in all her life so wanted to see something crushed.

Instead a kid puts his foot out and stops it.

That kid.

In one sense Iris has never seen him before. In another she has seen him a hundred times, on her way to her father's, has glimpsed him from her Monowheel, this kid with his too-cool-for-school slouch, in a gray wool baseball cap and a gray wool coat that has seen better days. He is always here, hanging out against the wall in front of a closed Novelty.

He doesn't do anything more than stop the ball with

his toe. Doesn't look up the road to see who dropped it, doesn't bend down to pick it up.

She steers the Monowheel over to him. It's easier now that she has two hands to guide it along.

"You're too kind. And I do mean that literally. You just rescued the world's crummiest birthday present," she says.

He doesn't reply.

She leans the Monowheel against the hitching post along the curb and bends to get the aquaball. She hopes it's cracked, squirting its guts out. What a pleasure it would be to watch that gruesome slug—that sardine-size parody of a woman—swimming frantically around as the water level falls. Not a mark on it, though. She doesn't know why she hates it so much. It isn't the mermaid's fault it's ugly, trapped, unasked for, unwanted.

"Shoot. I was hoping it would shatter into a thousand pieces. A girl can't catch a break."

This doesn't even earn her a chuckle, and she casts a quick, annoyed glance into his face—when she's witty, Iris expects to be appreciated—and sees it at last. He isn't a kid at all. He's a Clockwork, an old one, with a smiling, moonlike face of crackled ceramic. His chest is a scratched case of plasteel. Within is a coil of cloudy vinyl tubing where intestines belong, brass pipettes for bones, a basket of gold wires filled almost to the top

368 • FULL THROTTLE

with silver tokens instead of a stomach. His heart is a matte black vapor-drive.

A steel plate mounted to one side of his heart says COIN-OP FRIEND! LOYAL FAITHFUL COMPANION AND CONFIDANT. NEED HELP WITH GROCERIES? CAN LIFT UP TO ONE TON. KNOWS 30 CARD GAMES, SPEAKS ALL LANGUAGES, KEEPS SECRETS. A TOKEN FOR 30 MINUTES OF ABSOLUTE DEVOTION. GIRLS: LEARN HOW TO KISS FROM A PERFECT GENTLEMAN WHO WILL TELL NO TALES. BOYS: PRACTICE THE ANCIENT ART OF PUGILISM ON HIS ALMOST INDESTRUCTIBLE SHELL! THIS CLOCKWORK NOT RATED FOR ADULT/MATURE USE. Someone has scratched a cartoon penis below this last sentence.

Iris has not played with a Clockwork since she was small, not since Talk-to-Me-Tabitha, her childhood beloved, and Tabitha was perhaps a century more advanced. This thing is an antique, one of the novelties from the shuttered store directly behind him, likely planted on the street as an advertisement. A moldie-oldie from the days of Google and chunky VR headsets and Florida.

No one could steal him. His back is pressed to a magnetic charge plate installed in the brick wall. Iris is no longer sure he intentionally stopped the aquaball, suspects his foot was just there and halting her runaway mermaid was only a lucky accident. Or *unlucky* accident; a lucky accident would've been if it had imploded under the razorwheels of the hansom.

Iris turns her back on him and looks despairingly at the Monowheel she still has to push another half mile. The thought of steering it along the road makes her unpleasantly aware of the sweater sticking to her sweaty back.

Need help with groceries? Can lift up to one ton.

She swivels back, digs out her tokens—she has exactly two—and pushes first one, then the other into the slot on the Clockwork's chest. Silver credits clatter into the enormous pile of tokens in his stomach.

The vaporware heart in his chest expands and contracts with an audible thud. The numbers above the chrome plate on his chest make a ratcheting noise and roll over with a series of rapid clicks, to read 00:59:59.

And the seconds begin to tick down.

5.

He knew she would pay long before she dropped her tokens, knew when her back was still turned to him, just from the way she looked at her Monowheel and how her shoulders slumped at the sight of it. Body language says more than words ever do. And his processor, which is lethargic by the standards of modern computing, is still fast enough to complete two million clock cycles before she can get her hand out of her pocket with the coins in them. That's enough time to read and reread the complete works of Dickens.

Her body temperature is elevated, and she's sweating from labor but also from a frayed mood. The command line, which fills him always like breath, compels him to supply comfort with a bit of easy cleverness.

"You got three questions," he says, selecting for random grammatical errors. Informal speech always plays well with the young. "Let me answer them in order. First: What's my name? Chip. It's a joke. But it's also really my name."

The girl says, "What do you mean it's a—"

He taps one finger to his temple, indicating the logic boards hidden behind his ceramic face, and she smiles.

"*Chip.* Glad to meet you. What are my other two questions?"

"If you have to pay me, how can I really be your friend? The company that built me programmed me with one directive: For the next fifty-nine minutes, all I care about is you. I won't judge you and I won't lie to you. You are Aladdin and I am the genie. I'll execute any wish that's within my powers and isn't strictly forbidden by custom or law. I can't steal. I can't beat anyone up. There are certain adult functions I cannot perform owing to the 2072 Human-Clockwork Obscenity Laws—laws that have actually been repealed but remain a part of my OS."

"What's that mean?"

The command line impels a crude, comic response. Her social profile suggests a high probability that this will be well received.

"I can't eat pussy," he says. "Or take one up the ass."

"Holy shit," she says, a blush scalding her cheeks. Her embarrassment confirms he appeals to her. Physiology is confession.

"I have no tongue, so I cannot lick."

"This got real very quickly."

"I have no butthole, so I cannot—"

"Got it. Never even crossed my mind to ask. What was my third question?"

"Yes, of course I can carry your Monowheel. What happened to it?"

"Someone ripped the battery out. Can you carry it all the way to the Stacks?"

He unbolts himself from the charging plate, free for the first time in sixteen days. She unlocks the Monowheel from the hitching post. He grips the inner rail and lifts all 408.255 kilograms off the ground, slips it onto his shoulder. The tilt of her head implies satisfaction, while her body language suggests that the initial pleasure at solving a problem is fading, to be replaced by some other source of distress and exhaustion. *Probably.* Emotions cannot be known with any certainty, only hypothesized. A darting look of anxiety might suggest inner turmoil or merely the need to urinate. Apparently clever, witty remarks often shroud despair, while the statement "I'm dying" hardly ever indicates life-threatening physical trauma. Without certainty he follows the routines most likely to produce comfort and pleasure.

"I've answered three of your questions, so now you have to answer three of mine, fair?"

"I guess," she says.

"Got a name?"

"Iris Ballard."

Within a quarter second of learning her name, he has gathered every bit of information he can find on her in the socialverse, collecting half a gigabyte of unremarkable trivia and a single ten-month-old news report that might matter very much.

"I've known one Rapunzel, two Zeldas, and three Cleopatras, but I've never met an Iris."

"Do you remember *everyone* you've met? No, forget it. Of course you do. You probably have terabytes of memory you haven't used. What was Rapunzel like?"

"She had a shaved head. I didn't ask why."

Iris laughs. "Okay. What else?"

"You don't have a household Clockwork to help you with your busted Monowheel?"

Her smile slips. The subject is red-flagged as a threat to her approval. An algorithm ponders the possibilities, decides she is financially disadvantaged and that her lack of funds is a source of discomfort. The condition of poverty is new to her, probably a result of the events described in the unfortunate news story.

"I had a Talk-to-Me-Tabitha when I was little," she says. "I talked to her all day, from when I got home till when I went to bed. My dad used to come in at ten P.M. and say he was going to have to take her away and stick her in a closet if I didn't go to sleep. Nothing made me shut up faster than that. I hated the idea of him putting her in the closet, where she'd be all alone. But then she auto-upgraded, and after that she was always talking about how we could have a lot more fun together if I bought a Talk-to-Me-Tabitha Terrier or Talk-to-Me-Tabitha Smartglasses. She started working advertisements and offers into conversation. It got really gross, so I started doing intentionally mean things to her. I'd step on her if she was lying on the floor. One day my dad saw me swinging her against the wall and took her away. He resold her on Auctionz to teach me a lesson, even though I cried and cried. Honestly, that might be the only time in my life my father punished me for anything."

Her tone and expression suggest irritation, which he can't fathom. A lack of parental discipline should be a source of at least mild contentment, not disapproval. He marks this statement for further evaluation and will watch her for other signs of psychological malformation. Not that this will incline him to be any less devoted to her. He collected hundreds of tokens from a schizophrenic man named Dean. Dean believed he was being followed by a cabal of ballet dancers who intended to kidnap and castrate him. Chip dutifully watched for women in tutus and swore to defend Dean's genitals. It was all a long time ago.

"You had one more thing you were going to ask me?" she says. "Hopefully it won't be whether I'd like to take advantage of a very special offer. Marketing ruins the illusion that you're vaguely personlike."

He marks her contempt for advertising. Nothing to be done about it—he is required to peddle his own services later—but he marks it anyway.

"What are you doing to celebrate your birthday?" he asks. "Besides spending an hour with me, which is, I admit, going to be hard to top."

She stops walking. "How do you know it's my birthday?"

"You said."

"When did I say?"

"When you picked up your runaway fish."

"That was before I paid you."

"I know. I'm still aware of things when my meter isn't running. I still think. Your birthday?"

She frowns, processing. They have reached a fork in the conversation. It seems likely she remains in a state of guarded emotional distress. He banks a series of encouraging remarks and prepares three strategies for canceling out her unhappiness. Humans suffer terribly. Chip views lifting her spirits as much like lifting her Monowheel, a fundamental reason to act, to *be*.

"I've already celebrated it," she says, and they resume walking. "My dad gave me a pet leech with a human face and passed out, snoring into his oxygen tank. Now I'm going back to my mom's to think up an excuse—a *lie*—not to go out with friends tonight."

"I'm so sorry to hear your father isn't well."

"No you aren't," she says, her voice sharp. "Clockworks don't feel sorry about things. They execute programs. I don't need a hair dryer to offer me sympathy."

Chip does not take offense because he *cannot* take

offense. Instead he says, "May I ask what happened?" He already knows, reviewed the whole ugly story as soon as Iris identified herself, but a pretense of ignorance will give her license to talk, which may provide relief, a momentary distraction from her cares.

"He was in the Murdergame. He was a professional homicide victim. A Resurrection Man. You know. Someone will rent a private abattoir and work out her unhappy feelings by beating him to death with a hammer or shooting him or whatever. Then a cellular-rebuild program stitches him back together, just like new. He was one of the most popular hatchet victims in the twelve boroughs. He had a waiting list." She smiles without any pleasure. "He used to joke about how he was *literally* willing to die for me—and did at least twenty times a week."

"And then?"

"A bachelorette party. They hired him out for a stabbing. The whole crowd of them went at him with kitchen knives and meat cleavers. There was a power failure, but they were all so drunk they didn't even notice. Do you remember all the blackouts we had last February? His rebuild program couldn't connect with the server for repair instructions. He was dead for almost half an hour. Now he has the shakes and he forgets things. His insurance wouldn't cover his injuries because there was a company rule against having more than two assailants at a time, even though everyone ignores it. He's worse than completely broke, and the state board won't renew his license. He can't die for a living anymore, and he isn't fit for anything else."

"Have we agreed I shouldn't offer you sympathy? I don't want to overstep."

She flinches, as from a biting insect. "I wouldn't deserve your sympathy even if you had any to give. I'm a snotty, selfish, entitled little bitch. My dad lost everything, and I'm in a pissy mood because we're not doing what I wanted for my birthday. He got me the best gift he could, and I was going to drop it in front of a train. Tell me that doesn't sound ungrateful."

"It sounds like the latest disappointment on a stack of them. Ancient religions used to tell people that letting go of yearning is the highest form of spirituality. But Buddha had it wrong. Yearning is the difference between being human and being a Clockwork. Not to *want* is not to *live*. Even DNA is an engine of desire—driven to copy itself over and over. Nothing spiritual about a hair dryer. What did you want to do for your birthday?"

"Me and my friends were going to the top of the Spoke at sunset to see the stars come out. I've only ever seen them in pay-per-vision streams. Never for real. We were going to drink Sparklefroth and shoot sparks and then ride Drop Bubbles back to earth. After, we were going to put on Hideware and go down to the Cabinet Carnivals. My friends all think I'm getting a new face today, because that's what they got for their birthdays. No way *that's* happening. My mom is so cheap I bet she won't even buy me a new battery for my busted-ass Monowheel."

"And you can't tell your friends you can't afford a new face right now?"

"I can—if I want pity for my birthday. But Sparkle-froth tastes better."

"I can't help with the new face," he says. "Theft is prohibited. But if you want to see the stars come out from the top of the Spoke, it isn't too late. Sunset is in twenty-one minutes."

Iris looks toward the silver needle puncturing the mustard-colored clouds. "You need a ticket and reservations for the elevator." She has never been above the clouds, and they have never once cleared off in all her sixteen years. It's been overcast in the city for nearly three decades.

"You don't need an elevator. You've got me."

She catches in place. "What malarkey is this?"

"If I can carry a four-*hundred*-kilo wheel, I'm sure I can carry a forty-two-kilogram girl up a few stairs."

"It's not a few. It's three thousand."

"Three thousand and eighteen. I will need nine minutes from the bottom step. A Drop Bubble is eighty-three credits, a glass of Sparklefroth is eleven, a table is only by reservation—but the gallery in the Sun Parlor is free to all, Iris."

Her respiration has quickened. Rapid eye movements between himself and the Spoke telegraph her excitement.

"I . . . well . . . when I imagined it, I always thought I'd have a friend along."

"You will," he said. "What do you think you paid for?"

6.

The lobby is almost a quarter of a mile high, a dizzying cathedral of green glass. The air is cool and smells corporate. The glass barrels of the elevators vanish into pale clouds. The Spoke is so large it has its own climate.

They queue to pass through the scanners. The Clockwork guards might've been carved from soap, uniformed figures with featureless white heads and smooth white hands: a squad of living mannequins. Iris steps through the Profiler, which scans for weapons, biological agents, drugs, chemicals, threatening intentions, and debt. A low, discordant pulse sounds. A security Clockwork gestures for her to go through again. On her second pass, she clears the scanner without incident. A moment later Chip follows.

"Any idea why you tripped the Profiler?" Chip asks. "Debt? Or a desire to harm others?"

"If you've got debt, you can imagine doing harm to others," she says. She raises the aquaball she still carries under one arm. "Probably it caught me thinking about what I want to do with my mermaid. I was remembering how we planned to eat sushi at my birthday party."

"It's a pet, not a snack. Try to be good."

When Iris tilts her head back, she sees iridescent bubbles with people in them, hundreds of feet above her, floating here and there, pulling free of the clouds and drifting to earth. The sight of them—gleaming like ornaments on some impossibly huge Christmas tree—gives her an ache. She always thought someday she would ride in one herself.

Hammered-bronze doors open into the stairwell. Flights of black glass plates climb the walls, around and around, in a spiral that goes on into infinity.

"Get on my back," Chip says, sinking to one knee.

"The last time someone gave me a piggyback, I was probably six," she says, "someone" being her father.

"The last time I gave someone a piggyback," he says, "was twenty-three years before you were born. The

Spoke was still under construction then. I've never been up to the top either."

She straddles his back, puts her arms around the plasteel of his neck. He rises fluidly to his full height. The first step lights up when he steps on it—and the second, and the third. He bounds up them in an accelerating series of white pulses.

"How old *are* you?" she asks.

"I came online one hundred and sixteen years ago, almost a century before your own operating system began to function."

"Ha." They're moving so fast now that it makes her feel queasy. Her Monowheel doesn't go this fast at top speed. He leaps three steps at a time, keeping a steady, jolting rhythm. Iris cannot bear to look over the glass retaining wall on her right, cannot look at the black nautilus swirl of steps below them. For a while she is silent, eyes squeezed shut, pressing herself into his back.

Finally, just to be talking, she asks, "Who was the first person to put a coin in your meter?"

"A boy named Jamie. We were close for almost four years. He used to visit me once a week."

"That's where the money is," she says. "My dad had repeat clients, too. There was a woman who used to cut his throat every Sunday at one. She bled him dry, and he did the same to her—took her for every cent she had.

How much did you squeeze good old Jamie for before he got bored of you?"

"He didn't get bored. He died, when malware infected his enhanced immune system. He raved about cheap Viagra and Asian women who want English-speaking husbands for two awful days before the infection killed him. He was thirteen."

She shivers, has heard horror stories about corrupted bioware. "Awful."

"The price of being alive is that someday you aren't."

"Yeah. My meter is running, too. Isn't that the whole point of birthdays? To remind you the meter is running down? Someday I'll be dead, and you'll still be making new friends. Carrying other girls up other stairways." She laughs humorlessly.

"However old I myself may be, consider that in a very real sense my own life happens one token at a time, and there are sometimes days, or even weeks, between periods of activity. I've outlived Jamie by a hundred and three years in one sense. In another he spent far more time doing and being. And in still another sense, I've never lived at all—at least if we agree that life means personal initiative and choice."

She snorts. "Funny. People pay you to come to life, and people paid my dad to die, but you're both professional victims. You take money and let other people decide what happens to you. I guess maybe that's most work: being a victim for hire."

"Most work is about being of service."

"Same thing, isn't it?"

"Some work is about lying down for others, I suppose," he says, and she realizes he is leaping up the last flight of stairs to a wide black glass landing and another set of bronze doors. "And some work is about lifting people up."

He opens the doors.

A dying sun spears them in a shaft of light, seals them in dusky amber.

7.

At first it doesn't seem there are any walls. The Sun Parlor at the top of the Spoke is a small circular room beneath a lid of BluDiamond, as transparent as breath. The sun rests in a bed of bloodstained sheets. A bar of black glass, curved like the blade of a sickle, occupies the center of the room. A Clockwork gentleman stands behind it. He wears a bowler on the copper vase of his head, and his torso rides atop six copper legs, giving him the look of a jeweled, metal cricket in a hat.

"Are you here for the Danforth party?" the Clock-work attendant asks in a plummy voice. He presses fingertips of copper pipe together. "Ms. Paget, I presume? Mr. Danforth has checked in below with the others but indicated you would not be joining them this evening."

"I wanted it to be a surprise," Iris tells him . . . a lie so smooth that Chip can detect no trace of physiological change, no quickening of breath or alteration in skin temperature.

"Very good. The rest of your party is approaching in the elevator. If you would like to toast the maiden, you will be joined by the birthday girl in twenty seconds." The Clockwork gestures at a collection of champagne flutes filled with Sparklefroth.

Chip picks up a flute and hands it to Iris just as a hatch slides open in the floor. The elevator rises into the room, a bronze cage containing a flock of twelve-year-old girls in party dresses and new faces, accompanied by a weary man in a nice sweater—the birthday girl's father, no doubt. The grate opens. Chattering, laughing girls spill out.

"Are you sure you can't kill people?" Iris asks. "Because they're wearing about five thousand credits of Hideware on their faces, and I'm feeling murdery."

"Nothing ruins a birthday party like a multiple homicide."

"I should probably drink my Sparklefroth before the robowaiter introduces me as Ms. Paget, and they realize I'm crashing their party, and I get charged for a drink I can't afford."

"They're not going to hear him," Chip promises. "Get ready to shout happy birthday."

"Sparklefroth, French chocolate cake, and bubble rides, as the sun goes down on the twelfth year of Ms. Abigail Danforth's life!" cries the Clockwork waiter. "And happy day, your guests are all here, even—" But no one hears the last part of his statement.

Chip's head spins on his neck, 360 degrees, around and around, and at the same time he emits a piercing bottle-rocket whistle. Red, white, and blue sparks crackle and fly from his ears. A Wurlitzer organ plays the opening chords of "Happy Birthday" from inside his chest at a staggering volume.

Iris lifts her glass like she belongs and shouts, "Happy birthday!"

The kids shriek "Happy birthday!" and rush to collect flutes of Sparklefroth, while the sparks pouring from Chip's ears turn to cotton-candy clouds of pink and purple smoke. The girls sing. The room echoes with their gay noise. When the song is over, they erupt into gales of laughter and gulp Sparklefroth. Iris drinks with them. Her eyes widen. Her blond hair begins to lift and float around her head with electrical charge.

"Whoa," she says, and reaches for Chip's arm to steady herself.

A blue pop of electricity flies from her fingers. She twitches in surprise. Then, experimentally, she snaps her fingers. Another blue spark.

The party girls are zapping each other, provoking screams of hilarity and shock. The room is full of dazzle, flashing lights, loud crackling noises. It looks like Chinese New Year. Iris's presence has already been forgotten. The Clockwork waiter believes she belongs, while the partygoers accept her as someone who just happened to be there when the celebration began, nothing more.

"I'm electric," Iris says to Chip, her eyes wondering.

"Welcome to the club," he tells her.

8.

As the Sparklefroth begins to wear off, Iris turns from the crowd of girls to watch the sun slip out of the sky. The low-voltage drink has left her frizzy-haired and frazzled, keyed up in a way that is not entirely pleasant. It's the little girls in their Hideware. "Pampered bitches" is the phrase that comes to mind. Who buys thousand-token new faces for *children*?

The Hideware is a delicate, transparent mask that disappears when it adheres to the skin. New faces have moods, not features, and a person sees his or her own psychological projections. The birthday girl wears Girl-Next-Door. Iris knows it, because at one glimpse of her slightly upturned nose and her wry, knowing eyes, Iris felt almost overwhelmed by a desire to ask her something about sports. There's a girl in Celebrity, another wearing Copy-My-Homework, a Tell-Me-Anything, a Zen Sunrise. If Celebrity comes over to her, Iris will probably ask her to autograph her boob. The great pleasure of Hideware is the opportunities it gives you to humiliate others.

"Do you see them all? In their awful new faces?"

"Why awful?" Chip asks.

"They're awful because I don't have one. They're awful because I'm sixteen, and a sixteen-year-old shouldn't envy a twelve-year-old."

A face appears in the window next to hers, the ghostly reflection of a girl with bushy red hair and big ears. When Iris glances at her, she discovers that the redhead is wearing Tell-Me-Anything. Iris knows because she is seized by a sudden desire to blurt out the truth, that she lied about being part of their group so she could get a free glass of Sparklefroth. She quickly directs her stare back to the clouds, a turmoil of red and gold smoke.

"The sun is pretty dumb, huh?" says Tell-Me-Anything. "I mean, *so* it's really there. So what?"

"Boring," Iris agrees. "Maybe if it *did* something. But it just floats there making light."

"Yeah. I wish it was hot enough to set fire to something."

"Like what?"

"Like *anything*. The clouds. Some birds or something. Oh, *well*. After we get done with the stupid *scenic* part of the party we'll have fun. After the stars come out, we get to ride in Drop Bubbles. I know a secret about you." She says this last with no change in tone and waits with a sly smile for Iris to register it. Tell-Me-Anything continues, "The waiter thinks you're part of our group. He asked if I wanted to bring you a slice of cake, and he called you Ms. Paget, but you aren't Sydney Paget. She's at a funeral. She couldn't be here today. Here's your cake." She offers a saucer with a tiny round chocolate cake on it.

Iris accepts. She thinks, *I'm having cake at the top of the Spoke while the sun goes down, just like I wanted.* It is, oddly, even more delicious knowing she doesn't belong.

"Are you going to ride down in a Drop Bubble? Sydney's bubble is all paid for."

"I guess if no one is using it," Iris says cautiously.

"But if I *tell*, they won't let you. What will you give me not to tell?"

A bite of cake sticks in Iris's throat. It requires a conscious effort for her to swallow.

"Why would they let a Drop Bubble go to waste if it's paid for?"

"They're expensive. They're *so* expensive. Mr. Danforth is going to ask about a refund when he goes downstairs. But if you wait and go right after us, you could float down and land and walk out before he can get his money back. He has to talk to customer service, and it's a really long line. What would you do to keep me from telling?"

Iris hums to herself. "Tell you what, kid. Want a mermaid?" Lifting the aquaball under one arm to show it off.

The redhead wrinkles her nose. "Ugh. No thank you."

"What then?" Iris asks, not sure why she's indulging her pint-size extortionist.

"Have you ever seen a sunset before? A real one?"

"No. I've never been above the clouds before."

"Good. You aren't going to see this one either. You have to miss it. That's the deal. Liars don't get to have all the goodies. If you want a free ride in a Drop Bubble, you have to close your eyes until I say. You have to miss the last of the sunset."

Cake sits in Iris's stomach like a lump of wet concrete. She opens her mouth to tell the little blackmailer to take a long walk out an open window.

Chip speaks first. "I have an alternative suggestion. I have recorded this conversation. How about we play it for Mr. Danforth? I wonder how he'll feel about you tossing around threats and trying to cheat him out of his refund."

Tell-Me-Anything totters back a step, blinking rapidly. "No," she says. "You wouldn't. I'm only twelve. You wouldn't do that to a twelve-year-old. I'd cry."

Iris turns and for the first time looks Tell-Me-Anything right in her false new face, lets herself be swept up by the full psychotropic force of her mask.

"If there's one thing prettier than a sunset," Iris says, "it's seeing little shits cry."

9.

The clouds shimmer, piles of golden silk. Chip registers 1,032 variations in the light, ranging from canary to a hue the color of blood stirred into cream. There are shades here he's never witnessed, lighting up optic sensors that have not been tested since he was assembled in Taiwan. They watch until the sun drops into the slot of the horizon and is gone.

"I'm glad I got to see this. I'll never forget it," he tells Iris.

"Do you ever forget anything?"

"No."

"You saved my ass from a twelve-year-old supervillain. I owe you."

"No," he says. "I owe *you*. Twenty more minutes, to be exact."

A scattering of ancient stars fleck the gathering darkness. Chip knows all their names, although he has never directly seen any of them before.

The Clockwork waiter comes clitter-clattering from behind the bar on his cricket legs. A brass hatch opens in the floor, panels sliding away in a manner that suggests an iris widening in the dark. A quivering membrane fills the opening, an oily rainbow slick of light flashing across its surface.

"Who's ready to step into a dream and float back to earth?" cries the Clockwork waiter, gesturing with spindly arms. "Who's big enough and thirteen years old enough to go first?"

Girls scream *me me me me me me!* Chip observes Iris wrinkling her nose in disgust.

"How about the birthday girl? Abigail Danforth, step on up!"

The kid in the Girl-Next-Door face grabs her father's hand and hauls him to the edge of the hole. The girl hops up and down with excitement while Dad gazes uneasily over the rim of the open hatch.

"Step right onto the Drop Bubble surface. There is no reason for anxiety. The bubble will not pop, or we pledge to refund your money to your next of kin," the Clockwork waiter says.

Dad tests the quivering, transparent membrane with the toe of a polished loafer, and it yields slightly underfoot. He pulls his leg back, upper lip damp with sweat. The daughter, impatient to go, leaps into the center of the open hole. Immediately the glossy, glassy, semiliquid floor under her begins to sink.

"Come on, Dad, come on!"

And probably because she has a Girl-Next-Door face on and no one likes to look nervous in front of the Girl-Next-Door, Dad steps onto the soap-bubble floor beside her.

The ground sags beneath them. They sink slowly and steadily downward. Dad's eyes widen as the open hatch rises to his chest. He almost looks like he wants to grab the rim and pull himself back up. The girl hops up and down, trying to speed things along. The glassy soap bubble continues to expand, and Dad sinks out of sight. A moment later the Drop Bubble separates from the hatch and a trembling sheet of iridescent soapy stuff fills the opening once again.

"Who's next?" the Clockwork asks, and they leap and wave their hands, and the waiter begins arranging them into a line. The girl wearing Tell-Me-Anything casts a haunted, angry look over at Iris and Chip. Iris turns to face the night once more.

The sky is lit with stars, but Iris appears to be regarding her own reflection.

"Do you think I'm pretty?" she asks. "Please be honest. I don't want flattery. How do I measure up?"

"You're not bad."

One corner of her mouth twitches upward. "Give me the math, robot."

"The distance between your pupils and your mouth conforms closely to the golden ratio, which means you're a honey. Because of the way you cut your hair, few would ever notice that your left ear is a centimeter higher than ideal."

"Mm. That *does* make me sound smokin' hot. The firm that employed my dad already let me know they'd hire me the day I turn eighteen. I guess pretty girls are the most popular victims. They can earn five times what men earn. They can make a killing."

Chip can see more than a thousand gradients of color, but when it comes to emotion, he is color-blind, and knows it. Her statement suggests she's seeking praise, but other indicators imply dismay, irony, confusion, and self-hate. Absent a clear cue, he remains silent.

"Ms. Paget?" comes a modulated, electronic voice, and Iris turns. The Clockwork waiter stands behind them. "You're the only one left. Would you like to float back to the world below?"

"Can I take my friend?" Iris asks.

The Clockwork and Chip glance at each other and share a few megabytes of data in a quantum burst.

"Yes," the Clockwork waiter says. "The Drop Bubble can support up to seven hundred pounds without deformation. Your chance of dying accidentally remains one in one hundred and twelve thousand."

"Good," Iris tells him. "Because in my family no one dies without getting paid for it."

10.

They fall slowly into darkness.

The bubble, almost twelve feet in diameter, detaches and begins to spin lazily down through the gloom. Iris and Chip are standing when the Drop Bubble lets go of the hatch, but not for long. Iris's knees knock, not from fright but because her legs are so wobbly on the slippery-stretchy material under her feet. She loses her balance and plops onto her butt.

It is difficult to imagine Chip off-balance. He crosses his ankles and carefully sits across from her.

Iris leans forward to look through the glassy bottom of their bubble. She sees other bubbles, spread out below, floating here and there. Blue will-o'-the-wisps drift among them, constellations of bobbing, hovering lights: swarms of drones the size of wasps, armed with sapphire LEDs.

"This was just what I wanted for my birthday—only I was going to come here with my family and friends," Iris says. She cradles the aquaball in her lap, turning it absentmindedly in her hands. "I'm glad I didn't now. Those little girls were gross. That little creep playing her smug power games, trying to blackmail me. All of them casting spells on one another with their overpriced Hideware. My friends and I are older, but I'm not sure we're any better. Maybe sometimes it's best to experience something alone. Or just with one friend."

"Which is it? Are you alone? Or with a friend?"

The bubble carries them into cool, drifting mists. Birds of shadow dart through the clouds around them.

"To be a friend, you'd have to like me as much as I like you."

"I don't just like you, Iris. Until the meter runs down, I would do almost anything for you."

"That's not the same. That's a program, not a feeling. Clockworks don't feel."

"Just as well," he tells her. "We were talking about the genie in the bottle earlier, remember? Maybe the only way to survive being in the bottle is not to want anything different or better. If I could yearn for things I can't have, I'd go crazy. I'd be one long scream that went on and on for a hundred years, while my face keeps making this smile and I keep saying *Yes, sir, of course, ma'am.* Those girls disgust you because they like cake and parties, but if they *didn't* like it, if they couldn't want it, they'd be no better than me. In seventeen minutes I'll plug back into my charging plate and might not move again for a day, a week, a month. I once spent eleven weeks without collecting a single token. It didn't bother me in the slightest. But can *you* imagine not moving or speaking for eleven weeks?"

"No. I can't imagine it. I wouldn't wish it on my worst enemy." She hugs her knee to her chest. "You're right about one thing. Wanting what you can't have makes people crazy."

They emerge from the thin band of cloud and find

themselves sinking past the birthday girl and her father. The girl has her hands around her father's waist,
and the two of them turn slowly in silent dance, her
head on his chest. Both of them have their eyes closed.

There are only eleven minutes left on Chip's meter
when the bubble touches down in the landing zone: a
cordoned-off area where the floor is all springy green
hexagonal tiles. When the bubble hits those pad-
ded green hexagons, it bursts with a wet *smooch*. Iris
flinches and laughs as she is spattered by a soapy rain.

They were the last to leave the Sun Parlor but the first
to arrive on the ground floor. Iris can see the frizzy redhead in the Tell-Me-Anything mask, about four stories
above them, hands pressed to the wall of her bubble,
glaring down at them. Time to go. Without thinking,
Iris takes Chip's hand and runs. She doesn't realize until
they're outside that she's still laughing.

Fine grains of moisture hang suspended in the air.
She looks up for stars, but of course now that she and
Chip are below the clouds, the sky is its usual murky
blank.

The Monowheel is locked up at a hitching post. Chip
nods toward it.

"I don't have time to carry your Monowheel home for
you now," he says. "I hate to do this, Iris—it's scummy
and mercantile—but in thirty seconds an automatic

advertisement will play, inviting you to insert another coin. That's not something I choose to do. It exists outside my executive functions."

"I'll walk you back to your charging plate," Iris tells him, as if he'd said nothing. "We can say good night there. Leave the Monowheel. I'll get it later."

She still holds her hand in his. They walk, in no hurry now.

At the far end of the plaza, he cries out in a sudden, loud, falsely cheerful voice, "If you're having a good time, why should the fun stop here? It's just one slim coin for another thirty minutes of devotion! What do you say, Iris, old pal?"

He falls silent.

They cross the street and travel almost another block before he speaks again.

"You didn't find that distasteful?"

"No. It didn't bother me. What *will* bother me is if you pretend to feel regrets we both know you can't feel."

"I don't regret it. Regret is an inversion of desire, and it's true, I don't want things. But I can tell when a musician strikes the wrong note."

They have reached his corner. His meter has less than four minutes on it.

"I'll let you make it up to me," she says.

"Please."

"You were a good birthday gift, Chip. You carried me to the top of the Spoke. You gave me the sun and the stars. You saved me from blackmail, and you floated down to earth with me. For an hour you gave me back the life I had before my father got hurt." She leans toward him and kisses his cold mouth. It feels like kissing her reflection in the mirror.

"Did that make it up to you?" he asks.

She smiles. "Not quite. One more thing. Come with me."

He follows her past his charging plate and up onto the overpass. They climb the slight slope of the bridge until they're over the rails. She straddles the wide stone balustrade, one leg hanging over the tracks, one leg over the sidewalk, the aquaball in her lap.

"Chip. Will you climb up here and drop this thing in front of the next train? I'm not sure I can time it correctly. They're so fast."

"The mermaid was a gift from your father."

"It is. It was. And he meant well. But when I look at it, I feel like I'm looking at *him:* this helpless thing, trapped in a little space, that isn't good to anyone anymore and won't ever be free again. Every time I look at it, this ugly fish is going to remind me my dad won't ever be free again, and I don't want to think of him that way."

Chip climbs onto the balustrade and sits with both

feet hanging over the rails. "All right, Iris. If it will make you feel better."

"It will make me less sad. That's something, isn't it?"

"It is."

A faint, whistling, bottle-rocket sound begins to rise in the night, the next cannon-train coming toward them.

"You remind me of him, you know," Iris says.

"Your father?"

"Yes. He's as devoted to me as you are. In some ways you were filling in for him tonight. I was supposed to have the stars with him. I had them with you instead."

"Iris, the train is almost here. You should give me the aquaball."

She turns the glass globe over and over in her hands, does not offer it to him.

"You know how else you're like my father?" she says.

"How?"

"He used to die, every day, so I could have the things I wanted," she says. "And now it's your turn." And she puts her hand on Chip's back and shoves.

He drops.

The cannon-train punches through the darkness with a concussive boom.

By the time she carries the aquaball down the embankment, the train is long gone, rattling off into the south, leaving behind a smell like hot pennies.

Chip has been all but obliterated. She finds one of his ceramic hands on the blackened pebbles, a few feet from the rails, discovers shreds of his wool coat, still smoldering, among some slick, damp weeds. She spies a black diamond of battered plasteel—Chip's heart—and is able to pry the battery out of it. It is, miraculously, intact and should slot right into her Monowheel.

Tokens gleam between the rails, across the rocks. It almost seems there are as many silver coins on the ground as there were stars above the Spoke. She collects them until her fingers are so cold she can't feel them anymore.

On the walk back to the embankment, she kicks something that looks like a cracked serving plate. She picks it up and finds herself staring into Chip's blank smiling face and empty eye sockets. After a rare moment of indecision, she sticks it chin down in the soft gravel, planting it like a shovel. She leaves the aquaball next to it. She has no use for the kind of ugly, helpless thing born to live its life trapped in a bottle or a ball for the amusement of others. She has no use for victims. She intends never to be one herself.

She scrambles up the slope, grabbing brush to pull herself along, thinking that if she hurries, she can get to a RebootYu and buy some used Hideware before she has to meet her friends in the Carnival District. She collected seven hundred tokens in all, which might even be enough for a used Ophelia. And if that jealous bitch Joyce Brilliant thinks Iris is going to let her borrow it, she's got another think coming.

In another minute the mermaid is alone. It swims disconsolately out of the murk to gaze through the side of the aquaball at Chip's easy smile and empty eyes.

In a small, warbling voice, the pitiful creature inside the glass sphere begins to trill. Her song—a low-pitched, unearthly dirge, like the forlorn cries of the whales that have long been extinct—has no words. Perhaps there never are for grief.

Thumbprint

The first thumbprint came in the mail.

Mal was eight months back from Abu Ghraib, where she had done things she regretted. She had returned to Hammett, New York, just in time to bury her father. He died ten hours before her plane touched down in the States, which was maybe all for the best. After the things she had done, she wasn't sure she could've looked him in the eye. Although a part of her had wanted to talk to him about it and to see in his face how he judged her. Without him there was no one to hear her story, no one whose judgment mattered.

The old man had served, too, in Vietnam, as a medic. Her father had saved lives, jumped from a helicopter and dragged kids out of the paddy grass, under heavy

404 · FULL THROTTLE

fire. He called them kids, although he had been only twenty-five himself at the time. He'd been awarded a Purple Heart and a Silver Star.

They hadn't been offering Mal any medals when they sent her on her way. At least she hadn't been identifiable in any of the photographs of Abu Ghraib—just her boots in that one shot Graner took, with the men piled naked on top of each other, a pyramid of stacked ass and hanging sac. If Graner had just tilted the camera up a little, Mal would have been headed home a lot sooner, only it would have been in handcuffs.

She got back her old job at the Milky Way, keeping bar, and moved into her father's house. It was all he had to leave her, that and the car. The old man's ranch was set three hundred yards from Hatchet Hill Road, backed against the town woods. In the fall Mal ran in the forest, wearing a full ruck, three miles through the evergreens.

She kept the M4A1 in the downstairs bedroom, broke it down and put it together every morning, a job she could complete by the count of twelve. When she was done, she put the components back in their case with the bayonet, cradling them neatly in their foam cutouts—you didn't attach the bayonet unless you were about to be overrun. Her M4 had come back to the U.S. with a civilian contractor, who brought it with him on his company's private jet. He had been an interrogator for hire—there'd been a lot of them at Abu Ghraib in the final months before the arrests—and he said it was the least he could do, that she had earned it for services rendered, a statement that left her cold.

Come one night in November, Mal walked out of the Milky Way with John Petty, the other bartender, and they found Glen Kardon passed out in the front seat of his Saturn. The driver's-side door was open, and Glen's butt was in the air, his legs hanging from the car, feet twisted in the gravel, as if he had just been clubbed to death from behind.

Not even thinking, she told Petty to keep an eye out, and then Mal straddled Glen's hips and dug out his wallet. She helped herself to a hundred and twenty dollars cash, dropped the wallet back on the passenger-side seat. Petty hissed at her to hurry the fuck up, while Mal wiggled the wedding ring off Glen's finger.

"His wedding ring?" Petty asked when they were in her car together. Mal gave him half the money for being her lookout but kept the ring for herself. "Jesus, you're a demented bitch."

Petty put his hand between her legs and ground his thumb hard into the crotch of her black jeans while she drove. She let him do that for a while, his other hand groping her breast. Then she elbowed him off her.

"That's enough," she said.

"No it isn't."

She reached into his jeans, ran her hand down his hard-on, then took his balls and began to apply pressure until he let out a little moan, not entirely of pleasure.

"It's plenty," she said. She pulled her hand from his pants. "You want more than that, you'll have to wake up your wife. Give her a thrill."

Mal let him out of the car in front of his home and peeled away, tires throwing gravel at him.

Back at her father's house, she sat on the kitchen counter, looking at the wedding ring in the cup of her palm. A simple gold band, scuffed and scratched, all the shine dulled out of it. She wondered why she had taken it.

Mal knew Glen Kardon, Glen and his wife, Helen, both. The three of them were the same age, had all gone to school together. Glen had a magician at his tenth-birthday party, who had escaped from handcuffs and a straitjacket as his final trick. Years later Mal would become well acquainted with another escape artist who managed to slip out of a pair of handcuffs, a Ba'athist. Both of his thumbs had been broken, making it possible for him to squeeze out of the cuffs. It was easy if you could bend your thumb in any direction—all you had to do was ignore the pain.

And Helen had been Mal's lab partner in sixth-grade biology. Helen took notes in her delicate cursive, using different-colored inks to brighten up their reports, while Mal sliced things open. Mal liked the scalpel, the way the skin popped apart at the slightest touch of the blade to show what was hidden behind it. She had an instinct for it, always somehow knew just where to put the cut.

Mal shook the wedding ring in one hand for a while and finally dropped it down the sink. She didn't know what to do with it, wasn't sure where to fence it. Had no use for it, really.

When she went down to the mailbox the next morning, she found an oil bill, a real-estate flyer, and a plain white envelope. Inside the envelope was a crisp sheet of typing paper, neatly folded, blank except for a single thumbprint in black ink. The print was a clean impression, and among the whorls and lines was a scar, like a fishhook. There was nothing on the envelope—no stamp, no addresses, no mark of any kind. The postman had not left it.

In her first glance, she knew it was a threat and that whoever had put the envelope in her mailbox might still be watching. Mal felt her vulnerability in the sick clench of her insides and had to struggle against the conditioned impulse to get low and find cover. She looked to either side but saw only the trees, their branches waving in the cold swirl of a light breeze. There was no traffic along the road and no sign of life anywhere.

The whole long walk back to the house, she was aware of a weakness in her legs. She didn't look at the thumbprint again but carried it inside and left it with the other mail on the kitchen counter. She let her shaky legs carry her on into her father's bedroom, her bedroom now. The M4 was in its case in the closet, but her father's .45 automatic was even closer—she slept with it under the pillow—and it didn't need to be assembled. Mal slid the action back to pump a bullet into the chamber. She got her field glasses from her ruck.

Mal climbed the carpeted stairs to the second floor and opened the door into her old bedroom under the eaves. She hadn't been in there since coming home, and the air had a musty, stale quality. A tatty poster of Alan Jackson was stuck up on the inverted slant of the roof. Her dolls—the blue corduroy bear, the pig with the queer silver-button eyes that gave him a look of blindness—were set neatly in the shelves of a bookcase without books.

Her bed was made, but when she went close, she was surprised to find the shape of a body pressed into it, the pillow dented in the outline of someone's head. The idea occurred that whoever had left the thumbprint had been inside the house while she was out, and had taken a nap up here. Mal didn't slow down but stepped straight up onto the mattress, unlocked the window over it, shoved it open, and climbed through.

In another minute she was sitting on the roof, holding the binoculars to her eyes with one hand, the gun in the other. The shingles had warmed in the sun and provided a pleasant ambient heat beneath her. From where she sat on the roof, she could see in every direction.

She remained there for most of an hour, scanning the trees, following the passage of cars along Hatchet Hill Road. Finally she knew she was looking for someone who wasn't there anymore. She hung the binoculars from her neck and leaned back on the hot shingles and closed her eyes. It had been cold down in the driveway, but up on the roof, on the lee side of the house, out of the wind, she was comfortable, a lizard on a rock.

When Mal swung her body back into the bedroom, she sat for a while on the sill, holding the gun in both hands and considering the impression of a human body on her blankets and pillow. She picked up the pillow and pressed her face into it. Very faintly she could smell a trace of her father, his cheap corner-store cigars, the waxy tang of that shit he put in his hair, same stuff Reagan had used. The thought that he had sometimes been up here, dozing in her bed, gave her a little chill. She wished she were still the kind of person who could hug a pillow and weep over what she had lost. But in truth maybe she had never been that kind of person.

When she was back in the kitchen, Mal looked once more at the thumbprint on the plain white sheet of paper. Against all logic or sense, it seemed somehow familiar to her. She didn't like that.

He had been brought in with a broken tibia, the Iraqi everyone called the Professor, but a few hours after they put him in a cast, he was judged well enough to sit for an interrogation. In the early morning, before sunrise, Corporal Plough came to get him.

Mal was working in Block 1A then and went with Anshaw to collect the Professor. He was in a cell with eight other men: sinewy, unshaved Arabs, most of them dressed in Fruit of the Loom jockey shorts and nothing else. Some others, who had been uncooperative with CI, had been given pink-flowered panties to wear. The panties fit more snugly than the jockeys, which were all extra large and baggy. The prisoners skulked in the gloom of their stone chamber, giving Mal looks so feverish and sunken-eyed they appeared deranged. Glancing in at them, Mal didn't know whether to laugh or flinch.

"Walk away from the bars, women," she said in her clumsy Arabic. "Walk away." She crooked her finger at the Professor. "You. Come to here."

He hopped forward, one hand on the wall to steady himself. He wore a hospital johnny, and his left leg was in a cast from ankle to knee. Anshaw had brought a pair of aluminum crutches for him. Mal and Anshaw were coming to the end of a twelve-hour shift, in a week of twelve-hour shifts. Escorting the prisoner to CI with Corporal Plough would be their last job of the night. Mal was twitchy from all the Vivarin in her system, so much she could hardly stand still. When she looked at lamps, she saw rays of hard-edged, rainbow-shot light emanating from them, as if she were peering through crystal.

The night before, a patrol had surprised some men planting an IED in the red, hollowed-out carcass of a German shepherd, on the side of the road back to Baghdad. The bombers scattered, yelling, from the spotlights on the Hummers, and a contingent of men went after them.

An engineer named Leeds stayed behind to have a look at the bomb inside the dog. He was three steps from the animal when a cell phone went off inside the dog's bowels, three bars of "Oops! . . . I Did It Again." The dog ruptured in a belch of flame and with a heavy thud that people standing thirty feet away could feel in the marrow of their bones. Leeds dropped to his knees, holding his face, smoke coming out from under his gloves. The first soldier to get to him said his face peeled off like a cheap black rubber mask that had been stuck to the sinew beneath with rubber cement.

Not long after, the patrol grabbed the Professor—so named because of his horn-rimmed glasses and because he insisted he was a teacher—two blocks from the site of the explosion. He broke his leg jumping off a high berm, running away after the soldiers fired over his head and ordered him to halt.

Now the Professor lurched along on the crutches, Mal and Anshaw flanking him and Plough walking behind. They made their way out of 1A and into the predawn morning. The Professor paused, beyond the doors, to take a breath. That was when Plough kicked the left crutch out from under his arm.

The Professor went straight down and forward with a cry, his johnny flapping open to show the soft paleness of his ass. Anshaw reached to help him back up. Plough said to leave him.

"Sir?" Anshaw asked. Anshaw was just nineteen. He had been over as long as Mal, but his skin was oily and white, as if he had never been out of his chemical suit.

"Did you see him swing that crutch at me?" Plough asked Mal.

Mal did not reply but watched to see what would happen next. She had spent the last two hours bouncing on her heels, chewing her fingernails down to the skin, too wired to stop moving. Now, though, she felt stillness spreading through her, like a drop of ink in water, calming her restless hands, her nervous legs.

Plough bent over and pulled the string at the back of the johnny, unknotting it so it fell off the Professor's shoulders and down to his wrists. His ass was spotted with dark moles and relatively hairless. His sac was drawn tight to his perineum. The Professor glanced up over his shoulder, his eyes too large in his face, and spoke rapidly in Arabic.

"What's he saying?" Plough asked. "I don't speak Sand Nigger."

"He said don't," Mal answered, translating automatically. "He says he hasn't done anything. He was picked up by accident."

Plough kicked away the other crutch. "Get those."

Anshaw picked up the crutches.

Plough put his boot in the Professor's fleshy ass and shoved.

"Get going. Tell him get going."

A pair of MPs walked past, turned their heads to look at the Professor as they went by. He was trying to cover his crotch with one hand, but Plough kicked him in the ass again, and he had to start crawling. His crawl was awkward stuff, what with his left leg sticking out straight in its cast and the bare foot dragging in the dirt.

One of the MPs laughed, and then they moved away into the night.

The Professor struggled to pull his johnny up onto his shoulders as he crawled, but Plough stepped on it and it tore away.

"Leave it. Tell him leave it and hurry up."

Mal told him. The prisoner couldn't look at her. He looked at Anshaw instead and began pleading with him, asking for something to wear and saying his leg hurt while Anshaw stared down at him, eyes bulging, as if he were choking on something. Mal wasn't surprised that the Professor was addressing Anshaw instead of her. Part of it was a cultural thing. The Arabs couldn't cope with being humiliated in front of a woman. But also Anshaw had something about him that signified to others, even the enemy, that he was approachable. In spite of the nine-millimeter strapped to his outer thigh, he gave an impression of stumbling, unthreatening cluelessness. In the barracks he blushed when other guys were ogling centerfolds; he often could be seen praying during heavy mortar attacks.

The prisoner had stopped crawling once more. Mal poked the barrel of her M4 in the Professor's ass to get him going again, and the Iraqi jerked, gave a shrill sort of sob. Mal didn't mean to laugh, but there was something funny about the convulsive clench of his butt cheeks, something that sent a rush of blood to her head. Her blood was racy and strange with Vivarin, and watching the prisoner's ass bunch up like that was the most hilarious thing she had seen in weeks.

The Professor crawled past the wire fence, along the edge of the road. Plough told Mal to ask him where his friends were now, his friends who blew up the American GI. He said if the Professor would tell about his friends, he could have his crutches and his johnny back.

The prisoner said he didn't know anything about the IED. He said he ran because other men were running and soldiers were shooting. He said he was a teacher of literature, that he had a little girl. He said he had taken his twelve-year-old to Disneyland Paris once.

"He's fucking with us," Plough said. "What's a professor of literature doing out at two A.M. in the worst part of town? Your queer-fuck bin Laden friends blew the face right off an American GI, a good man, a man with a pregnant wife back home. Where do your friends— Mal, make him understand he's going to tell us where his friends are hiding. Let him know it would be better to tell us now, before we get where we're going. Let him know this is the easy part of his day. CI wants this motherfucker good and soft before we get him there."

Mal nodded, her ears buzzing. She told the Professor he didn't have a daughter, because he was a known homosexual. She asked him if he liked the barrel of her gun in his ass, if it excited him. She said, "Where is the house of your partners who make the dogs into bombs? Where is your homosexual friends go after murdering Americans with their trick dogs? Tell me if you don't want the gun in the hole of your ass."

"I swear by the life of my little girl I don't know who those other men were. Please. My child is named Alaya. She is ten years old. There was a picture of her in my pants. Where are my pants? I will show you."

She stepped on his hand and felt the bones compress unnaturally under her heel. He shrieked.

"Tell," she said. "Tell."

"I can't."

A steely clashing sound caught Mal's attention. Anshaw had dropped the crutches. He looked green, and his hands were hooked into claws, raised almost but not quite to cover his ears.

"You okay?" she asked.

"He's lying," Anshaw said. Anshaw's Arabic was not as good as hers, but not bad. "He said his daughter was twelve the first time."

She stared at Anshaw, and he stared back, and while they were looking at each other, there came a high, keening whistle, like air being let out of some giant balloon . . . a sound that made Mal's racy blood feel as if it were fizzing with oxygen, made her feel carbonated inside. She flipped her M4 around to hold it by the barrel in both hands, and when the mortar struck—out beyond the perimeter but still hitting hard enough to cause the earth to shake underfoot—she drove the butt of the gun straight down into the Professor's broken leg, clubbing at it as if she were trying to drive a stake into the ground. Over the shattering thunder of the exploding mortar, not even Mal could hear him screaming.

Mal pushed herself hard on her Friday-morning run, out in the woods, driving herself up Hatchet Hill, reaching ground so steep she was really climbing, not running. She kept going until she was short of breath and the sky seemed to spin, as if it were the roof of a carousel.

When she finally paused, she felt faint. The wind breathed in her face, chilling her sweat, a curiously pleasant sensation. Even the feeling of light-headedness, of being close to exhaustion and collapse, was somehow satisfying to her.

The army had her for four years before Mal left to become a part of the reserves. On her second day of basic training, she had done push-ups until she was sick, then was so weak she collapsed in it. She wept in front of others, something she could now hardly bear to remember.

Eventually she learned to like the feeling that came right before collapse: the way the sky got big, and sounds grew far away and tinny, and all the colors seemed to sharpen to a hallucinatory brightness. There was an intensity of sensation when you were on the edge of what you could handle, when you were physically tested and made to fight for each breath, that was somehow exhilarating.

At the top of the hill, Mal slipped the stainless-steel canteen out of her ruck, her father's old camping canteen, and filled her mouth with ice water. The canteen flashed, a silver mirror in the late-morning sun. She poured water onto her face, wiped her eyes with the hem of her T-shirt, put the canteen away, and ran on, ran for home.

She let herself in through the front door, didn't notice the envelope until she stepped on it and heard the crunch of paper underfoot. She stared down at it, her mind blank for one dangerous moment, trying to think who would've come up to the house to slide a bill under the door when it would've been easier to just leave it in the mailbox. But it wasn't a bill, and she knew it.

Mal was framed in the door, the outline of a soldier painted into a neat rectangle, like the human-silhouette targets they shot at on the range. She made no sudden moves, however. If someone meant to shoot her, he would have done it—there had been plenty of time—and if she was being watched, she wanted to show she wasn't afraid.

She crouched, picked up the envelope. The flap was not sealed. She tapped out the sheet of paper inside and unfolded it. Another thumbprint, this one a fat black oval, like a flattened spoon. There was no fishhook-shaped scar on this thumb. This was a different thumb entirely. In some ways that was more unsettling to her than anything.

No—the most unsettling thing was that this time he had slipped his message under her door, while last time he had left it a hundred yards down the road, in the mailbox. It was maybe his way of saying he could get as close to her as he wanted.

Mal thought police but discarded the idea. She had been a cop herself, in the army, knew how cops thought. Leaving a couple thumbprints on unsigned sheets of paper wasn't a crime. It was probably a prank, they would say, and you couldn't waste manpower investigating a prank. She felt now, as she had when she saw the first thumbprint, that these messages were not the perverse joke of some local snotnose but a malicious promise, a warning to be on guard. Yet it was an irrational feeling, unsupported by any evidence. It was soldier knowledge, not cop knowledge.

Besides, when you called the cops, you never knew what you were going to get. There were cops like her out there. People you didn't want getting too interested in you.

She balled up the thumbprint, took it onto the porch. Mal cast her gaze around, scanning the bare trees, the straw-colored weeds at the edge of the woods. She stood there for close to a minute. Even the trees were perfectly still, no wind to tease their branches into motion, as if the whole world were in a state of suspension, waiting to see what would happen next—only nothing happened next.

She left the balled-up paper on the porch railing, went back inside, and got the M4 from the closet. Mal sat on the bedroom floor, assembling and disassembling it, three times, twelve seconds each time. Then she set the parts back in the case with the bayonet and slid it under her father's bed.

Two hours later Mal ducked down behind the bar at the Milky Way to rack clean glasses. They were fresh from the dishwasher and so hot they burned her fingertips. When she stood up with the empty tray, Glen Kardon was on the other side of the counter, staring at her with red-rimmed, watering eyes. He looked in a kind of stupor, his face puffy, his comb-over disheveled, as if he had just stumbled out of bed.

"I need to talk to you about something," he said. "I was trying to think if there was some way I could get my wedding ring back. Any way at all."

All the blood seemed to rush from Mal's brain, as if she had stood up too quickly. She lost some of the feeling in her hands, too, and for a moment her palms were overcome with a cool, almost painful tingling.

She wondered why he hadn't arrived with cops, whether he meant to give her some kind of chance to settle the matter without the involvement of the police. She wanted to say something to him, but there were no words for this. She could not remember the last time she had felt so helpless, had been caught so exposed, in such indefensible terrain.

Glen went on. "My wife spent the morning crying about it. I heard her in the bedroom, but when I tried to go in and talk to her, the door was locked. She wouldn't let me in. She tried to play it off like she was all right, talking to me through the door. She told me to go to work, don't worry. It was her father's wedding ring, you know. He died three months before we got married. I guess that sounds a little—what do you call it? Oedipal. Like in marrying me she was marrying Daddy. Oedipal isn't right, but you know what I'm saying. She loved that old man."

Mal nodded.

"If they only took the money, I'm not sure I even would've told Helen. Not after I got so drunk. I drink too much. Helen wrote me a note a few months ago, about how much I've been drinking. She wanted to know if it was because I was unhappy with her. It would be easier if she was the kind of woman who'd just scream at me. But I got drunk like that, and the wedding ring she gave me that used to belong to her daddy is gone, and all she did was hug me and say thank God they didn't hurt me."

Mal said, "I'm sorry." She was about to say she would give it all back, ring and money both, and go with him to the police if he wanted—then caught herself. He had said "they": "If *they* only took the money" and "*they* didn't hurt me." Not "you."

Glen reached inside his coat and took out a white business envelope, stuffed fat. "I been sick to my stomach all day at work, thinking about it. Then I thought I could put up a note here in the bar. You know, like one of these flyers you see for a lost dog. Only for my lost ring. The guys who robbed me must be customers here. What else would they have been doing down in that lot, that hour of the night? So next time they're in, they'll see my note."

She stared. It took a few moments for what he'd said to register. When it did—when she understood he had no idea she was guilty of anything—she was surprised to feel an odd twinge of something like disappointment.

"Electra," she said.

"Huh?"

"A love thing between father and daughter," Mal said. "Is an Electra complex. What's in the envelope?"

He blinked. Now he was the one who needed some processing time. Hardly anyone knew or remembered that Mal had been to college, on Uncle Sam's dime. She had learned Arabic there and psychology too, although in the end she had wound up back here behind the bar of the Milky Way without a degree. The plan had been to collect her last few credits after she got back from Iraq, but sometime during her tour she had ceased to give a fuck about the plan.

At last Glen came mentally unstuck and replied, "Money. Five hundred dollars. I want you to hold on to it for me."

"Explain."

"I was thinking what to say in my note. I figure I should offer a cash reward for the ring. But whoever stole the ring isn't ever going to come up to me and admit it. Even if I promise not to prosecute, they wouldn't believe me. So I figured out what I need is a middleman. This is where you come in. So the note would say to bring Mallory Grennan the ring and she'll give you the reward money, no questions asked. It'll say they can trust you not to tell me or the police who they are. People know you. I think most folks around here will believe that." He pushed the envelope at her.

"Forget it, Glen. No one is bringing that ring back."

"Let's see. Maybe they were drunk, too, when they took it. Maybe they feel remorse."

She laughed.

He grinned, awkwardly. His ears were pink. "It's possible."

She looked at him a moment longer, then put the envelope under the counter. "Okay. Let's write your note. I can copy it on the fax machine. We'll stick it up around the bar, and after a week, when no one brings you your ring, I'll give you your money back and a beer on the house."

"Maybe just a ginger ale," Glen said.

Glen had to go, but Mal promised she'd hang a few flyers in the parking lot. She had just finished taping them up to the streetlamps when she spotted a sheet of paper, folded into thirds and stuck under the windshield wiper of her father's car.

The thumbprint on this one was delicate and slender,

an almost perfect oval, feminine in some way, while the first two had been squarish and blunt. Three thumbs, each of them different from the others.

She pitched it at a wire garbage can attached to a telephone pole, hit the three-pointer, got out of there.

The Eighty–second had finally arrived at Abu Ghraib, to provide force protection and try to nail the fuckers who were mortaring the prison every night. Early in the fall, they began conducting raids in the town around the prison. The first week of operations, they had so many patrols out and so many raids going that they needed backup, so General Karpinski assigned squads of MPs to accompany them. Corporal Plough put in for the job and, when he was accepted, told Mal and Anshaw they were coming with him.

Mal was glad. She wanted away from the prison, the dark corridors of 1A and 1B, with their smell of old wet rock, urine, flop sweat. She wanted away from the tent cities that held the general prison population, the crowds pressed against the chain-links who pleaded with her as she walked along the perimeter, black flies crawling on their faces. She wanted to be in a Hummer with open sides, night air rushing in over her. Destination: any-fucking-where else on the planet.

In the hour before dawn, the platoon they had been tacked onto hit a private home, set within a grove of palms, a white stucco wall around the yard and a wrought-iron gate across the drive. The house was stucco, too, and had a swimming pool out back, a patio and grill, wouldn't have looked out of place in SoCal. Delta Team drove their Hummer right through the gate, which went down with a hard metallic bang, hinges shearing out of the wall with a spray of plaster.

That was all Mal saw of the raid. She was behind the wheel of a two-and-a-half-ton troop transport for carrying prisoners. No Hummer for her, and no action either. Anshaw had another truck. She listened for gunfire, but there was none, the residents giving up without a struggle.

When the house was secure, Corporal Plough left them, said he wanted to size up the situation. What he wanted to do was get his picture taken chewing on a stogie and holding his gun, with his boot on the neck of a hog-tied insurgent. She heard over the walkie-talkie that they had grabbed one of the Fedayeen Saddam, a Ba'athist lieutenant, and had found weapons, files, personnel information. There was a lot of cornpone whoop-ass on the radio. Everyone in the Eighty-second looked like Eminem—blue eyes, pale blond hair in a crew cut—and talked like one of the Duke boys.

Just after sunup, when the shadows were leaning long away from the buildings on the east side of the street, they brought the Fedayeen out and left him on the narrow sidewalk with Plough. The insurgent's wife was still inside the building, soldiers watching her while she packed a bag.

The Fedayeen was a big Arab with hooded eyes and a three-day shadow on his chin, and he wasn't saying anything except "Fuck you" in American. In the basement, Delta Team had found racked AK-47s and a table covered in maps, marked all over with symbols, numbers, Arabic letters. They discovered a folder of photographs, featuring U.S. soldiers in the act of establishing checkpoints, rolling barbed wire across different roads. There was also a picture in the folder of George Bush Sr., smiling a little foggily, posing with Steven Seagal.

Plough was worried that the pictures showed places and people the insurgents planned to strike. He had already been on the radio a couple times, back to base, talking with CI about it in a strained, excited voice. He was especially upset about Steven Seagal. Everyone in Plough's unit had been made to watch *Above the Law* at least once, and Plough claimed to have seen it more than a hundred times. After they brought the prisoner out, Plough stood over the Fedayeen, yelling at him and sometimes swatting him upside the head with Seagal's rolled-up picture. The Fedayeen said, "More fuck you."

Mal leaned against the driver's-side door of her truck for a while, wondering when Plough would quit hollering and swatting the prisoner. She had a Vivarin hangover, and her head hurt. Eventually she decided he wouldn't be done yelling until it was time to load up and go, and that might not be for another hour.

She left Plough yelling, walked over the flattened gate and up to the house. She let herself into the cool of the kitchen. Red tile floor, high ceilings, lots of windows so the place was filled with sunlight. Fresh bananas in a glass bowl. Where did they get fresh bananas? She helped herself to one and ate it on the toilet, the cleanest toilet she had sat on in a year.

She came back out of the house and started down to the road again. On the way there, she put her fingers in her mouth and sucked on them. She hadn't brushed her teeth in a week, and her breath had a human stink on it.

When she returned to the street, Plough had stopped swatting the prisoner long enough to catch his breath. The Ba'athist looked up at him from under his heavy-lidded eyes. He snorted and said, "Is talk. Is boring. You are no one. I say fuck you still no one."

Mal sank to one knee in front of him, put her fingers

under his nose, and said in Arabic, "Smell that? That is the cunt of your wife. I fucked her myself like a lesbian, and she said it was better than your cock."

The Ba'athist tried to lunge at her from his knees, making a sound down in his chest, a strangled growl of rage, but Plough caught him across the chin with the stock of his M4. The sound of the Ba'athist's jaw snapping was as loud as a gunshot.

He lay on his side, twisted into a fetal ball. Mal remained crouched beside him.

"Your jaw is broken," Mal said. "Tell me about the photographs of the U.S. soldiers and I will bring a no-more-hurt pill."

It was half an hour before she went to get him the painkillers, and by then he'd told her when the pictures had been taken, coughed up the name of the photographer.

Mal was leaning into the back of her truck, digging in the first-aid kit, when Anshaw's shadow joined hers at the rear bumper.

"Did you really do it?" Anshaw asked her. The sweat on him glowed with an ill sheen in the noonday light. "The wife?"

"What? Fuck no. Obviously."

"Oh," Anshaw said, and swallowed convulsively. "Someone said . . ." he began, and then his voice trailed off.

"What did someone say?"

He glanced across the road, at two soldiers from the Eighty-second, standing by their Hummer. "One of the guys who was in the building said you marched right in and bent her over. Facedown on the bed."

She looked over at Vaughan and Henrichon, holding their M16s and struggling to contain their laughter. She flipped them the bird.

"Jesus, Anshaw. Don't you know when you're being fucked with?"

His head was down. He stared at his own scarecrow shadow, tilting into the back of the truck.

"No," he said.

Two weeks later Anshaw and Mal were in the back of a different truck, with that same Arab, the Ba'athist, who was being transferred from Abu Ghraib to a smaller prison facility in Baghdad. The prisoner had his head in a steel contraption, to clamp his jaw in place, but he was still able to open his mouth wide enough to hawk a mouthful of spit into Mal's face.

Mal was wiping it away when Anshaw got up and grabbed the Fedayeen by the front of his shirt and heaved him out the back of the truck, into the dirt road. The truck was doing thirty miles an hour at the time and was part of a convoy that included two reporters from MSNBC.

The prisoner survived, although most of his face was flayed off on the gravel, his jaw rebroken, his hands smashed. Anshaw said he leaped out on his own, trying to escape, but no one believed him, and three weeks later Anshaw was sent home.

The funny thing was that the insurgent really did escape, a week after that, during another transfer. He was in handcuffs, but with his thumbs broken he was able to slip his hands right out of them. When the MPs stepped from their Hummer at a checkpoint, to talk porno with some friends, the prisoner dropped out of the back of the transport. It was night. He simply walked into the desert and, as the stories go, was never seen again.

The band took the stage Friday evening and didn't come offstage until Saturday morning. Twenty minutes after one, Mal bolted the door behind the last customer. She started helping Candice wipe down tables, but she had been on since before lunch and Bill Rodier said to go home already.

Mal had her jacket on and was headed out when John Petty poked her in the shoulder with something.

"Mal," he said. "This is yours, right? Your name on it."

She turned. Petty was at the cash register, holding a fat envelope toward her. She took it.

"That the money Glen gave you, to swap for his wedding ring?" Petty turned away from her, shifting his attention back to the register. He pulled out stacks of bills, rubber-banded them, and lined them up on the bar. "That's something. Taking his money and fucking him all over again. If I plop down five hundred bucks will you fuck me just as nice?"

As he spoke, he put his hand back in the register. Mal reached under his elbow and slammed the drawer on his fingers. He squealed. The drawer began to slide open again on its own, but before he could get his mashed fingers out, Mal slammed it once more. He lifted one foot off the floor and did a comic little jig.

"Ohfuckgoddamnyouuglydyke," he said.

"Hey," said Bill Rodier, coming toward the bar carrying a trash barrel. "Hey."

She let Petty get his hand out of the drawer. He stumbled clumsily away from her, struck the bar with his hip, and wheeled to face her, clutching the mauled hand to his chest.

"You crazy bitch! I think you broke my fingers!"

"Jesus, Mal," Bill said, looking over the bar at Petty's hand. His fat fingers had a purple line of bruise across them. Bill turned his questioning gaze back in her direction. "I don't know what the hell John said, but you can't do that to people."

"You'd be surprised what you can do to people," she told him.

Outside, it was drizzling and cold. She was all the way to her car before she felt a weight in one hand and realized she was still clutching the envelope full of cash.

Mal kept on holding it, against the inside of her thigh, the whole drive back. She didn't put on the radio, just drove and listened to the rain tapping on the glass. She had been in the desert for two years, and she had seen it rain just twice during that time, although there was often a moist fog in the morning, a mist that smelled of eggs, of brimstone.

When she enlisted, she had hoped for war. She did not see the point of joining if you weren't going to get to fight. The risk to her life did not trouble her. It was an incentive. You received a two-hundred-dollar-a-month bonus for every month you spent in the combat zone, and a part of her had relished the fact that her own life was valued so cheap. Mal would not have expected more.

But it didn't occur to her, when she first learned she was going to Iraq, that they paid you that money for more than just the risk to your own life. It wasn't just a question of what could happen to you, but also a matter of what you might be asked to do to others. For her two-hundred-dollar bonus, she had left naked and bound men in stress positions for hours and told a nineteen-year-old girl that she would be gang-raped if she did not supply information about her boyfriend. Two hundred dollars a month was what it cost to make a torturer out of her. She felt now that she had been crazy there, that the Vivarin, the ephedra, the lack of sleep, the constant scream-and-thump of the mortars, had made her into someone who was mentally ill, a bad-dream version of herself. Then Mal felt the weight of the envelope against her thigh, Glen Kardon's pay-off, and remembered taking his ring, and it came to her that she was having herself on, pretending she had been someone different in Iraq. Who she'd been then and who she was now were the same person. She had taken the prison home with her. She lived in it still.

Mal let herself into the house, soaked and cold, holding the envelope. She found herself standing in front of the kitchen counter with Glen's money. She could sell him back his own ring for five hundred dollars if she wanted, and it was more than she would get from any pawnshop. She had done worse, for less cash. She stuck her hand down the drain, felt along the wet smoothness of the trap, until her fingertips found the ring.

Mal hooked her ring finger through it, pulled her hand back out. She turned her wrist this way and that, considering how the ring looked on her crooked, blunt finger. *With this I do thee wed.* She didn't know what she'd do with Glen Kardon's five hundred dollars if she swapped it for his ring. It wasn't money she needed. She didn't need his ring either. She couldn't say what it was she needed, but the idea of it was close, a word on the tip of her tongue, maddeningly out of reach.

She made her way to the bathroom, turned on the shower, and let the steam gather while she undressed. Slipping off her black blouse, she noticed she still had the envelope in one hand, Glen's ring on the third finger of the other. She tossed the money next to the bathroom sink, left the ring on.

She glanced at the ring sometimes while she was in the shower. She tried to imagine being married to Glen Kardon, pictured him stretched out on her father's bed in boxers and a T-shirt, waiting for her to come out of the bathroom, his stomach aflutter with the anticipation of some late-night, connubial action. She snorted at the thought. It was as absurd as trying to imagine what her life would've been like if she had become an astronaut.

The washer and dryer were in the bathroom with her. She dug through the Maytag until she found her Curt Schilling T-shirt and a fresh pair of Hanes. She slipped back into the darkened bedroom, toweling her hair, and glanced at herself in the dresser mirror, only she couldn't see her face, because a white sheet of paper had been stuck into the top of the frame and it covered the place where her face belonged. A black thumbprint had been inked in the center. Around the edges of the sheet of paper, she could see reflected in the mirror a man stretched out on the bed, just as she had pictured Glen Kardon stretched out and waiting for her, only in her head Glen hadn't been wearing gray-and-black fatigues.

She lunged to her side, going for the kitchen door. But Anshaw was already moving, launching himself at her, driving his boot into her right knee. The leg twisted in a way it wasn't meant to go, and she felt her ACL pop behind her knee. Anshaw was right behind her by then, and he got a handful of her hair. As she went down, he drove her forward and smashed her head into the side of the dresser.

A black spoke of pain lanced down into her skull, a nail gun fired straight into the brain. She was down and flailing, and he kicked her in the head. That kick didn't hurt so much, but it took the life out of her, as if she were no more than an appliance and he had jerked the power cord out of the wall.

When he rolled her onto her stomach and twisted her arms behind her back, she had no strength in her to resist. He had the heavy-duty plastic ties, the flex cuffs they used on the prisoners in Iraq sometimes. He sat on her ass and squeezed her ankles together and put the flex cuffs on them, too, tightening until it hurt, and then some. Black flashes were still firing behind her eyes, but the fireworks were smaller and exploding less frequently now. She was coming back to herself, slowly. Breathe. Wait.

When her vision cleared, she found Anshaw sitting above her, on the edge of her father's bed. He had lost weight, and he hadn't any to lose. His eyes peeked out, too bright at the bottoms of deep hollows, moonlight reflected in the water at the bottom of a long well. In his lap was a bag, like an old-fashioned doctor's case, the leather pebbled and handsome.

"I observed you while you were running this morning," he began, without preamble. Using the word "observed," like he would in a report on enemy troop movements. "Who were you signaling when you were up on the hill?"

"Anshaw," Mal said. "What are you talking about, Anshaw? What is this?"

"You're staying in shape. You're still a soldier. I tried to follow you, but you outran me on the hill this morning. When you were on the crest, I saw you flashing a light. Two long flashes, one short, two long. You signaled someone. Tell me who."

At first she didn't know what he was talking about;

then she did. Her canteen. Her canteen had flashed in the sunlight when she tipped it up to drink. She opened her mouth to reply, but before she could, he lowered himself to one knee beside her. Anshaw unbuckled his bag and dumped the contents onto the floor. He had a collection of tools: a pair of heavy-duty shears, a Taser, a hammer, a hacksaw, a portable vise. Mixed in with the tools were five or six human thumbs.

Some of the thumbs were thick and blunt and male, and some were white and slender and female, and some were too shriveled and darkened with rot to provide much of any clue about the person they had belonged to. Each thumb ended in a lump of bone and sinew. The inside of the bag had a smell, a sickly-sweet, almost floral stink of corruption.

Anshaw selected the heavy-duty shears.

"You went up the hill and signaled someone this morning. And tonight you came back with a lot of money. I looked in the envelope while you were in the shower. So you signaled for a meeting, and at the meeting you were paid for intel. Who did you meet? CIA?"

"I went to work. At the bar. You know where I work. You followed me there."

"Five hundred dollars. Is that supposed to be tips?"

She didn't have a reply. She couldn't think. She was looking at the thumbs mixed in with his mess of tools.

He followed her gaze, prodded a blackened and shriveled thumb with the blade of the shears. The only identifiable feature remaining on the thumb was a twisted, silvery fishhook scar.

"Plough," Anshaw said. "He had helicopters doing flyovers of my house. They'd fly over once or twice a day. They used different kinds of helicopters on different days to try and keep me from putting two and two together. But I knew what they were up to. I started watching them from the kitchen with my field glasses, and one day I saw Plough at the controls of a radio-station traffic copter. I didn't even know he knew how to pilot a bird until then. He was wearing a black helmet and sunglasses, but I still recognized him."

As Anshaw spoke, Mal remembered Corporal Plough trying to open a bottle of Red Stripe with the blade of his bayonet and the knife slipping, catching him across the thumb, Plough sucking on it and saying around his thumb, *Motherfuck, someone open this for me.*

"No, Anshaw. It wasn't him. It was just someone who looked like him. If he could fly a helicopter, they would've had him piloting Apaches over there."

"Plough admitted it. Not at first. At first he lied.

But eventually he told me everything, that he was in the helicopter, that they'd been keeping me under surveillance ever since I came home." Anshaw moved the tip of the shears to point at another thumb, shriveled and brown, with the texture and appearance of a dried mushroom. "This was his wife. She admitted it, too. They were putting dope in my water to make me sluggish and stupid. Sometimes I'd be driving home and I'd forget what my own house looked like. I'd spend twenty minutes cruising around my development before I realized I'd gone by my place twice."

He paused, moved the tip of the shears to a fresher thumb, a woman's, the nail painted red. "She followed me into a supermarket in Poughkeepsie. This was while I was on my way north, to see you. To see if you had been compromised. This woman in the supermarket, she followed me aisle to aisle, always whispering on her cell phone. Pretending not to look at me. Then, later, I went into a Chinese place and noticed her parked across the street, still on the phone. She was the toughest to get solid information out of. I almost thought I was wrong about her. She told me she was a first-grade teacher. She told me she didn't even know my name and that she wasn't following me. I almost believed her. She had a photo in her purse, of her sitting on the grass with a bunch of little kids. But it was tricked up. They used Photoshop to stick her in that picture. I even got her to admit it in the end."

"Plough told you he could fly helicopters so you wouldn't keep hurting him. The first-grade teacher told you the photo was faked to make you stop. People will tell you anything if you hurt them badly enough. You're having some kind of break with reality, Anshaw. You don't know what's true anymore."

"You *would* say that. You're part of it. Part of the plan to make me crazy, make me kill myself. I thought the thumbprints would startle you into getting in contact with your handler, and they did. You went straight to the hills to send him a signal. To let him know I was close. But where's your backup now?"

"I don't have backup. I don't have a handler."

"We were friends, Mal. You got me through the worst parts of being over there, when I thought I was going crazy. I hate that I have to do this to you. But I need to know who you were signaling. And you're going to tell. Who did you signal, Mal?"

"No one," she said, trying to squirm away from him on her belly.

He grabbed her hair and wrapped it around his fist, to keep her from going anywhere. She felt a tearing along her scalp. He pinned her with a knee in her back. She went still, head turned, right cheek mashed against the nubbly rug on the floor.

"I didn't know you were married. I didn't notice the ring until just tonight. Is he coming home? Is he part of it? Tell me." Tapping the ring on her finger with the blade of the shears.

Mal's face was turned so she was staring under the bed at the case with her M4 and bayonet in it. She had left the clasps undone.

Anshaw clubbed her in the back of the head, at the base of the skull, with the handles of the shears. The world snapped out of focus, went to a soft blur, and then slowly her vision cleared and details regained their sharpness, until at last she was seeing the case under the bed again, not a foot away from her, the silver clasps hanging loose.

"Tell me, Mal. Tell me the truth now."

In Iraq the Fedayeen had escaped the handcuffs after his thumbs were broken. Cuffs wouldn't hold a person whose thumb could move in any direction . . . or someone who didn't have a thumb at all.

Mal felt herself growing calm. Her panic was like static on a radio, and she had just found the volume, was slowly dialing it down. He would not begin with the shears, of course, but would work his way up to them.

He meant to beat her first. At least. She drew a long, surprisingly steady breath. Mal felt almost as if she were back on Hatchet Hill, climbing with all the will and strength she had in her, for the cold, open blue of the sky.

"I'm not married," she said. "I stole this wedding ring off a drunk. I was just wearing it because I like it."

He laughed: a bitter, ugly sound. "That isn't even a good lie."

And another breath, filling her chest with air, expanding her lungs to their limit. He was about to start hurting her. He would force her to talk, to give him information, to tell him what he wanted to hear. She was ready. She was not afraid of being pushed to the edge of what could be endured. She had a high tolerance for pain, and her bayonet was in arm's reach, if only she had an arm to reach.

"It's the truth," she said, and with that, PFC Mallory Grennan began her confession.

The Devil on the Staircase

I was
born in
Sulle Scale
the child of a
common bricklayer.

                                          The
                                      village
                                  of my birth
                                nested in the
                            highest sharpest
                          ridges, high above
                        Positano, and in the
                      cold spring the clouds
                    crawled along the streets
                  like a procession of ghosts.

                         It was eight hundred and twenty
                      steps from Sulle Scale to the world
                      below. I know. I walked them again and
                   again with my father, following his tread,
                from our home in the sky, and then back again.
           After his death I walked them often enough alone.

Up

      and   each

         down   with   step

            carrying   until   it

               freight   seemed as

                                             if the bones

                                          in my knees were

                                       being ground up into

                                       sharp white splinters.

The
cliffs
were mazed
with crooked
staircases, made
from brick in some
places, granite in others.
Marble here, limestone there,
clay tiles, or beams of lumber.
When there were stairs to build my

father built them. When the steps were
washed out by spring rains it fell to him
to repair them. For years he had a donkey to
carry his stone. After it fell dead, he had me.

                                    I
                                hated
                              him of
                           course.
                      He had his
                    cats and he
                sang to them
            and poured them
          saucers of milk and
       told them foolish stories
     and stroked them in his lap
   and when one time I kicked one—
I do not remember why—he kicked me to
  the floor and said not to touch his babies.

So I
carried
his rocks
when I should
have been carrying
schoolbooks, but I cannot
pretend I hated him for that.

I had no use for school, hated to
study, hated to read, felt acutely the
stifling heat of the single room schoolhouse,
the only good thing in it my cousin, Lithodora, who
read to the little children, sitting on a stool with her
back erect, chin lifted high, and her white throat showing.

                               I

                          often

                      imagined

                   her throat

                was as cool as

             the marble altar

           in our church and I

         wanted to rest my brow

       upon it as I had the altar.

     How she read in her low steady

    voice, the very voice you dream of

   calling to you when you're sick, saying

  you will be healthy again and know only the

 sweet fever of her body. I could've loved books

if I had her to read them to me, beside me in my bed.

I
knew
every
step of
the stairs

between Sulle
Scale and Positano,
long flights that dropped
through canyons and descended
into tunnels bored in the limestone,
past orchards and the ruins of derelict
paper mills, past waterfalls and green pools.
I walked those stairs when I slept, in my dreams.

                                          The
                                        trail
                                  my father
                              and I walked
                          most often led
                      past a painted red
                  gate, barring the way
              to a crooked staircase.
          I thought those steps led to
      a private villa and paid the gate
  no mind until the day I paused on the
way down with a load of marble and leaned
on it to rest and it swung open to my touch.
My
father,
he lagged
thirty or so
stairs behind me.

I stepped through the
gate onto the landing to
see where these stairs led.
I saw no villa or vineyard below,
only the staircase falling away from
me down among the sheerest of sheer cliffs.

                                    "Father,"
                            I called out
                        as he came near,
                    the slap of his feet
                echoing off the rocks and
            his breath whistling out of him.
        "Have you ever taken these stairs?"

When
he saw
me standing
inside the gate
he paled and had my
shoulder in an instant.
He hauled me back onto the
main staircase and cried out,
"How did you open the red gate?"

                                    "It was
                            open when
                        I got here,"
                    I said. "Don't

                                                they lead all the
                                              way down to the sea?"
"No."
"But it
looks as if
they go all the
way to the bottom."

                                                        "They go
                                                    farther than
                                                  that," my father
                                              said and he crossed
                                              himself. Then he said
                                            again, "The gate is always
                                          locked." And he stared at me,
                                      the whites of his eyes showing. I
                                  had never seen him look at me so, had
                              never thought I would see him afraid of me.
Lithodora
laughed when
I told her and
said my father was
old and superstitious.
She told me that there was
a tale that the stairs beyond
the painted gate led down to hell.
I had walked the mountain a thousand

times more than Lithodora and wanted to
know how she could know such a story when
I myself had never heard any mention of it.

                                                         She said
the old folks
never spoke of it,
but had put the story
down in a history of the
region, which I would know
if I had ever read any of the
teacher's assignments. I told her
I could never concentrate on books when
she was in the same room with me. She laughed.
But when I tried to touch her throat she flinched.

My
fingers
brushed her
breast instead
and she was angry
and she told me that
I needed to wash my hands.

                  After
my father
died—he was
walking down the
stairs with a load

                                    of tiles when a stray
                                  cat shot out in front of
                                  him and rather than step on
                                it, he stepped into space and
                              fell fifty feet to be impaled upon
                            a tree—I found a more lucrative use
                        for my donkey legs and yardarm shoulders.
                    I entered the employ of Don Carlotta, who kept
                a terraced vineyard in the steeps of Sulle Scale.
I hauled
his wine down
the eight hundred
odd steps to Positano,
where it was sold to a rich
Saracen, a prince it was told,
dark and slender and more fluent
in my language than myself, a clever
young man who knew how to read things:
musical notes, the stars, a map, a sextant.

                                              Once I
                                            stumbled
                                          on a flight
                                        of brick steps
                                      as I was making my
                                    way down with the Don's
                                  wine and a strap slipped and

the crate on my back struck the

cliff wall and a bottle was smashed.

I brought it to the Saracen on the quay.

He said either I drank it or I should have,

for that bottle was worth all I made in a month.

He told me I could consider myself paid and paid well.

He laughed and his white teeth flashed in his black face.

I was

sober when

he laughed at

me but soon enough

had a head full of wine.

Not Don Carlotta's smooth and

peppery red mountain wine but the

cheapest Chianti in the Taverna, which

I drank with a passel of unemployed friends.

Lithodora

found me after

it was dark and she

stood over me, her dark

hair framing her cool, white

beautiful, disgusted, loving face.

She said she had the silver I was owed.

She had told her friend Ahmed that he had

insulted an honest man, that my family traded

in hard labor, not lies, and he was lucky I had not —

"— did
you call
him friend?"
I said. "A monkey
of the desert who knows
nothing of Christ the lord?"

                        The way that
                     she looked at me
                then made me ashamed.
           The way she put the money in
         front of me made me more ashamed.
      "I see you have more use for this than
    you have for me," she said before she went.

I almost
got up to go
after her. Almost.
One of my friends asked,
"Have you heard the Saracen
gave your cousin a slave bracelet,
a loop of silver bells, to wear around
her ankle? I suppose in the Arab lands, such
gifts are made to every new whore in the harem."

                            I came
                         to my feet
                      so quickly my
                   chair fell over.

                                    I grabbed his throat
                                 in both hands and said,
                              "You lie. Her father would
                            never allow her to accept such
                            a gift from a godless blackamoor."

But
another
friend said
the Arab trader
was godless no more.
Lithodora had taught Ahmed
to read Latin, using the Bible
as his grammar, and he claimed now
to have entered into the light of Christ,
and he gave the bracelet to her with the full
knowledge of her parents, as a way to show thanks
for introducing him to the grace of our Father who art.

                                                    When
                                                 my first
                                              friend had
                                           recovered his
                                          breath, he told
                                    me Lithodora climbed
                                      the stairs every night
                                    to meet with him secretly

in empty shepherds' huts or in
the caves, or among the ruins of
the paper mills, by the roar of the
waterfall, as it leapt like liquid silver
in the moonlight, and in such places she was
his pupil and he a firm and most demanding tutor.

He
always
went ahead
and then she
would ascend the
stairs in the dark
wearing the bracelet.
When he heard the bells he
would light a candle to show her
where he waited to begin the lesson.

I
was
so drunk.

I set
out for
Lithodora's
house, with no
idea what I meant
to do when I got there.

I came up behind the cottage
where she lived with her parents
thinking I would throw a few stones
to wake her and bring her to her window.
But as I stole toward the back of the house
I heard a silvery tinkling somewhere above me.

She was
already on
the stairs and
climbing into the
stars with her white
dress swinging from her
hips and the bracelet around
her ankle so bright in the gloom.

My
heart
thudded,
a cask flung
down a staircase:
doom doom doom doom.
I knew the hills better
than anyone and I ran another
way, making a steep climb up crude
steps of mud to get ahead of her, then
rejoining the main path up to Sulle Scale.

I still had the silver coin the Saracen prince
had given her, when she went to him and dishonored
me by begging him to pay me the wage I was properly owed.
                                              I put
                                        his silver
                                     in a tin cup
                              I had and slowed
                          to a walk and went
                    along shaking his Judas
              coin in my old battered mug.
              Such a pretty ringing it made in
                    the echoing canyons, on the stairs,
              in the night, high above Positano and the
        crash and sigh of the sea, as the tide consummated
the desire of water to pound the earth into submission.
At
last,
pausing
to catch my
breath, I saw
a candle flame leap
up off in the darkness.
It was in a handsome ruin,
a place of high granite walls
matted with wildflowers and ivy.

A vast entryway looked into a room
with a grass floor and a roof of stars,
as if the place had been built, not to give
shelter from the natural world, but to protect a
virgin corner of wildness from the violation of man.

                                        Then
                                  again it
                            seemed a pagan
                      place, the natural
                setting for an orgy hosted
          by fauns with their goaty hooves,
      their flutes and their furred cocks.
  So the archway into that private courtyard
of weeds and summer green seemed the entrance
  to a hall awaiting revelers for a private bacchanal.

He
waited
on spread
blanket, with
a bottle of the
Don's wine and some
books and he smiled at
the tinkling sound of my
approach but stopped when I
came into the light, a block of
rough stone already in my free hand.

                                              I
                                          killed
                                       him there.

I did
not kill
him out of
family honor
or jealousy, did
not hit him with the
stone because he had laid
claim to Lithodora's cool white
body, which she would never offer me.

                                              I
                                            hit
                                       him with
                                    the block of
                                  stone because I
                           hated his black face.

After
I stopped
hitting him,
I sat with him.
I think I took his
wrist to see if he had
a pulse, but after I knew
he was dead, I went on holding

his hand listening to the hum of the
crickets in the grass, as if he were a
small child, *my* child, who had only drifted
off after fighting sleep for a very long time.

What

brought

me out of

my stupor was

the sweet music

of bells coming up

the stairs toward us.

I leapt
up and ran
but Dora was
already there,
coming through the
doorway, and I nearly
struck her on my way by.
She reached out for me with
one of her delicate white hands
and said my name but I did not stop.
I took the stairs three at a time, running
without thought, but I was not fast enough and
I heard her when she shouted *his* name, once and again.

I

don't

know where

I was running.

Sulle Scale, maybe,

though I knew they would

look for me there first once

Lithodora went down the steps and

told them what I had done to the Arab.

I did not slow down until I was gulping for

air and my chest was filled with fire and then

I leaned against a gate at the side of the path —

you know

what gate —

and it

swung open

at first touch.

I went through the

gate and started down

the steep staircase beyond.

I thought no one will look for

me here and I can hide a while and —

No.

I

thought,

these stairs

will lead to the

road and I will head

                                north to Napoli and buy

                        a ticket for a ship to the U.S.

                    and take a new name, start a new —

No.

Enough.

The truth:

                                        I

                                 believed

                              the stairs

                           led down into

                         hell and hell was

                    where I wanted to go.

The

steps

at first

were of old

white stone, but

as I continued along

they grew sooty and dark.

Other staircases merged with

them here and there, descending

from other points on the mountain.

I couldn't see how that was possible.

I thought I had walked all the flights of

stairs in the hills, except for the steps I

was on and I couldn't think for the life of me
where those other staircases might be coming from.

                                        The
                                     forest
                                  around me
                               had been purged
                            by fire at some time
                         in the not so far-off past,
                      and I made my descent through
                   stands of scorched, shattered pines,
                the hillside all blackened and charred.
             Only there had been no fire on that part of
          the hill, not for as long as I could remember.
       The breeze carried on it an unmistakable warmth.
    I began to feel unpleasantly overheated in my clothes.
I
followed
the staircase
round a switchback
and saw below me a boy
sitting on a stone landing.

                                        He
                                     had a
                                  collection
                               of curious wares

                                                  spread on a blanket.

                            There was a windup tin

                        bird in a cage, a basket of

                white apples, a dented gold lighter.

            There was a jar and in the jar was light.

         This light would increase in brightness until

      the landing was lit as if by the rising sun, and

   then it would collapse into darkness, shrinking to a

single point like some impossibly brilliant lightning bug.

He

smiled

to see me.

He had golden

hair and the most

beautiful smile I have

ever seen on a child's face

and I was afraid of him—even

before he called out to me by name.

I pretended I didn't hear him, pretended

he wasn't there, that I didn't see him, walked

right past him. He laughed to see me hurrying by.

                                                        The

                                                  farther

                                             I went the

                                        steeper it got.

                                There seemed to be

a light below, as if
somewhere beyond a ledge,
through the trees, there was
a great city, on the scale of Roma,
a bowl of lights like a bed of embers.
I could smell food cooking on the breeze.

If
it was
food — that
hungry-making
perfume of meat
charring over flame.

Voices
ahead of me:
a man speaking
wearily, perhaps
to himself, a long
and joyless discourse;
someone else laughing, bad
laughter, unhinged and angry.
A third man was asking questions.

"Is
a plum
sweeter after
it has been pushed
in the mouth of a virgin

to silence her as she is taken?
And who will claim the baby child
sleeping in the cradle made from the
rotten carcass of the lamb that laid with
the lion only to be eviscerated?" And so on.

                                        At
                                       the
                                      next
                                    turn in
                                  the steps
                                they finally
                              came into sight.
                          They lined the stairs:
                        half a dozen men nailed on
                      to crosses of blackened pine.
                    I couldn't go on and for a time
                  I couldn't go back; it was the cats.
                One of the men had a wound in his side,
              a red seeping wound that made a puddle on
            the stairs, and kittens lapped at it as if it
          were cream and he was talking to them in his tired
        voice, telling all the good kitties to drink their fill.
I
did
not go

```
close enough
to see his face.
                                              At
                                            last
                                      I returned
                                   the way I had
                                come on shaky legs.
                             The boy awaited me with
                            his collection of oddities.
"Why
not sit
and rest your
sore feet, Quirinus
Calvino?" he asked me.
And I sat down across from
him, not because I wanted to but
because that was where my legs gave out.
```

Neither of us spoke at first. He smiled across the blanket spread with his goods, and I pretended an interest in the stone wall that overhung the landing there. That light in the jar built and built until our shadows lunged against the rock like deformed giants, before the brightness winked out and plunged us back into our shared darkness. He offered me a skin of water but I knew better than to take anything from that child. Or thought I knew better. The light in the jar began to grow again, a single floating point of perfect whiteness, swelling like a balloon. I tried to look at it, but felt a pinch of pain in the back of my eyeballs and glanced away.

"What is that? It burns my eyes," I asked.

"A little spark stolen from the sun. You can do all sorts of wonderful things with it. You could make a furnace with it, a giant furnace, powerful enough to warm a whole city, and light a thousand Edison lights. Look how bright it gets. You have to be careful, though. If you were to smash this jar and let the spark escape, that same city would disappear in a clap of brightness. You can have it if you want."

"No, I don't want it," I said.

"No. Of course not. That isn't your sort of thing. No matter. Someone will be along later for this. But take something. Anything you want," he said.

"Are you Lucifer?" I asked in a rough voice.

"Lucifer is an awful old goat who has a pitchfork and hooves and makes people suffer. I hate suffering. I only want to help people. I give gifts. That's why I'm here. Everyone who walks these stairs before their time gets a gift to welcome them. You look thirsty. Would you like an apple?" Holding up the basket of white apples as he spoke.

I was thirsty—my throat felt not just sore, but singed,

as if I had inhaled smoke recently, and I began to reach
for the offered fruit, almost reflexively, but then drew
my hand back for I knew the lessons of at least one book.
He grinned at me.

"Are those—" I asked.

"They're from a very old and honorable tree," he said.
"You will never taste a sweeter fruit. And when you eat
of it, you will be filled with ideas. Yes, even one such as
you, Quirinus Calvino, who barely learned to read."

"I don't want it," I said, when what I really wanted
to tell him was not to call me by name. I could not bear
that he knew my name.

He said, "Everyone will want it. They will eat and
eat and be filled with understanding. Why, learning
how to speak another language will be as simple as, oh,
learning to build a bomb. Just one bite of the apple away.
What about the lighter? You can light anything with this
lighter. A cigarette. A pipe. A campfire. Imaginations.
Revolutions. Books. Rivers. The sky. Another man's
soul. Even the human soul has a temperature at which
it becomes flammable. The lighter has an enchantment
on it, is tapped into the deepest wells of oil on the planet,
and will set fire to things for as long as the oil lasts,
which I am sure will be forever."

"You have nothing I want," I said.

"I have something for everyone," he said.

I rose to my feet, ready to leave, although I had nowhere to go. I couldn't walk back down the stairs. The thought made me dizzy. Neither could I go back up. Lithodora would have returned to the village by now. They would be searching the stairs for me with torches. I was surprised I hadn't heard them already.

The tin bird turned its head to look at me as I swayed on my heels, and blinked, the metal shutters of its eyes snapping closed, then popping open again. It let out a rusty cheep. So did I, startled by its sudden movement. I had thought it a toy, inanimate. It watched me steadily and I stared back. I had, as a child, always had an interest in ingenious mechanical objects, clockwork people who ran out of their hiding places at the stroke of noon, the woodcutter to chop wood, the maiden to dance a round. The boy followed my gaze, and smiled, then opened the cage and reached in for it. The bird leaped lightly onto his finger.

"It sings the most beautiful song," he said. "It finds a master, a shoulder it likes to perch on, and it sings for this person all the rest of its days. The trick to making it sing for you is to tell a lie. The bigger the better. Feed it a lie, and it will sing you the most marvelous little tune. People love to hear its song. They love it so much, they don't even care they're being lied to. He's yours if you want him."

"I don't want anything from you," I said, but when I said it, the bird began to whistle: the sweetest, softest melody, as good a sound as the laughter of a pretty girl, or your mother calling you to dinner. The song sounded a bit like something played on a music box, and I imagined a studded cylinder turning inside it, banging the teeth of a silver comb. I shivered to hear it. In this place, on these stairs, I had never imagined I could hear something so right.

He laughed and waved his hand at me. The bird's wings snapped from the side of its body, like knives leaping from sheaths, and it glided up and lit on my shoulder.

"You see," said the boy on the stairs. "It likes you."

"I can't pay," I said, my voice rough and strange.

"You've already paid," said the boy.

Then he turned his head and looked down the stairs and seemed to listen. I heard a wind rising. It made a low, soughing moan as it came up through the channel of the staircase, a deep and lonely and restless cry. The boy looked back at me. "Now go. I hear my father coming. The awful old goat."

I backed away and my heels struck the stair behind me. I was in such a hurry to get away I fell sprawling across the granite steps. The bird on my shoulder took off, rising in widening circles through the air, but when

I found my feet it glided down to where it had rested
before on my
shoulder
and I began
to run back up
the way I had come.

I
climbed
in haste for
a time but soon
was tired again and
had to slow to a walk.
I began to think about what
I would say when I reached the
main staircase and was discovered.
"I will confess everything and accept
my punishment, whatever that is," I said.
The tin bird sang a gay and humorous ditty.

It
fell
silent
though as
I reached the
gate, quieted by
a different song not
far off: a girl's sobs.

I listened, confused, and
crept uncertainly back to where
I had murdered Lithodora's beloved.
I heard no sound except for Dora's cries.
No men shouting, no feet running on the steps.
I had been gone half the night, it seemed to me, but
when I reached the ruins where I had left the Saracen
and looked upon Dora it was as if only minutes had passed.

                                        I
                                     came
                                  toward
                                 her and
                              whispered
                           to her, afraid
                        almost to be heard.
                     The second time I spoke
                  her name she turned her head
               and looked at me with red-rimmed
            hating eyes and screamed to get away.
         I wanted to comfort her, to tell her I was
      sorry, but when I came close she sprang to her
   feet and ran at me, striking me and flaying at my
face with her fingernails while she cursed my name.
I meant
to put my
hands on her

shoulders to hold
her still but when I
reached for her they found
her smooth white neck instead.

                                        Her
                                    father
                                and his
                            my unemployed
                        friends discovered
                    me weeping over her.
                Running my fingers through
            the silk of her long black hair.
        Her father fell to his knees and took
            her in his arms and for a while the hills
        rang with her name repeated over and over again.

Another
man, who held
a rifle, asked me
what had happened and
I told him — I told him —
the Arab, that monkey from the
desert, had lured her here and when
he couldn't force her innocence from her,
he throttled her in the grass and I found them
and we fought and I killed him with a block of stone.

                                              And
                                            as I
                                          told it
                                        the tin bird
                                      began to whistle
                                    and sing, the most
                                  mournful and sweetest
                                melody I had ever heard
                              and the men listened until
                            the sad song was sung complete.

I
held
Lithodora
in my arms as
we walked back down.
And as we went on our way
the bird began to sing again as
I told them the Saracen had planned
to take the sweetest and most beautiful
girls and auction their white flesh in Araby —
a more profitable line of trade than selling wine.
The bird was by now whistling a marching song and the
faces of the men who walked with me were rigid and dark.

                                            Ahmed's
                                          men burned
                                        along with the

Arab's ship, and

sank in the harbor.

His goods, stored in a

warehouse by the quay, were

seized and his money box fell

to me as a reward for my heroism.

No

one

ever

would've

imagined when

I was a boy that

one day I would be

the wealthiest trader

on the whole Amalfi coast,

or that I would come to own the

prized vineyards of Don Carlotta, I

who once worked like a mule for his coin.

No

one

would've

guessed that

one day I would

be the beloved mayor

of Sulle Scale, or a man

of such renown that I would be

invited to a personal audience with
his holiness the pope himself, who thanked
me for my many well-noted acts of generosity.
The
springs
inside the
pretty tin bird
wore down, in time,
and it ceased to sing,
but by then it did not matter
if anyone believed my lies or not,
such was my wealth and power and fame.

However.
Several years
before the tin bird
fell silent, I woke one
morning in my manor to find
it had constructed a nest of wire
on my windowsill, and filled it with
fragile eggs made of bright silver foil.
I regarded these eggs with unease but when I
reached to touch them, their mechanical mother
nipped at me with her needle-sharp beak and I did
not after that time make any attempt to disturb them.
Months
later the

nest was filled
with foil tatters.
The young of this new
species, creatures of a new
age, had fluttered on their way.
                                        I
                                    cannot
                                  tell you
                             how many birds
                           of tin and wire and
                        electric current there
                   are in the world now — but I
               have, this very month, heard speak
          our newest prime minister, Mr. Mussolini.
      When he sings of the greatness of the Italian
     people and our kinship with our German neighbors,
   I am quite sure I can hear a tin bird singing with him.
Its tune plays especially well amplified over modern radio.
I don't
live in the
hills anymore.
It has been years
since I saw Sulle Scale.
I discovered, as I descended
at last into my senior years, that

I could no longer attempt the staircases.

I told people it was my poor sore old knees.

But in truth I

developed a

fear of

heights.

Twittering from the Circus of the Dead

WHAT IS TWITTER?

"Twitter is a service for friends, family, and co-workers to communicate and stay connected through the exchange of quick, frequent answers to one simple question: What are you doing? . . . Answers must be under 140 characters in length and can be sent via mobile texting, instant message, or the Web."

—from twitter.com

TYME2WASTE I'm only trying this because I'm so bored I wish I was dead. Hi Twitter. Want to know what I'm doing? Screaming inside.
8:17 PM – 28 Feb from Tweetie

TYME2WASTE My, didn't that sound melodramatic.
8:19 PM – 28 Feb from Tweetie

TYME2WASTE Lets try this again. Hello Twitterverse.
I am Blake and Blake is me. What am I doing? Counting
seconds.
8:23 PM – 28 Feb from Tweetie

TYME2WASTE Only about 50,000 more until we pack up
and finish what is hopefully the last family trip of my life.
8:25 PM – 28 Feb from Tweetie

TYME2WASTE It's been all downhill since we got to
Colorado. And I don't mean on my snowboard.
8:27 PM – 28 Feb from Tweetie

TYME2WASTE We were supposed to spend the break
boarding and skiing but it's too cold and won't stop snowing
so we had to go to plan B.
8:29 PM – 28 Feb from Tweetie

TYME2WASTE Plan B is Mom and I face off in a contest
to see who can make the other cry hot tears of rage and
hate first.
8:33 PM – 28 Feb from Tweetie

TYME2WASTE I'm winning. All I have to do to make Mom leave the room at this point is walk into it. Wait, I'm walking into the room where she is now . . .
8:35 PM – 28 Feb from Tweetie

TYME2WASTE She's such a mean bitch.
10:11 PM – 28 Feb from Tweetie

TYME2WASTE @caseinSD, @bevsez, @harmlesspervo yay my real friends! I miss San Diego. Home soon.
10:41 PM – 28 Feb from Tweetie

TYME2WASTE @caseinSD Hell no I'm not afraid Mom is going to read any of this. She's never going to know about it.
10:46 PM – 28 Feb from Tweetie

TYME2WASTE After she made me take down my blog, it's not like I'm ever going to tell her.
10:48 PM – 28 Feb from Tweetie

TYME2WASTE You know what bitchy thing she said to me a couple hours ago? She said the reason I don't like Colorado is because I can't blog about it.
10:53 PM – 28 Feb from Tweetie

TYME2WASTE She's always saying the Net is more real for me and my friends than the world. For us nothing really happens till someone blogs about it.
10:55 PM – 28 Feb from Tweetie

TYME2WASTE Or writes about it on their Facebook page. Or at least sends an instant message about it. She says the internet is "life validation."
10:55 PM – 28 Feb from Tweetie

TYME2WASTE Oh and we don't go online because it's fun. She has this attitude that people socially network 'cause they're scared to die. It's deep.
10:58 PM – 28 Feb from Tweetie

TYME2WASTE She sez no one ever blogs their own death. No one instant-messages about it. No one's Facebook status ever says "dead."
10:59 PM – 28 Feb from Tweetie

TYME2WASTE So for online people, death doesn't happen. People go online to hide from death and wind up hiding from life. Words right from her lips.
11:01 PM – 28 Feb from Tweetie

TYME2WASTE Shit like that, she ought to write fortune cookies for a living. You see why I want to strangle her. With an ethernet cable.
11:02 PM – 28 Feb from Tweetie

TYME2WASTE Little bro asked if I could blog about him having sex with a certain goth girl from school to make it real, but no one laughed.
11:06 PM – 28 Feb from Tweetie

TYME2WASTE I told Mom, no, the reason I hate Colorado is 'cause I'm stuck with her and it's all waaaaay too real.
11:09 PM – 28 Feb from Tweetie

TYME2WASTE And she said that was progress and got this smug bitch look on her face and then Dad threw down his book & left the room.
11:11 PM – 28 Feb from Tweetie

TYME2WASTE I feel worst for him. A few more months and I'm gone forever, but he's stuck with her for life and all her anger and the rest of it.
11:13 PM – 28 Feb from Tweetie

TYME2WASTE I'm sure he wishes he just got us plane tickets now. Suddenly our van is looking like the setting for a cage-match duel to the death.
11:15 PM – 28 Feb from Tweetie

TYME2WASTE All of us jammed in together for 3 days. Who will emerge alive? Place your bets, ladies and germs. Personally I predict no survivors.
11:19 PM – 28 Feb from Tweetie

TYME2WASTE Arrr. Fuck. Shit. It was dark when I went to bed and it is dark now and Dad says it's time to leave. This is so terribly wrong.
6:21 AM – 1 Mar from Tweetie

TYME2WASTE We're going. Mom gave the condo a careful search to make sure nothing got left behind, which is how she found me.
7:01 AM – 1 Mar from Tweetie

TYME2WASTE Damn, knew I needed a better hiding place.
7:02 AM – 1 Mar from Tweetie

TYME2WASTE Dad just said the whole trip ought to take between 35 and 40 hours. I offer this as conclusive proof there is no God.
7:11 AM – 1 Mar from Tweetie

TYME2WASTE Tweeting just to piss Mom off. She knows if I'm typing something on my phone, I'm obviously engaged in sin.
7:23 AM – 1 Mar from Tweetie

TYME2WASTE I'm expressing myself and staying in touch with my friends, and she hates it. Whereas if I was knitting and unpopular . . .
7:25 AM – 1 Mar from Tweetie

TYME2WASTE . . . then I'd be just like her when she was 17. And I'd also marry the first guy who came along and get knocked up by 19.
7:25 AM – 1 Mar from Tweetie

TYME2WASTE Coming down the mountain in the snow. Coming down the mountain in the snow. 1 more hairpin turn and my stomach's gonna blow . . .
7:30 AM – 1 Mar from Tweetie

TYME2WASTE My contribution to this glorious family moment is going to come when I barf on my little brother's head.
7:49 AM – 1 Mar from Tweetie

TYME2WASTE If we wind up in a snowbank and have a Donner Party, I know whose ass they'll be chewing on first. Mine.
7:52 AM – 1 Mar from Tweetie

TYME2WASTE Of course my survival skillz would amount to Twittering madly for someone to rescue us.
7:54 AM – 1 Mar from Tweetie

TYME2WASTE Mom would make a slingshot out of rubber from the tires, kill squirrels with it, make a fur bikini out of 'em, and be sad when we were rescued.
7:56 AM – 1 Mar from Tweetie

TYME2WASTE Dad would go out of his mind because we'd have to burn his books to stay warm.
8:00 AM – 1 Mar from Tweetie

TYME2WASTE Eric would put on a pair of my pantyhose. Not to stay warm. Just 'cause my little brother wants to wear my pantyhose.
8:00 AM – 1 Mar from Tweetie

TYME2WASTE I wrote that last bit 'cause Eric was looking over my shoulder.
8:02 AM – 1 Mar from Tweetie

TYME2WASTE But the sick bastard said wearing my pantyhose is the closest he'll probably come to getting laid in high school.
8:06 AM – 1 Mar from Tweetie

TYME2WASTE He's completely gross but I love him.
8:06 AM – 1 Mar from Tweetie

TYME2WASTE Mom taught him to knit while we were snowed in here in happy CO and he knitted himself a cocksock, and then she was sorry.
8:11 AM – 1 Mar from Tweetie

TYME2WASTE I miss my blog, which she had no right to make me take down.
8:13 AM – 1 Mar from Tweetie

TYME2WASTE But Twittering is better than blogging because my blog always made me feel like I should have interesting ideas to blog about.
8:14 AM – 1 Mar from Tweetie

TYME2WASTE But on Twitter every post can only be 140 letters long. Which is enough room to cover every interesting thing to ever happen to me.
8:15 AM – 1 Mar from Tweetie

TYME2WASTE True. Check it out.
8:15 AM – 1 Mar from Tweetie

TYME2WASTE Born. School. Mall. Cell phone. Driver's permit. Broke my nose playing trapeze at 8–there goes the modeling career. Need to lose 10 lbs.
8:19 AM – 1 Mar from Tweetie

TYME2WASTE Think that covers it.
8:20 AM – 1 Mar from Tweetie

TYME2WASTE It's snowing in the mountains but not down here, snow falling in the sunlight in a storm of gold. Good-bye beautiful mountains.
9:17 AM – 1 Mar from Tweetie

TYME2WASTE Hello not so beautiful Utah desert. Utah is brown and puckered like Judy Kennedy's weird nipples.
9:51 AM – 1 Mar from Tweetie

TYME2WASTE @caseinSD Yes she does have weird nipples. And it doesn't make me a lesbo for noticing. Everyone notices.
10:02 AM – 1 Mar from Tweetie

TYME2WASTE Sagebrush!!!!!! W00T!
11:09 AM – 1 Mar from Tweetie

TYME2WASTE Now Eric is trying on my pantyhose. He's bored. Mom thinks it's funny, but Dad is stressed.
12:20 PM – 1 Mar from Tweetie

TYME2WASTE Dared Eric to wear a skirt in the diner to get our takeout. Dad says no. Mom is still laughing.
12:36 PM – 1 Mar from Tweetie

TYME2WASTE I promised him if he does it I'll invite a certain hot goth to the pool party in April so he can see her in her tacky bikini.
12:39 PM – 1 Mar from Tweetie

TYME2WASTE There's no way he'll do it.
12:42 PM – 1 Mar from Tweetie

TYME2WASTE ZOMG hes doing it. Dad is going into the diner with him to make sure he isn't killed by offended Mormons.
12:44 PM – 1 Mar from Tweetie

TYME2WASTE Eric came back alive. Eric saves the day. I'm actually glad to be in the van right now.
12:59 PM – 1 Mar from Tweetie

TYME2WASTE Dad says Eric sat at the bar and talked football with this big trucker guy. Trucker guy was fine with the skirt and pantyhose.
1:03 PM – 1 Mar from Tweetie

TYME2WASTE He's still wearing it. The skirt. Maybe he's a closet transvestite! Sicko. Course that would be fun. We could shop together.
1:45 PM – 1 Mar from Tweetie

TYME2WASTE @caseinSD Yes we do have to invite a certain goth to the pool party now. She probably won't even come. I think sunlight burns her.
2:09 PM – 1 Mar from Tweetie

TYME2WASTE Every time I start to fall asleep, the van hits a bump and my head falls off the seat.
11:01 PM – 1 Mar from Tweetie

TYME2WASTE Trying to sleep.
11:31 PM – 1 Mar from Tweetie

TYME2WASTE I give up trying to sleep.
1:01 AM – 2 Mar from Tweetie

TYME2WASTE Oh fuck Eric. He's asleep and he looks like he's having a wet dream about a certain goth chick.
1:07 AM – 2 Mar from Tweetie

TYME2WASTE Meanwhile I'd have a better chance of sleeping if there were only steel pins inserted under my eyelids.
1:09 AM – 2 Mar from Tweetie

TYME2WASTE I'm so happy right now. I just want to hold this moment for as long as I can.
6:11 AM – 2 Mar from Tweetie

TYME2WASTE I just want to be home. I hate Mom. I hate everyone in the van. Including myself.
8:13 AM – 2 Mar from Tweetie

TYME2WASTE Okay. This is why I was happy earlier. It was 4 in the morning and Mom pulled into a rest area and then she came and got me.
10:21 AM – 2 Mar from Tweetie

TYME2WASTE She said it was my turn to drive. I said my permit is only for driving in Cali, and she said just get behind the wheel.
10:22 AM – 2 Mar from Tweetie

TYME2WASTE She told me if I got pulled over to wake her up and we'd switch and everything would be all right.
10:23 AM – 2 Mar from Tweetie

TYME2WASTE So she went to sleep in the passenger seat and I drove. We were down in the desert and the sun came up behind me.
10:25 AM – 2 Mar from Tweetie

TYME2WASTE And then there were coyotes in the road. In the red sunlight. They were all over the interstate, and I stopped so I wouldn't hit them.
10:26 AM – 2 Mar from Tweetie

TYME2WASTE Their eyes were gold and the sun was in their fur and there were so many, this huge pack. Just standing there like they were waiting for me.
10:28 AM – 2 Mar from Tweetie

TYME2WASTE I wanted to take a picture with my cell phone, but I couldn't figure out where I left it. While I was looking for it, they disappeared.
10:31 AM – 2 Mar from Tweetie

TYME2WASTE When Mom woke up, I told her all about them. And then I thought she'd be mad I didn't shake her awake to see them, so I said I was sorry.
10:34 AM – 2 Mar from Tweetie

TYME2WASTE And she said she was glad I didn't wake her up, because that moment was just for me. And for maybe three seconds I liked her again.
10:35 AM – 2 Mar from Tweetie

TYME2WASTE But then in the place we ate breakfast I was looking at my e-mail for a sec. & I heard Mom saying to the waitress, We apologize for her.
10:37 AM – 2 Mar from Tweetie

TYME2WASTE I guess the waitress was standing there waiting for my order and I didn't notice.
10:40 AM – 2 Mar from Tweetie

TYME2WASTE But I didn't sleep all night and I was tired and zoned out and that's why I didn't notice, not 'cause I was looking at my phone.
10:42 AM – 2 Mar from Tweetie

TYME2WASTE And Mom had to trot out her stories about being a waitress herself and that it was demeaning not to be acknowledged.
10:45 AM – 2 Mar from Tweetie

TYME2WASTE Just to rub it in. And she can be completely right and I can still hate the way she makes me feel like shit at every opportunity.
10:46 AM – 2 Mar from Tweetie

TYME2WASTE I napped, but I don't feel better.
4:55 PM – 2 Mar from Tweetie

TYME2WASTE Dad of course has to go the slowest possible route by way of every back road. Mom says he missed a turn and added 100 miles to the trip.
6:30 PM – 2 Mar from Tweetie

TYME2WASTE Now they're fighting. OMG I want out of this van.
6:37 PM – 2 Mar from Tweetie

TYME2WASTE Eric, I am psychically willing you to find some reason for us to get off the road. Put on the pantyhose again. Say you have to pee.
6:49 PM – 2 Mar from Tweetie

TYME2WASTE Anything. Please.
6:49 PM – 2 Mar from Tweetie

TYME2WASTE No no NO Eric, no. I wanted you to think up a GOOD reason not to get off the road but not this . . . this is going to be bad.
6:57 PM – 2 Mar from Tweetie

TYME2WASTE Mom doesn't want to pull over either. Write it down, kids, first time in two years we've agreed on anything.
7:00 PM – 2 Mar from Tweetie

TYME2WASTE Oh Dad is being a prick now. He says there was no point in taking back roads if we weren't going to find some culture.
7:02 PM – 2 Mar from Tweetie

TYME2WASTE We are driving up to something called the Circus of the Dead. The ticket guy looks really REALLY sick. Not funny-sick. SICK-sick.
7:06 PM – 2 Mar from Tweetie

TYME2WASTE Sores around his mouth and few teeth and I can smell him. He's got a pet rat. His pet rat dived in his pocket and came out with the tickets.
7:08 PM – 2 Mar from Tweetie

TYME2WASTE No it wasn't cute. None of us want to touch the tickets.
7:10 PM – 2 Mar from Tweetie

TYME2WASTE Boy, they're really packing them in. Show starts in 15 min but the parking lot is ½ empty. The big top is a black tent with holes in it.
7:13 PM – 2 Mar from Tweetie

TYME2WASTE Mom says to be sure to keep doing whatever I'm doing on my phone. She wouldn't want me to look up and see something happening.
7:17 PM – 2 Mar from Tweetie

TYME2WASTE Oh that was shitty. She just said to Dad that I'll love the circus because it'll be just like the internet.
7:18 PM – 2 Mar from Tweetie

TYME2WASTE YouTube is full of clowns, message boards are full of fire-breathers, and blogs are for people who can't live without a spotlight on them.
7:20 PM – 2 Mar from Tweetie

TYME2WASTE I'm going to tweet like 5 times a minute and make her insane.
7:21 PM – 2 Mar from Tweetie

TYME2WASTE The usher is a funny old Mickey Rooney type with a bowler and a cigar. He also has on a hazmat suit. He says so he can't get bitten.
7:25 PM – 2 Mar from Tweetie

TYME2WASTE I almost fell twice on the walk to our seats. Guess they're saving $ on lights. I'm using my iPhone as a flashlight. Hope there isn't a fire.
7:28 PM – 2 Mar from Tweetie

TYME2WASTE God this is the stinkiest circus ever. I don't know what I'm smelling. Are those the animals? Call PETA.
7:30 PM – 2 Mar from Tweetie

TYME2WASTE I can't believe how many people there are. Every seat is taken. Don't know where this crowd came from.
7:31 PM – 2 Mar from Tweetie

TYME2WASTE They must've had us park in a secondary parking lot. Oh wait, they just flipped on a spotlight. Showtime. Beating heart, restrain yourself.
7:34 PM – 2 Mar from Tweetie

TYME2WASTE Well, that got Eric and Dad's attention. The ringmistress came out on stilts and she's practically naked. Fishnets and top hat.
7:38 PM – 2 Mar from Tweetie

TYME2WASTE She's weird. She talks like she's stoned. Did I mention there are zombies in clown outfits chasing her around?
7:40 PM – 2 Mar from Tweetie

TYME2WASTE The zombies are waaay gross. They have on big clown shoes and polka dot outfits and clown makeup.
7:43 PM – 2 Mar from Tweetie

TYME2WASTE But the makeup is flaking off, and beneath it they're all rotted and black. Yow! They almost grabbed her. She's quick.
7:44 PM – 2 Mar from Tweetie

TYME2WASTE She says she's been a prisoner of the circus for 6 weeks and that she survived because she learned the stilts fast.
7:47 PM – 2 Mar from Tweetie

TYME2WASTE She said her boyfriend couldn't walk on them and fell down and was eaten his first night. She said her best friend was eaten the 2nd night.
7:49 PM – 2 Mar from Tweetie

TYME2WASTE She walked right up to the wall under us and begged someone to pull her over and rescue her, but the guy in the front row just laughed.
7:50 PM – 2 Mar from Tweetie

TYME2WASTE Then she had to run away in a hurry before Zippo the Zombie knocked her off her stilts. It's all very well choreographed.
7:50 PM – 2 Mar from Tweetie

TYME2WASTE You can totally believe they're trying to get her.
7:51 PM – 2 Mar from Tweetie

TYME2WASTE They rolled a cannon out. She said, Here at the Circus of the Dead we always begin things with a bang. She read it off a card.
7:54 PM – 2 Mar from Tweetie

TYME2WASTE She walked up to a tall door and rapped on it, and for a minute I didn't think they were going to let her out of the ring, but then they did.
7:55 PM – 2 Mar from Tweetie

TYME2WASTE Two men in hazmat suits just led a zombie out. He's got a metal collar around his neck with a black stick attached.
7:56 PM – 2 Mar from Tweetie

TYME2WASTE They're using the stick to hold him at a distance so he can't grab them.
7:57 PM – 2 Mar from Tweetie

TYME2WASTE Eric says he has fantasies about a certain goth girl putting him in a rig like that.
7:58 PM – 2 Mar from Tweetie

TYME2WASTE This show would be a great date for the two of them. It's got a hint of sex, a whiff of bondage, and it's really really morbid.
7:59 PM – 2 Mar from Tweetie

TYME2WASTE They put the zombie in the cannon.
8:00 PM – 2 Mar from Tweetie

TYME2WASTE Auuuughhh! They pointed the cannon at the crowd and fired it and fucking pieces of zombie went everywhere.
8:03 PM – 2 Mar from Tweetie

TYME2WASTE The guy in the row in front of us got smashed in the mouth with a flying shoe. He's bleeding and everything.
8:05 PM – 2 Mar from Tweetie

TYME2WASTE Fucking yuck! There's still a foot inside the shoe! It's totally realistic looking.
8:08 PM – 2 Mar from Tweetie

TYME2WASTE The guy sitting in front of us just walked off w/his wife to complain. Same dude who laffed at the ringmistress when she asked for help.
8:11 PM – 2 Mar from Tweetie

TYME2WASTE Dad had a zombie lip in his hair. I am so glad I didn't eat lunch. Looks like a gummy worm and it smells like ass.
8:13 PM – 2 Mar from Tweetie

TYME2WASTE Naturally Eric wants to keep it.
8:13 PM – 2 Mar from Tweetie

TYME2WASTE Here comes the ringmistress again. She says the next act is the cat's meo
8:14 PM – 2 Mar from Tweetie

TYME2WASTE OMG OMGthat was not funny. She almost fell down and the way they were snarling
8:16 PM – 2 Mar from Tweetie

TYME2WASTE The men in hazmat suits just wheeled in a lion in a cage. Yay, a lion! I am still girl enough to like a big cat.
8:17 PM – 2 Mar from Tweetie

TYME2WASTE Oh that's a really sad, sick-looking lion. Not fun. They're opening the cage and sending in zombies and he's hissing like a house cat.
8:19 PM – 2 Mar from Tweetie

TYME2WASTE Roawwwwr! Lion power. He's swatting them down and shredding them apart. He's got an arm in his mouth. Everyone cheering.
8:21 PM – 2 Mar from Tweetie

TYME2WASTE Eeeuuuw. Not so much cheering now. He's got one and he's tugging out its guts like he's pulling on one end of a tug rope.
8:22 PM – 2 Mar from Tweetie

TYME2WASTE They're sending in more zombies. No one laughing or cheering now. It's really crowded in there.
8:24 PM – 2 Mar from Tweetie

TYME2WASTE I can't even see the lion anymore. Lots of angry snarling and flying fur and walking corpses getting knocked around.
8:24 PM – 2 Mar from Tweetie

TYME2WASTE OH GROSS. The lion made a sound, like this scared whine, and now the zombies are passing around organ meat and hunks of fur.
8:25 PM – 2 Mar from Tweetie

TYME2WASTE They're eating. That's awful. I feel sick.
8:26 PM – 2 Mar from Tweetie

TYME2WASTE Dad saw I was getting upset and told me how they did it. The cage has a false bottom. They pulled the lion out through the floor.
8:30 PM – 2 Mar from Tweetie

TYME2WASTE You really get swept up in this thing.
8:30 PM – 2 Mar from Tweetie

TYME2WASTE The Mickey Rooney guy who led us back to the seats just showed up with a flashlight. He says we left the headlights on in the van.
8:31 PM – 2 Mar from Tweetie

TYME2WASTE Eric went to turn them off. He said he has to pee anyway.
8:32 PM – 2 Mar from Tweetie

TYME2WASTE The fireswallower just came out. He has no eyes, and there's some kind of steel contraption forcing his head back and his mouth open.
8:34 PM – 2 Mar from Tweetie

TYME2WASTE One of the men in the hazmat suits isFUCK ME.
8:35 PM – 2 Mar from Tweetie

TYME2WASTE They shoved a torch down his throat, and now he's burning! He's running around with smoke coming out of his mouth and
8:36 PM – 2 Mar from Tweetie

TYME2WASTE fire in his head coming out his eyes like a jack o lante
8:36 PM – 2 Mar from Tweetie

TYME2WASTE They just let him burn to death from the inside out. Realest thing I've ever seen.
8:39 PM – 2 Mar from Tweetie

TYME2WASTE What's even realer is the corpse after the hazmat guys sprayed it down with the fire extinguishers. It looks so sad and shriveled and black.
8:39 PM – 2 Mar from Tweetie

TYME2WASTE The ringmistress is back. She's really weaving around. I think something is wrong with her ankle.
8:40 PM – 2 Mar from Tweetie

TYME2WASTE She says someone from the audience has agreed to be tonight's sacrifice. She says he will be the lucky one.
8:41 PM – 2 Mar from Tweetie

TYME2WASTE He? I thought the sacrifice was usually a girl in this sort of situation.
8:41 PM – 2 Mar from Tweetie

TYME2WASTE Oh no he did not. They just wheeled Eric out, cuffed to a big wooden wheel. He winked on the way past. Psycho. Go, Eric!
8:42 PM – 2 Mar from Tweetie

TYME2WASTE They hauled out a zombie and chained him to a stake in the dirt. There's a box in front of him full of hatchets. Don't like where this is going.
8:43 PM – 2 Mar from Tweetie

TYME2WASTE Everyone's laughing now. The lion scene was a little grim, but we're back to funny again. The zombie threw the first hatchet in the crowd.
8:45 PM – 2 Mar from Tweetie

TYME2WASTE There was a thunk, and someone screamed like they got it in the head. Obvious plant.
8:45 PM – 2 Mar from Tweetie

TYME2WASTE Eric is spinning around and around on the wheel. He's telling the zombie to kill him before he throws up.
8:46 PM – 2 Mar from Tweetie

TYME2WASTE Eeeks! I'm not as brave as Eric. A knife just banged into the wheel next to his head. Like: INCHES. Eric screamed too. Bet he wishes now
8:47 PM – 2 Mar from Tweetie

TYME2WASTE OMGOMGO
8:47 PM – 2 Mar from Tweetie

TYME2WASTE Okay. He must be okay. He was still smiling when they wheeled him out of the ring. The hatchet went right in the side of his neck.
8:50 PM – 2 Mar from Tweetie

TYME2WASTE Dad says it's a trick. Dad says he's fine. He says later Eric will come out as a zombie. That it's part of the show.
8:51 PM – 2 Mar from Tweetie

TYME2WASTE Yep, looks like Dad's right. They've promised Eric will reemerge shortly.
8:53 PM – 2 Mar from Tweetie

TYME2WASTE Mom is wigging. She wants Dad to check on Eric.
8:54 PM – 2 Mar from Tweetie

TYME2WASTE She's being kind of crazy. She's talking about how the guy who sat in front of us never came back after he got hit by the shoe.
8:55 PM – 2 Mar from Tweetie

TYME2WASTE I don't really see what that has to do with Eric. And besides, if I got hit by a flying shoe . . .
8:55 PM – 2 Mar from Tweetie

TYME2WASTE Okay, Dad is going to check on Eric. Sanity restored.
8:56 PM – 2 Mar from Tweetie

TYME2WASTE Here comes the ringmistress again. This is why Eric agreed to go backstage. With the fishnets and black panties, she's very goth-hot.
8:56 PM – 2 Mar from Tweetie

TYME2WASTE She's being weird. She isn't saying anything about the next act. She says if she goes off script they don't let her out of the ring.
8:57 PM – 2 Mar from Tweetie

TYME2WASTE But she doesn't care. She says she twisted her ankle and she knows tonight is her last night.
8:58 PM – 2 Mar from Tweetie

TYME2WASTE She says her name is Gail Ross and she went to high school in Plano.
8:59 PM – 2 Mar from Tweetie

TYME2WASTE She says she was going to marry her boyfriend after college. She says his name was Craig and he wanted to teach.
9:00 PM – 2 Mar from Tweetie

TYME2WASTE She says she's sorry for all of us. She says they take our cars and dispose of them while we're in the tent.
9:01 PM – 2 Mar from Tweetie

TYME2WASTE She says 12,000 people vanish every year on the roads with no explanation, their cars turn up empty or not at all and no one will miss us.
9:02 PM – 2 Mar from Tweetie

TYME2WASTE Creepy stuff. Here's Eric. His zombie makeup is really good. Most of the zombies are black and rotted, but he looks like fresh kill.
9:03 PM – 2 Mar from Tweetie

TYME2WASTE Still got the hatchet in the neck. That looks totally fake.
9:03 PM – 2 Mar from Tweetie

TYME2WASTE He's not very good at being a zombie. He isn't even trying to walk slow. He's really going after the ringmistress.
9:04 PM – 2 Mar from Tweetie

TYME2WASTE oh shit I hope that's part of the show. He just knocked her down. Oh Eric Eric Eric. She hit the dirt really really hard.
9:05 PM – 2 Mar from Tweetie

TYME2WASTE They're eating her like they ate the lion. Eric is playing with guts. He's so gross. He's going totally Method.
9:07 PM – 2 Mar from Tweetie

TYME2WASTE Gymnastics now. They're making a human pyramid. Or maybe I should say an INhuman pyramid. They're surprisingly good at it. For zombies.
9:10 PM – 2 Mar from Tweetie

TYME2WASTE Eric is climbing the pyramid like he knows what he's doing. I wonder if they gave him backstage training or
9:11 PM – 2 Mar from Tweetie

TYME2WASTE He's up high enough to grab the wall around the ring. He's snarling at someone in the front row, just a couple feet from here. Wait
9:13 PM – 2 Mar from Tweetie

TYME2WASTE no lights fuck thta was stupid whyd they put out the
9:14 PM – 2 Mar from Tweetie

TYME2WASTE someones screaming
9:15 PM – 2 Mar from Tweetie

TYME2WASTE this is really dangerous its so dark and lots of people are screaming and getting up. im mad now you don't do this to people you don't
9:18 PM – 2 Mar from Tweetie

TYME2WASTE we need help we areacv
9:32 PM – 2 Mar from Tweetie

TYME2WASTE gtttttgggtttggtttttttttgggbbbnnnfrfffgt
9:32 PM – 2 Mar from Tweetie

TYME2WASTE I cant say anything theyll hear. were beinb ver y qiuet wevegot a plas
10:17 PM – 2 Mar from Tweetie

TYME2WASTE were off i70 mom says it was exit 331 but we drove a long way the last town we saw was called ucmba
10:19 PM – 2 Mar from Tweetie

TYME2WASTE cumba
10:19 PM – 2 Mar from Tweetie

TYME2WASTE the people in the stands were all dead except for us and a few others and they were roped together tethered
10:20 PM – 2 Mar from Tweetie

TYME2WASTE please someone send help call UT state police not making this up
10:22 PM – 2 Mar from Tweetie

TYME2WASTE @caseinSD lease help you know me you know I wouldnt isnta joke
10:23 PM – 2 Mar from Tweetie

TYME2WASTE have to be quiet so I can't call got the ringer is turned off
10:24 PM – 2 Mar from Tweetie

TYME2WASTE AZ state police mom says its arizona not UT our van is a white econlein
10:27 PM – 2 Mar from Tweetie

TYME2WASTE its quiet less screaming now less growling
10:50 PM – 2 Mar from Tweetie

TYME2WASTE theyre dragging people into piles
10:56 PM – 2 Mar from Tweetie

TYME2WASTE eating theyre eating them
11:09 PM – 2 Mar from Tweetie

TYME2WASTE the man who got hit by the shoe earlier walked by but he isn't like he was he hes dead now
11:11 PM – 2 Mar from Tweetie

TYME2WASTE just mom and me i love my mom shes so brave i love her so much so much i never ment it none of the bad things not one i am with her i am
11:37 PM – 2 Mar from Tweetie

TYME2WASTE imso csared
11:39 PM – 2 Mar from Tweetie

TYME2WASTE theyresearching to see if anyone is left with flashlights the men in hazmat soups i say go out mom says no
11:41 PM – 2 Mar from Tweetie

TYME2WASTE were here were waiting for help please forward this to everyone on twitter this is true not an internet prank believe believe believe pleves
12:03 AM – 3 Mar from Tweetie

TYME2WASTE ohgod it was dad went by mom sat up and said his name and mom and dad and mom and dad
12:09 AM – 3 Mar from Tweetie

TYME2WASTE notdad oh my oh bnb nnnb ;;/'./;'././/
12:13 AM – 3 Mar from Tweetie

TYME2WASTE /'/.
12:13 AM – 3 Mar from Tweetie

TYME2WASTE Were you SCARED by this TWITTER
FEED???!?!?
9:17 AM – 3 Mar from Tweetie

TYME2WASTE The FEAR–and THE FUN–is only just
BEGINNING!
9:20 AM – 3 Mar from Tweetie

TYME2WASTE "THE CIRCUS OF THE DEAD" featuring
our newest RINGMISTRESS the SEXY & DARING BLAKE THE
BLACKHEARTED.
9:22AM – 3 Mar from Tweetie

TYME2WASTE Watch as our newest QUEEN OF THE
TRAPEEZE introduces our PERVERSE & PERNICIOUS
performers ...
9:23 AM – 3 Mar from Tweetie

TYME2WASTE ... while DANGLING FROM A ROPE ABOVE
THE RAVENOUS DEAD!
9:23 AM – 3 Mar from Tweetie

TYME2WASTE A CIRCUS so SHOCKING it makes THE JIM ROSE CIRCUS look like THE MUPPET SHOW!
9:25 AM – 3 Mar from Tweetie

TYME2WASTE Now touring with stops in ALL CORNERS OF THE COUNTRY!
9:26 AM – 3 Mar from Tweetie

TYME2WASTE Visit our Facebook page and join our E-MAIL LIST to find out when we'll be in YOUR AREA.
9:28 AM – 3 Mar from Tweetie

TYME2WASTE STAY CONNECTED OR YOU DON'T KNOW WHAT YOU'LL MISS!
9:30 AM – 3 Mar from Tweetie

TYME2WASTE "THE CIRCUS OF THE DEAD" . . . Where YOU are the concessions! Other circuses promise DEATH-DEFYING THRILLS!
9:31 AM – 3 Mar from Tweetie

TYME2WASTE BUT ONLY WE DELIVER! (Tix to be purchased at box office day of show. No refunds. Cash only. Minors must be accompanied by adult.)
9:31 AM – 3 Mar from Tweetie

Mums

1.

When Jack comes downstairs for breakfast, Bloom is on the landline, talking to someone in a confidential, urgent tone of voice. Jack pays his mother no mind and helps himself to a bowl of granola. Cereals containing refined sugars and preservatives are not allowed in the McCourt household—the preservatives in sugar cereals are known to cause both autism and homosexuality. He carries his breakfast into the sitting room to watch *X-Men* on TV. *X-Men* is liberal media brainwashing and also frowned upon, but Jack's father is off to Wichita for a gun show, and his mother is less hung up about cartoons.

"Hey, kid," his mother says when she emerges from the kitchen. "You want to meet your great-great-great?"

"Meemaw?"

"You know she's going to turn a hundred this summer?"

"That isn't true."

"She's so old she was born before TV."

"No one was born before TV."

"Before cars. Maybe before horses. All the people in my family descend from trees," Bloom McCourt informs him. "You know how long a tree lives? There's trees alive today that were old when George Washington was born. We're descended from George Washington's people, too. I forget the details. You don't believe me she's about to be a hundred?"

"No."

"Want to ask her yourself?"

"Are we going to call her?"

His mother steps into the front hall. She opens the closet under the stairs and lifts out a drab and battered suitcase. Bloom sets it on the floor by her feet and gives him a pointed look.

"I was aiming to surprise you. You and I have never taken a trip together before. We'll get the bus in Cordia and zip on over to Joplin. We can catch a Greyhound to Minnesota there."

"What about Dad?"

"Your father knows all about Minnesota. You think anything can happen in this house without his know-about-it? Get dressed."

"Do I have to pack?"

She tipped her head at the suitcase by her feet. "Already done. I packed for both of us. Come on, now. Put on your hurry-up shoes."

Jack has never met any of his mother's people, not his grandfather Magnus, not his grandmother Devoted, and not his great-great-great-meemaw, who supposedly once babysat Ernest Hemingway. They are all of them Pentecostals and live up in northwestern Minnesota, on Lake Superior.

The first inkling he has that his father is *not* in on the plan to head north comes when they slip out through the back door instead of the front and cut across the brown January fields on foot. Until then Jack had assumed they would get a ride to the bus station in Cordia. Connor McCourt and his wife, Beth, share a three-room cottage at the end of the raked gravel drive, a quarter of a mile down the road. Jack's father allows them to stay there rent-free, part of the arrangement he has with them. The both of them are full-time help, available to do whatever needs doing, from farming to scullery work. Connor is off to the gun show with Jack's old man, but his fluorescent orange Road Runner is still here, parked alongside his bungalow.

"Why doesn't Beth drive us?"

"The Road Runner needs a new whatsit."

"Aren't we going to say good-bye?"

"Naw. It's her Saturday. We'll let her sleep in for once, kid. Give ol' Beth a break."

They walk swiftly toward the tree line, his mother hauling the suitcase in one hand and squeezing his cold fingers in the other. Jack can see Connor and Beth's cottage in its little stand of trees and wonders if Beth will look out the window and wonder why they're carrying a suitcase across the furrowed field.

They wade through a few yards of stiff, frozen brush and come out on the edge of the highway. His mother marches them east along the side of the road, gravel crunching under their heels. With every step they put between themselves and his father's sprawling red farmhouse, she seems more at ease with herself.

Jack and Bloom walk the ruler-straight highway in the strong, brassy morning light for around half an hour. His mother tells him about relations he will meet up north, people with colorful mental illnesses and amusing criminal histories. There is the aunt who fell in love with a parking meter and went to jail for taking a cutting torch to it so she could bring it home with her. There is the great-uncle who strangled some-one's poodle because he thought it was a Russian spy. Jack's great-great-grandfather used to walk in the Easter parade, naked except for a loincloth, carrying a hundred-pound mahogany cross on his back and wearing a crown of thorns, until the town ordered him to stop—the blood on his face was scaring children. Jack is at turns incredulous, bemused, and thrilled. She might almost be describing a nineteenth-century freak show instead of family.

He sees his father's F-150 coming before his mother does, Connor's Road Runner following right behind it.

"Hey," he says, pointing at the pickup, which is still half a mile away. "It's Dad. I thought he went to the gun show."

His mother looks back over her shoulder at the approaching vehicles. They travel another few yards, and then Bloom's feet catch up to her brain and they stop walking. She sets the suitcase down by her heels.

The truck eases to the side of the road, slowing in the chalky margin and throwing up a haze of dust. Jack's father sits at the wheel, staring at them from behind a pair of mirrored shades, Connor right beside him. The Road Runner parks behind the pickup, and Beth gets out. She stands holding the driver's-side door, looking frightened.

"Whyn't you come over here, Jack?" Beth calls. "I'll drive you back to the house. Grown-ups gotta talk."

Bloom tightens her grip on Jack's hand. He stares up at his mother, then catches a movement from the corner of his eye and glances behind them. There's another car coming, this one from the direction of town: a police cruiser. It glides along with the lights and siren off, and when it's about fifty feet away, it parks on the other side of the road.

Only then does Hank McCourt, Jack's father, the Separatist, climb out of the big beige F-150. Connor gets down from the other side, careful not to put his weight on his carbon foot. Jack's cousin is the luckiest man he knows: he has a twenty-first-century mechanical leg, that souped-up Road Runner, and Beth. Jack would commit multiple homicides to have even one of them.

Jack's father ambles toward them with his hands out to either side, palms down, in a gesture that seems to recommend calm. He's armed, a Glock in a black leather holster on his right hip, but that's no surprise. He only takes it off to shower.

"Get in the Road Runner, Jack," Hank says. "Beth will drive you home."

Jack looks at his mother. She nods and releases his hand. Bloom picks up the suitcase and moves to follow, but Hank steps between them. He reaches for the handle of the suitcase—a husbandly thing to do—but then he puts his palm against Bloom's chest to keep her from taking another step.

"No. Not you. You can go wherever you were going."

"You can't just take him away from me, Hank."

"And you can?"

"What's going on here?" This from the lawman standing in the road behind Jack's mother. "Hank, what can you tell me?"

Two town cops have spilled out of the cruiser. Jack recognizes the one doing the talking, one of his father's friends, a hefty white-haired cop with a swollen nose full of twisty purple veins. The other is a scrawny kid who hangs a few steps back, hands resting on his gun belt. A white stick pokes out of the corner of his mouth. A lollipop, maybe.

"My wife decided to walk off with the boy, take him who knows where without discussing it."

"He's my son," Bloom says.

"He's Hank's son, too," says the white-haired lawman. Spaulding. Rudy Spaulding. That's his name. "Are you leaving your husband, Mrs. McCourt?"

"We're both leaving him," Bloom says. She glares at Hank, both of them clutching the handle of her suitcase.

Hank looks past her to Spaulding. "She's a danger to my son, Rudy. She's probably a danger to herself, too, but I can't do anything about that. I want my kid home, with me, and with his educator, Beth. She handles the homeschooling."

"*We* do the homeschooling," Bloom says. She wrenches at the suitcase. "Will. You. Let. *Go?*"

Hank gives it a twist as he releases his grip, and the suitcase falls open. Piles of clothes flop onto the gravel. A bottle of gin strikes the pavement with a clink. Bloom's shoulders leap in surprise.

"That's not mine," she says. "I don't drink anymore. I didn't—"

She raises her head and stares at Hank, spots of color high in her cheeks.

"This isn't yours either," Hank says, bending and digging through the pile and coming up with a money clip stuffed full of twenties. He looks at Rudy Spaulding. "I was on my way to Wichita when I noticed I didn't have this. That's why I turned around."

"He's lying," Bloom says. "I didn't take his money. He planted that, like he planted the bottle."

"What about these pills?" Spaulding asks, bending and picking up an orange plastic tube. "He plant these, too?"

"I have a prescription for those," Bloom says. She snatches for the bottle, but Spaulding turns a shoulder to her, keeps it out of reach. "I *need* those."

"What for?" Spaulding asks, squinting at the label.

"I get bad ideas," she says.

"You said it. Running off with my kid was one of them," Hank tells her.

"They help. Jack needs help also. It's not too late. He doesn't have to wind up with a head full of my crazy—or yours, Hank."

"The only thing he can get from the mainstream medical establishment is a bunch of feel-good pills to make him docile. Easy to herd. No thank you."

Spaulding grips Bloom's arm. "Tell you what, Mrs. McCourt. Why don't you come into town and unload your troubles to me? I'm a good listener."

"Fuck you, Rudy Spaulding," Bloom spits. "He's setting me up with his money clip and his bottle of gin, and you're helping him because you want to suck his dick. You want to get down on the gun range with him and oil his pistol."

"Oh, goodie," Spaulding says. "I get bored doing things the nice way." He turns her suddenly, almost yanking her off her feet, spinning her to face his cruiser. "Let's take a walk."

She shoots a furious look over one shoulder. Hank stares back from behind his mirrored shades.

"I'll get a lawyer," she says. "I'll drag your fascist ass into court."

"Do that. See who a judge thinks should have custody of our kid. An unstable drunk with a history of mental illness and an arrest record long as my arm? Or a decorated former marine who makes a point of employing disabled vets? We'll see how it goes. Rudy, that's good gin. All yours if you want it."

Rudy Spaulding frog-marches Bloom to the cruiser while she twists and spits. The young cadet tugs the bottle of gin out of the pile of clothes. He turns it flashing in the sunlight to inspect the label.

"Is Mom getting arrested?" Jack asks.

Hank puts his hand on his son's shoulder. "Probably. But don't let it weigh on your mind. She's had plenty of practice."

2.

Jack sits with his legs hanging over the side of a hole gouged deep into the earth. His mother stares up at him from the bottom of the pit with a sad, apologetic smile. She's buried to her neck so that only her dirty face is visible. Her hair is all worms: fat, glistening earthworms that flex and squirm. The bottom of the hole is lit with a flashing blue light.

A screen door slaps shut with a bang loud as a gunshot, and Jack comes awake sitting on the top of the stairs. He has been night-walking again. There've been times his mother has found him out in the yard at two in the morning, eating handfuls of dirt. Once he went down the road bare naked, carrying a trowel, slashing it at imaginary enemies. It has been worse in the three weeks since she left.

He can still see that flashing blue light, and at first he doesn't know why. Beth appears at the bottom of the stairs and looks up at him with eyes bloodshot from crying. She mounts the steps three at a time, pulls on his arm to bring him to his feet.

"Come on, buddy," she says, her voice grainy with emotion. "Back to bed."

He climbs under the covers, and she sits on the edge of the bed beside him. She smooths his hair down with one palm, thoughtlessly stroking him as if he were a cat. He can smell her hands, a spicy sweetness, like geraniums.

Red and blue lights strobe across the smooth white plaster ceiling, throbbing around the blinds. Jack hears low male voices outside and the staticky squabble of people talking on the police scanner.

It isn't the first time law has come around to the house. The ATF raided them two years before. The feds tossed the house but didn't find the guns, which were buried in a sack, six feet deep, out in the barn, directly beneath the parked John Deere.

The bedroom door eases open. Hank looks in on him.

"Jack? It's your mother."

"Oh. Did she come to get me?" He hopes not. He's perfectly cozy under his blankets, with Beth's hand gently stroking his hair, and he doesn't want to get up.

"No."

Hank McCourt crosses the room and sits down beside Beth. Beth takes his hand and gazes miserably up at him. The round lenses of Hank's spectacles flash crimson and sapphire.

"Your mother is coming home," Hank says.

Beth shuts her eyes, the muscles of her face straining against some powerful emotion.

"She is? You're not mad at her anymore?" Jack asks.

"I'm not mad at her anymore."

"Did the police bring her home?"

"No. Not yet. Jack, do you know why your mother wanted to leave?"

"Because you wouldn't let her drink."

He has been taught this like a mantra over the last three weeks, has heard it from all of them: his father, Beth, Connor. His mother has been sober for two years, but her self-restraint finally split and tore, like a wet paper sack. The only Jack that concerned her now came in a bottle.

"That's right," Hank says. "She wanted to go someplace she could drink and take her crazy pills. She chose those things over you. It's awful to think she needed those things more than she needed us. She was staying in the efficiency apartments near High Street Liquor. So she didn't have to go far to do her shopping, I suppose. She bought a bottle of gin this afternoon and took it into the bath with her. When she stood to get out, she slipped and cracked her head."

"Oh."

"She's dead."

"Oh."

"She was ill, you know. She was ill when I met her. I thought I could make her better, but I couldn't. It runs too deep in her family. Your mother had peculiar ideas, and she tried to drown them with drink. In the end she only drowned herself." He waits for Jack to reply to this, but Jack doesn't have anything to say. Finally his father adds, "If you need to cry, no one will think less of you."

Jack searches his emotions but can't find anything yet approximating grief. Later, maybe. When he has time to get his head around it.

"No, sir," he says.

His father studies him for a time, from behind the bright blinking lenses of his spectacles. Then he nods, perhaps with approval, and squeezes Jack's knee again and rises. They do not hug, and Jack isn't surprised. Jack is not a little boy anymore. He's thirteen. Thirteen-year-olds fought in the Civil War against Yankee oppression. Thirteen-year-old soldiers carry machine guns in Syria to this very day. Plenty of thirteen-year-olds are ready to die or kill, whichever might be required.

Hank lets himself out of the bedroom. Beth stays behind. Jack doesn't cry, but *she* does, holding him to her and shuddering with soft sobs.

When she's all cried out, she gives Jack a peck on the temple. He takes her hand, kisses her creamy white palm, and tastes that spicy-sweet geranium soap. After she's gone, the taste remains, as lovely as a trace of cake frosting on his lips.

3.

They bury his mother on a windy day in early March on their own land, out beyond the orchard. Jack is not sure this is legal. His father says who is going to stop us, and Jack supposes the answer is no one.

Bloom doesn't have a coffin, and she hasn't been embalmed. Hank says embalming people is a waste of time. "You don't need to poison someone after they're already dead. God knows she had enough poison in her when she was alive."

She's wound up in a dingy white sheet with a few old stains on it that look like coffee spills. Jack's father has wrapped loops of silver duct tape around her ankles and throat, to draw the sheet tight to her body. He digs the hole with some of his friends, Separatists like him.

They have come from all over the state to honor Hank's loss. They are a crowd of ten-gallon hats and cowboy mustaches and blank stares. Some of them stand at the graveside with their AR-15s over their shoulders, as if a twenty-one-gun salute might be called for. One man, fleshy, sunburnt, with goggling eyes and a shaved head, wears crossed bandoliers and chaps, like he is on his way to a weekend engagement at the Alamo.

When the hole is deep enough, Connor and some of the others hand the body down. Hank kneels in the grave with his wife's shrouded head in his lap, gently stroking her brow. Perhaps he whispers to her. Once he glances up and meets Jack's gaze. Behind his John Lennon spectacles, his father's eyes are bright and brimming with tears, although they do not spill over.

Jack has the terrible idea his mother's eyes are open, too, and she is staring at him through the taut white cotton. He can see how her lips are parted. The sheet has sunk a little into the pit of her gaping mouth. At any moment he expects her to groan—or shriek.

Beth clutches Jack to her side, as if to comfort him, although she is the one who is crying. His head knocks against her big soft breasts.

Connor offers a hand, but Jack's father ignores it and lifts himself out of the grave under his own power. He dusts his palms off, walks to Jack's side, and puts a hand on his shoulder.

"Do you want to throw dirt on her?"

"Why would I want to do that?"

Hank's head jerks, and he stares down to see if Jack is giving him lip. He seems to decide his son is genuinely curious, and his face softens.

"To honor her memory," Hank says.

"Oh," Jack says. He picks up a handful of soil but then just lets it trickle out of his fist. He doesn't feel like honoring her with a faceful of dirt.

"That's all right," Hank says. "Maybe you'd like to bring her some flowers one of these days."

Beth is the first to grab a clump of earth and toss it in. She almost seems angry, the way she flings it at the body. The dirt makes a resonant *thwock* falling on the tight sheet, like a child's hand slapping a toy drum. Others join her. The man with the crossed bandoliers finds a shovel and begins to fill in the hole. Some of the cowboys fire their six-guns and wahoo mournfully. A bottle of Bulleit Bourbon begins to go around.

In less than a half hour, she has been planted like a seed.

4.

Five weeks after they plant his mother in the soil, Jack is on his way into town with Beth and Connor. His father has loaned them the F-150. Connor has farm business at Cordia Agricultural Supply, and Beth tells Jack he has to come along to protect her. She says she's trying to take care of her teeth, and she's worried about the candy machine in the lobby. She never can control herself around SweeTarts. But if Jack comes with them, he can eat most of her tarts for her, and her teeth will stay white and bright and straight, and Connor will still want to kiss her.

"*Mmmmmm*maybe," Connor says, squinting at her with one eye, like a man contemplating a challenging assignment.

She laughs and gives him a kiss that turns into a bite, Beth chewing on his lower lip. On the walk to the truck, he casually swats her heart-shaped behind. Such casual intimacies make Jack sick at heart, and for an instant he's sorry that Connor ever came back from

Afghanistan—such an evil thing to wish, he feels he might wilt with shame. Longing should be a sweet thrill, but for Jack it is a worm in a rotten apple.

They are two miles from the farm and two miles from town when Beth casts a wild look out the window and shrieks, "Pull over!" as if she has seen someone mangled and bloody at the side of the road.

Connor jerks the wheel, the ex-soldier handling the truck like a man who has had to drive through gunfire more than once. The pickup flings a milky cloud of dust into the air as they batter to a tooth-rattling stop on the shoulder.

Beth cranes her head to peer through the rear window at a farm stand. "The sign says she's got quail eggs."

Connor stares at her.

"Don't you get sick of eggs out of a chicken's butt?" Beth asks. "Don't you ever wanna eat something different?"

"I just did," Connor says. "I just ate the goddamn steering wheel."

Beth and Jack walk hand in hand to the farm stand, with the morning sunlight on their faces.

The stand is no more than a plank table on wooden trestles, covered with a green-and-white check tablecloth. Wicker baskets contain masses of radishes and bunches of kale. An elderly woman sits in a folding chair, looking as if she has nodded off, chin touching her chest. Jack can tell she's elderly because she wears a striped T-shirt that leaves her arms bare, and those arms are hatched with wrinkles, pale blue veins showing through the skin. But he can't see her face because she wears a wide-brimmed green straw hat, and with her head down her features are hidden beneath the floppy brim. The hand-lettered cardboard sign reads:

Quail Eggs! Yum yum good!
Tobacco-Leaf Hunny!
Apple Butter!
Small cakes, big tomatoes,
Seeds for the Garden

Beth peers into a shoe box stuffed with hay and oohs over the speckled eggs inside.

"I've never had quail eggs before," she says.

"I have the remedy for that, dearie!" says the old lady, and she straightens and lifts her head.

The sun shines through the thin material of the green straw hat and casts her face in an otherworldly green light. When she grins, her mouth opens so wide it's like she's been poisoned by the Joker. She keeps her gray hair pulled tightly back off her high forehead, and she has a Roman aquiline nose, and it comes to Jack that she looks something like George Washington. No sooner has the thought crossed his mind than she winks at him, as if he has spoken out loud and she wants him to know she isn't offended in the slightest.

"I heard about you folk. You're the tax resisters, over there starting your own nation. I hope you don't want to buy quail eggs with your own money—I only deal in American tender." She laughs, a dry cackle that sends a shiver through Jack.

"Glad to pay in American," Beth replies, her smile tightening. "Why not? It isn't worth the paper it's printed on. Hasn't been since we left the gold standard in 1933. You'd be better off taking payment in cigarettes. At least they'll still be worth something when the country falls."

"Did you want to pay me in ciggies?" the old woman asks. "It'll spare me a trip to the Citgo after you buy my eggs."

"I know most of the people round here. Where are you from?"

"The federal guv'mint!" says the old lady. "I am an undercover Eff Bee Eye agent, and I'm wearing a wire right this instant!" She cackles again. "I'm the oldest Eff Bee Eye agent in history. J. Edgar Hoover gave me my badge his own self, and the dress I'm wearing, too! We had the same taste in clothes."

Beth inquires how much for a dozen quail eggs, and the old woman tells her four-eighty. Beth asks what tobacco honey tastes like, and the old woman says just like honey.

"Well, what's special about it, then?"

"Eat enough and it will give you cancer," says the old doll, keeping herself entertained.

Beth opens her hemp purse and produces a crumpled ten. "I need change."

"Are you sure? Didn't we just agree U.S. money is only worth what we imagine? How about I give you a dime and you imagine it was a dollar?"

"I don't have that big an imagination," Beth says.

"Now, that is unfortunate. The true survivalist— someone who has truly made survival their primary preoccupation—will find an imagination more handy than bullets or beans. The lack of one often leads to avoidable misfortune."

"Do I have to pay extra for all the wisdom?" Beth asks. "Or is that on the house?"

The old woman lifts a metal cashbox from under the table and counts out Beth's money. She offers it over with her great hungry grin. "Good conversation is even better than quail eggs, and sitting out here by myself so long, I worked up an appetite. I hope you didn't find me too tiresome."

While the ladies spar, Jack moves along the table of produce. He admires a few boxes of button-size wild strawberries and a carton of oily green peppers. He picks through a wooden box full of tiny envelopes of seeds. He pauses at one for "Candy Corn" with a doodle on it that shows an ear of corn with orange and yellow kernels.

"You can't plant candy corn," Jack says to himself.

The old lady replies as if he'd been talking to her. "You can plant anything. You can plant an idea. I used to live near a power plant—who knew you could grow one of them? Killers sometimes plant evidence to throw the police off the track."

Jack shoots her a startled look, his heart hurrying in his chest, but if she meant anything by that last statement, there's no telling it from her daffy smile and bright eyes. He picks through the seeds some more. Another envelope is marked "Rocket." The doodle shows the tip of a missile sticking out of the ground.

"You can't plant that either."

"There's rockets planted all over this country. Enough to kill everyone on the planet ten times over."

The next envelope is marked "Mums." The doodle shows a sunny golden flower with a smiling face peeking out of it. The flower wears a dress and holds a child's hand.

"Twenty-five cents," the old lady says. "Go on and

grow yourself a mum. Grow yourself lots of 'em. All the mums you could ever need."

"Come on, bud," Beth says, carrying her purchase away in a brown paper bag, hugging it to her lovely bosom.

The old lady picks the envelope of mums out of the box and holds it out to him. "Prettiest mums you ever did see. Pretty and *hardy.* Give 'em something to drink, a little sun, a little love, and they'll shoot up and love you right back, Jack."

Jack's shoulders jump in a nervous jerk of surprise. It alarms him to think she knows his name. But no— wait. She doesn't (can't) know it . . . she just liked the rhyme, "back" and "jack." Any boy can be a bud or a mac or a jack.

He fishes a quarter out of the pocket of his bib overalls. She snatches it like a bird snapping a seed out of the dirt. She gazes avidly down at it, then turns it so he can see the raised image of President Washington.

"Why, it's my portrait!" she caws. "A perfect likeness!"

"Jack!" Beth shouts. She's at the truck, one foot on the running board. "Come on!"

Jack takes his envelope of mums and trots after her.

"Everything good must be paid for," the old lady says. "And everything wicked, too . . . everything wicked, especially. Reaping time always comes round. The corn falls to the scythe, sure as water runs downhill! Ha-ha!" She claps her hands as if she has said something quite clever.

"Psycho bitch," Beth says when the truck is moving again. "I ought to be glad she didn't bite one of us." She sees Jack turning the manila envelope over in one hand. "What'd you get? You buy yourself some flowers?"

"Dad said I could plant something for Bloom," Jack says. He has taken to calling his mother by her first name, same as the others.

"Aw," Beth says. "You are a darling. Can I help?"

He nods and is grateful when she puts an arm around him. She holds him all the way to Cordia Agricultural, where Jack climbs out to help Connor pile forty-pound sacks of ammonium nitrate into the flatbed. After Connor clangs the tailgate shut, Jack and Beth buy tarts from the quarter candy machine.

"Mm," Beth says, crunching a tart in her small white teeth. "Sour. Love these. They taste like radioactivity. Like they ought to glow. Does that make sense?"

Jack nods, unable to reply. He's sucking on a whole radioactive mouthful of sour tarts. The way the sugar makes his heart race, it's easy to imagine that his bloodstream is nothing but sweet poison now.

5.

The greenhouse has a curved roof like an airplane hangar's, only the walls are made of heavy-duty plastic. The world beyond seems blurred, a child's watercolor of field and sky. Beth leads Jack to one of the plywood tables and finds a few cheap plastic flowerpots.

"Too bad we didn't get these started a couple weeks ago," Beth says. "We had frost on the ground yesterday morning, but I think Mr. Winter is gone for good now. The weather is turning, and mums need to get a good running start on spring. We'll begin them inside, just to be safe, and in six weeks they'll be big enough we can move them outside."

Beth has an associate's degree in agricultural science from the U of Iowa and knows what she's talking about. She has seen to Jack's education in biology and natural sciences for years. Bloom handled English and history and civics. His father is supposed to be doing that now, but they meet only a couple of times a week, when Hank isn't busy with the farm or off visiting friends in the Patriot movement. Jack has to say he preferred Bloom's reading list. They had Harry Potter and the Narnia books. For his father Jack is making his way through *Behold a Pale Horse*, which is less like a book, more like a collage of manifestos, rants, and confessions.

Even Connor gives Jack lessons. Connor taught Jack how to drive the F-150 through an obstacle course, how to assemble an AR-15 blindfolded, and how to make a pipe bomb. Connor's lessons are obviously the best, but they are infrequent, as Jack's cousin is often out of state doing "recon." Reconnaissance of what, Jack asked Connor once. Connor got him in a headlock and said, "What you don't know, you can't tell, even during enhanced interrogation, like this." And he twisted Jack's nipple until Jack squealed.

Beth hefts a white plastic bag of soil, and Jack leaps to help her with it. They fill pots with earth as damp and black as crumbs of chocolate cake. Jack peels open the manila packet and sticks a finger in to dig out the seeds.

"Ouch!" he cries, and yanks his thumb back. For an instant he had an impression of being bitten by a small animal—a mouse—and bright red blood gleams around the edges of his thumbnail.

He shakes the seeds out into his palm, and who knows, maybe they did bite him. With his blood on them, they look like the teeth of a carnivore, stained from their last meal.

"What are you doing, Jack?" Beth says. "You want to water 'em, not bleed all over 'em."

"'The tree of liberty must be refreshed from time to time with the blood of patriots,'" Jack intones ominously, and they both crack up, although Beth casts a shame-faced look around as she laughs. This solemnity is a favorite of Hank McCourt's, and so naturally it is a giddy delight—and a kind of disloyalty—to make fun of it.

6.

Beth says the mums won't be ready for the garden until early May, but two weeks after they put them in their pots Jack has a look at them and hurries to find her. Dawn is just pinking the sky, but it's a rare day Beth isn't awake by sunup. If she's got her ears on, she should be able to hear him, even from the cottage at the end of the gravel lane. He crosses the front porch and descends to the dooryard. The big oak in the yard seems heavy with leaves, but when he hollers her name, the leaves erupt into the scarlet morning, a hundred sparrows taking off at once.

"Where's the fire, bud?" Beth asks, and he turns on his bare heel. She's already up at the farmhouse, peering at him with drowsy eyes through the bellied-out screen door.

For the tiniest fraction of a moment, he's surprised

to see her there. At this hour he would expect her to be padding around her cottage in her nightdress, helping Connor with his leg and performing her morning ablutions. But then she often serves all three of her men breakfast in the farmhouse kitchen, and perhaps she wanted to get a jump on the biscuits.

He plunges back across the porch, grabs her hand, and tows her toward the greenhouse. He has one look at her and doesn't dare another. Her hair is mussed up from sleep, and in her fuzzy sweater and acid-washed jeans, she looks so gorgeous it makes him short of breath. He turns his gaze instead to her feet, which are white and clean and bare and dainty.

Her brow furrows when she sees the plants in their pots. The mums already have felty green ears tufting up out of the dirt, big as hands.

"Huh! Well, I wonder if that ol' be-yotch ripped you off, kiddo."

"They aren't mums?"

"They look like 'em. But they haven't had time to grow so much. Not in ten days. I don't know if these are mums or salad, but I have dark suspicions. I suspect this stuff is crap. Do you want to keep our great garden experiment going or chuck 'em?"

He narrows one eye at her, as he has seen Connor do

when he's about to crack wise. "Lettuce consider. Do you carrot all what we do?"

She needs a minute to get that one. When she does, she raps his shoulder with one knuckle.

"I guess *weed* better move them outside then. Get it? *Weed?* Get it?"

"Mm-hm," he says. "Did you walk up here in your bare feet? They must be cold."

"Yeah. You know I'm always in a hurry to get up here and start another day of whipping your scrawny ass into shape. Speaking of. Let's chuck some food into you, huh? These aren't the only things shooting up around here."

His heart is so light and his spirits so high that he's annoyed with himself for wondering why there was no dirt or grass on her feet if she walked up from the cottage barefoot. It's like a mouthful of sour milk—there's nothing to do with a thought like that but spit it out.

7.

They pat the earth down around the plantings and then sit together on their knees in front of Bloom's grave marker. The air is rich with the mineral scent of fresh-turned loam. Her headstone is rose marble and by some modern alchemy has a photograph printed right on it: a nineteen-year-old Bloom smiles demurely, eyes downcast, flowers in her hair, on her wedding day.

The breeze stirs the green leaves of what might or might not be mums, bunched together below her waist-high stone.

Jack is pleased with the effect and proud of the work they've done this morning and is taken off guard when he sees tears dripping off the end of Beth's upturned nose. He puts an arm around her—a not entirely unselfish act.

Beth wipes her hands across her cheeks and snuffles in a delightfully unfeminine way. "I wish I could have her back. She didn't just love you. She loved me, too, more than I ever deserved. If I loved her as well as she loved me, she'd still be alive."

"No," Jack says. "That isn't true."

"It is. I knew what would happen to her if she left us. I should've got on my knees in the dirt and begged your father to let her come back home. I knew she couldn't be out there on her own, not with all the rotten stuff banging around inside her head. And I let her go anyway, and what kind of person does that make me?"

Jack puts both arms around her and squeezes. "Don't be sad, Beth. You didn't make her slip in the bath."

Beth makes a sound somewhere between a sob and

a croak and squeezes him back. Her whole lean body, with its wiry muscles shifting under the skin, shudders.

"Besides," Jack says, "you helped with the flowers. You're telling her how much she meant to you now, just by planting them with me. Nothing says good-bye better than flowers."

8.

Jack wakes from restless, overheated dreams and discovers he is sick. There is a great feeling of weight, of heaviness, in his chest. He sits on the edge of the bed, in the dark of his bedroom, taking stock. He coughs, tentatively, and produces a gravelly rattle.

He needs to be watered, he thinks. No—he frowns. He needs *water*, not to *be* watered.

He crosses the cold plank floor in bare feet. At the doorway he thumps his breastbone with one fist and clears his throat and coughs again. He coughs brown flecks into one palm. Blood? He turns his hand this way and that in the gloom and decides he's looking at dirt.

Jack sways down the staircase. He feels pressure building in his chest, another cough getting ready to explode. He hears voices, but they're muffled, as if his ears are crammed with earth.

At the foot of the steps, he bends over and grips his

knees to cough his hardest cough—and something snags halfway up his throat. He tries to suck a breath and can't, and suddenly he's suffocating. Something tough and fibrous has caught in his gullet. He opens his mouth and sticks a finger in to force himself to gag and finds wiry threads sticking out of his throat. He grips them between thumb and forefinger and pulls. He makes watery, sick, choking sounds as he hauls out what appears to be a root: brown, hairy, dusty. He pulls and pulls, and it goes on and on, and then suddenly the last of it is out—the stem of a plant with a few greenish pods at one end and a string of his spit hanging off it.

Jack tosses it aside in revulsion, turns, and flies toward the kitchen. He is in a panic to find help and desperate to get the taste of soil out of his mouth, and as is often the way in dreams, he runs through parts of the house that don't exist. He runs through a room where the floorboards have been removed to show the dirt beneath. Someone has been digging graves here. He runs through a room where Beth reclines naked in a claw-footed tub, soaping one pink leg in the steam. She's not using a *bar* of soap but a *flower* of soap. *A geranium,* Jack thinks, the idea landing with a bewildering occult force. *A geranium!* She asks if he wants to get in with her, but he keeps running. He slaps through the swinging kitchen door and rushes to the sink and throws on the tap. The faucet leaps, jerks, doesn't produce anything—and then begins to bubble rusty-colored water. He stares. The water darkens and deepens in color, becoming viscous. It stinks not of blood but of fresh-turned earth.

"Wash your face," his mother says gently, and takes him by the hair and shoves his head into it.

Cold water wakes him.

He sways at the sink in the kitchen, catching clean, fresh, icy water in the bowl of his cupped hands and then splashing it into his own face. With each handful of water, he rinses away a little more of the night terrors. When he's in the middle of one, it feels as true as life—truer, in some ways, more compelling. But they melt as fast as snowflakes against bare skin. He drinks right from the tap, and by the time he stands straight and wipes his mouth, his heart is no longer racing and he feels sleepy and untroubled. He knows he's been night wandering because he can't remember coming downstairs, but he recalls almost nothing of his confused fantasies except Beth roasting her naked body pink in a hot bath. The clock on the oven reports it is just three minutes after 1:00 A.M.

As Jack fills a glass of water—he is still thirsty, his throat feels *dusty* somehow, and he wonders if he's been in the backyard eating dirt again—low male voices in the dining room catch his attention: his father and Connor.

They have not heard him shuffling around. Jack crosses the dark expanse of the kitchen to the swinging door, which gapes open, held ajar by an antique doorstop, a cast-iron ear of corn. Jack is about to say hello, then shuts his mouth. He remains in the darkness of the kitchen, peering silently at his father and his cousin.

Hank's laptop is open, and the screen shows an image of the federal building in Oklahoma City, after Timothy McVeigh's bomb collapsed the whole front of the structure. Jack has heard his father say, more than once, that Oklahoma City was the first move in a long game, but when Jack asks what game and who's playing, his father only pats him on the head and smiles fondly.

Hank has a hand on his nephew's shoulders. Connor leans over the table, his back to the kitchen. They're looking at maps. One is a printout of an urban area. Another is a hand-drawn diagram of a building.

"—is the easiest way to get a pass to enter the garage. Park on level A-1, leave the keys in it, and walk."

"ATF is the top floor?"

Hank's right hand makes little circles on Connor's back. "And there's an IRS office in the same building, on four. A small one, but still tasty—like the cherry on a sundae."

Connor thinks it over. Suddenly he laughs and lifts his chin. His face is almost in profile, and his eyes are shining with excitement, and his mouth is open slightly. Jack sees something, a quality of his cousin he has never before observed, but which he supposes was always there: stupidity.

"Can you imagine!" Connor says, and claps his hands—*bang!* "There'll be pieces of them falling three states away. It'll be raining chunks."

"There'll be pieces of them knocked into orbit," Hank agrees.

Connor bows his head to examine the maps once more. When he speaks again, his voice is somber. "You'll look after Beth?"

"I already do."

"That's right. Yes, you do. Better than I can." This last is said with a certain bitterness.

"*Shhh.* What got done to you over in the sand was a crime—but you didn't come home any less of a man. You came home *more* of a man, and little Bethy knows it. Beth knows what you can do, and so do I. Someday everyone will know."

Connor straightens. "I wish we were doing it tomorrow."

"The big regional ATF assembly is in October. That's soon enough."

"If we have till October. If *she* didn't tell anyone."

"She didn't."

"You can't be sure of that."

"I am, though. I'm sure of it. Beth got everything out of her. Bloom knew what would happen if we got raided by the feds again. She knew it would be like putting a gun to her son's head. I warned her. I told her more than once. I said if they came, I wouldn't hesitate—I'd put the boy in the ground myself before I let the law take him away from me. No. She was crazy, Connor. But she wasn't stupid."

Jack's glass slips. His fingers tighten on it before it can drop to the tiles.

He sets his glass down very carefully in the stainless-steel sink and flies back to his bed, like the shadow of an owl moving across a moon-washed field.

9.

He can't sleep. At ten to five he is up again and outside, legs trembly and stomach spoiled.

The sky shines a soft marigold. A streaming mist shimmers above the long, sloping fields, where green stalks of wheat are just beginning to prod their way out of the earth. He thinks he ought to pass a word with Bloom about what he's heard and walks in bare feet through the wet grass, all the way out to the family graveyard. He lets himself in through the wrought-iron gate, beaded with dew, and finds her grave, and sinks to his knees before it. The mums are coming up in bunches of oily green stalks, with broad dark leaves. No sign of flowers. Not yet. They need a little more time before they're ready to blossom.

He can't think about the rest of it now: something about the ATF, something about what happened to Connor in Afghanistan, where he was almost killed by friendly fire, victim of a drone strike operated by his own government. What happened to Connor below the belt is never discussed, but Jack knows the missing leg is not the worst of it. He has seen Connor with his pants down, has seen the scarred stump of his penis, a horrible thing with no head.

I'd put the boy in the ground myself before I let the law take him away from me. That thought goes off in Jack's mind again and again, and each time it is like a gunshot, bullet to the head. That and: *Beth got everything out of her.* There are shades of meaning in this declaration that Jack doesn't want to examine.

He has to do something with the sick, ugly energy coursing through him. It feels like if he doesn't break something, he'll puke, but there's nothing breakable in arm's reach, so instead he grabs a fistful of stalks protruding from the ground.

The roots of the mum are embedded surprisingly

deep, have an astonishing grip on the soil. He grits his teeth and *pulls,* and the dirt begins to fall away. It's almost as if the green stalks are attached to some absurdly heavy gourd. He pulls—shuts his eyes—pulls harder—and opens his eyes—and can't scream because there's no air left in his lungs.

He has pulled a head out of the ground.

Not a whole head. Only the top part, from the bridge of the nose up. It is a woman's face. No—more than that. It is his mother's face, though her skin is greenish and waxy and her hair isn't hair at all, but long, tough strands of green fiber, plant stalks. Her eyes are shut.

Jack flings himself back, almost to the foot of the grave. He struggles to cry out and can't force any sound from his throat.

Her eyes roll open. The eyeballs look like soft white onions. There are no irises, no pupils, no sign of sight. Then she winks.

Jack gets a shout out at last and runs.

10.

He creeps back for another look, just before lunch, when he has a break from the morning chores and the sun has cooked off the mist. He can see where he half tugged the mum out of the ground, but it has sunk back down, dirt crumbling and falling to cover . . . what? He can see the curve of something that might be a skull or could be nothing more than a big peeled stick in the dirt. He kicks loose soil over it to cover it up. When he's done, he spreads the earth around, smooths it out.

He tries not to feel the top of her head right under the dirt, but his hand moves helplessly to the other plants. Feeling one hard curve of skull after another. Six in all.

This time when Jack leaves, he forces himself to walk, although his legs tremble.

11.

Three days later he squeezes into the front seat of the truck, between Connor and his father, and they drive to the efficiency apartments on Stalwart, where his mother spent the last weeks of her life. The police have finally authorized Hank McCourt to collect his deceased wife's things. The apartment building is on a wide avenue of shops catering to diminished expectations: a check-cashing outfit, a vape shop, and a Baptist church with a white drive-thru sign out front that reads ALL FLESH IS GRASS AND JESUS IS THE LAWNMOWER.

Hank steers them under a white stucco arch and into a courtyard parking lot. The building is two stories and wraps around them on three sides. There's a swim-ming pool in the center of the courtyard, enclosed by chain-link fence, but the water is low and there's a filthy pair of white jockey underwear floating in the shal-low end.

His father rolls up to park beside a police car. A cop leans against the cruiser, a steel clipboard in one hand and his campaign hat in the other. The last time Jack saw this cadet, he was inspecting an unopened bottle of gin. Just like then, he has a slender white stick poking out of the corner of his mouth.

Hank hops down on his side. Jack follows Connor out the other. The junior cadet hands Hank the clip-board and shows him where to sign.

"Kid want to stay out with me?" the young cop asks.

"He'll be all right."

The cop meets Jack's gaze. "Want a smoke?" He of-fers him the box. At that moment Jack realizes what the cop has in his mouth: a candy cigarette.

Hank nods indulgently, although he takes a dim view of processed sugars, so Jack says, "Thank you, sir," and helps himself.

The apartment is a single room with a grubby wall-to-wall carpet the color of dirt. Directly opposite the front door is a sliding glass door open to the day. Somehow the brightness of the afternoon makes the room seem even gloomier.

Jack steps out of the entryway into the open space. There's a cot around the corner, the bed unmade. The air has a sour odor, like feet. A brown paper bag crammed with empty bottles of gin stands against one wall. Flies buzz around an open carton of Chinese food, next to a book called *How to Fight for Your Kids and Win—A Field Guide to Divorce.* Jack wanders over and peeks into the box of Chinese. At first it seems the noodles are squirming. But they aren't noodles.

The three of them pack Bloom's belongings while the cop watches.

Jack finds his mother's clothes in neat piles under the bed and puts them in a box. He discovers an empty pill bottle: clozapine. Sounds like "clothespin," what you'd use to clamp down on something, which makes sense—this is what she used to clamp down on the bad thoughts in her head. Jack discovers another bottle of gin, two-thirds empty, tangled in her bedsheets.

"Funny thing is," the junior cadet says, "liquor store right next door, and the guy who runs the place says he never saw her."

"People don't like to shit where they eat, do they?" Connor says, scratching the back of his neck.

When they've carried the last cardboard box to the pickup, the junior cadet shuts the sliding glass door and thumbs the lock. When he steps back, the door shudders open a few inches anyway.

"That's right," the cadet says. "Lock is bust. What a craphole this place is. She's prolly fortunate she drank herself to death before someone could walk in and murder her."

"My son is in the room," Hank says, in that mild tone that is scarier than if he yelled.

The cop lowers his head and thumps it against the glass. He looks shamefacedly over his shoulder.

"Ah, gosh," he says. "I am so sorry."

Jack removes the last little toothpick of candy cigarette from the corner of his mouth and lifts it in a gesture he hopes will be understood to mean, *All is forgiven.*

On the walk to the truck, though, he discovers that his hands are sticky with candy-cigarette spit. He says just a minute and goes back in to wash them.

The bathroom is a tiny closet with a rosy pink tub, a toilet, and a sink somehow impossibly crammed into it. He doesn't look in the tub, intentionally averts his gaze from the place she drowned, won't even look at it in the mirror. Instead he stares into the sink, where some of his mother's hair still clogs the drain. They look like the fibers of dirty roots: a bad thought. Jack runs lukewarm water and scrubs his hands and lathers them with the little bar of soap. Then he pauses and lowers his head and breathes in the odor of his soap-slippery hands and tries to think where he has smelled this fragrance before, this particular spicy-sweet scent of geraniums.

12.

They have one more stop before they head home. Hank turns the truck into the lot at Motorsports Madnezzz, and Connor lowers himself laboriously down to the asphalt. The disabled veteran limps inside, leaving Jack alone with his father.

Hank leans back, one arm hanging out the window, and turns his head to fondly consider his child. Country music twangs on the radio.

"What do you know, Jack?" his father asks, and Jack's heart skips, and for a moment he thinks his father has somehow guessed the terrible certainty that has begun to harden in Jack's thoughts.

"Not a thing," Jack says. "I don't know a single thing."

"That's not true," his dad tells him. "You know your rights under the Constitution. You know how to pull weeds and how to drive this truck. You know how to safely operate a firearm, and you can make an improvised explosive device or a simple detonator from scratch. You know your mother loved you and would've died for you."

"Did she?" Jack asks.

"Did she . . . ?"

Die for me, Jack doesn't say. Instead he says, "Love me? She walked away and drank herself to death. Just like the policeman said. She took clothes-a-pin."

His father laughs without humor. "Clozapine. She would've pumped *you* full of that stuff if she could've. The Medical Establishment would like to have all of us on it, to make us less likely to question or resist." He looks out the open window, drums his fingers on the steel window frame. "She loved you in her way. A mother's love is planted deep. You can't uproot that. There's no one who can replace her. Although there *is* Beth. God knows Beth thinks the world of you. And she's a good example of what an upright and dutiful woman can be. I'm glad you have Beth in your life. That's a girl who knows how to keep her hands clean."

"Of course," Jack says. "She uses soap."

And then he surprises himself by laughing—a slightly crazed, crow caw of a laugh. Suddenly he has remembered where he last smelled that particular sweet odor of geraniums. If his father knew half of what was in his head, he might not think clozapine was such a bad idea.

His father frowns, but then the doors to Motorsports Madnezzz open and Connor emerges. He has a big white fifty-gallon tank of liquid nitromethane. A man in a Lynyrd Skynyrd shirt follows him out, carrying a tank himself. Hank gets out and lowers the tailgate, and they pile the tanks in.

"I got two more for you," says the guy in the Skynyrd shirt. He has a grungy little beard and oily hair sticking up in odd places. "I can't wait to see you racin' again, Connor. 'Bout time you saddled up. When are you putting tires on the track?"

"Look for me at Caledonia in August. But don't blink or you'll miss me."

"Same Road Runner? I always thought that ride was the bomb."

Connor grins. "Brother, you got no idea."

13.

The sow has had piglets, and in the afternoons Jack likes to go out and throw scraps to them, to watch them dance on their little trotters. More than once he has dozed off in the sweet grass outside their enclosure, their shrill, girlish shrieks following him into sleep, a sound like children being skinned alive. He feels a bit sleepy now, leaning over the fence, feeding them pork rinds out of a bag, and doesn't notice for several minutes that they are one piglet short. There are four hopping beneath his feet, grinning their hobgoblin smiles, when there should be five. Their mother, all 630 pounds of her, snores on the far side of the pen. One ear twitches at flies.

He hops the fence and ducks into the hog house, a long, open-faced shed. The interior is ripe with the green smell of pig shit. He kicks at the hay the sow uses for her bed, wondering if he will find a dead piglet with a black face. It wouldn't be the first time the sow has accidentally sat on one of her young and suffocated it. But no.

Jack steps back out into the bright glare of the day. He has a crowd of piglets underfoot, hopping at his ankles, grunting for attention and hoping he will drop more rinds. He ignores them and walks the length of the fence. As he approaches the far southwestern corner of the enclosure, the piglets fall away behind him, let him go on alone.

The pigs have trampled their pen to a floor of churned, sun-baked mud, except in the corners, where there are tufts of weeds and pale grass. As he approaches the nearest corner, he sees what looks like a fat pink lump of sausage, tangled in the grass. He slows. He smells something bad, like offal, like a warm split intestine in the sunshine. He shades his eyes with his hand.

The missing piglet is tangled in roots and weeds.

There are tough wiry roots wrapped around and around its throat. Each little leg is bound up in more loops of weed. Roots twist around to fill its open mouth and cram deep into its throat.

As Jack stares, the roots seem to tighten. A fresh tendril squirms like a grass snake and pushes itself into the piglet's half-open right eye with a faintly audible *splort!*

Jack doesn't know he's dropped the pork rinds until he finds himself on the other side of the pen, gasping for air, bent over and clutching his knees.

The piglets creep carefully toward the dropped bag, nervously monitoring that mass of squirming roots in the corner of the pen. The bravest of them grabs the bag by one flap and runs away with it, squealing triumphantly, while the others give chase.

14.

Jack McCourt has never felt less like going to sleep. He has a digital clock beside the bed, but he hardly looks at it. Instead he watches a rectangle of silver moonlight rise on the wall. It climbs higher and higher, moving from right to left across the room, raking the ceiling. Then it falls toward his bureau, dropping ever lower, until it vanishes. When he does peek at the time, it is almost 3:00 A.M.

His mother believed in astral spirits, and maybe there's something to it. He is so quiet, slipping down the back stairs, he might be a ghost of himself. He lets himself into the greenhouse—the air is so steamy and warm it's like stepping into a bathroom after someone has had a long, hot shower—and finds a trowel. Jack takes it with him to the graveyard.

He will tear up the mums, he thinks, when he gets to his mother's plot, and he will see they are only plants. Something has come loose in his mind, like a nut slipping on a pipe, and bad-dream ideas are leaking out. He can't be surprised. It runs in the family. Not for nothing did his mother want the clozapine.

Only when he arrives at her pink marble gravestone, he understands he isn't going to find ordinary plants with hairy, dirty roots.

The head of the slaughtered piglet is here, balanced carefully on the top of her marker. Its eyes are gone, and the sockets have been filled with white and yellow daisies. It smiles idiotically.

The mums beneath her gravestone are three feet high and obscure everything chiseled into the marble except her first name, which now reads as a command: BLOOM! He cannot think, at first, how the decapitated head of the piglet could've gotten out here unless someone carried it out. The swine enclosure is more than two football fields away. Then it comes to him that the mums must have root systems that reach all the way to the house. Perhaps this lump of pig has been carried all this distance *underground*. Is that possible? There is a lot of dried filth on the piglet's face.

Jack grips a handful of stems and pulls. Whatever is below the soil is heavy, so heavy. Dirt falls away.

The top of his mother's head comes out of the earth. Her eyes are shut. Her face is slick, and there's a grub on her filthy brow.

He uses his hands to clear the dirt back from her nose, to unearth her mouth. Her eyes roll open. The onions in her head stare blindly out at him.

"Jack," she whispers, and smiles.

15.

"You aren't my mother," he says when he gets his breath back.

"We're all your mother," she says, and his eyes dart to the other plants. "We grew you. Before you grew us."

"My mother is in the dirt," he says.

"Yes, but we don't have to stay here."

That's not what he meant.

"I'm imagining you."

"Give me your hand."

He holds out his palm, close to her face. At the last instant, he thinks her mouth will suddenly distend, open into a grotesque horror-movie maw full of teeth, and she'll bite his hand off at the wrist.

Instead she closes her eyes and rests her cheek against his palm. The texture is not quite right, not quite flesh. It's more rubbery, like the outer skin of an eggplant. But she's warm, and she gently kisses the ball of his thumb, as his mother did a thousand times in life. He shivers with relief and pleasure.

He didn't know until right then how much he missed her.

16.

"Jack," says the second mum when he tugs her head up out of the black, cake-dough soil.

"Jack," says the third.

"Jack, Jack, Jack," the mums singsong into the night as he clears the dirt away from their heads, six in all, buried up to their necks in the dirt. One of them has grown wrong. She has a dent in the right side of her face, and her right eye won't open. The whole face has a mis-shapen gourdlike quality to it, and there are hundreds of tiny ants crawling in and out of a black gouge in her right temple. She grins toothlessly. When she tries to say his name, it comes out, *"hhhHHhhack! Haaa-ack!"*

17.

He says, "Are you a plant? Or an animal?"

"They're only different categories in people's heads. There are really only two categories, Jack. Alive . . . and dead." The first head he'd dug up does all the talking. The others stare at her with their slick white onion eyeballs. "I didn't want to go. I didn't want to leave you."

"It wasn't your fault."

"Wasn't it?" She smiles, eyelids sinking with a certain sly suggestion.

He looks back at the farmhouse and spits.

"They're going to do something bad, Jack," she says. "Your father is going to do something bad."

"He already did something bad."

"hhhhhhHHHHHAAAAaaants! Haa-ants! Haants in my p-p-pants!" says the mum with ants crawling in and out of the hole in her temple.

"No, love," says Mum #2. "Not in your pants. They're in your brains."

"Grains?" says the deformed mother. "G-grains? Haaants in the grain!"

A few of the other mums sigh.

"He's going to do something worse than what got done to me," says Mum #1.

"I know. I know what he's going to do and how he's going to do it. He's got all of it out in the barn: the fertilizer and the nitro. Connor is going to use it to blow people up." Jack almost adds, *And kill himself while he's at it, and then Dad can marry*— but he won't even allow himself to finish the thought.

"You need to go. You need to warn people."

"Why didn't *you* warn people?"

Mum #1 smiles sadly, wistfully. "He had you. He said he'd kill you if I told. He'd shoot you, and then he'd shoot himself. I thought Meemaw could help us, but she didn't get here until after I was gone."

"She didn't get here at all."

"Yes she did," she says, and the smile is sly again. "You've already met her."

The other heads are nodding. A black, three-inch centipede falls out of the dirty root-tangle of Mum #2's hair and onto her forehead. It crawls down the bridge of her nose, and then her tongue pokes out of her mouth and reaches up and licks it off. There is a crunch as she closes her teeth on it.

Jack says, "You were a seed. I planted you myself. You can't really be my mum. You're just pretending.

You're like that movie. The one where the plants wrap up people who are sleeping and grow copies."

"We are rooted in your blood, Jack McCourt. And in hers. We draw from her strength even now. Our roots are tough and hardy and grow fast, to find what we need."

He thinks of the piglet and shudders. "You must be thirsty. We've been in a dry spell. Do you want me to get the watering can?"

"We're not thirsty for that," Mum #1 confesses.

"No," he says. "Do you want another piglet?"

"Maybe something with a little more juice in it," she says. "We're almost strong enough, Jack, to pull up roots and have us some fun. We could paint the farm red tonight, boy!"

"It's already red."

"Redder," says Mum #3, and she laughs a hoarse, smoker's laugh.

"Tell me what you want," Jack says.

"How about you walk that sow over here," Mum #1 suggests.

"Sow!" says the one with ants all over her face, and her tongue lolls out, and she slobbers on her lips. "Sow—*now!*"

"Okay," Jack says. "I understand. Mom? I don't want to stay here one more night."

"No," she says. "You won't have to. Just do this last

thing for us? Bring us a sow to build up a little strength. And then, Jack—"

"We'll help you do the rest," say five of the six heads at the same time. The sixth head, the deformed mum, licks ants off her cheek and smacks her lips.

As he reels out of the graveyard, the first poisonous line of crimson light shows in the east. The edge of the world glows like an ember.

18.

Jack is in the kitchen when Beth wanders in, her hair mussed up from sleep and her feet bare. He always expects her to enter from the porch, through the screen door, but instead she lets herself into the kitchen from the front hall, doing up the top button on her flannel shirt as she approaches. Is it *her* flannel shirt? It looks like a man's. It looks like one of his father's.

When she sees him on the far side of the kitchen counter, her chubby, pale face darkens with a blush and her fingers lose their grip on the button. The flannel shirt springs open to show her pretty, freckled breastbone.

"Jack, I—" she begins, but Jack doesn't have time for her explanations or, worse, her confession. He reels around the kitchen counter, holding his right hand up in the gesture that means "hello" but also "halt." Blood falls in fat drops from the bright line raked across his palm.

"Oh, Beth. Oh, Beth, quick, quick, come with me. I did something stupid. I did something really, really bad," he says, and is interested to find he is close to genuine tears, his eyes tingling and the world blurring.

"Jack! You're bleeding. We ought to do something about that hand—"

"No, no, *no*, please, just come, just come see what I *did*, Beth, you've got to help me, please—"

"Of course I will," Beth says, and clutches him to her, thoughtlessly squeezing his face to her bosom. Only a few weeks ago, such an intimacy would've dizzied him, but now he finds it as repulsive as a centipede crawling over his face.

With his uninjured hand, he tows her by the elbow to the back door. Blood plinks and plops on the tiles.

"I let her out of the pen, and she wouldn't go back in," he says in his choked voice. "I thought I could scare her."

"Oh, Jack," Beth says. "One of the pigs?"

"The sow," he says, leading her out into the pearly, brassy light of dawn. He hurries her across the dewy grass, past the kitchen garden, through the open gate of the graveyard. "I'm so stupid. I think she's going to die."

He slows as they approach his mother's headstone and the plants growing in a wild tumult before it. They've all cleverly sunk back into the ground, so nothing is visible except the disturbed earth and their tufted green branches. He lets go of Beth, and she takes another few steps forward, looking around, puzzled. When she frowns, Jack can see she has a small second chin, and it strikes him that someday she will be unpleasantly fat. Then he thinks, *No, she will never be fat.*

"Jack," Beth says, and her voice has a note of caution in it. "I don't see anything. What are you playing at?"

He reaches behind his back and grips the handle of the trowel, jammed down into the back of his jeans. He means to drive the point of the blade into her calf, but she turns at the last instant, and he sinks it, with a gritty crunch, into her thigh, above her left knee. She cries out and sits down among the mums with a thud. Beth draws a long, quivering breath and holds it, staring at the trowel buried in her leg. She rests her shoulders back against Bloom McCourt's headstone.

"Get her," Jack says to the mums. "Finish her off! She's yours!"

The plants do not stir.

Beth lifts her chin and gazes at him with bewildered eyes, brimming with tears.

"Have you lost your mind?" she asks.

"Get her! Kill the sow!" he shouts at the mums,

something almost like hysteria in his tone, but there is no response.

"Are you out of your god*damn* mind?" Beth asks again.

Jack stares into her pale face, at her damp eyes and quivering, girlish chin.

"Oh, for goodness' sake," Jack says. "I think I am."

His hand finds the handle of the trowel. He yanks it out of her leg. Then he puts it back in, this time in her chest. She tries to scream, but the third blow sinks into her mouth, cutting it open wide. The fourth finds her throat.

For a long time after, there is only the sound of digging, although Jack never once sinks the trowel into soil.

19.

Once he's done making a red, chewed-up clay of Beth's breasts and face, he tries to dig up his mums. He pulls up plant after plant and finds only the twisted white claws of roots, dirt falling off them. The sixth plant is sickly, the leaves full of holes, ants crawling up and down the roots.

Jack touches his head, which feels queer, and leaves red fingerprints on his face. Whether he has marked himself with Beth's blood or his own, he could not say.

He wonders if this is what it feels like to be hungover. His arm is sore from sticking her so many times. Butchering a full-grown woman is tiring work.

What exactly was he thinking when he led her out here anyway? It's already hard to recall. He can never truly remember his night terrors when they fade. They are like one of those flowers that only open by moonlight, and the night is well over, the sky is brightening, turning a shade of lemon.

Beth, with her slashed, savaged mouth yawning wide, gapes blindly at the coming dawn.

20.

Jack is a while in the barn. The forty-pound plastic sacks of ammonium nitrate are piled against one wall, the white cans of nitromethane lined up next to them. He works by the shaded steel lamp on the plywood table, crafting a simple explosive out of a couple inches of copper pipe, black gunpowder, cotton swabs, and some other bits and pieces. He caps either end of the pipe, feeds a fuse punched through a hole in one end. He works in a kind of half-awake trance, without second-guessing himself, without second thoughts. There is no going back now. There is only going forward.

After due consideration he nestles the nitro tanks here

and there among the heavy-duty plastic sacks of fertilizer. He uses electrical tape to secure his homemade
IED to one of the cans, directly beneath the valve—then
rotates the tank so the gleaming copper pipe is out of
sight, facing the wall.

By the time he leaves the barn, the sun is snagged
in the branches of the big oak beyond the house and
the entire tree is aglow like a burning skeletal hand of
glory. The grass rustles in the breeze, a hundred thousand burning filaments of green light.

21.

"Dad," Jack says. He pushes aside the shower curtain.
"Dad! I did something bad, I did something really, really bad. I need help."

His father stands, broad-shouldered and powerfully
built, in the hot and foaming spray. His face looks curiously naked without his spectacles. He twists his head
around and stares nearsightedly down at his son. Hank
McCourt's face is almost innocent in its shock.

"I went out, I went to Mom's grave—sometimes I go
out in the morning, just to spend time with her—only
I heard something moving in the corn," Jack says, his
words almost running together while tears run down his
cheeks. "I went in to see what it was, and a man tried to

grab me. A man in a black helmet and a flak jacket, and he had a gun. He tried to grab me, and I hit him in the neck, I . . . I . . ."

Jack produces the blood-sticky trowel in one shaking hand, holds it out for a moment, and lets it drop to the floor.

"I think I killed him, Dad," Jack says.

His father turns off the water and grabs for a towel.

"Did it say anything on the flak vest?" his father asks.

"I don't know, I don't know," Jack moans. "I think . . . I think it said ATF? Dad, there's more of them out there. I saw two other black helmets in the corn, and, Dad, oh, Dad, Beth came to look for me, and I think they got her," Jack says, all breathless. "I heard her shout."

His father pushes past him. In the bedroom he grabs his jeans off the floor and steps into them, cinches his belt. The Glock is in its holster as always. Jack put it back after unloading the magazine.

"Dad, I don't think any of the other men in the corn know about the one I stabbed, I don't think they've found his body yet, but what's going to happen when they do?" His voice rises to a keening wail, and his whole body is shaking. It isn't hard to feel sick with grief. His mother is in the dirt, and she's not even a plant either, just food for plants. His mother is never coming back. Also, Jack's brain itches. He has been wondering in the last few moments if there might be ants in his head. It's been itching ever since he finished murdering Beth.

"What's going to happen," his father says, "is we're going to put a hurt on them like they never knew they could be hurt. But first we need the guns in the barn."

He doesn't bother with a shirt or shoes but plunges out of the room in nothing more than his jeans, leaving behind a cloud of steam and Ivory soap smell. Ivory soap, not geranium-scented hotel-room soap. Maybe the crazy old thing at the farm stand was just a crazy old thing, not his hundred-year-old witchy grandmother come to give him magic seeds so he could grow a new mum. Maybe there is nothing in the garden but dirt and roots and plants and Beth's corpse and a piglet Jack himself slaughtered in his sleep.

But Bloom McCourt didn't drink, not anymore, and the sliding glass door in her hotel room didn't lock, and Jack knows what he smelled on Beth's hands. He didn't dream that. His father sent Beth to visit Bloom as a sympathetic friend, to find out who she might've told about the explosive materials in the barn. Once Beth made sure Bloom hadn't told anyone, she smashed his mother's head in, and watched her drown, and planted the empty bottles of gin. Jack might suffer from night terrors, but not idiocy, and the facts have been in front of him for some time now.

Jack hurries after his father. As Hank crosses the porch, he grabs the clapper in the old rusted dinner bell and gongs it, once, twice, a third time: the signal for a raid.

His father crosses the dirt apron in front of the farmhouse, angling toward the barn. He doesn't seem to notice that Jack has moved the F-150. As Hank reaches the big double swinging doors, Jack sees Connor coming up the road, moving in a jerky, hopping stride, his eyes wild and his shirt unbuttoned, a hunting rifle in both hands.

"What . . . ?" Connor cries.

"They're here," Jack's father says. "It's happening. They've got Beth, so she's out of it. We move quick enough, we can cut through them like a knife through butter, shoot our way through their line and get to the east side of Long Field. The old Jeep is parked in the corn shed. We could be in Iowa by lunch. There's plenty of men in the movement who will hide us. But we need the guns buried under the tractor."

"Fuck!" Connor says, and staggers into the darkness of the barn.

His father yanks himself up into the John Deere. Connor hurries to the air compressor, flips it on, and grabs the big post-hole digger. They can have their fully automatic machine guns in five minutes if they work quickly.

Jack watches from the open double doors long enough to be sure they're both occupied, and then he walks to the pile of ammonium nitrate against the wall. There's a box of kitchen matches on the worktable, next to an oil lamp. Jack lights the fuse on his improvised pipe bomb, constructed just exactly the way Connor taught him.

Jack walks back to the big double doors of the barn like a sleepwalker, but he isn't sleepwalking—he's got his eyes wide open, and the morning is bright and blue and clear. He swings the doors shut and locks them with the big Yale padlock. The two men won't be able to get out the side door either. He has already backed his father's Ford F-150 against it, so it can't be forced open.

He strolls down the gravel lane, a thirteen-year-old American boy in Converse All-Stars, with dirt on his nose and blood on his hands. A child of the land that grew him.

Behind him someone shouts in surprise. Connor? One of them throws himself into the double doors, which shudder and quake and remain closed. His father yells Jack's name. Now both of them hit the double doors, with a splintering crunch. A few pieces of wood go flying, but the lock holds. Jack turns back, halfway down the drive, to see if they will kick their way out—and that's when he sees ropy greenish vines, slithering up out of the soil, long cables of root that crawl up the sides of the barn, run across the double doors in trembling threads, binding them shut. The next time the two men hit the doors, the panels barely move. The cords draw tight around the base of the barn, a net around a fish. Jack smiles and rubs at the queer feeling in the left side of his head. She promised she'd help.

The barn disappears in a silent, obliterating flash. A gust of wind picks Jack up like a leaf and flings him weightlessly into the sky.

22.

When Jack McCourt comes to, he is lying in a great feather bed of violet blooms. He has wound up in one of Beth's flower beds, out in front of the cottage she shared with Connor. Sweet green fronds stroke his cheeks, and a fuzzy flower kisses his left temple. He can't hear a thing, and there's a trickle of blood running from one ear. He can taste blood in his mouth.

The barn is gone. It is hard to even look at the place where it stood. There is an orchid of light rising there, a stem of fire, with petals of flame spreading out from the top. The F-150 has been tossed a hundred feet to the east, a black charred wreck flipped on its side. One half of the farmhouse has collapsed in on itself, a balsa-wood dollhouse that has been kicked by a giant.

Blackened beams stick out of the ruin, trickling smoke into the brightness of the day.

A part of Jack doesn't want to get up. He has not felt so at peace since the morning he left the house with Bloom to go and see her family. There among the flowers, he feels as happy and comfortable as a child curled up beside his mother on a lazy summer morning. When he forces himself up at last, it's with a lazy sigh of regret.

His balance is screwy. He reels halfway across the little dirt drive and then catches himself against the hood of Connor's sweet '71 Road Runner, the car he's always wanted. Well. It's his now. He can't have Connor's cool carbon-fiber leg, and he doesn't yearn for Beth anymore, but the car is all his. He may only be thirteen, but he's tall enough to reach the pedals and is already a perfectly competent driver.

Jack steers the Road Runner down the drive and onto the lane, away from the collapsing farmhouse and the ruin of the barn. The barn isn't a barn at all anymore. It's a crater: a dish filled with flames. Shingles are still falling, along with sparks.

He rolls down his window and swings out onto the highway. Warm air rushes in, carrying a blast of the fresh, fragrant summer, every tree in full green flourish. Sunlight embraces him, as warm and gentle and kind as a mother's touch.

Jack McCourt has not been behind the wheel long, though, when he sees a woman in a wide-brimmed green straw hat standing at the side of the road, holding a suitcase in one hand. As the car rushes by her, she lifts her head and shows him a wide, toothy grin, the smile of someone who's been poisoned by the Joker. She stands in profile to him. It is like looking at the face on a dollar bill.

He whisks by her but lifts his foot from the gas, begins to slow, steers himself onto the gravel margin of the road. It occurs to him that he is still unconscious, never came fully awake after he was flattened by the explosion that took the barn, and this is one of his waking dreams, no different from those half-recalled fantasies of talking plants. His great-great-great-grandmother is older than TV, too old to have traveled all this way. And yet he thinks this might be the very woman herself and believes she's been waiting all morning for him to finish his business at the farm and come get her. She walks toward the car, smiling to herself as she approaches. Whatever she is—a figment of madness or his own true blood—he welcomes the company. Better, he believes, than traveling alone.

In the Tall Grass
with Stephen King

← →

He wanted quiet for a while instead of the radio, so you could say what happened was his fault. She wanted fresh air instead of the A/C for a while, so you could say it was hers. But since they never would have heard the kid without both of those things, you'd really have to say it was a combination, which made it perfect Cal-and-Becky, because they had run in tandem all their lives. Cal and Becky DeMuth, born nineteen months apart. Their parents called them the Irish Twins.

"Becky picks up the phone and Cal says hello," Mr. DeMuth liked to say.

"Cal thinks party and Becky's already written out the guest list," Mrs. DeMuth liked to say.

Never a cross word between them, even when Becky, at the time a dorm-dwelling freshman, showed up at Cal's off-campus apartment one day to announce she was pregnant. Cal took it well. Their folks? Not quite so sanguine.

The off-campus apartment was in Durham, because Cal chose UNH. When Becky (at that point unpregnant, if not necessarily a virgin) made the same college choice two years later, you could have cut the lack of surprise and spread it on bread.

"At least he won't have to come home every damn weekend to hang out with her," Mrs. DeMuth said.

"Maybe we'll get some peace around here," Mr. DeMuth said. "After twenty years, give or take, all that togetherness gets a little tiresome."

Of course they didn't do *everything* together, because Cal sure as hell wasn't responsible for the bun in his sister's oven. And it had been solely Becky's idea to ask Uncle Jim and Aunt Anne if she could live with them for a while—just until the baby came. To the senior DeMuths, who were stunned and bemused by this turn of events, it seemed as reasonable a course as any. And when Cal suggested he *also* take the spring semester off so they could make the cross-country drive together, their folks didn't put up much of a fuss. They even agreed that Cal could stay with Becky in San Diego until the baby was born. Calvin might be able to find a little job and chip in on expenses.

"Pregnant at nineteen," Mrs. DeMuth said.

"*You* were pregnant at nineteen," Mr. DeMuth said.

"Yes, but I was *married*," Mrs. DeMuth pointed out.

"And to a damned nice fellow," Mr. DeMuth felt compelled to add.

Mrs. DeMuth sighed. "Becky will pick the first name and Cal will pick the second."

"Or vicey versa," Mr. DeMuth said—also with a sigh. (Sometimes married couples are also Irish Twins.)

Becky's mother took Becky out for lunch one day not long before the kids left for the West Coast. "Are you sure you want to give the baby up for adoption?" she asked. "I know I don't have a right to ask—I'm only your mother—but your father is curious."

"I haven't entirely made up my mind," Becky said. "Cal will help me decide."

"What about the father, dear?"

Becky looked surprised. "Oh, he gets no say. He turned out to be a fool."

Mrs. DeMuth sighed.

↑

So there they were in Kansas, on a warm spring day in April, riding in an eight-year-old Mazda with New Hampshire plates and a ghost of New England road salt still splashed on the rocker panels. Quiet instead of the radio, open windows instead of the A/C. As a result, both of them heard the voice. It was faint but clear.

"Help! *Help!* Somebody *help* me!"

Brother and sister exchanged startled looks. Cal, currently behind the wheel, pulled over immediately. Sand rattled against the undercarriage.

Before leaving Portsmouth they had decided they would steer clear of the turnpikes. Cal wanted to see the Kaskaskia Dragon in Vandalia, Illinois; Becky wanted to make her manners to the World's Biggest Ball of Twine in Cawker City, Kansas (both missions accomplished); the pair of them felt they needed to hit Roswell and see some extraterrestrial shit. Now they were well south of the Twine Ball—which had been hairy, and fragrant, and altogether more impressive than either of them had anticipated—out on a leg of Route 73. It was a well-maintained stretch of two-lane blacktop that would take them the rest of the way across the flat serving platter of Kansas to the Colorado line. Ahead of them were miles of road with nary a car or truck in sight. Ditto behind.

On their side of the highway, there were a few houses,

a boarded-up church called the Black Rock of the Re-deemer (which Becky thought a queer name for a church, but this *was* Kansas), and a rotting Bowl-a-Drome that looked as if it might last have operated around the time the Trammps were committing pop music arson by lighting a disco inferno. On the other side of 73, there was nothing but high green grass. It stretched all the way to a horizon that was both illimitable and unremarkable.

"Was that a—" Becky began. She was wearing a light coat unzipped over a midsection that was just beginning to bulge; she was well along into her sixth month.

He raised a hand without looking at her. He was looking at the grass. "*Shhh.* Listen!"

They heard faint music coming from one of the houses. A dog gave a phlegmy triple bark—*roop-roop-roop*—and went still. Someone was hammering a board. And there was the steady, gentle susurration of the wind. Becky realized she could actually *see* the wind, combing the grass on the far side of the road. It made waves that ran away from them until they were lost in the distance.

Just when Cal was beginning to think they hadn't after all heard anything—it wouldn't be the first time they'd imagined something together—the cry came again.

"*Help! Please help me!*" And, "*I'm lost!*"

This time the look they exchanged was full of alarmed understanding. The grass was incredibly tall (for such an expanse of grass to be more than six feet high this early in the season was an anomaly that wouldn't occur to them until later). Some little kid had wandered into it, probably while exploring, almost certainly from one of the houses down the road. He had become disoriented and wandered in even deeper. He sounded about eight, which would make him far too short to leap up and find his bearings that way.

"We should haul him out," Cal said.

"Pull in to the church parking lot. Let's get off the side of the road."

He left her on the margin of the highway and turned into the dirt lot of the Redeemer. A scattering of dust-filmed cars was parked here, windshields beetle bright in the glare of the sun. That all but one of these cars appeared to have been there for days—even weeks—was another anomaly that would not strike them then. But it would later.

While he took care of the car, Becky crossed to the other shoulder. She cupped her hands to her mouth and shouted, "Kid! *Hey, kid!* Can you hear me?"

After a moment he called back, *"Yes! Help me! I've been in here for DAYS!"*

Becky, who remembered how little kids judged time, guessed that might mean twenty minutes or so. She looked for a path of broken or trampled grass where the kid had gone in (probably making up some video game or stupid jungle movie in his head as he did), and couldn't see one. But that was all right; she pegged the voice as coming from her left, at about ten o'clock. Not too far in either. Which made sense; if he'd gotten in very far, they wouldn't have heard him, even with the radio off and the windows open.

She was about to descend the embankment, to the edge of the grass, when there came a second voice, a woman's—hoarse and confused. She had the groggy rasp of someone who has just come awake and needs a drink of water. Badly.

"Don't!" shouted the woman. "*Don't!* Please! *Stay away!* Tobin, stop calling! Stop calling, honey! He'll hear you!"

"Hello?" Becky yelled. "What's going on?"

Behind her she heard a door slam. Cal, on his way across the street.

"We're lost!" the boy shouted. "Please! Please, my mom is hurt, please! Please help!"

"No!" the woman said. "No, Tobin, no!"

Becky looked around to see what was taking Cal so long.

He had crossed a few dozen feet of the dirt parking lot and then hesitated by what looked like a first-generation Prius. It was filmed with a pale coat of road dust, almost completely obscuring the windshield. Cal hunched slightly, shaded his eyes with one hand, and squinted through the side window, at something in the passenger seat. Frowning to himself for a moment and then flinching, as if from a horsefly.

"Please!" the boy said. "We're lost, and I can't find the road!"

"Tobin!" the woman started to call, but her voice went choked. As if she didn't have the spit for talk.

Unless this was an elaborate prank, something was very wrong here. Becky DeMuth was not conscious of her hand drifting to press against the tight, beach-ball-firm curve of her abdomen. Nor did she connect the way she felt then with the dreams that had been bothering her for close to two months now, dreams she'd not discussed even with Cal—the ones about driving at night. A child shouted in those dreams, too.

She dropped down the embankment in two long-legged steps. It was steeper than it looked, and when she reached the bottom, it was clear the grass was even higher than she thought, closer to seven feet than six.

The breeze gusted. The wall of grass surged and retreated in a soft, shushing tide.

"Don't look for us!" the woman called.

"Help!" said the boy, contradicting her, almost shouting over her—and his voice was close. Becky could hear him just off to the left. Not close enough to reach in and grab, but surely no more than ten or twelve yards from the road.

"I'm over here, buddy," she called to him. "Keep walking toward me. You're almost to the road. You're almost out."

"Help! Help! I still can't find you!" the boy said, his voice even closer now. This was followed by a hysterical, sobbing laugh that cooled Becky's skin.

Cal took a single skipping step down the embankment, slid on his heels, and almost fell on his ass. The ground was wet. If Becky hesitated to wade into the thick grass and go get the boy, it was because she didn't want to soak her shorts. Grass that high would hold enough water, suspended in glittering drops, to make a small pond.

"What are you doing?" Cal asked.

"There's a woman with him," Becky said. "She's being weird."

"Where are you?" the boy cried, almost babbled, from just a few feet away in the grass. Becky looked for a flash of his pants or shirt but didn't see them. He was just a little bit too far in for that. "Are you coming? *Please!* I can't find my way out!"

"Tobin!" the mother yelled, her voice distant and strained. "Tobin, *stop!*"

"Hang on, kid," Cal said, and stepped into the grass. "Captain Cal, to the rescue. Da-da-da!"

By then Becky had her cell phone out, cupped in one hand, and was opening her mouth to ask Cal if they should call the highway patrol or whatever they had out here that was blue.

Cal took one step, then another, and suddenly all Becky could see of him was the back of his blue denim shirt and his khaki shorts. For no rational reason at all, the thought of him moving out of sight caused her pulse to jump.

Still, she glanced at the face of her little black touch-screen Android and saw that she had the full complement of five bars. She dialed 911 and hit CALL. As she lifted the phone to her ear, she took a long step into the grass.

The phone rang once, and then a robot voice announced that her call was being recorded. Becky took another step, not wanting to lose sight of the blue shirt and light brown shorts. Cal was always so *impatient.* Of course, so was she.

Wet grass began to whicker against her blouse, shorts, and bare legs. *"From the bathing machine came a din,"* Becky thought, her subconscious coughing up part of a half-digested limerick, one of Edward Gorey's. *"As of jollification within. It was heard far and wide and the something something tide blah blah.*" She had written a paper on limericks for her freshman lit class that she had thought was rather clever, but all she got for her trouble was a head full of dumb rhymes she couldn't forget and a C-plus.

A human voice supplanted the robot. "Kiowa County 911, what is your location and the nature of your emergency, caller?"

"I'm on Route 73," Becky said. "I don't know the name of the town, but there's some church, the Rock of the Redeemer or something . . . and this broken-down old roller-skating rink—no, I guess it's a bowling alley—and some kid is lost in the grass. His mother, too. We hear them calling. The kid's close, the mother not so much. The kid sounds scared, the mother just sounds—" *Weird,* she meant to finish but didn't get the chance.

"Caller, we've got a very bad connection here. Please restate your—"

Then nothing. Becky stopped to look at her phone and saw a single bar. While she was watching, it disappeared, to be replaced by NO SERVICE. When she looked up, her brother had been swallowed by the green.

Overhead, a jet traced a white contrail across the sky at thirty-five thousand feet.

"Help! Help me!"

The kid was close, but maybe not quite as close as Cal had thought. And a little farther to the left.

"Go back to the road!" the woman screamed. Now *she* sounded closer, too. *"Go back while you still can!"*

"Mom! Mommy! They want to HELP!"

Then the kid just screamed. It rose to an ear-stabbing shriek, wavered, suddenly turned into more hysterical laughter. There were thrashing sounds—maybe panic, maybe the sounds of a struggle. Cal bolted in that direction, sure he was going to burst into some beaten-down clearing and discover the kid—Tobin—and his mother being assaulted by a knife-wielding maniac out of a Quentin Tarantino movie. He got ten yards and was just realizing that *had* to be too far when the grass snarled around his left ankle. He grabbed at more grass on his way down and did nothing but tear out a double handful that drooled sticky green juice down his palms to his wrists. He fell full-length on the oozy ground and managed to snork mud up both nostrils. Marvelous. How come there was never a tree around when you needed one?

He got to his knees. "Kid? Tobin? Sing—" He sneezed mud, wiped his face, and now smelled grass goo when he inhaled. Better and better. A true sensory bouquet. "Sing out! You too, Mom!"

Mom didn't. Tobin did.

"Help me pleeease!"

Now the kid was on Cal's *right,* and he sounded quite a lot deeper in the grass than before. How could that be? *He sounded close enough to grab.*

Cal turned around, expecting to see his sister, but there was only grass. *Tall* grass. It should have been broken down where he ran through it, but it wasn't. There was only the smashed-flat place where he'd gone full-length, and even there the greenery was already springing back up. Tough grass they had here in Kansas. Tough, *tall* grass.

"Becky? Beck?"

"Chill, I'm right here," she said, and although he couldn't see her, he would in a second; she was practically on top of him. She sounded disgusted. "I lost the 911 chick."

"That's okay, just don't lose *me.*" He turned in the other direction and cupped his hands to his mouth. "Tobin!"

Nothing.

"Tobin!"

"What?" Faint. Jesus Christ, what was the kid doing? Lighting out for Nebraska? *"Are you coming? You have to keep coming! I can't find you!"*

"KID, STAND STILL!" Shouting so loud and so hard it hurt his vocal cords. It was like being at a Metallica concert, only without the music. *"I DON'T CARE HOW SCARED YOU ARE, STAND STILL! LET US COME TO YOU!"*

He turned around, once more expecting to see Becky, but he saw only the grass. He flexed his knees and jumped. He could see the road (farther away than he expected; he must have run quite some distance without realizing it). He could see the church—Holy Hank's House of Hallelujah, or whatever it was called—and he could see the Bowl-a-Drome, but that was all. He didn't really expect to see Becky's head—she was only five-two—but he *did* expect to see her route of passage through the grass. The wind was combing through it harder than ever, though, and that made it seem like there were dozens of possible paths.

He jumped again. Soggy ground squashed each time he came down. Those little licking peeks back at Highway 73 were maddening.

"Becky? *Where the hell are you?*"

←

Becky heard Cal bellow for the kid to stand still no matter how scared he was and let them come to him. Which sounded like a good plan, if only her idiot brother would let her catch up. She was winded, she was wet, and she was for the first time feeling truly pregnant. The good news was that Cal was close, on her right at one o'clock.

Fine, but my sneakers are going to be ruined. In fact, the Beckster believes they're ruined already.

"Becky? Where the hell are you?"

Okay, this was strange. He was still on her right, but now he sounded closer to five o'clock. Like, almost *behind* her.

"Here," she said. "And I'm going to *stay* here until you get to me." She glanced down at her Android. "Cal, do you have any bars on your phone?"

"I don't have any idea. It's in the car. Just keep yakking until I get to you."

"What about the kid? And the crazy mom? She's gone totally dark."

"Let's get back together—*then* we'll worry about them, okay?" he said. Becky knew her brother, and she didn't like the way he sounded. This was Cal being worried and trying not to show it. "For now just talk to me."

Becky considered, then began to recite, stamping her muddy sneakers in time. "There once was a guy named *McSweeny,* who spilled some gin on his *weenie.* Just to be *couth,* he added *vermouth,* then slipped his girl a *martini.*"

"Oh, that's charming," he said. Now directly behind her, almost close enough to reach out and touch, and why was that such a relief? It was only a *field,* for God's sake.

"Hey, you guys!" The kid. Faint. Not laughing now, just sounding lost and terrified. *"Are you looking for me? I'm scared!"*

"YES! YES, OKAY! HANG ON," her brother hollered. "Becky? Becky, keep talking."

Becky's hands went to her bulge—she refused to call it a baby bump, that was so *People* magazine—and cradled it lightly. "Here's another. There once was a woman named *Jill,* who swallowed an exploding p*i*—"

"Stop, stop. I overshot you somehow."

Yup, his voice was now coming from ahead. She turned around again. "Quit goofing, Cal. This is *not* funny." Her mouth was dry. She swallowed, and her throat was dry, too. When it made that click sound, you knew you were dry. There was a big bottle of Poland

Spring water in the car. Also a couple of Cokes in the backseat. She could see them: red cans, white letters.

"Becky?"

"What?"

"There's something wrong here."

"What do you mean?" Thinking, *As if I didn't know.*

"Listen to me. Can you jump?"

"Of *course* I can jump! What do you think?"

"I think you're going to have a baby this summer, that's what I think."

"I can still— Cal, stop walking away!"

"I didn't move," he said.

"You did, you must have! You still *are!*"

"Shut up and listen. I'm going to count to three. On three you put your hands over your head like a ref signaling the field goal's good and jump just as high as you can. I'll do the same. You won't need to get much air for me to see your hands, 'kay? And I'll come to you."

"Oh, whistle and I'll come to you, my lad," she thought—no idea where it had come from, something else from freshman lit, maybe—but one thing she *did* know was that he could *say* he wasn't moving but he *was,* he was getting farther away all the time.

"Becky? *Beck—*"

"All right!" she screamed. *"All right, let's do it!"*

"*One! Two!*—" he cried. "*THREE!*"

At fifteen Becky DeMuth had weighed eighty-two pounds—her father called her "Stick"—and ran hurdles with the varsity team. At fifteen she could walk from one end of the school to the other on her hands. She wanted to believe she was *still* that person; some part of her had honestly expected to remain that person for her entire life. Her mind had still not caught up to being nineteen and pregnant—not eighty-two pounds but a hundred and thirty. She wanted to grab air—*Houston, we have liftoff*—but it was like trying to jump while giving a small child a piggyback (when you thought about it, that was pretty much the case).

Her eyeline only cleared the top of the grass for a moment, affording her the briefest glimpse back the way she'd come. What she saw, though, was enough to make her almost breathless with alarm.

Cal and the road. *Cal* . . . and the *road.*

She came back down, felt a shock of impact jolt up through her heels and into her knees. The squodgy ground under her left foot melted away. She dropped and sat down in the rich black muck with another jolt of impact, a literal whack in the ass.

Becky thought she had walked twenty steps into the grass. Maybe thirty at most. The road should've been close enough to hit with a Frisbee. It was instead as if she had walked the length of a football field and then some. A battered red Datsun, zipping along the highway, looked no bigger than a Matchbox car. A hundred and forty yards of grass—a softly flowing ocean of watered green silk—stood between her and that slender blacktop thread.

Her first thought, sitting in the mud, was, *No. Impossible. You didn't see what you think you saw.*

Her second thought was of a weak swimmer, caught in a retreating tide, pulled farther and farther from shore, not understanding how much trouble she was in until she began to scream and discovered that no one on the beach could hear her.

As shaken as she was by the sight of the improbably distant highway, her brief glimpse of Cal was just as disorienting. Not because he was far away but because he was really close. She had seen him spring up above the grass less than ten feet from her, but the two of them had been screaming for all they were worth just to make themselves heard.

The muck was warm, sticky, placental.

The grass hummed furiously with insects.

"Be careful!" the boy shouted. *"Don't you get lost, too!"*

This was followed by another brief burst of laughter—a giddy, nervous sob of hilarity. It wasn't Cal, and it wasn't the kid, not this time. It wasn't the woman either. This laughter came from somewhere to her left, then died out, swallowed by bug song. It was male and had a quality of drunkenness to it.

Becky suddenly remembered one of the things Weirdo Mom had shouted: *Stop calling, honey! He'll hear you!*

What the fuck?

"*What the* fuck?" shouted Cal, as if he were echoing her. She wasn't surprised. *Ike and Mike, they think alike*, Mrs. DeMuth liked to say. *Frick and Frack, got two heads but just one back*, Mr. Demuth liked to say.

A pause in which there was only the sound of the wind and the *reeeee* of the bugs. Then, bellowing at the top of his lungs: "*WHAT THE FUCK IS THIS?*"

✓

Cal had a brief period, about five minutes later, when he lost it a little. It happened after he tried an experiment. He jumped and looked at the road and landed and waited, and then, after he had counted to thirty, he jumped and looked again.

If you wanted to be a stickler for accuracy, you could say he was already losing it a little, to even think he needed to *try* such an experiment. But by then re-

ality was starting to feel much like the ground underfoot: liquid and treacherous. He could not manage the
simple trick of walking toward his sister's voice, which
came from the right when he was walking left and from
the left when he was walking right. Sometimes from
ahead and sometimes from behind. And no matter which
direction he walked in, he seemed to move farther from
the road.

He jumped and fixed his gaze on the steeple of the
church. It was a brilliant white spear set against the background of that bright blue, almost cloudless sky. Crappy
church, divine, soaring steeple. *The congregation must
have paid through the nose for that baby,* he thought.
Although from here—maybe a quarter of a mile off, and
never mind that was crazy, he had walked less than a
hundred feet—he could not see the peeling paint or the
boards in the windows. He couldn't even make out his
own car, tucked in with the other distance-shrunken
cars in the lot. He could, however, see the dusty Prius.
That one was in the front row. He was trying not to dwell
on what he had glimpsed in the passenger seat—a bad
dream detail that he wasn't ready to examine just yet.

On that first jump, he was turned to face the steeple
dead-on, and in any normal world he should've been able
to reach it by walking through the grass in a straight line,
jumping every now and then to make minor course cor-

rections. There was a rusting, bullet-peppered sign between the church and the bowling alley, diamond-shaped with a yellow border: SLOW CHILDREN X-ING maybe. He couldn't be sure—he had left his glasses in the car, too.

He dropped back down into the squidgy muck and began to count.

"Cal?" came his sister's voice, from somewhere behind him.

"Wait," he shouted.

"Cal?" she said again, from somewhere to his left. "Do you want me to keep talking?" And when he didn't reply, she began to chant in a desultory voice, from somewhere in front of him: "There once was a girl went to Yale—"

"Just shut up and wait!" he screamed again.

His throat felt dry and tight, and swallowing took an effort. Although it was close to two in the afternoon, the sun seemed to hover almost directly overhead. He could feel it on his scalp and the tops of his ears, which were tender, beginning to burn. He thought if he could just have something to drink—a cold swallow of spring water, or one of their Cokes—he might not feel so frayed, so anxious.

Drops of dew burned in the grass, a hundred miniature magnifying glasses refracting and intensifying the light.

Ten seconds.

"Kid?" Becky called, from somewhere on his right (*No. Stop. She's not moving. Get your head under control.*) She sounded thirsty, too. Croaky. "Are you still with us?"

"Yes! Did you find my mom?"

"*Not yet!*" Cal shouted, thinking it really had been a while since they'd heard from her. Not that she was his main concern just then.

Twenty seconds.

"Kid?" Becky said. Her voice came from behind him again. "Everything's going to be all right."

"*Have you seen my dad?*"

Cal thought: *A new player. Terrific. Maybe William Shatner's in here, too. Also Mike Huckabee . . . Kim Kardashian . . . the guy who plays Opie on* Sons of Anarchy, *and the entire cast of* The Walking Dead.

He closed his eyes, but the moment he did, he felt dizzy, as if he were standing on the top of a ladder beginning to sway underfoot. He wished he hadn't thought of *The Walking Dead.* He should have stuck with William Shatner and Mike Huckabee. He opened his eyes again and found himself rocking on his heels. He steadied himself with some effort. The heat made his face prickle with sweat.

Thirty. He'd been standing in this one spot for thirty

seconds. He thought he should wait a full minute but couldn't, and so he jumped for another look back at the church.

A part of him—a part he'd been trying with all his will to ignore—already knew what he was going to see. This part had been providing an almost jovial running commentary: *Everything will have moved, Cal, good buddy. The grass flows, and you flow, too. Think of it as becoming one with nature, bro.*

When his tired legs lofted him into the air again, he saw that the church steeple was now off to his *left*. Not a lot—just a little. He had drifted far enough to his right so that he was no longer seeing the front of that diamond-shaped sign but the silver aluminum *back* of it. Also, though he wasn't sure, he thought it was all just a little farther away than it had been. As if he had backed up a few steps while he was counting to thirty.

Somewhere, the dog barked again: *roop, roop*. Somewhere a radio was playing. He couldn't make out the song, just the thump of the bass. The insects thrummed their single lunatic note.

"Oh, come on," Cal said. He had never been much for talking to himself—as an adolescent he'd cultivated a Buddhist-skateboarder vibe and had prided himself on how long he could serenely maintain his silence—but he was talking now, and hardly aware of it. "Oh, come the *fuck* on. This is . . . this is *nuts.*"

He was walking, too. Walking for the road—again, hardly without knowing it.

"Cal?" Becky shouted.

"This is just nuts," he said again, breathing hard, shoving at the grass.

His foot caught on something, and he went down knee-first into an inch of swampy water. Hot water—not lukewarm, *hot,* as hot as bathwater—splashed up onto the crotch of his shorts, providing him with the sensation of having just pissed himself.

That broke him a little. He lunged back to his feet. Running now. Grass whipping at his face. It was sharp-edged and tough, and when one green sword snapped him under the left eye, he felt it, a sharp stinging. The pain gave him a nasty jump, and he ran harder, going as fast as he could now.

"*Help me!*" the kid screamed, and how about this? "Help" came from Cal's left, "me" from his right. It was the Kansas version of Dolby stereo.

"*This is nuts!*" Cal screamed again. "*This is nuts, it's nuts, it's fucking nuts!*" The words running together, "itsnutsitsnuts," what a stupid thing to say, what an inane observation, and he couldn't stop saying it.

He fell again, hard this time, sprawling chest-first. By now his clothes were spattered with earth so rich, warm, and dark that it felt and even smelled somewhat like fecal matter.

Cal picked himself back up, ran another five steps, felt grass snarl around his legs—it was like putting his feet into a nest of tangling wire—and goddamn if he didn't fall a third time. The inside of his head buzzed, like a cloud of flies.

"Cal!" Becky was screaming. "Cal, stop! *Stop!*"

Yes, stop. If you don't, you'll be yelling "help me" right along with the kid. A fucking duet.

He gulped at the air. His heart galloped. He waited for the buzzing in his head to pass, then realized it wasn't in his head after all. They really were flies. He could see them shooting in and out through the grass, a swarm of them around something through the shifting curtain of yellow-green, just ahead of him.

He pushed his hands into the grass and parted it to see.

A dog—it looked like it had been a golden retriever—was on its side in the mire. Limp brownish red fur glittered beneath a shifting mat of bluebottles. Its bloated tongue lolled between its gums, and the cloudy marbles of its eyes strained from its head. The rusting tag of its collar gleamed amid its fur. Cal looked again at the tongue. It was coated a greenish white. Cal didn't want to think why. The dog's dirty, wet, flyblown coat looked like a filthy golden carpet tossed on a heap of bones. Some of that fur drifted—little fluffs of it—on the warm breeze.

Take hold. It was his thought but in his father's steadying voice. Making that voice helped. He stared at the dog's caved-in stomach and saw lively movement there. A boiling stew of maggots. Like the ones he'd seen squirming on the half-eaten hamburgers lying on the passenger seat of that damned Prius. Burgers that had been there for days. Someone had left them, walked away from the car and left them, and never come back, and never—

Take hold, Calvin. If not for yourself, for your sister.

"I will," he promised his father. "I will."

He stripped the snarls of tough greenery from his ankles and shins, barely feeling the little cuts the grass had inflicted. He stood.

"Becky, where are you?"

Nothing for a long time—long enough for his heart to abandon his chest and rise into his throat. Then, incredibly distant, *"Here! Cal, what should we do? We're lost!"*

He closed his eyes again, briefly. *That's the kid's line.* Then he thought, *Le kid, c'est moi.* It was almost funny.

"We keep calling," he said, moving toward where her voice had come from. "We keep calling until we're together again."

"But I'm so thirsty!" She sounded closer now, but Cal didn't trust that. No, no, no.

"Me too," he said. "But we're going to get out of this, Beck. We just have to keep our heads." That he had already lost his—a little, only a little—was one thing he'd never tell her. She had never told him the name of the boy who knocked her up, after all, and that made them sort of even. A secret for her, now one for him.

"What about the kid?"

Ah, Christ, now she was fading again. He was so scared that the truth popped out with absolutely no trouble at all, and at top volume.

"Fuck the kid, Becky! This is about us now!"

↓

Directions melted in the tall grass, and time melted as well: a Dalí world with Dolby sound. They chased each other's voice like weary children too stubborn to give up their game of tag and come in for dinner. Sometimes Becky sounded close, sometimes she sounded far; he never once saw her. Occasionally the kid yelled for someone to help him, once so close that Cal sprang into the grass with his hands outstretched to snare him before he could get away, but there was no kid. Only a crow with its head and one wing torn off.

There is no morning or night here, Cal thought, *only eternal afternoon.* But even as this idea occurred to him, he saw that the blue of the sky was deepening and the squelchy ground beneath his sodden feet was growing dim.

If we had shadows, they'd be getting long and we might use them to move in the same direction at least, he thought, but they had no shadows. Not in the tall grass. He looked at his watch and wasn't surprised to see it had stopped even though it was a self-winder. The grass had stopped it. He felt sure of it. Some malignant vibe in the grass, some paranormal *Fringe* shit.

It was half past nothing when Becky began to sob.

"Beck? *Beck?*"

"I have to rest, Cal. I have to sit down. I'm so thirsty. And I've been having cramps."

"Contractions?"

"I guess so. Oh, God, what if I have a miscarriage out here in this fucking field?"

"Just sit where you are," he said. "They'll pass."

"Thanks, Doc, I'll—" Nothing. Then she began

screaming. *"Get away from me! Get away! DON'T TOUCH ME!"*

Cal, now too tired to run, ran anyway.

↘

Even in her shock and terror, Becky knew who the madman had to be when he brushed aside the grass and stood before her. He was wearing tourist clothes— Dockers and mud-clotted Bass Weejuns. The real give-away, however, was his T-shirt. Although it was smeared with mud and a dark maroon crust that was almost certainly blood, she could see the ball of spaghetti-like string and knew what was printed aboveit—WORLD'S BIGGEST BALL OF TWINE, CAWKER CITY, KANSAS. Didn't she have a shirt just like it neatly folded in her suitcase?

Tobin's dad. In the mud- and grass-smeared flesh.

"Get away from me!" She leaped to her feet, hands cradling her belly. *"Get away! DON'T TOUCH ME!"*

Dad grinned. His cheeks were stubbly, his lips red. "Calm down. Want to see my wife? Or hey! Want to get out? It's easy."

She stared at him, openmouthed. Cal was shouting, but for the moment she paid no attention.

"If you could get out," she said, "you wouldn't still be *in*."

He tittered. "Right idea. Wrong conclusion. I was just going to hook up with my boy. Already found my wife. Want to meet her?"

She said nothing.

"Okay," he said, and turned from her. He started into the grass. Soon he would melt away, just as her brother had, and Becky felt a stab of panic. He was clearly mad—you only had to look into his eyes or listen to his text-message vocal delivery to know that—but he was *human*.

He stopped and turned back, grinning. "Forgot to introduce myself. My bad. Ross Humbolt's the name. Real estate's the game. Poughkeepsie. Wife's Natalie. Little boy's Tobin. Sweet kid! Smart! You're Becky. Brother's Cal. Last chance, Becky. Come with me or die." His eyes dropped to her belly. "Baby, too."

Don't trust him.

She didn't, but she followed just the same. At what she hoped was a safe distance. "You have no idea where you're going."

"Becky? Becky!" Cal. But far away. Somewhere in North Dakota. Maybe Manitoba. She supposed she should answer him, but her throat was too raw.

"I was just as lost in the grass as you two," he said. "Not anymore. Kissed the stone." He turned briefly and regarded her with roguish, mad eyes. "Hugged it, too. *Whsssh.* See it then. All those little dancing fellas. See everything. Clear as day. Back to the road? Straight shot! If I'm line, I'm dine. Wife's right up here. You have to meet her. She's my honey. Makes the best martini in America. There once was a guy named McSweeny, who spilled some gin on his . . . *ahem!* Just to be couth, he added vermouth. I guess you know the rest." He winked at her.

In high school Becky had taken a gym elective called Self-Defense for Young Women. Now she tried to remember the moves and couldn't. The only thing she could remember . . .

Deep in the right pocket of her shorts was a key ring. The longest and thickest key fit the front door of the house where she and her brother had grown up. She separated it from the others and pressed it between the first two fingers of her hand.

"*Here* she is!" Ross Humbolt proclaimed jovially, parting high grass with both hands, like an explorer in some old movie. "Say hello, Natalie! This young woman is going to have a *critter!*"

There was blood splashed on the grass beyond the swatches he was holding open, and Becky wanted to stop, but her feet carried her forward, and he even stepped aside a little, like in one of those other old movies where the suave guy says, "After you doll," and they enter the swanky nightclub where the jazz combo's playing only this was no swanky nightclub this was a beaten-down swatch of grass where the woman Natalie Humbolt if that was her name was lying all twisted with her eyes bulging and her dress pushed up to show great big red divots in her thighs and Becky guessed she knew now why Ross Humbolt of Poughkeepsie had such red lips and one of Natalie's arms was torn off at the shoulder and lying ten feet beyond her in crushed grass already springing back up and there were more great big red divots in the arm and the red was still wet because . . . because . . .

Because she hasn't been dead that long, Becky thought. *We heard her scream. We heard her* die.

"Family's been here a while," Ross Humbolt said in a chummy, confidential tone as his grass-stained fingers settled around Becky's throat. He hiccupped. "Folks can get pretty hungry. No Mickey D's out here! Nope. You can drink the water that comes out of the ground—it's gritty and awful damn warm, but after a while you don't mind that—only we've been in here for *days.* I'm full now, though. Full as a tick." His bloodstained lips descended into the cup of her ear, and his beard stubble tickled her skin as he whispered, "Want to see the rock? Want to lay on it naked and feel me in you, beneath the pinwheel stars, while the grass sings our names? Poetry, eh?"

She tried to suck a chestful of air to scream, but nothing came down her windpipe. In her lungs was a sudden, dreadful vacancy. He screwed his thumbs into her throat, crushing muscle, tendon, soft tissue. Ross Humbolt grinned. His teeth were stained with red, but his tongue was a yellowish green. His breath smelled of blood, also like a fresh-clipped lawn.

"The grass has things to tell you. You just need to learn to listen. You need to learn how to speak *Tall Weed,* honey. The rock knows. After you see the rock, you'll understand. I've learned more from that rock in two days than I learned in twenty years of schooling."

He had her bent backward, her spine arched. She bent like a high blade of grass in the wind. His green breath gushed in her face again.

"'Twenty years of schoolin' and they *will* put you on the day shift,'" he said, and laughed. "That's some good old rock, isn't it? Dylan. Child of Yahweh. Bard of Hibbing, and I ain't ribbing. I'll tell you what. The stone in the center of this field is a *good old* rock, but it's a *thirsty* rock. It's been working on the gray shift since before red men hunted on the Osage Cuestas, been working since a glacier brought it here during the last ice age, and oh, girl, it's *so* fucking thirsty."

She wanted to drive her knee into his balls, but it was all too much effort. The best she could do was lift her foot a few inches and then gently set it down again. Lift the foot and set it down. Lift and set. She seemed to be stamping her heel in slow motion, like a horse ready to be let out of a stall.

Constellations of black and silver sparks exploded at the edges of her vision. *Pinwheel stars,* she thought. It was oddly fascinating, watching as new universes were born and died, appearing and winking out. She would soon be winking out herself, she understood. This did not seem such a terrible thing. Urgent action was not required.

Cal was screaming her name from very far away. If he had been in Manitoba before, now he was down a mineshaft in Manitoba.

Her hand tightened on the key ring in her pocket. The teeth of some of those keys were digging into her palm. Biting.

"Blood is nice, tears are better," Ross said. "For a thirsty old rock like that. And when I fuck you on the stone, it'll have some of both. Has to be quick, though. Don't want to do it in front of the kid." His breath *stank*.

She pulled her hand out of her pocket, the end of her house key protruding between her pointer and middle fingers, and jabbed her fist into Ross Humbolt's face. She just wanted to push his mouth away, didn't want him breathing on her, didn't want to smell the green stink of him anymore. Her arm felt weak, and the way she punched at him was lazy, almost friendly—but the key caught him under the left eye and raked down his cheek, sketching a jaggedy line in blood.

He flinched, snapping his head back. His hands loosened; for an instant his thumbs were no longer burrowing into the soft skin in the hollow of her throat. A moment later he tightened his grip again, but by then she'd drawn a single whooping breath. The sparks—the pinwheel stars—bursting and flaring at the periphery of her vision faded out. Her head went clear, as clear as if someone had dashed icy water into her face. The next time she punched him, she put her shoulder behind it and sank the key into his eye. Her knuckles jarred against bone. The key popped through his cornea and into the liquid center of the eyeball.

He did not scream. He made a kind of doglike bark, a woofing grunt (*roop!*), and wrenched her hard to one side, trying to yank her off her feet. His forearms were sunburned and peeling. Close up she could see that his nose was peeling, too, badly, the bridge of his nose sizzling with sunburn. He grimaced, showing teeth stained pink and green.

Her hand fell away, let go of the key ring. It continued to dangle from the welling socket of his left eye, the other keys dancing against one another and bouncing against his stubbly cheek. Blood slicked the entire left side of Humbolt's face, and that eye was a glimmering red hole.

The grass seethed around them. The wind rose, and the tall blades thrashed and flailed at Becky's back and legs.

He kneed her in the belly. It was like being clubbed with a piece of stove wood. Becky felt pain and something worse than pain, in a low place where abdomen met groin. It was a kind of muscular contraction, a twisting, as if there were a knotted rope in her womb and someone had just yanked it tight, tighter than it was supposed to go.

"Oh, Becky! Oh, girl! Your ass—your ass is grass now!" he screamed, a note of mad hilarity wavering in his voice.

He kneed her in the stomach again and then a third time. Each blow set off a fresh, black, poisonous detonation. *He's killing the baby,* Becky thought. Something trickled down the inside of her left leg. Whether it was blood or urine, she could not have said.

They danced together, the pregnant woman and the one-eyed madman. They danced in the grass, feet squelching, his hands on her throat. The two of them had staggered in a wavering semicircle around the corpse of Natalie Humbolt. Becky was aware of the dead body to her left, had glimpses of pale, bloody, bitten thighs, rumpled jean skirt, and Natalie's exposed grass-stained granny panties. And her arm—Natalie's arm in the grass, just behind Ross Humbolt's feet. Natalie's dirty, severed arm (how had he removed it? had he torn it off like a chicken drumstick?) lay with fingers slightly curled, filth under her cracked fingernails.

Becky threw herself at Ross, heaved her weight forward. He stepped back, put his foot on that arm, and it turned beneath his heel. He made an angry, grunting cry of distress as he spilled over, pulling her with him. He did not let go of her throat until he hit the ground, his teeth coming together with an audible *clack!*

He absorbed most of the impact, the springy mass of his suburban-dad gut softening her own fall. She shoved herself off him, began to scramble on all fours into the grass.

Only she couldn't move quickly. Her insides pulsed with a dreadful weight and feeling of tension, as if she had swallowed a medicine ball. She wanted to vomit.

He caught her ankle and pulled. She fell flat, onto her hurt, throbbing stomach. A lance of rupturing pain went through her abdomen, a feeling of something bursting. Her chin struck the wet earth. Her vision swarmed with black specks.

"Where are you going, Becky DeMuth?" She had not told him her last name. He couldn't know that. "I'll just find you again. The grass will show me where you're hiding, the little dancing men will take me right to you. Come here. You don't need to go to San Diego now. No decisions about the baby will be necessary. All done now."

Her vision cleared. She saw, right in front of her, on a flattened bit of grass, a woman's straw purse, the contents dumped out, and amid the mess a little pair of manicuring scissors—they almost looked more like pliers than scissors. The blades were gummy with blood. She didn't want to think how Ross Humbolt of Poughkeepsie might have used that tool, or how she herself might now use it.

Nevertheless, she closed her hand around it.

"Come here, I said," Ross told her. "*Now*, bitch." Hauling on her foot.

She twisted and shoved herself back at him, with Natalie Humbolt's manicure scissors in one fist. She struck him in the face, once, twice, three times, before he began to scream. It was a scream of pain, even if, before she was done with him, it had turned into great, sobbing guffaws of laughter. She thought, *The kid laughed, too.* Then for quite a while she thought nothing. Not until after moonrise.

→

In the last of the day's light, Cal sat in the grass, brushing tears off his cheeks.

He never gave way to full-on weeping. He only dropped onto his butt, after who knew how much fruitless wandering and calling for Becky—she had long since stopped replying to him—and then for a while his eyes were tingling and damp and his breath a little thick.

Dusk was glorious. The sky was a deep, austere blue, darkening almost to black, and in the west, behind the church, the horizon was lit with the infernal glow of dying coals. He saw it now and then, when he had the energy to jump and look and could persuade himself there was some point in looking around.

His sneakers were soaked through, which made them heavy, and his feet ached. The insides of his thighs itched. He took off his right shoe and dumped a dingy trickle of water from it. He wasn't wearing socks, and his bare foot had the ghastly white, shriveled look of a drowned thing.

He removed the other sneaker, was about to dump it, then hesitated. He brought it to his lips, tipped back his head, and let gritty water—water that tasted like his own stinking foot—run over his tongue.

He had heard Becky and the Man, a long way off in the grass. Had heard the Man speaking to her in a gleeful, inebriated voice, lecturing her almost, although Cal had not been able to make out much of what was actually said. Something about a rock. Something about dancing men. Something about being thirsty. A line from some old folk song. What had the guy been singing? *"Twenty years of writing and they put you on the night shift."* No—that wasn't right. But something close to that. Folk music wasn't an area of expertise for Cal; he was more of a Rush fan. They'd been surfing on *Permanent Waves* all the way across the country.

Then he heard the two of them thrashing and struggling in the grass, heard Becky's choked cries and the man ranting at her. Finally there came screams—screams that were terribly like shouts of hilarity. Not Becky. The Man.

By that point Cal had been hysterical, running and jumping and screaming for her. He shouted and ran for a long time before he finally got himself under control, forced himself to stop and listen. He had bent over, clutching his knees and panting, his throat achy with thirst, and had turned his attention to the silence.

The grass hushed.

"Becky?" he had called again, in a hoarsened voice. "Beck?"

No reply except for the wind slithering in the weeds.

He walked a little more. He called again. He sat. He tried not to cry.

And dusk was glorious.

He searched his pockets, for the hundredth hopeless time, gripped by the terrible fantasy of discovering a dry, linty stick of Juicy Fruit. He had bought a package of Juicy Fruit back in Pennsylvania, but he and Becky had shared it out before they reached the Ohio border. Juicy Fruit was a waste of money. That citrus flash of sugar was always gone in four chews and—

—he felt a stiff paper flap and withdrew a book of matches. Cal did not smoke, but they had been giving them away free at the little liquor store across the street from the Kaskaskia Dragon in Vandalia. It had a picture of the thirty-five-foot-long stainless-steel dragon on the cover. Becky and Cal had paid for a fistful of tokens and spent most of the early evening feeding the big metal dragon, to watch jets of burning propane erupt from its nostrils. Cal imagined the dragon set down in the field and went dizzy with pleasure at the thought of it exhaling a gassy plume of fire into the grass.

He turned the matchbook over in his hand, thumbing soft cardboard.

Burn the field, he thought. *Burn the fucking field.*

The tall grass would go the way of all straw when fed to flame.

He visualized a river of burning grass, sparks and shreds of toasted weed drifting into the air. It was such a strong mental image that he could close his eyes and almost *smell* it, the somehow wholesome late-summer reek of burning green.

And what if the flames turned back on him? What if it caught Becky out there somewhere? What if she was passed out and woke to the stink of her own burning hair?

No. Becky would stay ahead of it. *He* would stay ahead of it. The idea was in him that he had to *hurt* the grass, show it he wasn't taking any more shit, and then it would let him—let them both—go. Every time a strand of grass brushed his cheek, he felt it was teasing him, having fun with him.

He rose on sore legs and yanked at the grass. It was tough old rope, tough and sharp, and it hurt his hands, but he wrenched some loose and crushed it into a pile and knelt before it, a penitent at a private altar. He tore a match loose, put it against the strike strip, folded the cover against it to hold it in place, and yanked. Fire spurted. His face was close, and he inhaled a burning whiff of sulfur.

The match went out the moment he touched it to the wet grass, the stems heavy with a dew that never dried and dense with juice.

His hand shook when he lit the next.

It hissed as he touched it to the grass, and it went out. Hadn't Jack London written a story about this?

Another. Another. Each match made a fat little puff of smoke as soon as it touched the wet green. One didn't even make it into the grass but was huffed out by the gentle breeze as soon as it was lit.

Finally, when there were six matches left, he lit one and then, in desperation, touched it to the book itself. The paper matchbook ignited in a hot white flash, and he dropped it into the nest of singed but still-damp grass. For a moment it settled in the top of this mass of yellow-green weeds, a long, bright tongue of flame rising up from it.

Then the matchbook burned a hole in the damp grass and fell into the muck and went out.

He kicked at the whole mess in a spasm of sick, ugly despair. It was the only way to keep from crying again.

Afterward he sat still, eyes shut, forehead against his knee. He was tired and wanted to rest, wanted to lie on his back and watch the stars appear. At the same time, he did not want to lower himself into the clinging muck, didn't want it in his hair, soaking the back of his shirt. He was filthy enough as it was. His bare legs were striped from the flogging the sharp edges of the grass had given him. He thought he should try walking toward the road again—before the light was completely gone—but could hardly bear to stand.

What caused him to rise at last was the faraway sound of a car alarm going off. But not just *any* car alarm, no. This one didn't go *wah-wah-wah* like most of them; this one went *WHEEK-honk, WHEEK-honk, WHEEK-honk.* So far as he knew, only old Mazdas wheek-honked like that when they were violated, flashing their headlights in time.

Like the one in which he and Becky had set out to cross the country.

WHEEK-honk, WHEEK-honk, WHEEK-honk.

His legs were tired, but he jumped up anyway. The road was closer again (not that it mattered), and yes, he could see a pair of flashing headlights. Not much else, but he didn't need to see much else to guess what was going on. The people along this stretch of the highway would know all about the field of tall grass across from the church and the defunct bowling alley. They would know to keep their own children on the safe side of the road. And when the occasional tourist heard cries for help and disappeared into the tall grass, determined to do the Good Samaritan bit, the locals visited the cars and took whatever there was worth taking.

They probably love this old field. And fear it. And worship it. And—

He tried to shut off the logical conclusion but couldn't.

And sacrifice to it. The swag they find in the trunks and glove compartments? Just a little bonus.

He wanted Becky. Oh, God, how he wanted Becky. And oh, God, how he wanted something to eat. He couldn't decide which he wanted more.

"Becky? *Becky?*"

Nothing. Overhead, stars were now glimmering.

Cal dropped to his knees, pressed his hands into the mucky ground, and dredged up more water. He drank it, trying to filter the grit with his teeth. *If Becky was with me, we could figure this out. I know we could. Because Ike and Mike, they think alike.*

He got more water, this time forgetting to filter it and swallowing more grit. Also something that wriggled. A bug, or maybe a small worm. Well, so what? It was protein, right?

"I'll never find her," Cal said. He stared at the darkening, waving grass. "Because you won't let me, will you? You keep the people who love each other apart, don't you? That's Job One, right? We'll just circle around and around, calling to each other, until we go insane."

Except Becky had *stopped* calling. Like Mom, Becky had gone dar—

"It doesn't have to be that way," a small clear voice said.

Cal's head jerked around. A little boy in mud-spattered clothes was standing there. His face was pinched and filthy. In his right hand he held a dead crow by one yellow leg.

"Tobin?" Cal whispered.

"That's me." The boy raised the crow to his mouth and buried his face in its belly. Feathers crackled. The crow nodded its dead head as if to say, *That's right, get right in there, get to the meat of the thing.*

Cal would have said he was too tired to spring after his latest jump, but horror has its own imperatives, and he sprang anyway. He tore the crow out of the boy's muddy hands, barely registering the guts unraveling from its open belly. Although he did see the feather stuck to the side of the boy's mouth. He saw that very well, even in the gathering gloom.

"You can't eat that! *Jesus*, kid! What are you, crazy?"

"Not crazy, just hungry. And the crows aren't bad. I couldn't eat any of Freddy. I loved him, see. Dad ate some, but I didn't. Course, I hadn't touched the rock then. When you touch the rock—hug it, like—you can see. You just know a lot more. It makes you hungrier, though. And like my dad says, a man's meat and a man's gotta eat. After we went to the rock, we separated, but he said we could find each other again anytime we wanted."

Cal was still one turn back. "Freddy?"

"He was our golden. Did great Frisbee catches. Just like a dog on TV. It's easier to find things in here once they're dead. The field doesn't move dead things around." His eyes gleamed in the fading light, and he looked at the mangled crow, which Cal was still holding. "I think most birds steer clear of the grass. I think they know and tell each other. But some don't listen. *Crows* don't listen the most, I guess, because there are quite a few dead ones in here. Wander around for a while and you find them."

Cal said, "Tobin, did you lure us in here? Tell me. I won't be mad. Your father made you do it, I bet."

"We heard someone yelling. A little girl. She said she was lost. That's how *we* got in. That's how it *works.*" He paused. "My dad killed your sister, I bet."

"How do you know she's my sister?"

"The rock," he said simply. "The rock teaches you to hear the grass, and the tall grass knows everything."

"Then you must know if she's dead or not."

"I could find out for you." Tobin said, "No. I can do better than that. I can show you. Do you want to go see? Do you want to check on her? Come on. Follow me."

Without waiting for a reply, the kid turned and walked into the grass. Cal dropped the dead crow and bolted after him, not wanting to lose sight of him even for a second. If he did, he might wander around forever without finding him again. *I won't be mad,* he'd told Tobin, but he *was* mad. *Really* mad. Not mad enough to kill a kid, of course not (*probably* of course not), but he wasn't going to let the little Judas goat out of his sight either.

Only he did, because the moon rose above the grass, bloated and orange. *It looks pregnant,* he thought, and when he looked back down, Tobin was gone. He forced his tired legs to run, shoving through the grass, filling his lungs to call. Then there was no more grass to shove. He was in a clearing—a real clearing, not just beaten-down grass. In the middle of it, a huge black rock jutted out of the ground. It was the size of a pickup truck and inscribed all over with tiny dancing stick-men. They were white and seemed to float. They seemed to *move.*

Tobin stood beside it, then put out one hand and touched it. He shivered—not in fear, Cal thought, but in

pleasure. "Boy, that feels good. Come on, Cal. Try it."
He beckoned.

Cal walked toward the rock.

↗

There was a car alarm for a bit, and then it stopped.
The sound went into Becky's ears but made no connection to her brain. She crawled. She did it without
thinking. Each time a fresh cramp struck her, she
stopped with her forehead pressed against the muck
and her bottom in the air, like one of the faithful saluting Allah. When the cramp passed, she crawled some
more. Her mud-smeared hair was stuck to her face.
Her legs were wet with whatever was running out
of her. She felt it running out of her but didn't think
about it any more than she had thought about the car
alarm. She licked water off the grass as she crawled,
turning her head this way and that, flicking her
tongue like a snake, *snoop-sloop*. She did it without
thinking.

The moon came up, huge and orange. She twisted her
head to look at it, and when she did, the worst cramp yet
hit her. This one didn't pass. She flopped over onto her
back and clawed her shorts and panties down. Both were
soaked dark. At last a clear and coherent thought came,

forking through her mind like a stroke of heat lightning: *The baby!*

She lay on her back in the grass with her bloody clothes around her ankles and her knees spread and her hands in her crotch. Snotty stuff squelched through her fingers. Then came a paralyzing cramp, and with it something round and hard. A skull. Its curve fit her hands with sweet perfection. It was Justine (if a girl), or Brady (if a boy). She had been lying to all of them about not having made up her mind; she'd known from the first that this baby was going to be a keeper.

She tried to shriek, and nothing came out but a whispery *hhhhaaaahhh* sound. The moon peered at her, a bloodshot dragon's eye. She pushed as hard as she could, her belly like a board, her ass screwed down into the mucky ground. Something tore. Something *slid.* Something arrived in her hands. Suddenly she was empty down there, so empty, but at least her hands were full.

Into the red-orange moonlight, she raised the child of her body, thinking, *It's all right, women all over the world give birth in fields.*

It was Justine.

"Hey, baby girl," she croaked. "Oooh, you're so small."

And so silent.

↑↓

Close up, it was easy to see that the rock wasn't from Kansas. It had the black, glassy quality of volcanic stone. The moonlight cast an iridescent sheen on its angled surfaces, creating slicks of light in tones of jade and pearl.

The stick-men and the stick-women held hands as they danced into curving waves of grass. He could not tell if these images had been carved into the stone or were painted on it.

From eight steps back, they seemed to float just slightly above the surface of that great chunk of what was probably not obsidian.

From *six* steps back, they seemed to hang suspended just *beneath* the black, glassy surface, objects sculpted from light, hologram-like. It was impossible to keep them in focus. It was impossible to look away.

Four steps from the rock, he could *hear* it. The rock emitted a discreet buzz, like the electrified filament in a tungsten lamp. He could not *feel* it, however—he was not aware of the left side of his face beginning to pink, as if from sunburn. He had no sensation of heat at all.

Get away from it, he thought, but found it curiously difficult to step backward. His feet didn't seem to move in that direction anymore.

"I thought you were going to take me to Becky."

"I said we were going to check on her. We are. We'll check with the stone."

"I don't care about your goddamn— I just want Becky."

"If you touch the rock, you won't be lost anymore," Tobin said. "You won't ever be lost again. You'll be redeemed. Isn't that nice?" He absentmindedly removed the black feather that had been stuck to the corner of his mouth.

"No," Cal said. "I don't think it is. I'd rather stay lost." Maybe it was just his imagination, but the buzzing seemed to be getting louder.

"No one would rather stay lost," the boy said amiably. "Becky doesn't want to stay lost. She miscarried. If you can't find her, I think she'll probably die."

"You're lying," he said, without any conviction.

He might've inched a half step closer. A soft, fascinating light had begun to rise in the center of the rock, behind those floating stick figures—as if that buzzing tungsten he could hear was embedded about two feet beneath the surface of the stone and someone was slowly dialing it up.

"I'm not," the boy said. "Look close and you can see her."

Down in the smoked-quartz interior of the rock, he

saw the dim lines of a human face. He thought at first he was looking at his own reflection. But although it was similar, it wasn't his. It was Becky, her lips peeled back in a doglike grimace of pain. Clots of filth smeared one side of her face. Tendons strained in her throat.

"Beck?" he said, as if she might be able to hear him.

He took another step forward—he couldn't help himself—leaning in to see. His palms were raised before him, in a kind of *go-no-further* gesture, but he could not feel them beginning to blister from whatever was radiating from the stone.

No, too close, he thought, and tried to fling himself backward but couldn't get traction. Instead his heels slid, as if he stood at the top of a mound of soft earth giving way beneath him. Only the ground was flat; he slid forward because the *stone* had him, it had its own gravity, and it drew him as a magnet draws iron scrap.

Deep in the vast, jagged crystal ball of the great rock, Becky opened her eyes and seemed to stare at him in wonder and terror.

The buzzing rose in his head.

The wind rose with it. The grass flung itself from side to side, ecstatically.

In the last instant, he became aware that his flesh was burning, that his skin was boiling in the unnatural climate that existed in the immediate space right around the rock. He knew when he touched the stone that it would be like setting his palms on a heated frying pan, and he began to scream—

—then stopped, the sound catching in his suddenly constricted throat.

The stone wasn't hot at all. It was cool. It was blessedly cool, and he laid his face upon it, a weary pilgrim who has finally arrived at his destination and can rest at last.

← →

When Becky lifted her head, the sun was either coming up or going down, and her stomach hurt, as if she were recovering from a week of stomach flu. She swiped the sweat off her face with the back of one arm, pushed herself to her feet, and walked out of the grass, straight to the car. She was relieved to discover that the keys were still hanging from the ignition. Becky pulled out of the lot and eased on up the road, driving at a leisurely pace.

At first she didn't know where she was going. It was hard to think past the pain in her abdomen, which came in waves. Sometimes it was a dull throb, the soreness of overworked muscles; other times it would intensify without warning into a sharp, somehow watery pain that lanced her through the bowels and burned in her crotch. Her face was hot and feverish, and even driving with the windows down didn't cool her off.

Now it was coming on for night, and the dying day smelled of fresh-mown lawns and backyard barbecues and girls getting ready to go out on dates and baseball under the lights. She rolled through the streets of Durham, in the dull red glow, the sun a bloated drop of blood on the horizon. She sailed past Stratham Park, where she had run with her track team in high school. She took a turn around the baseball field. An aluminum bat clinked. Boys shouted. A dark figure sprinted for first base with his head down.

Becky drove distracted, chanting one of her limericks to herself, only half aware she was doing it. She whisper-sang the oldest one she'd been able to find when she was researching her paper for freshman lit, a limerick that had been written well before the form devolved into grotty riffs on fucking, although it pointed the way in that direction:

"'A girl once hid in tall grass,'"
she crooned.

"'And ambushed any boy who walked past.
As lions eat gazelles,

so many men fell,
and each tasted better than the last."

A girl, she thought, almost randomly. *Her girl.* It
came to her, then, what she was doing. She was out looking for her girl, the one she was supposed to be babysitting, and oh, Jesus, what an unholy fucking mess—the
kid had wandered off on her, and Becky had to find her
before the parents got home, and it was getting dark fast,
and she couldn't even remember the little shit's name.

She struggled to remember how this could've happened. For a moment the recent past was a maddening
blank. Then it came to her. The girl wanted to swing in
the backyard, and Becky said *Go on, that's fine,* hardly
paying any attention. At the time she was text-messaging
with Travis McKean. They were having a fight. Becky
didn't even hear the back screen door slapping shut.

what am i supposed to tell my mom, Travis said,
i don't even know if I want to stay in college let alone
start a family. And this gem: if we get married will i
have to say I DO to your bro too? hes always around sitting on your bed reading skateboreding magazine, i m
amazed he wasn't sitting there watching the night i got
you pregnant. you want a family you should start one
with him

She had made a little scream down in her throat and chucked the phone against the wall, leaving a dent in the plaster, hoped the parents came back drunk and didn't notice. (Who were the parents anyway? Whose house was this?) Beck had wandered to the picture window that looked into the backyard, pushing her hair away from her face, trying to get her calm back—and saw the empty swing moving gently in the breeze, chains softly squalling. The back gate was open to the driveway.

She went out into the jasmine-scented evening and shouted. She shouted in the driveway. She shouted in the yard. She shouted until her stomach hurt. She stood in the center of the empty road and yelled "Hey, kid, hey!" with her hands cupped around her mouth. She walked down the block and into the grass and spent what felt like days pushing through the high weeds, looking for the wayward child, her lost responsibility. When she emerged at last, the car was waiting for her and she took off. And here she was, driving aimlessly, scanning the sidewalks, a desperate, animal panic rising inside her. She had lost her girl. Her girl had gotten away from her—wayward child, lost responsibility—and who knew what would happen to her, what might be happening to her right now? The not-knowing made her stomach hurt. It made her stomach hurt *bad*.

A storm of little birds flowed through the darkness above the road.

Her throat was dry. She was so fucking thirsty she could hardly stand it.

Pain knifed her, went in and out, like a lover.

When she drove past the baseball field for a second time, the players had all gone home. *Game called on account of darkness,* she thought, a phrase that caused her arms to prickle with goose bumps, and that was when she heard a child shout.

"BECKY!" shouted the little girl. "IT'S TIME TO EAT!" As if Becky were the one who was lost. "IT'S TIME TO COME EAT!"

"WHAT ARE YOU DOING, LITTLE GIRL?" Becky screamed back, pulling over to the curb. "YOU COME HERE! YOU COME HERE RIGHT NOW!"

"YOU'LL HAVE TO FIIIND ME!" screamed the girl, her voice giddy with delight. "FOLLOW MY VOICE!"

The shouts seemed to be coming from the far side of the field, where the grass was high. Hadn't she already looked there? Hadn't she tramped all through the grass trying to find her? Hadn't she gotten a little lost in the grass herself?

"'THERE WAS AN OLD FARMER FROM LEEDS!'" the girl shouted.

Becky started across the infield. She took two steps, and there was a tearing sensation in her womb, and she cried out.

"'WHO SWALLOWED A BAG FULLA SEEDS!'" the girl trilled, her voice vibrato with barely controlled laughter.

Becky stopped, exhaled the pain, and when the worst of it had passed, she took another cautious step. Immediately the pain returned, worse than before. She had a sensation of things shearing inside, as if her intestines were a bedsheet, stretched tight, beginning to rip down the middle.

"BIG BUNCHES OF GRASS," the girl yodeled, "SPROUTED OUT OF HIS ASS!"

Becky sobbed again, took a third staggering step, almost to second base now, the tall grass not far away, and then another bolt of pain ran her through, and she dropped to her knees.

"AND HIS BALLS GREW ALL SHAGGY WITH WEEDS!" the girl yelled, voice quivering with laughter.

Becky gripped the sagging, empty waterskin of her stomach and shut her eyes and lowered her head and waited for relief, and when she felt the tiniest bit better, she opened her eyes

↓↑

and Cal was there, in the ashy light of dawn, looking down at her. His own eyes were sharp and avid.

"Don't try to move," he said. "Not for a while. Just rest. I'm here."

He was naked from the waist up, kneeling beside her. His scrawny chest was very pale in the dove-colored half-light. His face was sunburned—badly, a blister right on the end of his nose—but aside from that he looked rested and well. No, more than that: He looked bright-eyed and bushy-tailed.

"The baby," she tried to say, but nothing would come out, just a scraping click, the sound of someone trying to pick a rusty lock with rusty tools.

"Are you thirsty? Bet you are. Here. Take this. Put it in your mouth." He pushed a soaked, cold twist of his T-shirt into her mouth. He had saturated it with water and rolled it up into a rope.

She sucked at it desperately, an infant hungrily nursing.

"No," he said, "no more. You'll make yourself sick." Taking the wet cotton rope away from her, leaving her gasping like a fish in a pail.

"Baby," she whispered.

Cal grinned at her—his best, zaniest grin. "Isn't she *great*? I've got her. She's perfect. Out of the oven and baked just right!"

He reached to the side and lifted up a bundle wrapped in someone else's T-shirt. She saw a little snub of bluish nose protruding from the shroud. No, not a shroud. Shrouds were for dead bodies. It was swaddling. She had delivered a child here, out in the high grass, and hadn't even needed the shelter of a manger.

Cal, as always, spoke as if he had a direct line to her private thoughts. "Aren't you the little Mother Mary? Wonder when the wise men will show up! Wonder what gifts they'll have for us!"

A freckled, sunburned boy, his eyes set a little far apart, appeared behind Cal. He was bare-chested, too. It was probably his shirt wound around the baby. He bent over, hands on his knees, to look at her swaddled infant.

"Isn't she wonderful?" Cal asked, showing the boy.

"Scrumptious," the boy said.

Becky closed her eyes.

→ ←

She drove in the dusk, the window down, the breeze fanning her hair back from her face. The tall grass bordered both sides of the road, stretched ahead of her as far as she could see. She would be driving through it the rest of her life.

"'A girl once hid in tall grass,'" she sang to herself. "'And ambushed any boy who walked past.'"

The grass rustled and scratched at the sky.

← ←

She opened her eyes for a few moments, later in the morning.

Her brother was holding a doll's leg in one hand, filthy from the mud. He stared at her with a bright, stupid fascination while he chewed on it. It was a lifelike thing, chubby and plump-looking, but a little small and also a funny pale blue color, like almost-frozen milk. *Cal, you can't eat plastic*, she thought of saying, but it was just too much work.

The little boy sat behind him, turned in profile, licking something off his palms. Strawberry jelly, it looked like.

There was a sharp smell in the air, an odor like a freshly opened tin of fish. It made her stomach rumble. But she was too weak to sit up, too weak to say anything, and when she lowered her head against the ground and shut her eyes, she sank straight back into sleep.

← ← ←

This time there were no dreams.

← ← ← ←

Somewhere a dog barked: *roop-roop*. A hammer began to fall, one ringing whack after another, calling Becky back to consciousness.

Her lips were dry and cracked, and she was thirsty once more. Thirsty *and* hungry. She felt as if she'd been kicked in the stomach a few dozen times.

"Cal," she whispered. "Cal."

"You need to eat," he said, and put a string of something cold and salty in her mouth. His fingers had blood on them.

If she'd been anywhere near in her right mind she might've gagged. But it tasted good, a salty-sweet strand of something, with the fatty texture of a sardine. It even smelled a little like a sardine. She sucked at it much as she had sucked at the wet rope of Cal's shirt.

Cal hiccupped as she sucked the strand of whatever it was into her mouth, sucked it in like spaghetti and swallowed. It had a bad aftertaste, bitter-sour, but even that was sort of nice. Like the food equivalent of the taste you got after drinking a margarita and licking some of the salt off the rim of your glass. Cal's hiccup sounded almost like a sob of laughter.

"Give her another piece," said the little boy, leaning over Cal's shoulder.

Cal gave her another piece. "Yum-yum. Get that li'l baby right down."

She swallowed and shut her eyes again.

← ← ← ← →

When she next found herself awake, she was over Cal's shoulder and she was moving. Her head bobbed, and her stomach heaved with each step.

She whispered, "Did we eat?"

"Yes."

"*What* did we eat?"

"Something scrumptious."

"Cal, what did we eat?"

He didn't answer, just pushed aside grass spattered with maroon droplets and walked into a clearing. In the center was a huge black rock. Standing beside it was a little kid.

There you are, she thought. *I chased you all over the neighborhood.*

Only that hadn't been a rock. You couldn't chase a *rock.* It had been a *girl.*

A girl. *My* girl. My responsi—

"WHAT DID WE EAT?" She began to pound him, but her fists were weak, weak. *"OH, GOD! OH, MY JESUS!"*

He set her down and looked at her first with surprise and then amusement. "What do you think we ate?" He looked at the boy, who was grinning and shaking his head, the way you do when someone's just pulled a really hilarious boner. "Beck . . . honey . . . we just ate some of the *grass*. Grass and seeds and so on. Cows do it all the time."

"'There was an old farmer from Leeds,'" the boy sang, and put his hands to his mouth to stifle his giggles. His fingers were red.

"I don't believe you," Becky said, but her voice sounded faint. She was looking at the rock. It was incised all over with little dancing figures. And yes, in this early light they *did* seem to dance. To be moving around in rising spirals, like the stripes on a barber pole.

"Really, Beck. The baby is . . . is *great*. Safe. Touch the rock and you'll see. You'll understand. Touch the rock and you'll be—"

He looked at the boy.

"*Redeemed!*" Tobin shouted, and they laughed together.

Ike and Mike, Becky thought. *They laugh alike.*

She walked toward it . . . put her hand out . . . then drew back. What she had eaten hadn't tasted like grass. It had tasted like sardines. Like the final sweet-salty-bitter swallow of a margarita. And like . . .

Like me. *Like licking sweat from my own armpit. Or . . . or . . .*

She began to shriek. She tried to turn away, but Cal had her by one flailing arm and Tobin by the other. She should have been able to break free from the child at least, but she was still weak. And the rock. It was pulling at her, too.

"Touch it," Cal whispered. "You'll stop being sad. You'll see the baby is all right. Little Justine. She's better than all right. She's *elemental.* Becky—she *flows.*"

"Yeah," Tobin said. "Touch the rock. You'll see. You won't be lost out here anymore. You'll understand the grass then. You'll be *part* of it. Like Justine is part of it."

They escorted her to the rock. It hummed busily. Happily. From inside there came the most wondrous glow. On the outside, tiny stick-men and stick-women danced with their stick-hands held high. There was music. She thought, *All flesh is grass.*

Becky DeMuth hugged the rock.

→ → → →   →

There were seven of them in an old RV held together by spit, baling wire, and—perhaps—the resin of all the dope that had been smoked inside its rusty walls. Printed on one side, amid a riot of red and orange psychedelia, was the word FURTHUR, in honor of the 1939 International Harvester school bus in which Ken Kesey's Merry Pranksters had visited Woodstock during the summer of 1969. Back then all but the two oldest of these latter-day hippies had yet to be born.

Just lately the twenty-first-century Pranksters had been in Cawker City, paying homage to the World's Biggest Ball of Twine. Since leaving they had busted mega-amounts of dope, and all of them were hungry.

It was Twista, the youngest of them, who spotted the Black Rock of the Redeemer, with its soaring white steeple and oh-so-convenient parking lot. "Church picnic!" he shouted from his seat beside Pa Cool, who was driving. Twista bounced up and down, the buckles on his bib overalls jingling. "Church picnic! Church picnic!"

The others took it up. Pa looked at Ma in the rearview. When she shrugged and nodded, he pulled *Furthur* into the lot and parked beside a dusty Mazda with New Hampshire license plates.

The Pranksters (all wearing Ball of Twine souvenir T-shirts and all smelling of superbud) piled out. Pa and Ma, as the eldest, were the captain and first mate of the good ship *Furthur,* and the other five—MaryKat, Jeepster, Eleanor Rigby, Frankie the Wiz, and Twista—were perfectly willing to follow orders, pulling out the barbecue, the cooler of meat, and—of course—the beer. Jeepster and the Wiz were just setting up the grill when they heard the first faint voice.

"Help! *Help!* Somebody help me!"

"That sounds like a woman," Eleanor said.

"Help! Somebody please! I'm lost!"

"That's not a woman," Twista said. "That's a little kid."

"Far out," MaryKat said. She was cataclysmically stoned, and it was all she could think to say.

Pa looked at Ma. Ma looked at Pa. They were pushing sixty now and had been together a long time—long enough to have couples' telepathy.

"Kid wandered into the grass," Ma Cool said.

"Mom heard him yelling and went after him," Pa Cool said.

"Maybe too short to see their way back to the road," Ma said. "And now—"

"—they're both lost," Pa finished.

"Jeez, that sucks," Jeepster said. *"I* got lost once. It was in a mall."

"Far out," MaryKat said.

"Help! Anybody!" That was the woman.

"Let's go get them," Pa said. "We'll bring 'em out and feed 'em up."

"Good idea," the Wiz said. "Human kindness, man. Human fuckin' kindness."

Ma Cool hadn't owned a watch in years but was good at telling time by the sun. She squinted at it now, measuring the distance between the reddening ball and the field of grass, which seemed to stretch to the horizon. *I bet all of Kansas looked that way before the people came and spoiled it all,* she thought.

"It *is* a good idea," she said. "It's going on for five-thirty, and I bet they're really hungry. Who's going to stay and set up the barbecue?"

There were no volunteers. Everyone had the munchies, but none of them wanted to miss the mercy mission. In the end, all of them trooped across Route 73 and entered into the tall grass.

FURTHUR. →   →   →   →

You Are Released

GREGG HOLDER IN BUSINESS

Holder is on his third scotch and playing it cool about the famous woman sitting next to him when all the TVs in the cabin go black and a message in white block text appears on the screens. AN ANNOUNCEMENT IS IN PROGRESS.

Static hisses from the public-address system. The pilot has a young voice, the voice of an uncertain teenager addressing a crowd at a funeral.

"Folks, this is Captain Waters. I've had a message from our team on the ground, and after thinking it over, it seems proper to share it with you. There's been an incident at Andersen Air Force Base in Guam, and—"

The PA cuts out. There is a long, suspenseful silence.

"—I am told," Waters continues abruptly, "that U.S. Strategic Command is no longer in contact with our forces there or with the regional governor's office. There are reports from offshore that . . . that there was a flash. Some kind of flash."

Holder unconsciously presses himself back into his seat, as if in response to a jolt of turbulence. What the hell does that mean, "there was a flash"? Flash of what? So many things can flash in this world. A girl can flash a bit of leg. A high roller can flash his money. Lightning flashes. Your whole life can flash before your eyes. Can Guam flash? An entire island?

"Just say if they were nuked, please," murmurs the famous woman on his left in that well-bred, moneyed, honeyed voice of hers.

Captain Waters continues, "I'm sorry I don't know more, and that what I do know is so . . ." His voice trails off again.

"Appalling?" the famous woman suggests. "Disheartening? Dismaying? Shattering?"

"Worrisome," Waters finishes.

"Fine," the famous woman says, with a certain dissatisfaction.

"That's all I know right now," Waters says. "We'll share more information with you as it comes in. At this time we're cruising at thirty-seven thousand feet, and we're about halfway through your flight. We should arrive in Boston a little ahead of schedule."

There's a scraping sound and a sharp click, and the monitors start playing films again. About half the people in business class are watching the same super-hero movie, Captain America throwing his shield like a steel-edged Frisbee, cutting down grotesques that look like they just crawled out from under the bed.

A black girl of about nine or ten sits across the aisle from Holder. She looks at her mother and says, in a voice that carries, "Where is Guam, precisely?" Her use of the word "precisely" tickles Holder—it's so teacherly and unchildlike.

The girl's mother says, "I don't know, sweetie. I think it's near Hawaii." She isn't looking at her daughter. She's glancing this way and that with a bewildered expression, as if reading an invisible text for instructions. *How to discuss a nuclear exchange with your child.*

"It's closer to Taiwan," Holder says, leaning across the aisle to address the child.

"Just south of Korea," adds the famous woman.

"I wonder how many people live there," Holder says.

The celebrity arches an eyebrow. "You mean as of this moment? Based on the report we just heard, I should think very few."

ARNOLD FIDELMAN IN COACH

The violinist Fidelman has an idea the very pretty, very sick-looking teenage girl sitting next to him is Korean. Every time she slips her headphones off—to speak to a flight attendant or to listen to the recent announcement—he's heard what sounds like K-pop coming from her Samsung. Fidelman himself was in love with a Korean for several years, a man ten years his junior, who loved comic books and played a brilliant if brittle viol, and who killed himself by stepping in front of a Red Line train. His name was So as in "so it goes" or "so there we are" or "little Miss So-and-So" or "so what do I do now?" So's breath was sweet, like almond milk, and his eyes were shy, and it embarrassed him to be happy. Fidelman always thought So was happy, right up to the day he leaped like a ballet dancer into the path of a fifty-two-ton engine.

Fidelman wants to offer the girl comfort and at the same time doesn't want to intrude on her anxiety. He mentally wrestles with what to say, if anything, and finally nudges her gently. When she pops out her earbuds, he says, "Do you need something to drink? I've got half a can of Coke that I haven't touched. It isn't germy—I've been drinking from the glass."

She shows him a small, frightened smile. "Thank you. My insides are all knotted up."

She takes the can and has a swallow.

"If your stomach is upset, the fizz will help," he says. "I've always said that on my deathbed the last thing I want to taste before I leave this world is a cold Coca-Cola." Fidelman has said this exact thing to others, many times before, but as soon as it's out of his mouth, he wishes he could have it back. Under the circumstances it strikes him as a rather infelicitous sentiment.

"I've got family there," she says.

"In Guam?"

"In Korea," she says, and shows him the nervous smile again. The pilot never said anything about Korea in his announcement, but anyone who's watched CNN in the last three weeks knows that's what this is about.

"Which Korea?" says the big man on the other side of the aisle. "The good one or the bad one?"

The big man wears an offensively red turtleneck that brings out the color in his honeydew melon of a face. He's so large he overspills his seat. The woman sitting next to him—a small, black-haired lady with the high-strung intensity of an overbred greyhound—has been crowded close to the window. There's an enamel

American flag pin in the lapel of his suit coat. Fidelman already knows they could never be friends.

The girl gives the big man a startled glance and smooths her dress over her thighs. "South Korea," she says, declining to play his game of good versus bad. "My brother just got married in Jeju. I'm on my way back to school."

"Where's school?" Fidelman asks.

"MIT."

"I'm surprised you could get in," says the big man. "They've got to draft a certain number of unqualified inner-city kids to meet their quota. That means a lot less space for people like you."

"People like what?" Fidelman asks, enunciating slowly and deliberately. *People. Like. What?* Nearly fifty years of being gay has taught Fidelman that it is a mistake to let certain statements pass unchallenged.

The big man is unashamed. "People who are qualified. People who earned it. People who can do the arithmetic. There's a lot more to math than counting out change when someone buys a dime bag. A lot of the model immigrant communities have suffered because of quotas. The Orientals especially."

Fidelman laughs—sharp, strained, disbelieving laughter. But the MIT girl closes her eyes and is still, and Fidelman opens his mouth to tell the big son of a bitch off and then shuts it again. It would be unkind to the girl to make a scene.

"It's Guam, not Seoul," Fidelman tells her. "And we don't know what happened there. It might be anything. It might be an explosion at a power station. A normal accident and not a . . . catastrophe of some sort." The first word that occurred to him was "holocaust."

"Dirty bomb," says the big man. "Bet you a hundred dollars. He's upset because we just missed him in Russia."

"He" is the Supreme Leader of the DPRK. There are rumors someone took a shot at him while he was on a state visit to the Russian side of Lake Khasan, a body of water on the border between the two nations. There are unconfirmed reports that he was hit in the shoulder, hit in the knee, not hit at all; that a diplomat beside him was hit and killed; that one of the Supreme Leader's impersonators was killed. According to the Internet, the assassin was either a radical anti-Putin anarchist, or a CIA agent masquerading as a member of the Associated Press, or a K-pop star named Extra Value Meal. The U.S. State Department and the North Korean media, in a rare case of agreement, insist there were no shots fired during the Supreme Leader's visit to Russia, no assassination attempt at all. Like many following the story, Fidelman takes this to mean the Supreme Leader came very close to dying indeed.

It is also true that eight days ago a U.S. submarine patrolling the Sea of Japan shot down a North Korean test missile in North Korean airspace. A DPRK spokesman called it an act of war and promised to retaliate in kind. Well, no. He had promised to fill the mouths of every American with ashes. The Supreme Leader himself didn't say anything. He hasn't been seen since the assassination attempt that didn't happen.

"They wouldn't be that stupid," Fidelman says to the big man, talking across the Korean girl. "Think about what would happen."

The small, wiry, dark-haired woman stares with a slavish pride at the big man sitting beside her, and Fidelman suddenly realizes why she tolerates his paunch intruding on her personal space. They're together. She loves him. Perhaps adores him.

The big man replies placidly, "Hundred dollars."

LEONARD WATERS IN THE COCKPIT

North Dakota is somewhere beneath them, but all Waters can see is a hilly expanse of cloud stretching to the horizon. Waters has never visited North Dakota and when he tries to visualize it, imagines rusting antique farm equipment, Billy Bob Thornton, and furtive acts of buggery in grain silos. On the radio the controller in Minneapolis instructs a 737 to ascend to flight level three-six-zero and increase speed to Mach Seven Eight.

"Ever been to Guam?" asks his first officer, with a false fragile cheer.

Waters has never flown with a female copilot before and can hardly bear to look at her, she is so heart-breakingly beautiful. Face like that, she ought to be on magazine covers. Up until the moment he met her in the conference room at LAX, two hours before they flew, he didn't know anything about her except that her name was Bronson. He had been picturing someone like the guy in the original *Death Wish*.

"Been to Hong Kong," Waters says, wishing she weren't so terribly lovely.

Waters is in his mid-forties and looks about nineteen, a slim man with red hair cut to a close bristle and a map of freckles on his face. He is only just married and soon to be a father: a photo of his gourd-ripe wife in a sundress has been clipped to the dash. He doesn't want to be attracted to anyone else. He feels ashamed of even spotting a handsome woman. At the same time, he doesn't want to be cold, formal, distant. He's proud of his airline for employing more female pilots, wants to approve, to support. All gorgeous women are an affliction upon his soul. "Sydney. Taiwan. Not Guam, though."

"Me and friends used to freedive off Fai Fai Beach. Once I got close enough to a blacktip shark to pet it. Freediving naked is the only thing better than flying."

The word "naked" goes through him like a jolt from a joy buzzer. That's his first reaction. His second reaction is that of course she knows Guam—she's ex-navy, which is where she learned to fly. When he glances at her sidelong, he's shocked to find tears in her eyelashes.

Kate Bronson catches his gaze and gives him a crooked, embarrassed grin that shows the slight gap between her two front teeth. He tries to imagine her with a shaved head and dog tags. It isn't hard. For all her cover-girl looks, there is something slightly feral underneath, something wiry and reckless about her.

"I don't know why I'm crying. I haven't been there in ten years. It's not like I have any friends there."

Waters considers several possible reassuring statements and discards each in turn. There is no kindness in telling her it might not be as bad as she thinks, when in fact it is likely to be far worse.

There's a rap at the door. Bronson hops up, wipes her cheeks with the back of her hand, glances through the peephole, turns the bolts.

It's Vorstenbosch, the senior flight attendant, a

plump, effete man with wavy blond hair, a fussy manner, and small eyes behind his thick gold-framed glasses. He's calm, professional, and pedantic when sober and a potty-mouthed swishy delight when drunk.

"Did someone nuke Guam?" he asks without preamble.

"I don't have anything from the ground except we've lost contact," Waters says.

"What's that mean, specifically?" Vorstenbosch asks. "I've got a planeload of very frightened people and nothing to tell them."

Bronson thumps her head, ducking behind the controls to sit back down. Waters pretends not to see. He pretends not to notice that her hands are shaking.

"It means—" Waters begins, but there's an alert tone, and then the controller is on with a message for everyone in ZMP airspace. The voice from Minnesota is sandy, smooth, untroubled. He might be talking about nothing more important than a region of high pressure. They're taught to sound that way.

"This is Minneapolis Center with high-priority instructions for all aircraft on this frequency. Be advised we have received instructions from U.S. Strategic Command to clear this airspace for operations from Ellsworth. We will begin directing all flights to the closest appropriate airport. Repeat, we are grounding all commercial and recreational aircraft in the ZMP. Please remain alert and ready to respond promptly to our instructions." There is a momentary hiss, and then, with what sounds like real regret, Minneapolis adds, "Sorry about this, ladies and gents. Uncle Sam needs the sky this afternoon for an unscheduled world war."

"Ellsworth Airport?" Vorstenbosch says. "What do they have at Ellsworth Airport?"

"The 28th Bomb Wing," Bronson says, rubbing her head.

VERONICA D'ARCY IN BUSINESS

The plane banks steeply and Veronica D'Arcy looks straight down at the rumpled duvet of cloud beneath. Shafts of blinding sunshine stab through the windows on the other side of the cabin. The good-looking drunk beside her—he has a loose lock of dark hair on his brow that makes her think of Cary Grant, of Clark Kent—unconsciously squeezes his armrests. She wonders if he's a white-knuckle flier or just a boozer. He had his first scotch as soon as they reached cruising altitude, three hours ago, just after 10:00 A.M.

The screens go black and another AN ANNOUNCEMENT

IS IN PROGRESS. Veronica shuts her eyes to listen, focusing the way she might at a table read as another actor reads lines for the first time.

CAPTAIN WATERS (V.O.)

Hello, passengers, Captain Waters again. I'm afraid we've had an unexpected request from air traffic control to reroute to Fargo and put down at Hector International Airport. We've been asked to clear this airspace, effective immediately—

(uneasy beat)

—for military maneuvers. Obviously the situation in Guam has created . . . um, complications for everyone in the sky today. There's no reason for alarm, but we are going to have to put down. We expect to be on the ground in Fargo in forty minutes. I'll have more information for you as it comes in.

(beat)

My apologies, folks. This isn't the afternoon any of us were hoping for.

If it were a movie, the captain wouldn't sound like a teenage boy going through the worst of adolescence. They would've cast someone gruff and authoritative. Hugh Jackman, maybe. Or a Brit, if they wanted to suggest erudition, a hint of Oxford-acquired wisdom. Derek Jacobi, perhaps.

Veronica has acted alongside Derek off and on for almost thirty years. He held her backstage the night her mother died and talked her through it in a gentle, reassuring murmur. An hour later they were both dressed as Romans in front of 480 people, and God, he was good that night, and she was good, too, and that was the evening she learned she could act her way through anything, and she can act her way through this, too. Inside, she is already growing calmer, letting go of all cares, all concern. It has been years since she felt anything she didn't decide to feel first.

"I thought you were drinking too early," she says to the man beside her. "It turns out I started drinking too late." She lifts the little plastic cup of wine she was served with her lunch and says "Chin-chin" before draining it.

He turns a lovely, easy smile upon her. "I've never been to Fargo, although I did watch the TV show." He narrows his eyes. "Were you in *Fargo*? I feel like you were. You did something with forensics, and then Ewan McGregor strangled you to death."

"No, darling. You're thinking of *Contract: Murder*, and it was James McAvoy with a garrote."

"So it was. I knew I saw you die once. Do you die a lot?"

"Oh, all the time. I did a picture with Richard Harris, it took him all day to bludgeon me to death with a candlestick. Five setups, forty takes. Poor man was exhausted by the end of it."

Her seatmate's eyes bulge, and she knows he's seen the picture and remembers her role. She was twenty-two at the time and naked in every scene, no exaggeration. Veronica's daughter once asked, "Mom, when exactly did you discover clothing?" Veronica had replied, "Right after you were born, darling."

Veronica's daughter is beautiful enough to be in movies herself, but she makes hats instead. When Veronica thinks of her, her chest aches with pleasure. She never deserved to have such a sane, happy, grounded daughter. When Veronica considers herself—when she reckons with her own selfishness and narcissism, her indifference to mothering, her preoccupation with her career—it seems impossible that she should have such a good person in her life.

"I'm Gregg," says her neighbor. "Gregg Holder."

"Veronica D'Arcy."

"What brought you to L.A.? A part? Or do you live there?"

"I had to be there for the apocalypse. I play a wise old woman of the wasteland. I assume it will be a wasteland. All I saw was a green screen. I hope the real apocalypse will hold off long enough for the film to come out. Do you think it will?"

Gregg looks out at the landscape of cloud. "Sure. It's North Korea, not China. What can they hit us with? No apocalypse for us. For them, maybe."

"How many people live in North Korea?" This from the girl on the other side of the aisle, the one with the comically huge glasses. She has been listening to them intently and is leaning toward them now in a very adult way.

Her mother gives Gregg and Veronica a tight smile and pats her daughter's arm. "Don't disturb the other passengers, dear."

"She's not disturbing me," Gregg says. "I don't know, kid. But a lot of them live on farms, scattered across the countryside. There's only the one big city, I think. Whatever happens, I'm sure most of them will be okay."

The girl sits back and considers this, then twists in her seat to whisper to her mother. Her mother squeezes her eyes shut and shakes her head. Veronica wonders if she even knows she is still patting her daughter's arm.

"I have a girl about her age," Gregg says.

"I have a girl about *your* age," Veronica tells him. "She's my favorite thing in the world."

"Yep. Me, too. *My* daughter, I mean, not yours. I'm sure yours is great as well."

"Are you headed home to her?"

"Yes. My wife called to ask if I would cut a business trip short. My wife is in love with a man she met on Facebook, and she wants me to come take care of the kid so she can drive up to Toronto to meet him."

"Oh, my God. You're not serious. Did you have any warning?"

"I thought she was spending too much time online, but to be fair, she thought I was spending too much time being drunk. I guess I'm an alcoholic. I guess I might have to do something about that now. I think I'll start by finishing this." And he swallows the last of his scotch.

Veronica has been divorced—twice—and has always been keenly aware that she herself was the primary agent of domestic ruin. When she thinks about how badly she behaved, how badly she used Robert and François, she feels ashamed and angry at herself, and so she is naturally glad to offer sympathy and solidarity to the wronged man beside her. Any opportunity to atone, no matter how small.

"I'm so sorry. What a terrible bomb to have dropped on you."

"What did you say?" asks the girl across the aisle, leaning toward them again. The deep brown eyes behind those glasses never seem to blink. "Are we going to drop a nuclear bomb on them?"

She sounds more curious than afraid, but at this her mother exhales a sharp, panicked breath.

Gregg leans toward the child again, smiling in a way that is both kindly and wry, and Veronica suddenly wishes she were twenty years younger. She might've been good for a fellow like him. "I don't know what the military options are, so I couldn't say for sure. But—"

Before he can finish, the cabin fills with a nerve-shredding sonic howl.

An airplane slashes past, then two more flying in tandem. One is so near off the port wing that Veronica catches a glimpse of the man in the cockpit, helmeted, face cupped in some kind of breathing apparatus. These aircraft bear scant resemblance to the 777 carrying them east—these are immense iron falcons, the gray hue of bullet tips, of lead. The force of their passing causes the whole airliner to shudder. Passengers scream, grab each other. The punishing sound of the bombers crossing their path can be felt intestinally, in the bowels. Then they're gone, having raked long contrails across the bright blue.

A shocked, shaken silence follows.

Veronica D'Arcy looks at Gregg Holder and sees he has smashed his plastic cup, made a fist, and broken it into flinders. He notices what he's done at the same time and laughs and puts the wreckage on the armrest.

Then he turns back to the little girl and finishes his sentence as if there had been no interruption. "But I'd say all signs point to 'yes.'"

SANDY SLATE IN COACH

"B-1s," her love says to her, in a relaxed, almost pleased tone of voice. He has a sip of beer, smacks his lips. "Lancers. They used to carry a fully nuclear payload, but black Jesus did away with them. There's still enough firepower on board to cook every dog in Pyongyang. Which is funny, because usually if you want cooked dog in North Korea, you have to make reservations."

"They should've risen up," Sandy says. "Why didn't they rise up when they had a chance? Did they *want* work camps? Did they want to starve?"

"That's the difference between the Western mind-set and the Oriental worldview," Bobby says. "There, individualism is viewed as aberrant." In a murmur he adds, "There's a certain ant-colony quality to their thinking."

"Excuse me," says the Jew in the middle aisle, sitting next to the Asian girl. He couldn't be any more Jewish if he had the beard and his hair in ringlets and the prayer shawl over his shoulders. "Could you lower your voice, please? My seatmate is upset."

Bobby *had* lowered his voice, but even when he's trying to be quiet, he has a tendency to boom. This wouldn't be the first time it's got them in trouble.

Bobby says, "She shouldn't be. Come tomorrow morning, South Korea will finally be able to stop worrying about the psychopaths on the other side of the DMZ. Families will be reunited. Well. Some families. Cookie-cutter bombs don't discriminate between military and civilian populations."

Bobby speaks with the casual certainty of a man who has spent twenty years producing news segments for a broadcasting company that owns something like seventy local TV stations and specializes in distributing content free of mainstream media bias. He's been to Iraq, to Afghanistan. He went to Liberia during the Ebola outbreak to do a piece investigating an ISIS plot to weaponize the virus. Nothing scares Bobby. Nothing rattles him.

Sandy was an unwed pregnant mother who'd been cast out by her parents and was sleeping in the supply room of a gas station between shifts on the day Bobby bought her a Quarter Pounder and told her he didn't care who the father was. He said he would love the baby as much as if it were his own. Sandy had already scheduled the abortion. Bobby told her, calmly, quietly, that if she came with him, he would give her and the child a good, happy life, but if she drove to the clinic, she would murder a child and lose her own soul. She had gone with him, and it had been just as he said, all of it. He had loved her well, had adored her from the first; he was her miracle. She did not need the loaves and fishes to believe. Bobby was enough. Sandy fantasized, sometimes, that a liberal—a Code Pinker, maybe, or one of the Bernie people—would try to assassinate him, and she would manage to step between Bobby and the gun to take the bullet herself. She had always wanted to die for him. To kiss him with the taste of her own blood in her mouth.

"I wish we had phones," the pretty Asian girl says suddenly. "Some of these planes have phones. I wish there was a way to call—someone. How long before the bombers get there?"

"Even if we could make calls from this aircraft," Bobby says, "it would be hard to get a call through. One of the first things the U.S. will do is wipe out communications in the region, and they might not limit themselves to just the DPRK. They won't want to risk agents in the South—a sleeper government—coordinating a counterstrike. Plus, everyone with family in the Korean Peninsula will be calling right now. It would be like trying to call Manhattan on 9/11, only this time it's *their* turn."

"Their turn?" says the Jew. "*Their* turn? I must've missed the report that said North Korea was responsible for bringing down the World Trade Towers. I thought that was al-Qaeda."

"North Korea sold them weapons and intel for years," Bobby lets him know. "It's all connected. North Korea has been the number one exporter of Destroy America Fever for decades."

Sandy butts her shoulder against Bobby and says, "Or they used to be. I think they've been replaced by the Black Lives Matter people." She is actually repeating something Bobby said to friends only a few nights before. She thought it was a witty line, and she knows he likes hearing his own best material repeated back to him.

"Wow. Wow!" says the Jew. "That's the most racist thing I've ever heard in real life. If millions of people are about to die, it's because millions of people like *you* put unqualified, hate-filled morons in charge of our government."

The girl closes her eyes and sits back in her chair.

"My wife is *what* kind of people?" Bobby asks, lifting one eyebrow.

"Bobby," Sandy cautions him. "I'm fine. I'm not bothered."

"I didn't ask if you were bothered. I asked this gentleman what kind of people he thinks he's talking about."

The Jew has hectic red blotches in his cheeks. "People who are cruel, smug—and ignorant."

He turns away, trembling.

Bobby kisses his wife's temple and then unbuckles his seat belt.

MARK VORSTENBOSCH IN THE COCKPIT

Vorstenbosch is ten minutes calming people down in coach and another five wiping beer off Arnold Fidelman's head and helping him change his sweater. He tells Fidelman and Robert Slate that if he sees either of them out of their seats again before they land, they will both be arrested in the airport. The man Slate accepts this placidly, tightening his seat belt and placing his hands in his lap, staring serenely forward. Fidelman looks like he wants to protest. Fidelman is shaking helplessly, and his color is bad, and he calms down only when Vorstenbosch tucks a blanket in around his legs. As he's leaning toward Fidelman's seat, Vorstenbosch whispers that when the plane lands, they'll make a report together and that Slate will be written up for verbal and physical assault. Fidelman gives him a glance of surprise and appreciation, one gay to another, looking out for each other in a world full of Robert Slates.

The senior flight attendant himself feels nauseated and steps into the head long enough to steady himself. The cabin smells of vomit and fear, fore and aft. Children weep inconsolably. Vorstenbosch has seen two women praying.

He touches his hair, washes his hands, draws one deep breath after another. Vorstenbosch's role model has always been the Anthony Hopkins character from *The Remains of the Day*, a film he has never seen as a tragedy but rather as an encomium to a life of disciplined service. Vorstenbosch sometimes wishes he were British. He recognized Veronica D'Arcy in business right off, but his professionalism requires him to resist acknowledging her celebrity in any overt way.

When he has composed himself, he exits the head

and begins making his way to the cockpit to tell Captain Waters they will require airport security upon landing. He pauses in business to tend to a woman who is hyperventilating. When Vorstenbosch takes her hand, he is reminded of the last time he held his grandmother's hand—she was in her coffin, and her fingers were just as cold and lifeless. Vorstenbosch feels a quavering indignation when he thinks about the bombers—those idiotic hot dogs—blasting by so close to the plane. The lack of simple human consideration sickens him. He practices deep breathing with the woman, assures her they'll be on the ground soon.

The cockpit is filled with sunshine and calm. He isn't surprised. Everything about the work is designed to make even a crisis—and this *is* a crisis, albeit one they never practiced in the flight simulators—a matter of routine, of checklists and proper procedure.

The first officer is a scamp of a girl who brought a brown-bag lunch onto the plane with her. When her left sleeve was hiked up, Vorstenbosch glimpsed part of a tattoo, a white lion, just above the wrist. He looks at her and sees in her past a trailer park, a brother hooked on opioids, divorced parents, a first job in Walmart, a desperate escape to the military. He likes her immensely—how can he not? His own childhood was much the same, only instead of escaping to the army, he went to New York to be queer. When she let him into the cockpit last time, she was trying to hide tears, a fact that twists Vorstenbosch's heart. Nothing distresses him quite like the distress of others.

"What's happening?" Vorstenbosch asks.

"On the ground in ten," says Bronson.

"Maybe," Waters says. "They've got half a dozen planes stacked up ahead of us."

"Any word from the other side of the world?" Vorstenbosch wants to know.

For a moment neither replies. Then, in a stilted, distracted voice, Waters says, "The U.S. Geological Survey reports a seismic event in Guam that registered about six-point-three on the Richter scale."

"That would correspond to two hundred and fifty kilotons," Bronson says.

"It was a warhead," Vorstenbosch says. It's not quite a question.

"Something happened in Pyongyang, too," Bronson says. "An hour before Guam, state television switched over to color bars. There's intelligence about a whole bunch of high-ranking officials being killed within minutes of one another. So we're either talking a palace coup or we tried to bring down the leadership with some surgical assassinations and they didn't take it too well."

"What can we do for you, Vorstenbosch?" says Waters.

"There was a fight in coach. One man poured beer on another—"

"Oh, for fuck's sake," Waters says.

"—and they've been warned, but we might want Fargo PD on hand when we put down. I believe the victim is going to want to file charges."

"I'll radio Fargo, but no promises. I get the feeling the airport is going to be a madhouse. Security might have their hands full."

"There's also a woman in business having a panic attack. She's trying not to scare her daughter, but she's having trouble breathing. I have her huffing into an airsickness bag. But I'd like emergency services to meet her with an oxygen tank when we get down."

"Done. Anything else?"

"There are a dozen other mini-crises unfolding, but the team has it in hand. There is one *other* thing, I suppose. Would either of you like a glass of beer or wine in violation of all regulations?"

They glance back at him. Bronson grins.

"I want to have your baby, Vorstenbosch," she says. "We would make a lovely child."

Waters says, "Ditto."

"That's a yes?"

Waters and Bronson look at each other.

"Better not," Bronson decides, and Waters nods.

Then the captain adds, "But I'll have the coldest Dos Equis you can find as soon as we're parked."

"You know what my favorite thing about flying is?" Bronson asks. "It's always a sunny day up this high. It seems impossible anything so awful could be happening on such a sunny day."

They are all admiring the cloudscape when the white and fluffy floor beneath them is lanced through a hundred times. A hundred pillars of white smoke thrust themselves into the sky, rising from all around. It's like a magic trick, as if the clouds had hidden quills that have suddenly erupted up and out. A moment later the thunderclap hits them and with it turbulence, and the plane is *kicked*, knocked up and to one side. A dozen red lights stammer on the dash. Alarms shriek. Vorstenbosch sees it all in an instant as he is lifted off his feet. For a moment Vorstenbosch floats, suspended like a parachute, a man made of silk, filled with air. His head clubs the wall. He drops so hard and fast it's as if a trapdoor has opened in the floor of the cockpit and plunged him into the bright fathoms of the sky beneath.

JANICE MUMFORD IN BUSINESS

"Mom!" Janice shouts. "Mom, lookat! What's that?"

What's happening in the sky is less alarming than what's happening in the cabin. Someone is screaming: a bright silver thread of sound that stitches itself right through Janice's head. Adults groan in a way that makes Janice think of ghosts.

The 777 tilts to the left and then rocks suddenly hard to the right. The plane sails through a labyrinth of gargantuan pillars, the cloisters of some impossibly huge cathedral. Janice had to spell "cloisters" (an easy one) in the Englewood Regional.

Her mother, Millie, doesn't reply. She's breathing steadily into a white paper bag. Millie has never flown before, has never been out of California. Neither has Janice, but unlike her mother she was looking forward to both. Janice has always wanted to go up in a big airplane; she'd also like to dive in a submarine someday, although she'd settle for a ride in a glass-bottomed kayak.

The orchestra of despair and horror sinks away to a soft diminuendo (Janice spelled "diminuendo" in the first round of the State Finals and came thi-*i-i-i-is* close to blowing it and absorbing a humiliating early defeat). Janice leans toward the nice-looking man who has been drinking iced tea the whole trip.

"Were those rockets?" Janice asks.

The woman from the movies replies, speaking in her adorable British accent. Janice has only ever heard British accents in films, and she loves them.

"ICBMs," says the movie star. "They're on their way to the other side of the world."

Janice notices that the movie star is holding hands with the much younger man who drank all the iced tea. Her features are set in an expression of almost frosty calm. Whereas the man beside her looks like he wants to throw up. He's squeezing the older woman's hand so hard his knuckles are white.

"Are you two related?" Janice asks. She can't think why else they might be holding hands.

"No," says the nice-looking man.

"Then why are you holding hands?"

"Because we're scared," says the movie star, although she doesn't look scared. "And it makes us feel better."

"Oh," Janice says, and then quickly takes her mother's free hand. Her mother looks at her gratefully over the bag that keeps inflating and deflating like a paper lung. Janice glances back at the nice-looking man. "Would you like to hold my hand?"

"Yes, please," the man says, and they take each other's hand across the aisle.

"What's I-C-B-M stand for?"

"Intercontinental ballistic missile," the man says.

"That's one of my words! I had to spell 'interconti-nental' in the regional."

"For real? I don't think I can spell 'intercontinental' off the top of my head."

"Oh, it's easy," Janice says, and proves it by spelling it for him.

"I'll take your word for it. You're the expert."

"I'm going to Boston for a spelling bee. It's Interna-tional Semifinals, and if I do well *there*, I get to go to Washington, D.C., and be on television. I didn't think I'd ever go to either of those places. But then I didn't think I'd ever go to Fargo either. Are we still landing at Fargo?"

"I don't know what else we'd do," says the nice-looking man.

"How many ICBMs was that?" Janice asks, craning her neck to look at the towers of smoke.

"All of them," says the movie star.

Janice says, "I wonder if we're going to miss the spelling bee."

This time it is her mother who responds. Her voice is hoarse, as if she has a sore throat or has been crying. "I'm afraid we might, sweetie."

"Oh," Janice says. "Oh, no." She feels a little like she did when they had Secret Santa last year and she was the only one who didn't get a gift, because her Secret Santa was Martin Cohassey and Martin was out with mononucleosis.

"You would've won," her mother says, and shuts her eyes. "And not just the semifinals either."

"They aren't till tomorrow night," Janice says. "Maybe we could get another plane in the morning."

"I'm not sure anyone will be flying tomorrow morning," says the nice-looking man apologetically.

"Because of something happening in North Korea?"

"No," her friend across the aisle says. "Not because of something that's going to happen there."

Millie opens her eyes and says, "*Shhh.* You'll scare her."

But Janice isn't scared—she just doesn't understand. The man across the aisle swings her hand back and forth, back and forth.

"What's the hardest word you ever spelled?" he asks.

"'Anthropocene,'" Janice says promptly. "That's the word I lost on *last* year, at semis. I thought it had an *i* in it. It means 'in the era of human beings.' As in 'the Anthropocene era looks very short when compared to other geological periods.'"

The man stares at her for a moment and then barks with laughter. "You said it, kid."

The movie star stares out her window at the enormous white columns. "No one has ever seen a sky like this. These towers of cloud. The bright sprawling day caged in its bars of smoke. They look like they're holding up heaven. What a lovely afternoon. You might soon get to see me perform another death, Mr. Holder. I'm not sure I can promise to play the part with my usual flair." She shuts her eyes. "I miss my daughter. I don't think I'm going to get to—" She opens her eyes and looks at Janice and falls quiet.

"I've been thinking the same thing about mine," says Mr. Holder. Then he turns his head and peers past Janice at her mother. "Do you know how lucky you are?" He glances from Millie to Janice and back, and when Janice looks, her mother is nodding, a small gesture of acknowledgment.

"Why are you lucky, Mom?" Janice asks her.

Millie squeezes her and kisses her temple. "Because we're together today, silly bean."

"Oh," Janice says. It's hard to see the luck in that. They're together *every* day.

At some point Janice realizes the nice-looking man has let go of her hand, and when she next looks over, he is holding the movie star in his arms, and she is holding him, and they are kissing each other, quite tenderly, and Janice is shocked, just *shocked*, because the movie star is a lot older than her seatmate. They're kissing just like lovers at the end of the film, right before the credits roll and everyone has to go home. It's so outrageous that Janice just has to laugh.

A RA LEE IN COACH

For a moment at her brother's wedding in Jeju, A Ra thought she saw her father, who has been dead for seven years. The ceremony and reception were held in a vast and lovely private garden, bisected by a deep, cool, man-made river. Children threw handfuls of pellets into the current and watched the water boil with rainbow carp, a hundred heaving, brilliant fish in all the colors of treasure: rose-gold and platinum and new-minted copper. A Ra's gaze drifted from the kids to the ornamental stone bridge crossing the brook, and there was her father in one of his cheap suits, leaning on the wall, grinning at her, his big, homely face seamed with deep lines. The sight of him startled her so badly she had to look away, was briefly breathless with shock. When she looked back, he was gone. By the time she was in her seat for the ceremony, she had concluded that she'd only seen Jum, her father's younger brother, who cut his hair the same way. It would be easy, on such an emotional day, to momentarily confuse one for another—especially given her decision not to wear her glasses to the wedding.

On the ground the student of evolutionary linguistics at MIT places her faith in what can be proved, recorded, known, and studied. But now she is aloft and feeling more open-minded. The 777—all three hundred–odd tons of it—hurtles through the sky, lifted by immense, unseen forces. Nothing carries everything on its back. So it is with the dead and the living, the past and the present. *Now* is a wing, and history is beneath it, holding it up. A Ra's father loved fun—he ran a novelty factory for forty years, so fun was his actual business. Here in the sky, she is willing to believe he would not have let death get between him and such a happy evening.

"I'm so fucking scared right now," Arnold Fidelman says.

She nods. She is, too.

"And so fucking angry. *So* fucking angry."

She stops nodding. She isn't and chooses not to be. In this moment more than any other, she chooses not to be.

Fidelman says, "That motherfucker, Mr. Make-America-So-Fucking-Great over there. I wish we could bring back the stocks, just for one day, so people could hurl dirt and cabbages at him. Do you think this would be happening if Obama were in office? Any of this . . . *this* . . . lunacy? *Listen.* When we get down—*if* we get down. Will you stay with me on the jetway? To report what happened? You're an impartial voice in all this. The police will listen to you. They'll arrest that fat creep for pouring his beer on me, and he can enjoy the end of the world from a dank little cell, crammed in with shitty raving drunks."

She has shut her eyes, trying to place herself back in the wedding garden. She wants to stand by the man-made river and turn her head and see her father on the bridge again. She doesn't want to be afraid of him this time. She wants to make eye contact and smile back.

But she isn't going to get to stay in her wedding garden of the mind. Fidelman's voice has been rising along with his hysteria. The big man across the aisle, Bobby, catches the last of what he has to say.

"While you're making your statement to the police," Bobby says, "I hope you won't leave out the part where you called my wife smug and ignorant."

"Bobby," says the big man's wife, the little woman with the adoring eyes. "Don't."

A Ra lets out a long, slow breath and says, "No one is going to report anything to police in Fargo."

"You're wrong about that," Fidelman says, his voice shaking. His legs are shaking, too.

"No," A Ra says, "I'm not. I'm sure of it."

"Why are you so sure?" asks Bobby's wife. She has bright, birdlike eyes and quick, birdlike gestures.

"Because we aren't landing in Fargo. The plane stopped circling the airport a few minutes after the missiles launched. Didn't you notice? We left our holding pattern some time ago. Now we're headed north."

"How do you know that?" asks the little woman.

"The sun is on the left side of the plane. Hence we go north."

Bobby and his wife look out the window. The wife makes a low hum of interest and appreciation.

"What's north of Fargo?" the wife asks. "And why would we go there?"

Bobby slowly lifts a hand to his mouth, a gesture that might indicate he's giving the matter his consideration but which A Ra sees as Freudian. He already knows why they aren't landing in Fargo and has no intention of saying.

A Ra needs only to close her eyes to see in her mind exactly where the warheads must be now, well outside the earth's atmosphere, already past the crest of their deadly parabola and dropping back into gravity's well. There is perhaps less than ten minutes before they strike the other side of the planet. A Ra saw at least thirty missiles launch, which is twenty more than are needed to destroy a nation smaller than New England. And the thirty they have all witnessed rising into the sky are certainly only a fraction of the arsenal that has been unleashed. Such an onslaught can only be met with a proportional response, and no doubt America's ICBMs have crossed paths with hundreds of rockets sailing the other way. Something has gone horribly wrong, as was inevitable when the fuse was lit on this string of geopolitical firecrackers.

But A Ra does not close her eyes to picture strike and counterstrike. She prefers instead to return to Jeju. Carp riot in the river. The fragrant evening smells of lusty blossoms. Her father puts his elbows on the stone wall of the bridge and grins mischievously.

"This guy—" says Fidelman. "This guy and his goddamn wife. Calls Asians 'Orientals.' Talks about how your people are ants. Bullies people by throwing beer at them. This guy and his goddamn wife put reckless, stupid people just like themselves in charge of this country, and now here we are. The missiles are flying." His voice cracks with strain, and A Ra senses how close he is to crying.

She opens her eyes once more. "This guy and his goddamn wife are on the plane with us. We're *all* on this plane." She looks over at Bobby and his wife, who are listening to her. "However we got here, we're *all* on this plane now. In the air. In trouble. Running as hard as we can." She smiles. It feels like her father's smile. "Next time you feel like throwing a beer, give it to me instead. I could use something to drink."

Bobby stares at her for an instant with thoughtful, fascinated eyes—then laughs.

Bobby's wife looks up at him and says, "*Why* are we running north? Do you really think Fargo could be hit? Do you really think we could be hit *here*? Over the middle of the United States?" Her husband doesn't reply, so she looks back at A Ra.

A Ra weighs in her heart whether the truth would be a mercy or yet another assault. Her silence, however, is answer enough.

The woman's mouth tightens. She looks at her husband and says, "If we're going to die, I want you to know I'm glad I'll be next to you when it happens. You were good to me, Robert Jeremy Slate."

He turns to his wife and kisses her and draws back and says, "Are you kidding me? I can't believe a fat man like me wound up married to a knockout like you. It'd be easier to draw a million-dollar lottery ticket."

Fidelman stares at them and then turns away. "Oh, for fuck's sake. Don't start being human on me now." He crumples up a beery paper towel and throws it at Bob Slate.

It bounces off Bobby's temple. The big man turns his head and looks at Fidelman—and laughs. Warmly.

A Ra closes her eyes, puts her head against the back of her seat.

Her father watches her approach the bridge, through the silky spring night.

As she steps up onto the stone arch, he reaches out to take her hand and lead her on to an orchard, where people are dancing.

KATE BRONSON IN THE COCKPIT

By the time Kate finishes field-dressing Vorstenbosch's head injury, the flight attendant is groaning, stretched out on the cockpit floor. She tucks his glasses into his shirt pocket. The left lens was cracked in the fall.

"I have never, *ever* lost my footing," Vorstenbosch says, "in twenty years of doing this. I am the Fred Effing Astaire of the skies. *No.* The Ginger Effing Rogers. I can do the work of all other flight attendants, but backward and in heels."

Kate says, "I've never seen a Fred Astaire film. I was always more of a Sly Stallone girl."

"Serf," Vorstenbosch says.

"Right to the bone," Kate agrees, and squeezes his hand. "Don't try to get up. Not yet."

Kate springs lightly to her feet and slips into the chair beside Waters. When the missiles launched, the imaging system lit up with bogeys, a hundred red pinpricks and more, but there's nothing now except the other planes in the immediate vicinity. Most of the other aircraft are behind them, still circling Fargo. Captain Waters turned them to a new heading while Kate tended to Vorstenbosch.

"What's going on?" she asks.

His face alarms her. He's so waxy he's almost colorless.

"It's all happening," he says. "The president has been moved to a secure location. The cable news says Russia launched."

"Why?" she asks, as if it matters.

He shrugs helplessly but then replies, "Russia, or China, or both put defenders in the air to turn back our bombers before they could get to Korea. A sub in the South Pacific responded by striking a Russian aircraft carrier. And then. And then."

"So," Kate says.

"No Fargo."

"Where?" Kate can't seem to load more than a single word at a time. There is an airless, tight sensation behind her breastbone.

"There must be somewhere north we can land, away

from—from what's coming down behind us. There must be somewhere that isn't a threat to anyone. Nunavut maybe? They landed a 777 at Iqaluit last year. Short little runway at the end of the world, but it's technically possible, and we might have enough fuel to make it."

"Silly me," Kate says. "I didn't think to pack a winter coat."

He says, "You must be new to long-haul flying. You never know where they're going to send you, so you always make sure to have a swimsuit and mittens in your bag."

She *is* new to long-haul flying—she attained her 777 rating just six months ago—but she doesn't think Waters's tip is worth taking to heart. Kate doesn't think she'll ever fly another commercial aircraft. Neither will Waters. There won't be anywhere to fly *to*.

Kate isn't going to see her mother, who lives in Pennsyltucky, ever again, but that's no loss. Her mother will bake, along with the stepfather who tried to put a hand down the front of Kate's Wranglers when she was fourteen. When Kate told her mom what he'd tried to do, her mother said it was her own fault for dressing like a slut.

Kate will also never see her twelve-year-old half brother again, and that *does* make her sad. Liam is sweet, peaceful, and autistic. Kate got him a drone for Christmas, and his favorite thing in the world is to send it aloft to take aerial photographs. She understands the appeal. It has always been her favorite part of getting airborne, too, that moment when the houses shrink to the size of models on a train set. Trucks the size of ladybugs gleam and flash as they slide, frictionless, along the highways. Altitude reduces lakes to the size of flashing silver hand mirrors. From a mile up, a whole town is small enough to fit in the cup of your palm. Her half brother Liam says he wants to be little, like the people in the pictures he takes with his drone. He says if he were as small as they are, Kate could put him in her pocket and take him with her.

They soar over the northernmost edge of North Dakota, gliding in the way she once sliced through the bathwater-warm water off Fai Fai Beach, through the glassy bright green of the Pacific. How good that felt, to sail as if weightless above the oceanworld beneath. To be free of gravity is, she thinks, to feel what it must be like to be pure spirit, to escape the flesh itself.

Minneapolis calls out to them. "Delta 236, you are off course. You are about to vacate our airspace. What's your heading?"

"Minneapolis," Waters says, "our heading is zero-six-zero, permission to redirect to Yankee Foxtrot Bravo, Iqaluit Airport."

"Delta 236, why can't you land at Fargo?"

Waters bends over the controls for a long time. A drop of sweat plinks on the dash. His gaze shifts briefly, and Kate sees him looking at the photograph of his wife. "Minneapolis, Fargo is a first-strike location. We'll have a better chance north. There are two hundred and forty-seven souls onboard."

The radio crackles. Minneapolis considers.

There is a snap of intense brightness, almost blinding, as if a flashbulb the size of the sun has gone off somewhere in the sky, behind the plane. Kate turns her head away from the windows and shuts her eyes. There is a deep muffled *whump,* felt more than heard, a kind of existential shudder in the frame of the aircraft. When Kate looks up again, there are blotchy green afterimages drifting in front of her eyeballs.

Kate leans forward and cranes her neck. Something is glowing under the cloud cover, possibly as much as a hundred miles away behind them. The cloud itself is beginning to deform and expand, bulging upward.

As she settles back into her seat, there is another deep, jarring, muffled crunch, another burst of light. The inside of the cockpit momentarily becomes a negative image of itself. This time she feels a flash of heat against the right side of her face, as if someone has switched a sunlamp on and off.

Minneapolis says, "Copy, Delta 236. Contact Winnipeg Center one-two-seven-point-three." The air traffic controller speaks with an almost casual indifference.

Vorstenbosch sits up. "I'm seeing flashes."

"Us, too," Kate says.

"Oh, my God," Waters says. His voice cracks. "I should've tried to call my wife. Why didn't I try to call my wife? She's five months pregnant, and she's all alone."

"You can't," Kate says. "You couldn't."

"Why didn't I call and *tell* her?" Waters says, as if he hasn't heard.

"She knows," Kate tells him. "She already knows." Whether they are talking about love or the apocalypse, Kate couldn't say.

Another flash. Another deep, resonant, meaningful thump.

"Call now Winnipeg FIR," says Minneapolis. "Call now Nav Canada. Delta 236, you are released."

"Copy, Minneapolis," Kate says, because Waters has his face in his hands and is making tiny anguished sounds and can't speak. "Thank you. Take care of yourselves, boys. This is Delta 236. We're gone."

Story Notes and Acknowledgments

In the introduction I talked about some of the artists who most influenced me. One I left out was the novelist Bernard Malamud, author of *The Fixer* and *The Assistant,* who once suggested that a corpse in a coffin might be the perfect work of art, because "you got form, but you also got content."

The first good short story I ever wrote, "Pop Art," was heavily influenced by Malamud's "The Jewbird," and my ideas about collections were shaped by his. A book of stories isn't a novel and can't have the simple narrative drive of a novel. I think it should still try to have a feeling of progression, of connectedness. It's like a road trip. You're staying in a different inn every night: One evening it's a romantic Victorian B&B with a supposedly

704 • Story Notes and Acknowledgments

haunted gazebo out back, the next it's a cruddy Motel 6 with what looks like old bloodstains on the ceiling. The places where you stop to rest and dream are unique—but the road is the same, always waiting to carry you on to whatever's next. And when it's over, you've arrived someplace new, someplace (you hope) with a good view. A place to breathe deep and take it all in.

I hope it was a brisk, fun road trip for you. I hope you roared along at full throttle. It took a little longer for me: I wrote the oldest of these tales in 2006, while the most recent was finished a few scant months before we went to press. That's slightly more than a decade, which is also roughly how long I took to write the tales in my last collection of short stories, *20th Century Ghosts*. At that rate, barring tragedy (and can anyone bar tragedy?), I hope to write somewhere between thirty and fifty more short stories before I'm done.

That might be morbid, but if you've read this far, it's kind of late to complain.

Some readers are always curious to learn how a story got written and what was on the writer's mind when he wrote it. How did those bloodstains get on the ceiling in Room 217? And is there any *proof* that a pale woman in a lilac dress haunts the old gazebo in the yard? I don't have all the answers, but maybe I have a few. The interested should proceed. Those who are satisfied with the stories alone, thanks for riding with me this far. I hope you had a thrill. Let's do it again sometime.

INTRODUCTION: "WHO'S YOUR DADDY?"

I can hear you saying wh-a-a-*aaaaat*, the introduction gets its own story note? It does, but only to mention that it's the expression of some thoughts I've been thinking for a few years now. Elements of "Who's Your Daddy?" have appeared in somewhat different form, in essays such as "The Truck" (from *Road Rage*, IDW Publishing) and "Bring On the Bad Guys" (which first appeared on Goodreads). I'm sure I've also talked about Tom Savini's influence on my work elsewhere. It's probably just as well that I stick with fiction—I've got only so many stories to tell about myself and only so many different ways to tell them.

THROTTLE

Richard Matheson came home from World War II, sat down at his typewriter, and rattled off several spare, savage masterpieces of suspense: *I Am Legend, The Incredible Shrinking Man,* and *The Legend of Hell House* among them. Although he was genre-fluid—he wrote crime, westerns, war, and sci-fi, including one of the very best episodes of the original *Star Trek*—he left the deepest imprint on the horror genre. A good Richard Matheson story moves like an eighteen-wheeler, thundering downhill with no brakes, and God help anything in the way.

In fact, one of Matheson's most famous stories, "Duel," featured a runaway tanker trunk as the antagonist and was the inspiration for that Spielberg film we discussed back in the introduction.

In 2008 I was asked if I wanted to write a story for an anthology honoring Matheson's work. The idea was that each contributing writer would take one of Matheson's concepts and reinvent it, take it in a new, unexpected direction. No one had to twist my arm. I had hardly finished reading the e-mail before I knew what I wanted to do. I had instantly imagined a short story about a faceless trucker taking on a gang of outlaw bikers, in a chase that would soon devolve into a war in the sand.

I saw pretty quickly that I was going to have one problem writing the story, which is that I had never ridden a motorcycle in my life. But my dad had—he'd been hauling around on hogs since he was a teenager. So I pitched him my idea and asked if he wanted to write it with me. He said yes. And there we were, playing Truck again, twenty-six years after our last game.

The summer after we wrote "Throttle," I got my

motorcycle license and wound up buying a Triumph Bonneville. My dad is more of a Harley guy. One summer we went out for a ride together, me on my Bonnie and him on his Fat Boy. That was a good afternoon. When we got back, he said, "You got a decent set of wheels there—even if the engine does sound like a sewing machine."

DARK CAROUSEL

A book of stories can't be a novel, but as I said, I think it should have a sense of progression, of one thing flowing naturally into the next. So I guess it makes sense to go from the first story I ever wrote with my father to "Dark Carousel," which is probably the most shamelessly Stephen King thing I've ever put down on paper. It's practically a cover of "Riding the Bullet" or "The Road Virus Heads North." I didn't try to run from the kinds of stories that inspired it—I just let it be what it wanted to be. I even named my tragic brother and sister the Renshaws, after Renshaw, the steely hit man, in my father's story "Battleground," and I see echoes of that story in "Dark Carousel" as well.

Musicians can do cover songs by the artists they admire. The Black Crowes can cover "Hard to Handle" by Otis Redding, and the Beatles could do Buddy Holly whenever they wanted. But writers don't have the same privilege (when you "cover" another writer line for line, it's called plagiarism, and the author you admire will be contacting you through his lawyer). This is the next-best thing, an act of literary mimicry—maybe less like a cover and more like an actor performing a well-known real-life figure (Oldman doing Churchill, Malek doing Mercury).

"Dark Carousel" was first released as an audiobook *on vinyl,* as a double fuckin' album, read by Nate Corddry. How cool is that, man? And while we're talking about rock-n-rollas covering other artists, the "Dark Carousel" album included a sensational cover of the Rolling Stones' "Wild Horses" by an American guitar-slinger by the name of Matthew Ryan. It's worth hunting down a copy and dusting off your old turntable to give it a listen: Matt cut right to the emotional core of the Stones song, and my story, in one fell swoop.

WOLVERTON STATION

I wrote "Wolverton Station" while I was trekking around the United Kingdom to support the publication of *Horns.* I spent those days in the company of Jon Weir, a witty, self-effacing PR man who yanked me out of the way of a double-decker bus on the first morning of our tour. He was so shaken by the near miss he had to sit on the curb to get back his breath.

We spent most of that week riding British rail from one end of the country to the other and back again. Early on the trip, I half glimpsed an approaching stop—Wolverhampton—and suddenly had Warren Zevon howling in my head.

Jon and I popped into a bookstore that afternoon to do a signing, and while I was there, I bought myself a notebook. The first draft of "Wolverton Station" was written over the five days that followed, scribbled longhand entirely on trains. Hogwarts could've gone by out the right-hand window and I wouldn't have noticed.

And where does the story end? In a lot of ways, I feel that thematically it closes at almost the exact place *American Werewolf in London* begins: the pub.

Drinks on me, boys.

BY THE SILVER WATER OF LAKE CHAMPLAIN

Much as "Throttle" was written to honor Richard Matheson, "Silver Water" first appeared in *Shadow Show,* a collection assembled by editors Sam Weller and Mort Castle to celebrate Ray Bradbury. Theoretically it was inspired by "The Foghorn," one of the better-known bits of Bradburiana. But (don't tell Mort or Sam) the story is really my mom's fault. Bradbury didn't figure into it, not at first.

I was raised in Maine, but my earliest memories are of the United Kingdom, in the months after my little brother, Owen, was born. My parents were shaggy hippies, and after Ford pardoned Nixon, they wanted to get the fuck out of the States, were sick of the place. I think my dad was also attracted by the idea of being an expatriate writer, like Hemingway or Dos Passos. So they shuffled us all off to a damp, dark little house outside London.

I was a wee guy then and thrilled by the possibility of a dinosaur lurking in the depths of Loch Ness. I wouldn't shut up about it. Finally my mother loaded my brother, my sister, and myself onto a train, and we went to Scotland. My dad stayed in London to collaborate with Peter Straub on drinking a case of beer.

Only there were torrential the-end-is-nigh rains, and the roads to the ancient loch washed out. We got halfway there and had to turn back. And that is my first childhood memory—the rain sluicing across the windshield, a flood rushing crosswise across the blacktop, orange cones blocking our path. And later I remember the shiver of awe that rolled over me when I spotted the blackened Gothic spoke of the Walter Scott Monument, stabbing at the low, swollen clouds.

Decades later—on the road with Jon Weir for that same *Horns* book tour—I glimpsed the Scott Monument and it all came rushing back to me, the whole futile quest to reach Loch Ness. How odd that even as a six-year-old, I was fixated on monsters.

I mused on my memories of that attempted family trip to Loch Ness for days and by the end of the tour had come up with a story I was never going to write, about some kids finding Nessie's washed-up corpse. I didn't dare try it—I could do the kids, and I could do the beast, but I wasn't sure I could write convincingly about Scotland.

America has a few lake monsters of its own, however. The most famous is Champ, a plesiosaur rumored to paddle about Lake Champlain. At some point I came across an apparently true news item from the mid-1930s, about a ferry striking a half-submerged lake creature, colliding hard enough to damage the boat. In an instant I had an explanation for the death of the monster, and a way to transplant my story to the United States, where I felt I was on stronger footing as a writer. I already had a first draft when I was invited to contribute to *Shadow Show*, and so I seasoned it with a bit more Bradbury to show my appreciation for a writer whose work did so much to help me find my own voice.

Sometimes life really is like a novel; the earlier scenes foreshadow what's to come and certain motifs make regular appearances. A long time ago, in a different century, I spent a week with Tom Savini on the set of *Creepshow* and got my first inkling of what I might want to be when I grew up. Here in 2019, *Creepshow* is returning as a TV show on a streaming horror network by the name of Shudder. Tom Savini's protégé, Greg Nicotero, is the driving creative force behind the show, and "By the Silver Water of Lake Champlain" is one of the stories they decided to bring to life. And would you believe Savini himself is directing? Keep an eye out for it.

FAUN

This story, on the other hand, is a pretty conscious descendant of Bradbury's "The Sound of Thunder." In stories of Oz, Narnia, and Wonderland, the little door to topsy-turvy land is always discovered by a child who needs something: to learn the value of home, or to serve a cause bigger than herself, or to avoid creepy old fellas like Charles Lutwidge Dodgson. I couldn't help but wonder, though, what might happen if an enchanted portal were found by someone with a more mercantile heart and a lot less moral fiber.

There's a debt here to C. S. Lewis, but the tale also owes a lot to the work of Lawrence Block. Block has something of a knack for the savage final twist. When he asked me to contribute a story to an anthology he was putting together, *At Home in the Dark*, I knew I wanted to write something that would reflect his values and instincts. Hopefully "Faun" does. What a pleasure to have read and enjoyed Larry for so many years and to now get to trade e-mails with him!

LATE RETURNS

I hate the idea of dying when I'm only halfway through a book.

ALL I CARE ABOUT IS YOU

One of these days, I'll learn how to write a story with a happy ending.

I've written a lot in this collection about creative parents and the power of influence. Nietzsche had a fine saying, however: One repays a teacher badly by remaining always a student. "All I Care About Is You" is, I think, its own thing, with its own rhythms and ideas and emotional texture. It appeared in *The Weight of Words,* an anthology of stories inspired by the protean art of Dave McKean, but, as with "Silver Water," I already had a draft before I was asked to jump in. Contributors were offered a selection of illustrations and asked to pick one and write a story about it. As it happened, though, there was a piece among them that looked as if it had been specifically crafted for "All I Care About Is You," almost as if McKean knew what I was going to write before I wrote it. And maybe he did.

I'm not entirely kidding. The best works of art have a tendency to fall through time differently than human beings. They remember, but they also anticipate. A good piece can mean different things to different people at different times, and all of those meanings are true, even if they contradict one another. McKean didn't know what I was going to write and didn't need to. His imagination knew what might be written, and that was enough.

THUMBPRINT

"Thumbprint" is the oldest story here. It was composed in 2006, after PS Publishing released their edition of *20th Century Ghosts* but before the publication of *Heart-Shaped Box.* I was, at the time, dimly aware that I was in trouble. Professionally, things had never looked better, but psychologically, I was beginning to tussle with anxiety and the pressure to write another novel. I had already begun a couple of things that didn't make it past page ten. Stories roared to life and were shot down before they took their first steps. "Thumbprint" was the only thing that made it through the enfilade, a nasty story about a hard, resilient woman who came back from Iraq with blood on her conscience, only to find herself stalked by an unseen hunter here in the States. In retrospect I guess Mal was tough enough to make it home from the sand and tough enough to carry me through this particular story. It was published in *Postscripts* in 2007. Later, comic-book writer Jason Ciaramella and artist Vic Malhotra adapted "Thumbprint" into a bare-knuckled graphic novel, heavy on the war, light on the peace.

THE DEVIL ON THE STAIRCASE

```
I bet
this is
the first
short story
you've read
all year that was
```

```
written in staircases
instead of paragraphs.
```

The first draft of the story was written in longhand while I was on a holiday in Positano. Because it was a vacation, I didn't intend to be writing anything, since one conventional definition of a vacation is "a time in which you are not working." Only I get restless when I don't write. I don't feel like myself anymore. A couple days into the trip, on a hike up one of the Amalfi coast's vertiginous staircases, this idea popped into my head, and by next morning I was scratching away.

That first draft looked like any other story. But when I began typing up a second draft, the title looked like this, before I centered it:

The Devil
on the Staircase

Which to my eye seemed like two steps leading downward. I remembered Malamud's comment about form matching content and went to work rebuilding my flights of fancy into flights of stairs.

Trivia for design buffs: The staircases work only when printed in a monotype such as `Courier` where every letter takes up exactly as much space as any other letter. Reprint my staircases of words in a font like Caslon or Fournier and they melt apart.

TWITTERING FROM THE CIRCUS OF THE DEAD

I made one mistake in this story. Back when I wrote it, it seemed reasonable to imagine that a kid facing the undead hordes would turn to social media for help. Truth is, though, here in 2019 it's clearer than ever that social media won't save us from zombies—it's turning us into them.

MUMS

Sometimes I think the national crop is not wheat or corn but paranoia.

IN THE TALL GRASS

At the time of this writing, director Vincenzo Natali has just wrapped up a movie-length adaptation of this story for Netflix, and by the time *Full Throttle* is in bookstores, *In the Tall Grass* will most probably be available to stream in nearly 190 countries. That's a pretty wild result for a short story that was written in . . . six days.

Both here, and with "Throttle," the experience of working with my father has been the same. Ever see one of those Road Runner cartoons? I always feel like Wile E. Coyote strapped to the rocket, and my dad is the missile. We came up with this story over flapjacks in an International House of Pancakes, on a week when we were both in between projects. We started writing the next morning. It was first published across two issues of *Esquire*.

My brother, Owen, has also worked with our dad. They wrote a whole novel, *Sleeping Beauties*, a big, brawling, Dickensian story of wonder and suspense and ideas. That one comes across less like one rocket and more like a whole salvo of ballistic missiles. Check it out.

YOU ARE RELEASED

Did someone say something about launching the missiles?

My dad has always been a nervous, white-knuckle flier, and in 2018 he jointly edited a collection of stories about terror in the high skies (his copilot was horror and fantasy critic Bev Vincent). I fly quite a bit myself—I enjoy it, although I didn't always—and on one transatlantic trip I looked out my window and imagined the cloudscape suddenly punctured by dozens of rocket contrails. When my father asked if I wanted to contribute something to *Flight or Fright,* this idea was already well developed.

"You Are Released" is, I suppose, my attempt to write a David Mitchell story. Mitchell is the author of *Cloud Atlas, Black Swan Green,* and *The Thousand Autumns of Jacob de Zoet,* and over the last decade I've sort of fallen in love with his sentences—which float and dip and soar like kites—and with his gift for kaleidoscopic narratives that quickly shift from one time and place and perspective to another. I learned a lot about the business of being a pilot from a book called *Skyfaring* by Mark Vanhoenacker, who is himself a bit David Mitchellian in tone. It was Vanhoenacker who drew attention to the rather poignant phrase "you are released," which is what traffic control always says to an aircraft as it crosses out of their airspace.

My thanks to retired airline pilot Bruce Black for talking me through proper procedure in the cockpit. His granular attention to detail made this a much better story. Usual caveat, however: any technical errors are mine and mine alone.

This may be a peculiar thing to say about a story that concerns the end of the world, but I wanna thank Bev and my dad for giving me a reason to write this one—it made me happy.

There wouldn't be a *Full Throttle* if not for the support, generosity, and kindness of the editors who first published nine of the stories herein: Christopher Conlon, Bill Schafer, Sam Weller, Mort Castle, Lawrence Block, Peter Crowther, Christopher Golden, Tyler Cabot, David Granger, and Bev Vincent. Jennifer Brehl, my editor at William Morrow, read, edited, and greatly improved each of these stories. A story in these pages was specifically written for Jim Orr—I am grateful to him for allowing me to share it with a wider audience and should add that the story in question wouldn't exist at all if not for Jim's generous contribution to the Pixel Project, an organization dedicated to reducing violence against women (see: thepixelproject.net).

Jen Brehl works with some of the best in publishing, many of whom went all out to craft and support the release of this book: Tavia Kowalchuk, Eliza Rosenberry, Rachel Meyers, William Ruoto, Alan Dingman, Aryana Hendraawan, Nate Lanman, and Suzanne Mitchell. Publisher Liate Stehlik makes it all happen. I am particularly grateful to copyeditor Maureen Sugden, who has unsnarled my grammatical catastrophes in every book, going all the way back to *Heart-Shaped Box*. I'm equally thankful for the team that works with Jen's UK counterpart, editor Marcus Gipps. My thanks to them as well: Craig Leyenaar, Brendan Durkin, Paul

Hussey, Paul Stark, Rabab Adams, Nick May, Jennifer McMenemy, and Virginia Woolstencroft—I owe you. The novelist Myke Cole looked over a couple stories here to make sure that when I wrote about guns I did so with a modicum of accuracy. If I fucked up, don't blame him.

I am so grateful to Vincenzo Natali for all his hard work to bring *In the Tall Grass* to the screen—and to Rand Holsten, who cut his way through the high weeds of Hollywood to make the deal happen in the first place. Thanks as well to Greg Nicotero and his team for including "Lake Champlain" in the first upcoming season of *Creepshow.*

My friend Sean Daily has been my screen agent for about a decade now and has worked up a really silly number of film and TV deals on my behalf, for everything from eight-hundred-page novels to thousand-word blog posts. My thanks to him for representing the stories in this book.

The oldest pieces in *Full Throttle* were agented by my longtime friend, the late Michael Choate. The more recent fiction has been shopped about by Laurel Choate, who keeps the business end of my life in good running order. My love and thanks to both.

How much do I owe to all the booksellers who have said such kind things about my stories and done so much to connect my books with a wide audience? My deepest thanks to every bookslinger who finds joy in connecting readers with stories. Your work matters and is a pure good.

And hey—how 'bout a little thanks for you, the reader? You could've been surfing Twitter, or staring at YouTube, or thumbing the shit out of a PlayStation controller, but you decided to read a book instead. I'm grateful to you for letting me share a little space in your head. I hope you had some fun. I'm already looking forward to next time.

The happiness of my days is the result of a collaborative effort with some of the most thoughtful and loving people I know: my parents, my sister, my brother and his family. I especially want to thank my three sons, Ethan, Aidan, and Ryan, for their humor and kindness and for their patience with their often distracted father. Finally, my thanks to Gillian, for marrying me and letting me have a place in her life and at her side. I love you so much. When we're together, I always feel like a king.

Joe Hill
Exeter, New Hampshire
The Witching Season, 2018

About the Author

J oe Hill has written screenplays, novels, comics, and many short stories, including this one.

A LITTLE SORROW

A man named Atkinson—as lonely as a castaway and as empty as a cupboard—found his way to a dank curio shop at the end of a nameless alley. He asked the shopkeep if he had something for the pain.

The shopkeep put his hand on a sickly child, with dark rings under his colorless eyes. "I can sell you a small persistent sorrow. Guaranteed for life, very little upkeep, and utterly faithful. This one has a faint odor of mothballs. Otherwise? Mint."

They soon agreed on a price, and Atkinson sank to one knee so the Little Sorrow could climb on his back, where it would remain for the rest of his natural life. The small child whispered that Atkinson was no good; his life had been for nothing; his mother had felt disgust for him from the first moment Atkinson fastened onto her breast. The child told him this with great solemnity and quiet conviction.

Atkinson staggered as he rose to his feet, felt a pinch in the small of his back, the weight already making him ache with fatigue. He inhaled deeply (a dizzying reek of mothballs) and let out a great sigh of effort—and relief.

"Company at last," he said, and he carried the whispering child out with him, feeling much lighter than when he had come in.

HARPER LUXE

THE NEW LUXURY IN READING

We hope you enjoyed reading
our new, comfortable print size and found it
an experience you would like to repeat.

Well — you're in luck!

HarperLuxe offers the finest in fiction and
nonfiction books in this same larger print size and
paperback format. Light and easy to read, HarperLuxe
paperbacks are for book lovers who want to see
what they are reading without the strain.

For a full listing of titles and
new releases to come, please visit our website:

www.HarperLuxe.com

SEEING IS BELIEVING!

RECEIVED FEB - - 2020